The Reality of Illusion

A NOVEL

Chuck Markussen & Stephen Lance

The Reality of Illusion

ISBN: 978-0-9994001-5-9 (print)
ISBN: 978-0-9994001-6-6 (ebook)

Editor: Leslie M. Carringer

Interior photos courtesy of:
Ray Poage (Chapter One)
Prairie Markussen (Chapter Two)
Don Lance (Chapters Three and Eighteen)
Dusty Hill (Chapters Six, Seven, and Twenty)
Walter Guiot (Chapter Eight)
Greg Latta (Chapter Thirteen)
Stephen Honsburger (Chapter Fifteen)
Stock media provided by [Vice_and_Virtue]/Pond5
    (Chapters Five and Eleven, and Cover)

Other interior photos: Stephen Lance

Acknowledgements

Steve and Chuck would like to thank Leslie M. Carringer for her extensive work editing this novel. She provided valuable feedback on everything from plot integrity and character development to grammar and spelling. We would also like to thank Dorothy Lance and Jerry Hill for their proofreading and editing contributions. Their efforts were much appreciated!

Thanks, as always, to Cathie Bishop and Dorothy Lance for their patience and tolerance during the writing, editing, and publishing of this novel. Their support and encouragement were essential.

Special thanks to Martha R. Miller, MD, and William P. Johnson, MD, for providing medical expertise and guidance in the development of this novel. Their time and effort were highly valued.

The Authors

Steve Lance and Chuck Markussen have over 75 combined years of aerospace engineering experience in the areas of tactical missile development, defense electronics, and modeling and simulation. Both moved to Tucson, AZ, with Hughes Missile Systems Group in 1994 and retired from Raytheon Company in February, 2011. This is their third collaborative novel.

Disclaimer

Authors' Note

The Reality of Illusion is the sequel to *The Reality of Chaos* and is the third book in the *Reality* series. The first in the series, *The Reality of Fiction*, was published in 2014. Many of the characters developed in the first two novels continue their lives in *The Reality of Illusion*, and several new characters are introduced. A list of the principal characters and their roles in these novels is provided below.

The Characters

Amhurst, Becky
Software Project Manager at Alpha Defense Electronics.
From: Birmingham, Alabama
Education: PhD Computer Science, Stanford

Burdan, Frank
Lead guitar player for Logan Fletcher's jazz band, The Fourth
Harmonics.
From: Denver, Colorado
Education: Culinary, Institute of Culinary Education NYC

Chu, Luana
CEO of a high-tech software company. Jason Stone's significant other.
From: Kapalua, Hawaii
Education: English, Computer Science & Math, Stanford

Crandall, Richard
Independently wealthy computer expert.
From: Littlehampton, England
Education: PhD Math, University of Oxford

Crandall (Remington), Yvette
Homeless girl taken in by Richard Crandall who is now his heir and
assists him in his predictive chaos modeling.
From: London, England
Education: Berkeley Academy, London, studying math and computer
science

Enfield, Arthur
Driver, butler, and cook for Diana Foster.
From: London, England
Education: BA, London Metropolitan University

Fishburne, Colin
Friend of Yvette Crandall (Remington).
From: London, England
Education: Berkeley Academy, London, studying math and computer science

Fletcher, Cathie
Author of high-tech espionage novels. Wife of Logan Fletcher. Sorority sister of Joy Johnson.
From: Thousand Oaks, CA
Education: PhD English Literature, USC

Fletcher, Logan
Retired aerospace engineer and married to Cathie. Longtime friend of Chuck Johnson. Leader of the jazz band The Fourth Harmonics.
From: Plymouth Meeting, PA
Education: BA Music, Temple University, MS Computer Science, University of Arizona

Foster, Diana
Independently wealthy aristocrat. Friend of Richard Crandall.
From: Manchester, England
Education: PhD Physics, University of Oxford

Hernandez, Ramón
Chief lieutenant and bodyguard to cartel boss Carlos Velasquez.
From: Zihuatanejo, Mexico
Education: Street smarts

Heskin, Carl
Epidemiologist working at the CDC.
From: Glens Falls, NY
Education: MD, NYU

Johnson, Chuck
Retired Navy SEAL who worked for the CIA. Now works for Stone
Security Services. Married to Joy Johnson. Longtime friend of Logan
Fletcher.
From: Philadelphia, PA
Education: BA Criminal Justice, U.S. Naval Academy

Johnson, Joy
Wife of Chuck Johnson and sorority sister of Cathie Fletcher.
From: Washington, D.C.
Education: BS Business, USC

Johnson, Marcus
Son of Chuck and Joy Johnson. Works for the CIA.
From: San Francisco, CA
Education: BS Business, USC

Kittle, Garrett
Drummer in Logan's jazz band, The Fourth Harmonics.
From: Grass Valley, CA
Education: BA Music Performance, Curtis Institute of Music

Lewis, Judy
Jazz singer and friend of Logan Fletcher's family.
From: Tucson, AZ
Education: MS Music Performance, University of Arizona

Lister, Emma
Former administrative Assistant to Smythe-Montgomery. Now running his enterprise.
From: London, England
Education: MBA, University of Oxford

Morris, Tyrone
Medical doctor and longtime friend of Chuck Johnson. Skilled bass player.
From: Philadelphia, Pennsylvania
Education: MD, Temple

O'Neil, Gail
Computer software expert at Alpha Defense Electronics working for Becky Amhurst. Wife of Randy O'Neil.
From: Holdrege, Nebraska
Education: MS Computer Science, UW-Madison

O'Neil, James Charles
Child of Randy and Gail O'Neil
From: Tucson, Arizona
Education: None

O'Neil, Randy
Worked for the CIA under the leadership of Chuck Johnson. Now a member of Stone Security Services. Married to Gail O'Neil.
From: Booth Harbor, Maine
Education: MS Security Studies, Boston College

Raynard, Jesse
An enigmatic individual with murky connections to Carlos Velasquez.
From: Unknown
Education: Unknown

Shorewood, Charlotte
Friend and assistant to Jesse Raynard.
From: Cape Town, South Africa
Education: MA in Theatre Arts, SDSU

Shukhov, Constantin
Epidemiologist and former staff member at the CDC.
From: St. Petersburg, Russia
Education: MD, Georgetown

Simms, Caldwell
Hitman for Carlos Velasquez.
From: St Andrews, Scotland
Education: The Royal Regiment of Scotland

Smythe-Montgomery, Conrad
Former multibillionaire with global influence.
From: Cambridge, England
Education: MA Political Science, Minor History, University of Oxford

Stone, Jason (AKA James Kulwicki)
Ex-Army Ranger weapons expert (guns and explosives). Founder of
Stone Security Services. Confidant and lover of Luana Chu.
From: San Diego, CA
Education: BA History, SDSU

Velasquez, Carlos (AKA The Viper)
Head of the largest drug cartel in Mexico and Central America.
From: Mexico City, Mexico
Education: Universidad Nacional Autónoma de México

Walkin, Gary
Avionics expert from Alpha Defense Electronics.
From: Milwaukee, Wisconsin
Education: MS Electrical Engineering, UCLA

Zanders, Martha
Epidemiologist and friend of Tyrone Morris
From: Bellingham, Washington
Education: MD, Johns Hopkins University

Berkeley Academy (as well as several other advanced academies and universities in London) had been the victim of a particularly insidious ransomware attack.

Prologue

Small Justice

The fog lay heavy over London, like drab, dank curtains reaching from the clouds to the streets. To the very soles of Yvette's shoes. By the sun, there was no telling the time of day, for the light was diffuse. But Yvette knew the time, 3:58 p.m., as she entered Berkeley Academy, the small private school she'd been attending since the traumatic situation with Sir Conrad Smythe-Montgomery had been resolved.

Nightmares still haunted her from the grim interlude that had divided her previous life from the present. What she *had been* was a remarkably bright street urchin, brought in out of the cold by her eccentric benefactor, Richard Crandall. She had been cared for and given an opportunity to learn at the price of playing a part in Crandall's perverse sexual fantasies, a role she never resented. As her intelligence and aptitude had become more apparent, she had taken on an unexpected additional role, that of junior collaborator for Richard's extraordinary research into the 'synergistic application of chaos theory and autoregressive stochastic processes for predictive analysis of geopolitical events.' Her first contribution had been to shorten the tongue-twisting name to the less precise but far more manageable 'predictive chaos.' She had proceeded to dazzle Crandall with her quick grasp of the arcane subject matter and algorithms.

After a few months, she was making minor corrections and modifications, primarily to the graphics and interface code. But not long after, she had begun contributing to the basic modeling; coding and debugging the algorithms scratched out by Crandall. At that time, he had resolved to put her on an aggressive schooling regimen more suited to her ability. During that same period, he began to have doubts about his unusual private relationship with Yvette.

The chaos ensuing from Smythe-Montgomery's emergence on the geopolitical landscape put Crandall's schemes and doubts on hold, and nearly cost him his life. After a lengthy convalescence, he had reinstituted his plans. His relationship with Yvette was now of a more conventional sort: de facto ward and guardian. And she had been enrolled in Berkeley Academy.

Computer science and mathematics had come easily to her. She had breezed through algebra and geometry, and had learned several computer languages, including the archaic FORTRAN still to be found in some of Crandall's older code. This semester had been the most challenging so far, with the introduction to calculus and probability, subjects quite beyond most students her age. But her continuous 'on-the-job training' and dedicated tutoring had helped her amaze her instructors.

As she entered the school, a gloom hung over her. Berkeley Academy (as well as several other advanced academies and universities in London) had been the victim of a particularly insidious ransomware attack. Computer systems had been locked for two days, and Berkeley's directors were seriously considering the demand of the attacker: a payment of £50,000 to release control of their computers. Concern that the academy might pay the ransom had cast the melancholy shroud over Yvette. If the directors hadn't yet met the demands, the computers would still be locked and unusable. Precisely what she hoped for. Patting her backpack, a smile replaced her frown as she recalled the argument she'd won with Crandall the previous evening.

***

'No, Yvette, I won't hear of it,' he said. 'The school must find its own solution.'

'But Richard, it's a simple variant of the Exquisite Primes malware.'

'If it's so simple, then the school's IT staff can manage well enough. Now, returning to time-varying statistics—'

'Simple *for you*, I meant. Exquisite Primes has done a lot of damage: schools, hospitals, government offices.'

'Yes, well, why should this instance be any different?'

'Because it's *my* school. And I can't learn the way you want me to learn with the computers all jacked up.'

He started slightly at her reversion to the cruder street language that had been her lingua franca when she first joined him.

'Besides,' she said, playing her trump card, 'you'd never tolerate such interference if it had originated with Smythe-Montgomery.'

He sighed, defeated. 'I suppose you'll want the advanced version of the malware removal software?'

'Oh, yes please,' she purred.

***

The despondent faces of the teachers, staff, and fellow students brought Yvette a sense of relief. The malware problem was unsolved, and she … well, Richard had accused her of wanting to show off, and there was some truth to that. She hid her self-satisfaction behind the knowledge that she would be doing the school a tremendous service, saving them thousands of pounds, and—a vindictive smile curled the corners of her mouth—someone would get what was coming to them.

The instructor for her first class of the day, statistics, entered the classroom with a forced smile.

'You can put away your tablets. Terribly sorry. Seems I'll be teaching you, as they say, old school today. If you'll turn to page forty-two—' He stopped, realizing that none of his students had a paper copy of the textbook. 'Oh, sod it,' he mumbled. The class tittered appreciatively.

Yvette's hand shot up, and her teacher gladly called on her, hoping for a reprieve while he tried to sort things out in his mind.

'I believe I have a solution to the school's malware problem,' she said, holding up a thumb drive. All eyes turned to her, and a few grunts of disbelief filled the room.

'Something you found on the internet?' Colin Fishburne asked sarcastically.

Colin, a brilliant student about Yvette's age, was a universally acknowledged wanker. Yvette referred to him as Colin Fishbreath.

'No. Something of value from Richard Crandall's lab. If you like, I can loan it to you after class and you can use it to repair your home computer. Another week without surfing for porn would probably kill you.'

Students laughed and clapped.

'Now that's enough, you lot,' the instructor said. 'Well, Ms. Crandall, your guardian has a reputation for a certain eccentric genius. However, I warn you, if you plug that drive into an infected computer, you may never use it again.'

'Oh, I doubt that,' Yvette muttered as she rose from her seat.

Murmurs ran through the class as students leaned forward in their chairs, and a number of bets were hastily arranged. Had Yvette cared to know, she would have discovered that the odds were running roughly ten-to-one against her.

The instructor motioned graciously to the disabled computer at the front of the classroom. 'Would you like me to ...' He motioned to the controls for the classroom projection system.

'Yes, certainly,' Yvette replied. *OK, now I am showing off*, she thought.

The screen filled with swirling numbers—prime numbers. They grew and shrank, floated and disappeared, to be replaced by others, all in a kaleidoscope of color. A stable dialogue box stated the terms of the ransom and the method for making payment. In the background, ABBA's 'Take a Chance on Me' played in a mind-numbing, endless loop. The class groaned.

Yvette calmly inserted the drive, moved to the keyboard, and typed in Ctrl+Alt+Del. The screen flickered and the numbers froze. The lyrics of the song slurred as though ABBA had recorded their hit song while drunk. Then another image began to appear, ghostly at first, but growing firmer and brighter with every moment: a huge, purple Jabberwocky. Flaming words beneath the Jabberwocky blazed: 'Clyde says, bugger off!'

Before a minute passed, the numbers had faded entirely and Clyde's caption had changed to 'Clyde now returns control to you.' He winked once and disappeared, replaced by the academy's home page. The class erupted in applause, the instructor joining in. Only Colin Fishbreath seemed displeased.

***

In the basement of a grim, windowless North Korean building, servers spun out of control, shuffling data at maniacal speed. Before the shocked technicians monitoring the malware attack could respond, grinding was heard and smoke drifted up from every machine. The technicians stared in frustration at blank screens and ruined hardware. Richard Crandall's *advanced* malware removal software had a very capable counterstrike algorithm.

'Stone, this really doesn't suck. I feel for the VPs of other companies who can't be here enjoying this.'

Chapter One

Starting a New Business

Near Puerto Barrios, Guatemala

A warm, steady rain splashed off the cracked asphalt, adding to the gloom of the night as much as to the oppressive humidity. The ditches alongside the road ran with muddy water and dead vegetation. Human waste and the corpses of animals blended in the steady rush, adding a charnel house smell and creating a deadly brew that was a breeding ground for disease as the water spilled into the harbor.

The truck driver forced the shifter into a lower gear with a gravelly, grinding sound and the truck began to slow. Rough canvas over a rusty metal frame enclosed the rear of his stake bed truck. In other circumstances, the bed might be filled with bananas or sacks of coffee, but tonight's cargo was considerably more valuable. Seated on the bare floor of splintering wood was a human cargo, mostly women and children, though a few grown men were mixed into the dispirited crush. Two men, better clothed and seated on empty crates at the tailgate, watched these people, anger and hate burning in their eyes. They were required to be angry and hateful; it allowed them to feel no sympathy, let alone mercy, for this forlorn group. Each guard had a shotgun resting across his knees, but it was unlikely that any fight remained in the people they guarded. Taken from small villages inland, they were doomed, and they knew it. Masked men had come at night, bursting into houses, grabbing people whom they had likely identified earlier. Who knew whether these same men might have passed through the village recently or posed as laborers in previous weeks as they selected their victims? There was always some resistance, but surprise and terror were often sufficient to cow villagers.

Occasionally, blood was shed, after which an unnatural quiet would settle, those not targeted staying indoors until the danger passed.

The truck came to a juddering halt near a small pier. The howling of a dog was heard, followed by an angry voice and sudden yelping. The two men in the back of the truck leaped to the ground and motioned with their shotguns for the others to follow. Once assembled in a ragged group on the pier, the people were herded to a crude walkway and a waiting boat.

One by one the prisoners were crowded in and the boat settled lower in the water. Guards in the boat took over as the two with the guns hurried back to the truck. There would be three more nights work for them, bringing similar groups from other inland towns and villages. Others, taken from the slums of larger cities in Central America, had already been brought on board the grimy cargo ship anchored in the harbor. No effort would be made to locate or rescue the poor and often homeless victims of these raids. They were the invisible. Never to be missed.

On the fourth night, the ship would be tied up at a larger pier and loaded with the legitimate cargo of sugar, coffee, and bananas that would arrive by train that day. It was a clever scheme to transport large numbers of illegals, destined primarily for the sex trade in the United Kingdom and Europe.

***

The captives were herded into the mess area for inspection by the captain, the last time they would be above the waterline for at least a week. Soon they would be forced into cramped, hidden compartments deep in the hold. In addition to sidearms, the ship's crew carried bright machetes, intended to frighten as much as to keep order. And though fear was a deterrent, the men had no hesitation in wielding their weapons. A slashed face or dismembered body would guarantee a quiet cruise.

'Well, what has Lopez brought me tonight?' the captain asked.

A large man, the captain had more the appearance of a street fighter than an honest merchant or seaman. Unruly black hair with only a smattering of silver matched a wild, unkempt beard. His face was leathery and pitted beneath jutting eyebrows, and his eyes were as dark and unfeeling as a shark's. He had achieved his rank by being more ruthless and less honest than his predecessors. Lies, betrayal, and murder had been his tools as he rose in the ranks.

One of the machete-wielding men shrugged. 'Fresh meat, anyway, captain. A few will fetch a good price.'

The captain eyed the people as though he were assessing cattle. Cattle that he found sadly lacking. At last he stepped forward and grabbed the chin of a young woman, barely more than a girl, with long black hair and terror-wide eyes. He tipped her head from side to side. 'This one will do for tonight. After all, she must learn her new trade.'

A bellow from nearby as a young man rushed forward, trying to defend the woman. But the captain had expected this, and he doubled the man over with a powerful blow to the solar plexus. When the man was secured between two of the ship's crew, the captain examined him closely.

'Well, who might you be, my brave one? A brother? A lover? Or just a silly fool?'

The young man summoned the last of his courage and spat in the captain's face.

The captain slowly wiped the spittle away. 'A fool,' he concluded. He nodded to his men, who twisted the captive's arms and bent him forward at the waist. The captain reached out his hand, and a machete was placed in it. He looked around the room coldly. 'As this is the first incident, I will show mercy.' He took a mighty swing with the machete. A sound like an ax striking damp wood filled the room as the captive's spine was severed. In two more blows, the head rolled away. The group stood frozen in horror while the ship's crew only grinned. At last, with ponderous slowness, the captain pointed the bloody machete at the woman he had first spoken to. 'My men will throw this carcass overboard and you will clean up this mess. Then you will shower and come to my cabin.'

The children were sobbing with fear now, as the older ones and the few adults tried to overcome their terror and comfort them.

'The rest of you,' the captain said, 'have witnessed the only act of mercy I will ever show. Obey! Cause no disturbance. Or, you will be dealt with most severely.' He turned to his men. 'Get them out of here.'

***

Breckenridge, Colorado

Stone added another log to the crackling fire, placing it across two others, partially consumed in flame, and directly over the glowing embers at the fire pit's center. Flames were already licking around this new addition before he sat back down. This spring day had been warm and sunny, though a recent snow still tempted plenty of skiers onto the nearby slopes. But the sun had turned the western sky bloody before disappearing a short time later, and now the evening air was chilly.

Randy shifted in his cushioned patio chair and stared into the flames, a Cuban cigar in his right hand, a glass of single malt scotch in the other. He was undecided which he should sample first, settling on the scotch. He took a pull on the cigar before the pleasant tingle of the fine spirit vanished. Fragrant smoke drifted into the night air.

'Stone, this really doesn't suck. I feel for the VPs of other companies who can't be here enjoying this.'

'Amen, brudda,' Chuck agreed from the other side of the fire pit. 'Though I suppose a little corporate chitting and chatting is in order.'

'What a buzzkill,' Randy said, followed immediately by the obligatory, 'boss.'

'Not anymore, Randolph. We are now co-equals in the budding enterprise inspired by our gracious host, the right honorable Jason Stone.'

'You must be confusing me with someone else,' Stone replied, with a wry smile. 'You know, a nice guy.'

'Oh, hell, you're nice enough. Luana seems to think so, anyway.'

'Yeah,' Stone said, 'that surprises the hell out of me most days.'

'Here's to inexplicable romances, including mine,' Randy said, holding his glass up. 'You know,' he continued, after the clink of glasses and another gentle pull at Stone's eighteen-year-old scotch, 'I've been wondering, never having been the vice president of anything, how all this is supposed to work. Back when I worked for the Agency, Chuck would just come into my office, rattle my cage, and dump a pile of work on me. Most of it was pretty dull, but some was fantastic. Then I got a paycheck. I never even wondered about who set up the office, bought the coffee and paper, paid for electricity, let alone about how the jobs came to land on my desk.'

'The painful part of freelancing,' Chuck grumbled.

'We're luckier than most,' Stone said. 'Diana was extremely generous, offering up the east wing of her mansion outside London for our European headquarters. We'll need to make a few mods and install some equipment, but Luana and I have talked, and she's helping with the purchases: computers, office furniture, STE phones ... paper. And Richard Crandall seems more than eager to get involved. I think he's looking for a little more adventure in his life.'

'That last dose of adventure nearly got him dead,' Chuck grumbled. 'Still, his unique expertise might come in handy.'

Randy gave a chuckle. 'And don't forget Yvette. I know she's dying to have John Steed and Emma Peel spending time with Richard and her.'

Stone shook his head. 'How the hell she sees me and Luana like that is a mystery.'

'You're kidding, right?' Randy asked. 'Have you seen the old *Avengers* TV series? You two are just the 21st-century equivalent. Luana is beautiful, Stone is—well, passable to look at. You jet around the world, meet with heads of state, have great adventures, and defeat the villain.'

'It's a silly fantasy,' Stone said, surprisingly grim. 'And she could have been killed more than once when we ...'

An awkward silence was broken when Chuck waved his empty glass. Stone smiled slightly and refilled the glass. 'OK,' Chuck said, 'and since Randy can't seem to tear himself away from his loving wife and bambino—what's his name again?'

'James Charles O'Neil. Named after you two ass clowns, God help me, though most people won't realize Jason's real name is James. Gail insisted.'

'To James Charles O'Grumpy,' Chuck said, raising his glass for another toast. 'As I was saying, since Randy can't be separated from his lovely wife and baby boy, the U.S. headquarters for SSS might as well be in Tucson. And guess what, Joy and I will be movin' there soon. So that's settled.'

More toasting, more drinking.

'We'll get matching equipment in Tucson,' Stone said. 'Luana's already picked out a building near Rita Ranch.'

'Where Gail and I will be living,' Randy added.

'I think Joy wants to be closer to the Fletchers, so we'll probably be on the north or northeast side of town.'

'Bigger bucks, boss,' Randy said, unable to break his old habit.

'Yeah, dang right. Which is why I'll be workin' till I kick the can.'

A loud snap in the fire as a log broke and fell, sending amber sparks into the clear night sky.

'Speaking of that—work I mean—umm, how do we get that exactly?' Randy asked.

Chuck and Stone exchanged a look consisting of amusement and incredulity, then burst into laughter.

'OK,' Randy said, scowling, 'I missed the joke. Care to enlighten me?'

Stone gestured graciously to Chuck. 'Still learning, eh, Grasshopper? Listen now to the masters.' After pausing for dramatic effect, he said one word: 'Connections.'

Randy blinked twice and looked from Chuck to Stone, no sign of understanding lighting his face.

'We know people,' Stone said. 'Chuck has connections. I have connections. These people know—sort of—what we do. How many times have you been contacted since you left the Agency and signed up with our shabby crew, Chuck?'

'Seven,' Chuck said. 'Two are bullshit, three are iffy, two are legit.'

'Legit?' Randy asked.

'Legit work for Stone Security Services. Good people, good work, good pay. How about you, Stone?'

'Twelve. Same sort of breakdown. But one was more interesting, and you'll never guess the source.' Neither Chuck nor Randy was willing to hazard a guess. 'Diana. And it's through her connection with The Salvation Army.' The same dull look was on both of his companions' faces. Stone laughed. 'Let me explain.'

***

Randy blinked saltwater from his eyes. How the hell had a relaxing night drinking scotch and smoking Cuban cigars led to this? Stone offered his hand and pulled Randy on board the *Saint Martin*, a dilapidated merchant ship anchored off Puerto Barrios, Guatemala. The ship was riding high, and a line of scum and weed showed along her hull. Painted black from the rail down to an orange-red that began near the waterline, the ship's sides were streaked with weeping rust. There was an overpowering smell of stale oil and fish, apparently the chief components of most meals aboard the freighter. But as Stone and Randy moved noiselessly forward, they were met with an even more powerful odor of human waste that made Randy's stomach lurch. Stone stopped and lifted an eyebrow. Randy forced his bile to settle and nodded.

***

'The Army does a lot of work to combat human trafficking,' Stone had said. 'Apparently, the donation of over £100 million made by Crandall and Yvette was directed specifically towards that mission. Now, with that kind of windfall, what could be accomplished? Well, use your imaginations. Offices sprang up all over the world: Africa, China, Indonesia, Central America. Money flowed in for food, shelter, and education. When people aren't hungry, ignorant, or hopeless, they're less desperate. Less vulnerable. It must've been working. Salvation Army offices in Honduras and Guatemala were being torched. A couple of them during the day, when people were there.'

Randy shook his head and a hard set came to Chuck's jaw.

'So, what to do?' Stone continued. 'Despite being an "army," the organization lacks ... enforcement capability. Appeals to local law agencies were met with polite refusal. Those not directly in the payroll of the cartels were too terrified to take action. Enter our heroine, Diana Foster. Turns out, when she's not honing her deadly fencing skills, she works for several charitable organizations.'

'Including The Salvation Army,' Randy offered.

'Yes. As a member of the international advisory board. Well, she just happens to know people.'

'Nasty, unsavory people,' Chuck said.

'And yet, with hearts of gold!' Randy added, with a crooked grin.

'Speak for yourself, Randy,' Stone said, as he refilled drinks. 'In any case, folks like us, who might be able to help.'

'So, we're being hired by The Salvation Army?'

'Not exactly,' Stone said. 'They won't get involved directly. Diana and Luana will be paying for our services.'

'Works for me and Randy,' Chuck said, 'but you won't make money this way.'

'Let's just say I'll be getting practice for our soon-to-come big score.'

Chuck smirked and Randy stifled a laugh.

'Yeah,' Stone grumbled, 'what bullshit. Just sit here and discuss my gullibility for a while. There's something I want to show you.' He rose and headed for his house.

***

Stone continued moving, eyes searching, but saw no activity on deck. True, it was 2:30 a.m. local time, but some sort of harbor watch was to be expected, and so far there was none. The smugglers apparently felt safe anchored well clear of the dock, despite the nature of their activities. Stone smiled grimly. After tonight, they might think differently.

A few muted sounds drifted across the empty harbor from the loading docks, occupied now by two container ships, but the machinery of loading and unloading the heavy cargos was silent for the night. By tomorrow evening, if Stone's intel was correct, the two ships would have sailed, and the *Saint Martin* would be docked to load their official cargo. Their true cargo, a sad collection of men, women, and children, had already been brought on board by small fishing craft. The boldness of this operation was an indicator of the value of this human cargo.

Stone halted. They had reached the stairs that would lead them to the bridge. He pulled an unusual, long-barreled weapon from his vest pocket. It was only the second time Randy had seen it, and he remembered well Stone's first demonstration of this gun.

***

When Stone returned from the house, he had brought a case, which Randy assumed contained one of Stone's usual favorites, an H&K pistol or a Glock, possibly even an Uzi. Chuck leaned in closer to a small table near the fire where Stone set the case down.

'Naturally, if we attempt the mission, we need to be discreet,' Stone said. 'No killing would be ideal, especially considering our clientele.' He shrugged. 'We'll see how that goes. But, among my usual tools, I'd want to bring this.'

He opened the case and Chuck gave a grunt of recognition. Randy looked from his former boss to Stone, puzzled. 'Sorry. It looks like an air pistol. A large, fancy air pistol. Like I used to shoot when I was a kid.'

Chuck snorted a laugh.

26

'*Close,*' *Stone said. He picked up the weapon, snapped it to a firing position, and pulled the trigger. The hiss of compressed gas sounded over the crackle of the fire. He pointed to a thin wooden post, no more than two inches wide, protruding from the deck about twenty paces away. It was one of several that supported the strings of decorative lights that illuminated the patio during Luana's social gatherings. '*Why don't you see if you can recover my round, Randy.*'

Randy moved off, his eyebrows raised. He could barely see the post in the coy flicker of light from the fire pit, and he wasn't sure how to recover a slug even if Stone had somehow managed to hit it.

'*Really?*' *Chuck asked. '*At this range?*'

'*Years of practice,*' *Stone replied.*

'*Show-off,*' *Chuck grumbled, just as Randy returned, his confusion supplanted by amazement. Between the forefinger and thumb of his right hand he gingerly held a tiny dart.*

'*Uh, don't touch the tip,*' *Stone said.*

'*I may be ignorant,*' *Randy said, as he carefully transferred the nasty little projectile to Stone, '*but I'm not stupid.*'

*Chuck picked up the gun. '*Automatic load? Shit, Stone, this is a major improvement—*'

'*Over what you used during the cold war?*' *Stone interjected.*

'*Kiss my ass,*' *Chuck snarled.*

'*What's in the cylinder?*' *Randy asked, inspecting the object cupped in Stone's hand.*

'*Could be anything. Cyanide is popular.*'

Randy flinched back and Stone laughed.

'*In this case, just a heavy-duty trank. Put it into the neck and your target is snoozing before he hits the ground. A body shot takes longer.*'

'*And you nailed that post at, what, fifty feet? In bad light.*'

'*It's a close-range weapon,*' *Stone said seriously.*

***

Randy saw the confidence in Stone's eyes. Stone had repeatedly commented that the key to success for any operation was planning. Since Chuck had drummed that mantra into Randy's head for years, he had no argument. He was a believer. The incredible scope of planning for this mission had surprised him, however. They'd derived their initial intel from a villager who'd escaped an early morning raid by armed thugs. He'd hidden, unable to offer any resistance, and had seen many villagers loaded onto a truck. They'd left the village on the only road, heading for the harbor. Other information had trickled in through discreet inquiries in Puerto Barrios. No one was unaware of the activities going on there, and local gossip provided the basis for their painstaking planning.

Randy had spent hours studying the *Saint Martin* and had been quizzed by Stone on the location of every hatch, companionway, and cabin, the size of the crew, their duties, even on their expected watch schedules or potential shore leave. At the end of these studies, Randy could have walked the ship blindfolded without being spotted. However, at this point they would not be avoiding the crew. It was time to take this ship, and the steps for doing so (along with at least a dozen contingency plans) had been drilled into his head. All he had to do was remain calm and alert. Oh, yeah. Just that.

Randy took a deep breath. A tiny smile curled the corners of his mouth and he nodded. Stone turned and moved silently up the stairs. There was a small window in the door to the bridge. From a crouching position, Stone slowly lifted a miniature periscope until the upper end peeked above the windowsill. A minute passed that seemed like an hour to Randy. Stone, looking puzzled, held up two fingers. They had been expecting no fewer than three on the bridge.

***

'There'll probably be three men on the bridge,' Stone had said.

'Why so many?' Randy asked.

'Yeah,' Chuck seconded, 'the boat's anchored in a harbor and you'll be hittin' it in the early a.m., so why so many?'

Stone shrugged. 'If it were a normal, innocent merchant ship I'd agree. But if it was me, I'd want a 24-hour coms person and a heavy— a guard who's actually there to protect the cargo.'

'You mean the people,' Randy said.

'It's just cargo to them. In an operation like this one, I'll bet the smugglers have their own first and second in command, their own guards, maybe even a business guy who'll seal the deal and collect payment in whatever port they land. The smugglers will be

independent of the ship's crew. There may even be mutual mistrust between the groups.'

'Can we use that?' Chuck asked.

Stone shook his head. 'I doubt it, except to the extent that one side may not be willing to die for the other.'

Chuck grunted. 'So, three on the bridge. What do we do?'

Stone grinned, but it was the grin of a big cat about to devour its prey. 'I open the door and shoot them—with this.' He held up the air gun. 'If I miss'—Chuck and Randy both snorted their disbelief—'or if they start thrashing around, Randy drops them. One shot to the head. No bullshit chivalry.'

'And where am I going to be?' Chuck asked.

'On shore. Monitoring communications and acting as lookout,' Stone said.

The eruption of creative vulgarity that followed as Chuck protested made no impression on Stone, who simply refilled his drink and lit another cigar. He waited until Chuck's anger was (mostly) spent. 'Imagine yourself in your thirties, Chuck,' Stone began, with provoking calm. 'You're in charge of an op. There's a high probability of unexpected kinetic action. There's a guy in your office, a former stud operator, but getting a little long in the tooth; maybe lost half a step. Odds are he'd be fine, but there's a finite probability that he moves too slow, takes a knife between the ribs or stops a round with his winning smile. Remember, you're in charge. You're responsible. Do you let him come along?'

Chuck's breathing was loud in the silence that followed. Finally he said, 'I'd tell him to go have sex with himself. Then I'd tell him he'd be putting the op and the people involved at risk, and that there was a better way for him to help.'

'Q.E.D.' Stone said quietly.

'Sorry, Q.E. what?' Randy asked.

'It means my sorry ass has been whipped by logic,' Chuck muttered. 'Jeez, Stone, at least refill my drink.'

'Ah, now that I'm happy to do.'

***

With an eerie calmness, Stone opened the door to the bridge. In what seemed a slow-motion action, he raised his pistol, fired once, shifted his aim and fired again. Randy was barely in the room before both targeted men slumped to the floor, never uttering more than a gasp of surprise. A tiny dart protruded from each of their necks.

Both Stone and Randy crouched low, Stone examining the two men, Randy enabling his coms gear. 'Two down. Stone's checking.'

Randy glanced over and Stone shook his head.

'Captain's not here. What do you see?'

Chuck wiped the lenses of his binoculars and scanned the ship, the shoreline, and the dock. 'All quiet. No activity at all on shore. As for the ship, I can't see a single guard anywhere. 'Course I'm blind to the port side, so don't assume anything.'

'Roger.'

'By the way, this job sucks. I'm cramped up in this moldy old attic. Water's dripping through the shingles. There's not a single person to shoot …'

'We'll contact you as soon as we've bagged the big dog,' Randy said, the grin on his face finding its way into his next words. 'Try not to get too bored.'

'Yeah, and you can kiss my—'

'Roger. Out.'

'Sounds like Chuck is holding up well,' Stone said. 'These two will be out for a while, but let's gag and tie 'em just to be sure.'

A few minutes later, Randy and Stone were moving stealthily down a dimly lit corridor heading for the captain's cabin. When they arrived they paused, listening. The only sound was a low, growling snore.

Randy backed to the other side of the hallway, crouching down and scanning from side to side, as Stone gently turned the doorknob and eased the door open. Unlocked. Apparently no one on this boat would be foolish enough to disturb the captain's repose. Stone smiled crookedly. Well, almost no one.

In the blackness of the cabin, Stone could barely see anything until the door was open an inch or two. As his eyes adjusted, he located the captain's bed, guided by the heaving snoring. An amorphous shape sprawled across it. Years of training had taught Stone to never assume. He shifted the angle of his periscope and was rewarded with the vague image of another person, a woman, huddled in a chair on the other side of the room. *Not too interested in staying in the same bed,* Stone thought. *Can't say I blame her.* He watched for a minute longer, then turned and caught Randy's eye. He silently held up one finger and pointed, giving an angle to the captain's location, and then a second finger followed by the direction. Randy nodded.

Stone stood and pulled his dart gun. Randy stepped in, close behind him. Stone swung the door open and fired, immediately moving into the room so Randy could follow. An instant later, he had a hand over the woman's mouth and kept repeating in rapid Spanish, 'Friends, a rescue. You're safe.'

After Stone checked the captain, he closed the door and turned on a small LED light. Crouching near the woman, he smiled and put a finger to his lips. Understanding lit her eyes and she nodded.

***

'Once you've got the captain in the bag?' Chuck had asked.

'We give him a mega-dose of stimulant to wake him up some. Then we get the specifics: How many crew? How many guards? Where are they stationed? And so on,' Stone replied.

'And he'll be just too happy to tell you?' Chuck said sarcastically.

'Yes, he will,' Stone said matter-of-factly. 'His life is not important to us, and we'll make that very clear.'

'Hmm,' Chuck muttered. 'Makes sense. The guy is in it for the money, not for glory. And he sure as hell won't nobly sacrifice himself for his greasy boss. What's next.'

'Simple,' Stone said, 'we take down the rest of the crew and release their prisoners.'

***

'Think she's got it right?' Randy asked. 'Or do we have to wake up Captain Pig?'

'We'll start by checking for port-side lookouts. That'll keep Chuck happy. If we can find one alone, we should be able to take him and have a talk. According to her, the crew and guards we expected are mostly on shore, partying. After all, they anticipated a nice, quiet time in port, with local authorities either bribed or terrified into cooperating. Still, a pretty sloppy operation.'

'But good for us. OK, I'll tell the woman to sit tight here till we come get her.'

'No. I go with,' she said urgently. She pointed at Randy.

'Whoa, you speak English?' he asked.

'Only little. I no stay with that.' This time, the finger pointed at the prone and still-snoring captain.

Randy turned to Stone, who was frowning. Finally he shrugged. 'What's your name.'

'Maria.'

'OK, Maria, you stay behind us, make no noise, and do exactly what you're told, right?'

'*Si!*'

***

As Randy and Stone worked their way aft, it seemed Chuck had been unduly concerned about lookouts until they saw the slumped form of a sailor collapsed against a bulkhead, a nearly empty bottle keeping him company. Stone, motioning for Randy and the woman to hang back, crept noiselessly to the man's side and relieved him of his knife, setting it aside. With one hand over his mouth and the other throttling him, Stone lowered him to the deck.

The sailor's eyes popped open, but they were bloodshot and unfocused. Stone rapped the man's head on the deck several times, which brought him to a terrified state of consciousness.

Randy moved to Stone's side as he began asking the man questions. How many men were on watch? A question for which they already had an answer. Where were the sailors? The guards? 'Whisper the answers,' Stone commanded, 'or I cut your throat.' Despite his dazed condition, the sailor had no difficulty believing Stone's threat. There wasn't the hint of softness in his dark-brown eyes. Randy watched, knowing that Stone was serious as a gallows. He and Stone concentrated as the man's sotto voce answers flowed in rapid Spanish. The woman crouched beside them, and no one saw her wrap the sailor's knife into the folds of her dress.

When they had the information they needed, Stone made a tight nod. Without a word, Randy reached around, took the air gun from Stone's holster, put it to the man's neck, and fired. Stone clamped his hand down on the man's mouth and whispered, *'Duerme bien.'* Sleep well. The man twitched once and was still.

'You not kill him?' the woman asked.

'No,' Stone said.

'Why?'

A good question. Stone's answer was immanently practical and held no trace of mercy. 'He's a sailor. We may need his help to sail the ship.'

***

'But aren't you forgetting something?' Chuck had asked.

'No, I don't think so,' Stone said, with a provoking smile.

Chuck leaned forward in his chair, and his voice rose half an octave. 'You've got a friggin' ship full of kidnapped people and a bunch of knocked out or dead—which I'd prefer—sex traffickers. Now what?'

'We sail the ship out to international waters, where you've arranged to have a company-contracted ship waiting to transfer everyone on board. We scuttle the bad guy's ship. Unless you want to keep her?'

Chuck's voice rose another half octave. 'And you know how to sail a freighter?'

'How hard can it be? Besides, I'll bet the sailors will be more than willing to help.'

'You are one arrogant, egotistical smartass, Stone,' Chuck said as he flopped back into the chair. 'Did you know that?'

'He knows,' Randy replied with a grin. 'And that's one of his better qualities.'

***

The sleeping guards and sailors had been even less trouble than expected. Most were drunk. Nearly comatose. The two most lively, including the first mate, were bound and gagged and dragged back to the bridge.

'I think we'll wake the captain, now,' Stone said. 'See if he's willing to be helpful. If he is, we'll chain him to that pipe near the starboard bulkhead.'

As Stone mentioned his plans, a gleam lit Maria's eyes. She glanced over to the unconscious captain, then lowered her head.

A few minutes later, the captain was standing, though still wobbly and supporting himself on the control console with one hand.

He stared in disbelief at his two men, now sitting on the deck under Randy's careful watch. 'Why should I help you?' he said, his lip curled in a snarl. 'You'll be caught by my compadres and cut up for fish bait.'

'That's not your concern,' Stone said easily. 'And you should know that I'm not with the police nor am I employed by any government. Which is to say, I'm not bound by any conventional rules in the treatment of prisoners.'

The captain considered Stone's words before saying, 'We are not so different, you and I. We have no master. We do work. We are paid. I can double your pay in one easy trip. No. Triple it! You work for me and you will see. Life can be very good. And there are certain … other benefits,' he went on, leering at Maria. 'You can even have this one. She is a wildcat!'

With a yell of rage, Maria flew across the cabin, the knife flashing in her hand. With all her strength, and the momentum of her charge, she drove the knife in low, below the man's belt.

The captain bent over double and his eyes bugged out. A piercing scream rattled the windows as gushing blood soaked his pants and he tumbled to the floor. Unperturbed, Stone kicked him in the side of the head and he was unconscious once again. Stone looked at the woman, who stood panting with rage, her eyes blazing, her chin held high, and gave her a terse nod. Then he turned to the two captive sailors. He pointed to the one on the left. 'I promote you to captain. If you refuse to cooperate, Maria will punish you. Nod if you wish to help.'

***

Breckenridge, Colorado

'Honestly,' Randy said, 'except for the fact that the CIA chose to return the ship to its owners rather than scuttle her, things went pretty much as planned.'

Randy was relating his experiences on board the *Saint Martin* to Luana on the patio of her home in Breckenridge as they waited for Stone and

Chuck to bring out a platter of raw steaks for their barbecue and another bottle or two of vino. The day had been fine—warm and dry—and they planned on eating outside.

'Jason has the ability to cast that illusion,' Luana said. 'Everything went exactly as planned. I've learned to ignore it. More than once he's had to rely on dumb luck and the intervention of a benevolent God, often in the form of his friends.'

Randy shrugged and took a drink. 'Excellent Cab. Perfect for steaks. But seriously, things went as smoothly as could be expected.'

'Meaning that only the captain of the *Saint Martin* was converted into a soprano?'

'Don't shed any tears for that bastard. If I'd been in charge, I'd have let him bleed out. Damn it, now I'm going to need my steak well done.'

'Well done?' Chuck asked, as he set the loaded platter on the tiled counter next to the grill. 'That's a waste of good meat. You know, Stone, I think Randy would rather have a hot dog.'

Stone laughed. 'Really? Well, if you insist.'

'No, I do not. Here, let me give you a hand.' Stone was juggling three bottles, two glasses, barbecue tools, and the bottle opener. 'Whoa,' Randy said, checking the labels, 'this is good stuff. But what's Chuck going to have? Got any Ripple?'

'Ah, touché, Grasshopper.'

When everyone had a drink and Stone was busily cooking, Luana said, 'So the plan is to meet in London? Open up the headquarters there?'

'Yeah,' Chuck said. 'Though "married with children"'—he motioned to Randy—'has to stop off in Tucson and say hello to the wife and bambino.'

'How about you, Chuck? Doesn't Joy want to see your smiling face?'

'You kidding? She's having the time of her life house-hunting with Cathie Fletcher in the Old Pueblo. Probably find something we can't afford.'

'You are the vice president of a very professional organization that's just had their first successful business venture,' Luana teased.

'Only wish we were getting paid,' he retorted.

'Oh, quit your griping, Chuck,' Randy said. 'Even though The Salvation Army isn't paying the bills, Diana and Luana have tossed in enough to keep us in steaks and Cab.'

'Hmph. Seems like we're just paying ourselves.'

'Can nothing cheer this man up?' Stone asked. 'Randy, how'd you manage to work for Mr. Cup-is-Half-Empty all those years?'

'Alcohol.'

'Fill Chuck's glass, would you,' Stone said. 'See if maybe it doesn't work on him.'

Chuck pulled out three cigars and passed them out. 'This'll cheer me up. Besides, I'm going to visit my son, Marcus, for a few days on the way to London. He finally got a break and I haven't seen him in a long time.'

'How's he doing?' Stone asked.

'Got his first real assignment as a CIA rookie.'

'Oh, Lord,' Randy moaned. 'I remember mine. I had this boss—a grumpy, old, mean SOB.'

'Hey, I wasn't that old,' Chuck countered. 'And I'm still just a sprightly lad.'

'Fine,' Stone said. 'You and the other sprightly lad go and get the plates and salad. These steaks have just about stopped mooing.'

***

After dinner, as a bottle of cognac was making the rounds, Stone pulled out a newspaper and began flipping pages.

'Jeez, Stone, are we boring you?' Chuck asked.

'Oh, he does this every evening,' Luana said, as she applied a Firestarter to several candles on the table. The sun had set, and only the palest blue lit the sky near the horizon. To the east, stars had already exploded into the night. 'Maybe he could explain,' Luana finished, fixing Stone with a meaningful look.

Stone folded the paper. 'Did you ever wonder what might be the next big thing?'

'You mean like Beyoncé or pickle ice cream?' Chuck said.

'I'm being serious, Johnson.'

For some reason, his words had a chilling effect. Randy took an incautious gulp of his cognac, coughed for a moment, and reached for the decanter to top off his glass. Chuck's smirk slid from his face. 'What d'ya mean?'

Stone lit a fresh cigar and blew a fragrant cloud into the night sky before answering. 'Think about it. In June of 1914, a newspaper reported the assassination of Austrian archduke Franz Ferdinand and his wife. Before you know it, we have World War I. Or how about an unknown loudmouth named Adolf being voted in as chancellor in Germany. No reason to really take notice. What was the first news article that mentioned blockading Cuba in 1962? Point is, every major story has a predicate. Most stories today are just fodder for the 24-hour news cycle. Come and gone in a flash. Some are ... different. Given the business we're in, some might lead to a fat payday.'

Chuck snorted laughter and Randy smiled.

Stone held up his hand in mock seriousness. 'Let me give you a sample.' He ruffled the newspaper and began reading:

'"North Korea to reenter nuclear negotiations." Wow. Exciting.

'"Ben and Jerry to introduce new flavor: Global Warming Sundae." Sounds delicious.

'"Tariffs to increase on agricultural exports."

'"Break-in at the CDC in Atlanta."

'"Russia vows to hold Crimea."

'"Mexican drug cartels fighting a bloody war for control of the drug trade.

'"China tests hypersonic aircraft."

'"Unexplained illness aboard Summerline cruise ship."

'You get the idea.

'Ah. Here's the best of all. "Shipload of sex trafficking victims rescued by CIA. All freed and offered asylum in the U.S."'

'Might have heard about that one,' Randy said. 'And you think we'll find our next job under the fold on page seventeen?'

'You never know,' Stone answered.

They were walking down the hall in the formerly disused wing of Diana's estate, the wing that would house the Triple S headquarters.

Chapter Two

London Headquarters

Alexandria, Virginia

'Dad!' The tall young man rose from his seat in the noisy restaurant and stepped into the aisle, his hand extended.

Chuck stood silently, contemplating his son. He was lean, but with a muscular build, and was several inches taller than Chuck. He stood there with confidence though there was a slight hesitation in his smile and a touch of uncertainty in his brown eyes. But his jaw was firm and his dark skin smooth from chin to brow. The look of a very capable man still a little awed by the reputation of his father. Chuck couldn't have been prouder. He ignored the offered hand, wrapping his arms around Marcus and slapping his back. Marcus did the same.

'Well look at you!' Chuck said when he stepped back. 'Nearly as handsome and studly as I was at your age.'

Marcus snorted and took his seat. 'And you're not so bad for a field man with a few miles on him and a few slug holes in him.'

'Yeah,' said Chuck as he sat, 'that's funny 'cause it's true. So have they got you out there spying on Chinese or shooting up bad guys?'

'Maybe. Maybe not. Actually, just not. My riskiest assignment so far was collating pages for my boss's report. See that.' He held up his thumb. 'Got a bad papercut.'

When Chuck stopped laughing, he said, 'Man, it's good to see you. Two T-bones, medium rare, salads with ranch, baked potatoes with everything,' he said briskly as a waiter appeared. 'And a couple of Pabst Blue Ribbon beers.' He turned to Marcus and raised an eyebrow.

'Who am I to argue with that?'

The waiter nodded. 'Yes, sir.'

'So, I've told you my war stories,' Marcus said. 'What the hell have you been up to? Mom said something about chasing Central American beauties. How come a corporate vice president has to do field work?'

''Cause there's only three of us and we're all VPs. Hey, if you joined, you could be, like, Junior Agent, Second Class. Then you'd get all the shit work and we'd sit in big offices and smoke cigars.'

'Fat chance. But seriously, Mom sounded worried about something you were up to.'

Chuck sighed. He pulled out a cigar and regarded it with longing.

Marcus shook his head. 'Not in here. Later we can take a walk.'

'Well, working with Jason Stone is never dull, that's for sure. OK, keep this under your hat. I haven't told even half of this to your mom.'

'Like she hasn't guessed!'

'Right,' Chuck said glumly, as he ran his hand along the stubble on his chin.

***

London

'A party?' Diana asked. 'Why that's a marvelous idea, Yvette. To celebrate the opening of the European headquarters of Stone Security Services.'

'Yes, I thought it would be fun. Of course, Richard said I shouldn't impose.'

'He would. The man wouldn't know a party—a real party—if it bit him on the bum.'

'And do you suppose,' Yvette said, stifling a giggle, 'I mean, would it be possible ...'

They were walking down the hall in the formerly disused wing of Diana's estate, the wing that would house the Triple S headquarters. It was usual now for Diana to use prosthetics. She'd lost her lower legs long ago in a brutal attack arranged by Smythe-Montgomery's jealous father, and she'd used her wheelchair for years. With the threat of the Smythe-Montgomery family removed, there was no fear that flaunting her mobility would bring about swift and brutal retribution. The hallway itself was still dusty and in serious want of cleaning, but the emblems of the Foster family—ancient swords, tapestries, and shields with the Foster coat of arms—were everywhere, and Diana had agreed with Yvette that these links to the past must stay.

Yvette's voice had trailed off just as they passed what had once been the formal dining room for House Foster. Diana took Yvette's meaning instantly and stopped at the entry door. In the gloom of the cavernous old banquet hall, sheet-covered furniture, long-dead candles, and dusty cobwebs were evident. 'Oh, I'm really not sure, dear. This room has been ignored for far longer than your lifetime. I only remember seeing it fully occupied when I was a child.' The memory clouded Diana's features as she saw crisp visions of long ago. A magical place for a youngster, full of light and color, wondrous smells, the clink of china, the bustling servants, candles all aglow, and unquenchable laughter. She put a hand to her mouth as her breath caught in her throat. 'You don't suppose … Could we put it to rights? Could we bring back just a hint of its old glory?'

'Yes, oh certainly,' Yvette said, bouncing on the balls of her feet with excitement. 'That is,' she added quickly, 'probably not. Not without help. But I think I know someone who would be willing to lend a hand.'

Diana eyed her suspiciously. 'All right, out with it. I've been warned, you know, by your crotchety old guardian. Would this hypothetical helper be a young gentleman? And would the price of his help be an invitation to our dinner party?'

Yvette felt waves of embarrassment rolling off her scorching face. 'Well, yes. Perhaps.'

Diana laughed until the tears came, and Yvette gradually brightened. 'You mean it might be OK? That is, if he helps—'

Diana reached out and folded Yvette in her arms. 'Of course, silly girl. Whether he helps or not, though the help would be most welcome. The question is, is he of good character and a good family? That is, would he be worthy of the brilliant and lovely Yvette Crandall?'

'Oh, of course.' The blush had returned in full force. 'Stop teasing! He's a friend from school, a classmate. We didn't get on too well, at first. His father is a rather famous professor and doctor of medicine specializing in communicable diseases, and his older brother is a London neurosurgeon. Intimidating to say the least. Made my friend defensive.'

'And now you and this classmate are getting on well? Not so extraordinary. And does this friend have a name?'

'Yes. It's Colin Fishburne.'

***

Diana called Richard Crandall as soon as Yvette left for the day, knowing she would be in transit. 'Do you know Mr. Fishburne, Richard?'

'Yes. A universally acknowledged wanker, according to Yvette. But that was a while ago. Since her escapade cleaning the malware from the school's computer, their relationship has thawed. It seems he put aside his resentment at her rise to fame and offered heartfelt congratulations; has been gracious and gentlemanly to a fault since. Not just to Yvette, but to all and sundry. So much so that the school's headmaster called me, wondering what other magic was on the thumb drive that cleared their computers. I told him I suspected it was love.'

'And are you ... are you OK with all this?'

'Ah, Diana, my life has been a muddle for an eternity. As you know, I've mended—moderated my ways,' he corrected himself quickly. 'What Yvette is to me today is not what she was several years ago. It causes occasional embarrassment, naturally, but I've been very clear that she must live her own life. I suspect she still consults Becky Amhurst, that impressive woman, from time to time and receives similar advice. I'm delighted for Yvette.'

'So this party—'

'Meets with my full approval. However, I seem to remember a rather large ballroom, near your dining room. And I would like to propose ... But wait. Has Yvette seen this room?'

'Oh yes. She's explored the house in its entirety. What on earth are you thinking, Richard?'

'Just this. Leave it as it is. Dusty and disused.'

'That's easy enough.'

'Until several days before the party. Then, with your permission, I'd like to keep Yvette occupied—several critical new algorithms to integrate into the predictive chaos model—and send over a team to clean and decorate. Also, with your permission, I'd like to hire a band, one with a Victorian flair. Perhaps even costumes. After dinner, we shall hold a ball. A modest affair, at which it would be my extreme pleasure to watch Yvette dance with her new friend, and where it would be even more pleasurable for me to engage you in a dance ... or two.'

42

When he'd finished, Crandall waited, expecting a tart rebuttal. Instead, he heard breathing. A bit erratic, but steadying at last. 'Oh, Richard! Will you ever cease to amaze? My noble friend, how could I do less than accept?'

***

'*The Fall of an Empire: The Tragic End of the Family Croker / Smythe-Montgomery*. I love the title, babe. Is it done?' Logan asked.

'Yes,' Cathie replied tentatively. 'Well, a pretty well polished draft, anyway. I'd like you to read it, now.'

'I'd love to. It'll give me something to do on the plane.'

'Are you going somewhere?'

'*We're* going somewhere. A formal dinner at the Castle Foster.'

'Castle? Don't be ridiculous.'

'Fine. But it's an invitation from Diana and Richard, and the party is at her estate in England. Chuck and Randy described it as pretty castle-like.'

'You're such a buffoon sometimes. It's why I love you. But I love you more when we get invited to grand parties in England. You are serious, aren't you?'

'Quite.'

'Who'll be there?'

'Diana. Duh! Richard. Beyond that point, I'm only guessing. But since it's a grand-opening celebration for Stone Security Service's European office, I'll assume Stone and Luana will be there. Chuck and Randy as well.'

'Their spouses?'

'Oddly enough, our invitation doesn't say. You can just call Joy and Gail and ask.'

'Crude, but effective.' She sat pondering. 'I've been dying to get back to England. And seeing everyone there will be so much fun.'

'That's not all. It seems there will be something of an old English ball following dinner, so full costume is required.'

'Really? In celebration of the opening of the Triple S office?'

'And something more. It would seem that this is the surprise "coming out" party for Ms. Yvette Crandall.'

***

Jesse Raynard sat impassively as the big Mercedes rounded another curve and kept climbing, the powerful engine barely noticing the incline. The headlights swept the private road, revealing the dense vegetation to either side. Carlos Velasquez, also known as the Viper, was conducting business in Guatemala, so he was staying at his fortress-like estate in the rugged, overgrown mountains. Jesse sniffed in disdain. The car had been stopped twice along the road by heavily armed men. A blind squirrel would know that this was the lair of the most powerful drug lord in Mexico, Honduras, and Guatemala. Intimidation and money had kept him safe in these countries, the local politicians and law enforcement either terrified or supportive—for a reasonable fee.

But Carlos was operating in an international market, as was evidenced by the fact that one of his ships, owned through a shell corporation, had been seized by the CIA. The CIA had kindly returned the vessel to its 'rightful owners' with more than a small hint that they knew the truth beneath the thin façade of 'cargo freighter.' The two sets of three numbers at the bottom of their terse note were puzzling to Carlos's people, and were assumed to be some sort of Agency identification code. Jesse sniffed again. One glance had revealed the numbers to be the latitude and longitude of the very estate they were now approaching.

The car was stopped for the third time at the perimeter of Carlos's compound. Once again, flashlights probed the dark interior of the vehicle, and the man in the front passenger's seat said, 'Jesse Raynard. Requested by the Viper.' The beams swung to the back seat, and Jesse nodded tolerantly. The look of surprise by the men outside never ceased to amuse, but it was late. Hopefully, this would be a short meeting.

A huge, wrought-iron gate swung open on silent hinges and the car moved forward. A brilliantly lit home of stone, stucco, and Spanish tile swung into view, but the car hurried past and was soon descending a shallow incline, at the end of which was a caretaker's house. For the first time this evening, a genuine smile lit Jesse's face. Deception was always appreciated by Raynard. And though there was little genius here, at least a Predator's Hellfire missiles—should the annoyed Americans choose to use them—would destroy only the flamboyant dwelling of the Viper, who was apparently staying in these modest lodgings.

'Ah, Raynard, so good of you to come,' Carlos said as soon as Jesse was ushered in. 'You have been most helpful to me in the past, and, as you see'—he spread his arms to indicate his adopted dwelling—'I have taken your ... concerns ... to heart.' The fact that half of the Viper's more extravagant furnishings had been shoehorned into a house completely unsuited to their size spoke to the foolish arrogance of the man.

Jesse made no reply. Carlos was serving pap. He would eventually come to the point.

'Yes, of great value to me in the past. And now, this irksome interference of the Americans has added to my other difficulties. Which you know, of course?' Cold, dark eyes pierced Jesse, who was relaxed and remained silent. 'Be careful, my friend,' Carlos said, his voice suddenly glacial. 'You are clever. Perhaps too clever.' He stared silently for what seemed minutes, then burst into laughter. 'Fine. You were never one for idle chitchat. Good. So, two other problems. First, I am still suffering from the removal of Sir Conrad. An alliance with such a man would have been useful. His proposals for product production and distribution were most interesting. His absence has exacerbated my difficulties with the other cartels.'

Jesse knew all this. Smythe-Montgomery had approached Carlos through his intelligent and gorgeous aid, Ms. Emma Lister. At that time, Smythe-Montgomery had global aspirations, with grand visions of a supply chain of drugs in the Americas that originated with Carlos, whom Smythe-Montgomery proposed to help gain control over the smaller producers. As Ms. Lister had put it, 'Sir Conrad prefers to work with one individual who controls production in your hemisphere. Preferably you. He will help you ... consolidate operations to achieve this end.' Her meaning had been clear. Unfortunately, with the sudden elimination of Smythe-Montgomery, Carlos had lost considerable status with the other cartels. Several were now making his life difficult.

'And second,' Carlos continued, 'is this sudden American interference. 'Who is behind it? You have informants. Perhaps ...'

Jesse held up a hand. 'I believe I can help with both your difficulties. Let's take the second first. As you say, I have friends who may be able to probe the reasons for the intervention of the CIA. But as I'm sure you know ...' Now Jesse was serving pap. Clearly, Carlos was as ignorant as

45

a lump of granite. 'Well, it's improbable that the CIA captured your ship. In a Guatemalan port, of all places! There are other agencies at work, possibly freelancers. We shall see.

'As to your first problem, I took the liberty of bringing something with me that might both amuse you and provide a convenient solution to these tedious disputes with other cartels. If one of your men would be so good? They insisted I leave it in the trunk.'

Carlos motioned imperiously, and two lackeys rushed from the room to retrieve the package from the trunk.

'It's a pleasant evening,' Jesse said. 'We could step outside. Perhaps a cigar and a drink? And I'll demonstrate the solution to your difficulties with the other cartels.'

Carlos shrugged. 'Fine. I'll assume this is worth my time and attention.' The threat was apparent.

Ten minutes later, Carlos stood with his mouth gaping. 'And you have how many?'

'Today? Fourteen. By week's end, sixty. More than enough.'

'And the chemical?'

It was Jesse's turn to grow cold. 'I'm offering you a gift. My failure is my death. Do you think I want to die?'

Carlos smiled.

Jesse nodded. 'Precisely. I will be busy with final preparations. My assistant, Charlotte, will contact you with updates. She'll also answer any of your questions. Acceptable?'

Carlos had met Charlotte once. A stunning South African beauty with a devil's wit. Also an aspiring Hollywood actress with only B-movie credits in her résumé, and clearly more than Raynard's assistant. 'Perfectly acceptable. And if this should turn out well—'

'Not "if," Viper. Never "if." You have my word.'

***

As the Mercedes drove off, Carlos called to one of his lieutenants, Ramón Hernandez. 'Talk with me,' Carlos said, offering the man a cigar.

'*Gracias, patrón*,' Ramón answered, accepting the cigar with a deferential nod of his head. 'Ah,' he said a moment later, as the fragrant smoke curled into the sky, '*muy bueno*!'

46

The night was heavy with moisture and the chirring of insects. A sliver of moon hung hazily in the velvet sky. All was peaceful, the strange visitor nearly forgotten.

Nearly.

Carlos walked over to the heavy wooden table where the focus of the recent demonstrations still sat. He reached out a hand and lifted the drone. 'Hmph. Heavier than it looks.' He set his cigar carefully on the edge of the table and hefted the machine with both hands. Six propellers were attached by tubes to the drone's main structure. A camera and a boxy appendage hung below. Carlos examined the underside. There were sixteen small tubes, now all empty, that would contain projectiles, the payload. As Raynard had explained it, drones such as this had been developed to reforest areas previously cleared or destroyed by fire. It was an ingenious method for quickly replanting areas before rains and erosion could wipe them clean. Each projectile was designed to penetrate the ground and deposit the seed of a desired tree type. Using GPS, a small fleet of these drones could plant acres of difficult terrain along a grid with precise spacing. No more sending crews crawling over rough terrain. No more labor-intensive planting. Simply load the drones, deploy them, and reload until an area was covered. Raynard had cleverly adapted the concept to suit the purpose of the Viper: to poison the crops of his competitors. A swarm of drones hidden by darkness and loaded with a toxic chemical could destroy a crop of poppies or marijuana in a single night and make the field unusable for a season. Raynard had predicted that only a few such demonstrations would be necessary before his rivals capitulated to Carlos's demands. It wouldn't do to poison all the Viper's *future* land.

'Amazing, eh *patrón*,' Ramón said. 'Raynard is quite brilliant. A good ally, yes?'

It was far more than a rhetorical question. Carlos snorted and set the drone back down on the table. 'Quite brilliant.' The words he left unsaid screamed out to the dark. He picked up his cigar and took a long, thoughtful pull. 'Jesse is also a chameleon.' He shook his head. 'No. More like this.' He blew a cloud of smoke that drifted, swirled, and disappeared into the night air, leaving no trace but the mild fragrance, soon gone. 'We met in Los Angeles, years ago. At that time, I was responsible for distribution from San Diego to Sacramento.'

'A heavy responsibility, *patrón.*'

'Yes. And I was betrayed. An *unfaithful* lieutenant,' he said, one eyebrow raised.

Ramón gave him a nervous half-smile.

'Raynard worked in Los Angeles. Had achieved a certain notoriety, I believe.' He took another draw from his cigar, and the smoke trickled from his lips in a thin stream. 'I suppose it involved being smoke. Here one instant, gone the next. And with what purpose? That is an unsolved mystery.

'I was being transported from the LA Courthouse, where my legal team had just failed me, to the Detention Center. Traffic was bad and got worse. There were sirens and we were stopped. Then my vehicle was hit from behind, hard. The guards cursed and one said something about a garbage truck. There was much shouting, cursing, then silence. The back doors of the van opened, and Raynard, dressed as a paramedic, entered, unlocked my bindings with the ease of a magician, and said this: "My name is Jesse Raynard. I'm looking for a new career and I think I'd enjoy working with you. If this is acceptable, please come with me. I have an SUV waiting.'

'Mother of God!' Ramón said.

'Yes. A miraculous salvation. A comfortable drive south, a change of name, and other miracles to follow. My former *patrón*, who might have objected to my return, suddenly dead of a mysterious disease. My rivals disposed of by brutally efficient means. And suddenly'—he spread his arms wide—'I am *patrón.*'

'Jesse Raynard did all this? Why?'

'An excellent question. Since then, Raynard has been nothing but helpful, but not always on my terms. Jesse appears when needed, performs some useful feat'—he nodded towards the drone—'and disappears.' Carlos shrugged. 'Raynard's companion, Charlotte, is both beautiful and intelligent. I have no problem dealing with her.'

'But something concerns you, *patrón*?'

'You said it yourself. Why? Oh, I pay Jesse well. Extraordinarily well. Still, there may be something more. I had hoped that with the aid of our British friend, I might be able to do without the enigma that is Jesse Raynard. That hope is now gone. Raynard may yet prove valuable, as with this deadly aircraft. Still, best to be prepared. When the time comes, and I sense it may be coming soon, you will be ready. At my command, you will kill Jesse Raynard.'

***

Yvette stuck out her lower lip and blew a drop of sweat off her nose. Who would have thought cleaning out the dusty dining hall would be such a task? She was standing in stocking feet on the old mahogany table and attempting, with the aid of paper towels and cotton swabs, to bring one of three large chandeliers back to a state of burnished brilliance. Music played from a Bluetooth speaker nearby, taking its signal from a playlist on her iPhone. A bit of an old classic now, 'Jessie's Girl,' but with a driving, thumping beat appropriate for cleaning. She and her cleaning companion, Colin Fishburne, had jointly chosen the music. A loud sneeze from near the sideboard drew her attention, and she looked over, smiling. She had been going to school with Colin for over half a year, but was seeing him for the first time. True, he had never come to class in a faded Offspring T-shirt and jeans that were ratty at the cuffs. In these clothes, he seemed a bit thin, something she'd never noticed, but wiry, if what she could see of his arms translated to the rest of his body. His thick brown hair, always meticulously coiffed at school, had just the right amount of unruliness. Then there were his eyes, a surprisingly deep sapphire blue. Distracting.

Colin returned the smile, then sneezed again. 'I say, where do you suppose dust comes from? I mean, when I look around this room I see wood, brass, stone, glass, leather, and wax. Which do you suppose is the villain? Which is the father of dust?'

Yvette laughed lightly. 'You're mad, you know. Quite mad.'

'Hmm. I've been called worse. By you!'

'That was ages ago. Before you stopped being a truly irredeemable wanker!'

'Such language! Tut. But I suppose you're right. It's hard to say why. Bloody great chip on my shoulder, I suppose. Always being compared to my father and older brother. Always falling short. And here I am, still struggling to identify a career and failing to live up to the Fishburne family expectations.'

'Nonsense. You're quite smart. Nearly as smart as me.'

A used dusting towel was quickly crumbled and sent sailing across the room, but Yvette was far too nimble to be hit.

'Now look what you've done!' she cried. 'Dust on the table. Mysterious, self-generating dust.'

Both were still laughing hard when Diana entered the room.

'Oh my! You've done wonders. Absolute wonders.' She scanned the room, which was filled with mid-afternoon light lancing in from the interior courtyard. The windows were spotless, washed inside and out; the floors swept and mopped; tables, chairs, and sideboard cleaned and oiled, showing a deep brown luster that had lain hidden for decades; the old brass—candelabras, chandeliers, cabinet hinges and handles—gleamed. Even the heirlooms of House Foster and several ornately framed paintings had been meticulously cleaned. 'In fact,' Diana said, 'it appears that the filthiest objects in the room now are the two of you.'

'But I'm not nearly done here.' Yvette pointed with a cotton swab towards the chandelier she was working on. 'And Colin hasn't finished oiling the doorframes.'

'My lord, Yvette. Well, another half hour, no more. Then the two of you get cleaned up. I've managed a shepherd's pie all on my own, and I want you two to share it with me. We might find a bottle of wine. You *can* stay for dinner, Colin, can't you?'

'That's very generous of you.' He glanced at Yvette who was willing him to give the correct answer. 'So, how could I say no? Thank you.'

'Ah, lovely. We'll eat in my somewhat less formal west-wing dining room in an hour or so. Come as soon as you're cleaned up.' She turned and walked to the door opening onto the main hallway, then stopped and looked back, her eyes shining. 'What you've accomplished is astonishing. I've not seen the room like this since I was a little girl. Well done!'

***

The next day, Crandall quenched Yvette's enthusiasm with a stack of sloppily written formulas that he insisted be coded and integrated into the predictive chaos model immediately.

'But this will take days! Gawd, your handwriting. The party is this Saturday.'

'Ah, so best get to it. I'd hate to see you miss such an auspicious event.'

'Richard, you are truly evil! No, you're having me on. But I had counted on shopping.'

'Your wardrobe is quite adequate, I'm sure. This is a party of friends, not the House of Lords. Now please'—he motioned to the stack of papers—'it's the job that's never begun that's never done!'

Yvette gave him a disemboweling look and picked up a nearby letter opener. 'Yvette Crandall, in the study, with the letter opener!'

Crandall laughed as he hastily withdrew.

***

The day of the party found Yvette up early, shuffling through her closet. Richard was correct; she had more than enough to choose from. She suddenly lowered her nervous hands and thought back to the days, not so many years ago, when she'd stolen from thrift stores to have a shirt and pants that weren't worn to tatters. Had she really been that girl? And more to the point, who was she now? This calmed her, and she reached out for a blue dress (not nearly the lovely deep blue of his eyes) that would be fine. She sighed. She had hoped for something a bit more suited to the grandeur of the newly restored dining room. *Childish fancies*, she thought.

A knock on her bedroom door distracted her. 'Yes?'

'Ah, I'm glad you're up,' said Crandall. 'When you're dressed, come to breakfast. There's been a slight change to the, let's say style, of this evening's party. But not to worry. Just join me when you're ready.'

Yvette was more than worried as she threw on jeans and a shirt, and hustled towards the kitchen.

'So, what's this change of style, Richard?' Yvette asked as she entered the room.

'Oh, nothing really. But you haven't even poured yourself a cup of coffee. Try a scone, they're quite delicious.'

'Richard Crandall!'

'Oh, very well. Diana thought, and I agreed, that it would be quite fun to have everyone dress in Victorian costume. Rather well suited to the lovely work you and Colin did in the dining hall.'

'It won't work. No one knows.'

'Actually, they do. It was in the invitations. I'm afraid I, well, it completely slipped my mind. But all the guests know. Even your young man knows.'

51

Yvette flopped into a chair, her eyes dull. 'He's not my young man,' was all she could think to say. Days lost, typing mathematical algorithms, running test cases, correlating results. Plus all the work of cleaning the dining hall. 'I suppose you'll be suitably dressed.'

'Here's my costume.' He reached around a doorway and brought back an aristocratic costume. A dashing blue/grey coat with silver embroidery liberally splashed around the cuffs and collar, a silver waistcoat, an elegant matching cravat, and high-waist flat-front pants.

Yvette glanced up, her chin quivering. 'It's wonderful, Richard,' she said, and hung her head.

Crandall flushed as waves of guilt rolled over him. Diana had warned him not to tease. 'Don't … oh, dear. I'm just an old jackass, as Diana so often reminds me, and I've carried the joke too far.' He reached back around the corner. 'Here is your costume. Not, I'm delighted to say, chosen by me, but by Diana herself. We took the liberty.'

Yvette raised her head, and two glistening tears rolled down her cheeks. 'Oh!' It was all she could say. The blue of Colin's eyes—deep and romantic—had been captured in silk that gleamed as though it were alive. Creamy lace highlighted the collar, hem, and seams; the short sleeves were off the shoulder. Dangling carelessly from the hanger was a string of pearls. Crandall held up his other hand. Looping silver wire, also dotted with pearls, glistened. 'For your hair, or so I'm told,' he said sheepishly. 'Shoes are—'

Yvette crossed the room fast as a cricket and threw her arms around Crandall's neck. 'You insane, wonderful man. Thank you!'

***

The evening approached with the breakneck speed of a glacier, at least that was Yvette's impression once she was satisfied with the fit of her costume. The thought of seeing so many old friends together for the first time in over a year—and the previous occasion under less-than-ideal circumstances—was no small part of her excitement. But she blushed that a far larger part was the anticipated dinner with Colin. Her random energy would have been a real trial for Crandall had she not focused it on running test simulations with the newly coded predictive chaos algorithms. Finally, feeling a sense of guilt, Crandall approached and put a gentle hand on her shoulder.

'That's enough, now. Go get dressed. Diana said we might come over early and welcome the guests with her.'

Yvette was up and gone in an instant, only her smile seeming to linger in the air like the Cheshire Cat's of *Alice in Wonderland* fame.

***

Lights already blazed in the main entry hall, competing with the ocher sunlight lighting the circular driveway. True, the fountain was still dry, but the flowerbed had been partially restored, and the summer blooms would be a cheerful end to the long lane of dead elm trees. Diana, in a long-sleeved, silver and black gown with a tall black choker, waited with Yvette at the doorway, the heavy doors thrown open to the mild early-evening air.

Though no horse-drawn carriages were expected, the three greeters still got a mild shock when a silver Aston Martin DB5 growled up to the entrance. Stone leaped out and went to the passenger side to open the door for Luana, who exited with her usual grace. The two wore their costumes with such amazing ease that Yvette imagined they'd stepped directly from a more gracious past, visitors only in the 21st century. After greetings at the top of the stairs, Stone excused himself. 'Gave my driver the evening off. I'd better move the car.'

Before he could get away, Yvette grabbed his elbow. 'For a moment,' she said, 'I thought James Bond would get out of that car.'

'Ah, no, just me,' Stone said, with a grin.

'Better and better.' Yvette gave him a light kiss on the cheek.

'Yes,' Luana said to Yvette, as Stone retreated, 'he couldn't resist. Thank God he couldn't find a 1928 Bentley worthy of John Steed.'

'Oh, lord,' Yvette said, bringing her hand to her mouth. 'I hadn't even thought of that!'

***

As more guests arrived, Richard and Diana divided hosting duties, Diana walking her guests to the dining hall, pointing out interesting historical items along the way. Logan, Cathie, Gail, and Randy arrived together in a limousine arranged by the hotel where they were staying. The newest O'Neil, James Charles, was unimpressed by the goings on, or at least conveyed that notion by being sound asleep. 'He'll stay that way for a while—I hope.' said Gail. Chuck and Joy arrived shortly after in a cab.

All had come appropriately dressed, but most seemed self-conscious, Chuck Johnson the least comfortable of all.

'Would you stop fussing with that?' Joy said, as Chuck dug a finger under his cravat and twisted his head from side to side for the twentieth time.

'How the hell did men even breath? Did they all have pencil necks? And these pants are constricting my muscular buttocks.'

Joy shook her head and walked away as Logan came up. 'Should have opted for the short pants of an earlier era,' he said, his eyes drifting over Chuck's costume. 'Then we could all be treated to a nice view of your shapely calves.'

'Up yours, Fletch,' Chuck replied, twisting and contorting still as the two walked from the entry hall.

Yvette's second surprise of the evening came as a second cab pulled up behind the Johnson's and a tall, elegant woman in a stunning burgundy gown exited: Becky Amhurst. From the opposite side, a man whom Yvette had never met got out, looking uncomfortable and tugging at his cuffs.

'Becky!' Yvette said, beaming. 'I had no idea you'd be here.'

Becky bypassed Yvette's extended hand and wrapped her in a hug. 'How are you?'

'Oh, just wonderful.'

Becky gave her a penetrating stare. 'I'll expect a full explanation for that boundless enthusiasm—later. Yvette, this is Gary Walkin, Chief Engineer for ARC Avionics. Gary, this is Yvette Crandall. Be a gentleman and say hello.'

'She's like this at work, too,' Gary said, shaking Yvette's hand. 'Nice to meet you. I've heard some stories—amazing stories. All good,' he added.

'We're lucky to be here,' Becky said. 'Good timing. Gary and I are on our way to Indonesia to see Gary's hot girlfriend—oops!—that is, for a meeting with our customers, Pacific-Indo-Asia Airlines. We have only the one night in London.'

'Oh, no!' Yvette groaned. 'When will we talk?'

'I'm free all day tomorrow. Our flight out doesn't leave till 9:00 p.m.'

Yvette brightened instantly.

'Hello,' Crandall said, walking up. 'Come inside and join the others.'

Yvette was alone in the massive doorway, hands clasped in front of her, anticipating the last guest's arrival. A short time later, an Austin Mini Cooper came circling around the drive. It slowed at the entrance, then drove on and parked near the Aston Martin. Even at this distance, Colin was recognizable as he got out of the car. He gave the Aston Martin an envious glance, then walked along the pathway to the entrance. He paused at the bottom of the steps, gazing up at Yvette.

'Wow!'

To his credit, he tripped only once as he ascended. The two stood regarding each other like newly discovered species.

Yvette reached out and ran a finger along the shoulder of his coat. 'It's much nicer than your Offspring T-shirt,' she finally said.

'And you, I mean ...'

A cough from inside the hallway caused them both to spin around, embarrassed.

'Well,' Diana said, 'I doubt there'll be too much of a scandal if you hug. Then come along to your scrubbed and polished dining hall to meet the others. You might also want a glass of wine. For the nerves.'

As Colin entered the hall, a woman approached with a determined stride and a serious expression (put there an instant after a barely perceptible wink in Yvette's direction).

'So, you're Yvette's boyfriend,' Becky said, her eyes narrowed, her features granite. She evaluated him slowly, and finally gave one terse, approving nod. 'You'd better be good to her. I have ways of punishing men who misbehave.'

'You really ought to believe that,' Randy said, as he came up behind Becky, giving her a light poke in the ribs that made her jump.

Becky rounded on him and burst into laughter. 'Oh, now you've ruined my entire hard-ass routine.' She turned back to Colin and stuck out her hand. 'Just joking. Nice to meet you, Colin. I'm Becky Amhurst, an occasional collaborator with the rest of this eclectic crew and, more importantly, a friend of Yvette's.'

A steady stream of introductions followed, and several minutes passed before Colin was able to have a quiet word with Yvette. 'I say, your friends are amazing. And every one with such a story. Aerospace engineers, retired CIA agents, corporate CEOs, and a genuine superspy. And then there's you. Brilliant and beautiful! I'm feeling a bit inadequate in this crowd.'

'Don't,' she said, taking his arm. 'A handsome, courtly gentleman with all his future ahead of him.'

Colin looked around. 'Really? Where?'

Yvette swatted his arm. 'And a comedian as well. Oh, looks like Diana is about to call us to the table.'

'Ladies and gentlemen. Thank you all so much for coming. To the executives of Triple S, thank you for refraining from talking business at this lovely gathering which, I must say, was made possible by my dear old friend, Richard Crandall, and my dear *much* newer friend, Yvette Crandall and *her* friend, Colin Fishburne.'

There was loud applause and Becky whistled.

'This old room,' Diana continued, 'hasn't seen such a gathering in decades. Its physical beauty was restored by Yvette and Colin, but the warmth ... the love ... is thanks to you all.'

Crandall stood. 'Please raise your glasses. To an extraordinary woman, my friend, and the hostess of this festive gathering. To Lady Diana Foster!'

Glasses clinked. 'To Lady Diana Foster!' echoed in the hall.

Colin glanced at Yvette, a horrified look on his face. '*Lady* Diana Foster?' he whispered.

Yvette nodded.

'Oh, gawd! And I wore an Offspring T-shirt.'

Yvette just smiled and patted his shoulder as Diana went on.

'Please take your seats and dinner will be served.'

Applause as the guests took their seats, with Stone heard to say, 'God bless England.' Luana rolled her eyes.

For Yvette, the dinner passed too quickly, as she and Colin would occasionally nudge each other below the table or exchange a smile for no apparent reason.

The main-course dishes had been cleared away by the serving staff Crandall had hired for the evening, and Yvette looked around for signs of tea, coffee, or dessert. Instead, Crandall tapped a knife on a wine glass and Diana rose. 'I hope you've enjoyed your meal. As a very special surprise for Yvette and Colin, thanks entirely to Richard, we'll be moving to the ballroom for after-dinner drinks and dessert, and also ...' She cocked her head, and, like magic, music began to filter into the silent dining hall. A Joseph Lanner waltz, '*Die Romantiker*' (The Romantics), snatched from the past.

Colin turned an accusatory face to Yvette, who only shrugged. 'I don't understand. The ballroom is a disaster. Far worse than this was.'

'I see Yvette and Colin are confused,' Crandall said. 'A mystery soon resolved. Please, follow me.'

Like the Pied Piper, Crandall led the assembly down the main hallway to a large set of oak doors. 'Please,' he said, indicating Yvette and Colin. They came forward, he threw the doors open, and they stepped into the grandeur of the past. Lights blazed from chandeliers and wall sconces; the marble floor gleamed in response. Large gilt mirrors lined the walls and tossed the blazing light all around. Candelabras placed on tables lent their own mellow light. At one end of the room, a string quartet, dressed in full costume, played on. Linen covered tables at the sides of the room held drinks and desserts. The central area was left open—for dancing.

Colin plucked up his courage and held out his arm, which Yvette took. They marched to the center of the ballroom. Colin bowed deeply, Yvette curtseyed, and they were off, dancing the waltz as though they were in exams with their dance instructor, Mrs. Glatchett. More applause and whistling. Then Crandall held out his arm to Diana. 'Would you do me the honor?'

'Ah, Richard. An old dog and a new trick. It would be my pleasure.'

Very soon, everyone was dancing. Some expertly. Some—among them, Stone and Randy—poorly, but with determination. Gary Walkin amazed Becky, being both graceful and skilled.

'Why, Gary, what woman would leave a man who can dance like this?'

'Only my wives,' he said, with a crooked smile.

***

The evening took on the characteristics of a fairy tale. Only rarely was there a hint of the serious work ahead, the real reason for the gathering of this peculiar group. Small conversations would spring up between the members of Triple S, and then furrowed brows and tightened jaw muscles hinted at work—possibly lethal work—to be done. But as a good hostess,

Diana would soon recall the miscreants to their social duties: to enjoy the evening and provide a charming background for Yvette and Colin. Whether the two required or even noticed Diana's efforts was uncertain. Their focus was far more intimate, and they were seldom apart—either dancing or sharing a dessert—until the late hours when the band played their final song, Strauss's waltz '*Jugendträume*' (Youthful Dreams) and slipped away.

Colin was the last guest to leave, standing and talking to Yvette at the main entrance, until, reluctantly, he made his way to his car and drove off.

Diana, who had waited quietly out of sight until the rumble of the Mini Cooper faded into the night, put an arm around Yvette. 'Did you have a pleasant evening?'

Yvette turned to her, her eyes sparkling, and what seemed a permanent flush coloring her cheeks. 'Oh … yes!' she gasped. 'So magical. Thank you so much! I will make it up to you. Possibly more cleaning or gardening. And I'll thank Richard properly and work on his models without complaining for … as long as he likes.'

Diana laughed. 'Enough of that. I'm just glad the grumpy old man said you should stay the night. Off to bed, now.'

The man in question was tied to a sturdy chair with unusually wide armrests, his arms pinned down with heavy leather straps at the wrists and elbows. This chair, in turn, was bolted to the floor.

Chapter Three

Odd Partners

'Ow,' Randy said, putting the flat of his hand to his forehead. 'That was a great party.'

Chuck grunted his assent as he poured himself a huge mug of coffee. 'You working for us now?' he growled (softly) in Logan's direction.

'Jeez, don't shout,' Logan whispered.

Only Stone seemed relatively fresh.

'What the hell's your secret?' Randy asked.

'Simple,' Stone said, 'I switched to water, straight up, after 11:00. But I will take a cup of coffee if you're pouring, Chuck.'

The four were gathered in a conventional, modern conference room, recently equipped with a main table, a dozen chairs, several desks holding computer monitors and keyboards, and, most importantly, a table with a coffee machine, cups, and a large box of *biscuits*. The fact that tall, stone-bordered windows looked out on the central courtyard of an ancient British estate hardly seemed to matter.

'How come the Brits call cookies biscuits?' Randy asked.

'Don't be crass, Randolph,' Chuck chided. 'It's 'cause they have way more class than us common folk from the colonies. Now be a good boy, or no biscuit!'

'Where's Luana?' Logan asked.

'She'll be along,' Stone said. 'Wanted us to get things organized among ourselves first.'

'That could take a while,' Randy said.

'There you go. No biscuit!'

A few more comments unworthy of a meeting of senior corporate executives filled the next several minutes, then Stone stood. 'OK. So, what's our next job? Any input? How about it, Randy?'

'Pretty quiet. The folks I feel comfortable contacting at the Agency aren't returning my calls, or if they do it's to ask about my life as a new father.'

'How about you, Chuck?'

'Crickets. Which is surprising. Seems to me we did them a good turn, ·snapping up a shipload of prisoners destined for the sex trade. Plus, that greasy old ship, what was it? The *San Luis Obispo*?'

Logan groaned.

'I think it was the *Saint Martin*, Chuck,' Stone said. 'And the funny thing is, I'm getting the silent treatment too. Oh, everyone I talk to is impressed, some even grateful, but something is fishy. That action should be opening doors. You should probe a little deeper, Chuck. Your son, Marcus, works at the Agency, doesn't he?'

'Yeah.'

'Maybe he could, you know, just listen. Let you know what he hears.'

'You don't think someone at the Agency is blackballing us, do you?'

Stone shrugged. 'I've heard crazier things. Could just be a turf issue. Maybe we overstepped.'

'Never thought I'd hear those words out of your mouth, Stone,' Chuck commented.

'Oh, I'm not saying anything. Just have Marcus keep his ears open. I've been trying to get some information from a friend at MI6, but no luck.'

'What does your newspaper say?' Randy asked.

Logan gave him a puzzled look.

'Stone picks up newspapers and tries to figure which insignificant story is going to grow into the next big thing,' Randy explained.

'Huh, sounds like a job for Crandall's predictive chaos model, if you ask me,' Logan said.

The other three turned to him, jaws slack, then glanced at each other sheepishly.

'You're kidding,' Logan said. 'You haven't engaged Crandall?'

'Ah, we were ...' Randy faded to silence.

'We'll do that,' Stone said. 'Should've already. Looks like you've earned your salary as an unpaid consultant.'

The next half hour didn't produce any action items more significant than the one Logan had stumbled on: engage Crandall and his models.

Second and third cups of coffee hadn't helped, and by the time Luana arrived, the men resembled four discontented toads.

'Nothing?' she asked.

'It's strange,' Stone said. 'I've asked Ganesh to put out feelers in the Middle East.'

'Ganesh? The buddy from your service days? The guy who helped get Elaya Andoori out of Iran?' Chuck asked.

'That's him. And I've been tempted to contact Elaya, but it doesn't seem right asking the head of a foreign government for a job.'

'The hell you say,' Chuck grumbled. 'We did save her ass and gave her a country back.'

'That's maybe a little exaggeration, Chuck.' Randy said.

'Bull! She was dead meat.'

'Fine,' Stone said, 'I'll contact her—discreetly.'

'You gentlemen are in fine spirits, I see,' Luana remarked. 'And where's Cathie?' she asked.

'Oh, she wouldn't get caught dead at a meeting like this,' Logan replied. 'Shopping, I think.'

'Well, I'll leave you to it. By the way, Jason,' she said, 'here's today's *Times*. You might want to look on page twelve.'

Stone grunted as he took the paper. He glanced at the front page, then shuffled his way to page twelve.

'What's it say, Stone?' Randy asked.

'Huh,' he said. 'It looks like there's a major drug war going on among the cartels from Mexico to Venezuela. They're calling it an attempted takeover, with the biggest fish trying to swallow all the others. Reports of gunfights in Sinaloa, Jalisco, and Guatemala City. Not too unusual, but here's something that is. Farms owned by smaller cartels are being methodically poisoned. At least, that's the claim. No one seems to know how it's happening.'

'Is everyone being hit?' Chuck asked. 'You know, the Agency talked about doing something like this, but of course it was highly … irregular. We never even took it to State.'

'All the cartels are being hit except for one.' Stone smiled grimly. 'The one that owns the *Saint Martin* has been magically immune. The cartel run by Carlos Velasquez.'

'Carlos the Viper,' Chuck said.

'The *who*?' Randy asked.

'Carlos Velasquez, aka the Viper. Took over Mexico's largest drug cartel under very mysterious circumstances.'

'Lead poisoning?' Chuck asked.

Stone shook his head. 'That would hardly be mysterious. The previous head of the cartel, the Viper's predecessor, got sick. Reported as a virulent form of the flu—aggressive and lethal—though no one else was infected. Hence, a mystery. And here's another one.' He flipped back a few pages. 'Let me read this. "An Arizona congressman, Brad Delaney, and his family were killed in a helicopter crash yesterday at a resort in the Bahamas where the family was vacationing. The pilot and two others— friends of the family—were also killed. Witnesses say the helo erupted in a fireball and plunged to the ground …" I'll skip ahead. At the end it says, "The helicopter, operated by Bahamian Sapphire Resorts, had passed a thorough safety inspection just three days earlier."'

'Pretty piss-poor inspection, I'd say,' Chuck mumbled.

'Wait a minute,' Randy said. 'Hey, Logan, wasn't Delaney the fire-eating congressman who was co-sponsoring an aggressive bill targeting the cartels?'

'You're right. I forget the exact details of the legislation, but it went specifically after the cartel bosses and their lieutenants. Hit 'em where it hurts. Sanctioning the individuals and squeezing their ability to move wealth. There was an international component, too, and he was close to convincing Mexico's president plus a few others to support the move.'

'I'll bet the number-one name on the sanctioning list was Carlos Velasquez.' Stone said grimly. 'It doesn't do to name names in the cartels. 'And here's a thought. I've been in a few rough helo landings and I've known dozens of pilots. Of all the failure modes I've ever heard of, exploding in midair—unless you're hit with a missile or RPG—isn't one of them.'

'Somebody put a bomb on board?' Randy asked.

'Or rigged a spectacular failure,' Chuck replied. 'The maintenance crew, right, Stone?'

'That's a good bet. Randy, why don't you call Bahamian Sapphire Resorts. Introduce yourself and Triple S. I'm sure they don't want a stain on their reputation. A hit job is a better answer for them. I'll get in touch with the maintenance company.'

'And say what?' Logan asked. 'Just curious.'

'I'm guessing they need a new mechanic because someone on their team—a relatively new person—suddenly quit. If not, then the guy is still there, and I could use a vacation in the Bahamas.'

'Pretty darn clever, Stone,' Logan said.

'Hey, we get paid to do this.'

'Really?' Randy asked.

Stone shrugged. 'It's a figure of speech. By the way, can you get this information over to Crandall, Chuck? We're assuming a connection, but I'd like to know what Deep Thought has to say.'

Chuck looked puzzled, but Logan laughed. 'The computer from *The Hitchhiker's Guide to the Galaxy*. The one that solved the meaning of life, the universe, and everything.'

'Loved the movie,' Randy said.

'Check out the six-part PBS version,' Logan said. 'It's a riot.'

'OK,' Stone said, 'we have some actions. I suggest we reconvene tomorrow with status.'

As everyone rose, Randy grabbed another section of the newspaper. 'Hey, Stone, here's a story you missed. It's a preview of an upcoming book on the life of Sir Conrad Smythe-Montgomery. "Ms. Fletcher, the well-known author of suspense/mystery novels, including the award-winning *A Tangled Web*, has ventured into the world of nonfiction with stunning success, writing an engaging biography of one of the most controversial and influential entrepreneurs in England's long history. Hers is a masterful work that reaches back to the Croker forebears of the eccentric billionaire and probes the multi-generational obsession that could not be satisfied by money or power. This arching family history is brought to a close outlining his detailed plans for world empire, the product of a delusional mind. A sweeping and deliciously scandalous work that highlights the 'story' in history."'

'Wow,' Chuck said. 'Not bad. Wonder who her lucky husband is?'

'Hey,' Randy said, 'it says here she's doing a series of events including book signings in less than a month. I thought she hadn't finished.'

'Turns out she was a lot closer than she let on, even to me,' Logan said. 'That plus a lot of pressure from her UK publisher. It's been over a year since the drama with Smythe-Montgomery came to its violent, blood-splattering conclusion. There's still plenty of buzz, but Eccles, that's the publisher's name, doesn't want to let events get stale. "Strike while the iron is hot," he says.'

'Are you coming back to the UK with her?'

Logan shook his head. 'Not a chance. My love of book signings just about matches hers of corporate meetings for Triple S.'

Stone laughed. 'Well, we still have most of the day to make some calls. Something is going on within the cartels. It may not mean work for us, but it just might.'

***

'Ah, Pepito, I hope you are comfortable?'

The man in question was tied to a sturdy chair with unusually wide armrests, his arms pinned down with heavy leather straps at the wrists and elbows. This chair, in turn, was bolted to the floor.

Pepito glared at the man, but said nothing. He had been grabbed by four hard men, drugged, and driven to a location he could not have identified. He might have been unconscious for minutes or for days. He was in a single-room house, barely bigger than a farmer's hut. There was electricity, as evidenced by the bright lights hung from overhead. He could hear the rhythmic drumming of a gas-powered generator outside. Two walls had curtain-less windows, though there was nothing but blackness outside. Apparently, he was sufficiently isolated that no one would see what took place in the house. Several other lights stood on tripods to either side of a video camera, facing him. He swallowed painfully. He had seen the recordings of interrogations. Men captured by rival cartels and brutally tortured until they revealed every bit of information they knew, usually followed by a perfunctory execution.

'You've noticed the camera, I see. Very good. It's not turned on at the moment, so we have the opportunity for a private chat. I'll begin. You work for the Viper. In fact, you're a senior advisor, which is merely a euphemism for a hired butcher who carries out orders and controls his own organization of ... what is it? Sixty men?' The interrogator cocked his head and smiled. 'So, not so communicative just yet. Very well. We will get the precise number and all their names quite soon. Where was I? Ah, in your position, you know many things. For instance, you know the brand of cigar favored by your *patrón*. You know how many women he has seen in the last week. And, let me see, you know exactly how he is poisoning our crops.'

The questioner pulled a large caliber handgun from his belt and set it on a nearby table. 'Now you will answer questions. When we are done, I will put one .45 hollow-point round through your head. Simple. You feel nothing. There is no shame in this, though, to be sure, it would be a disappointment to me. I prefer a long, slow conversation, as between two old friends.' He motioned to another table, covered with a cloth. 'Here I keep the tools to make our conversation both lively and productive. Now, I always like to start with a very easy question, which is this. Will you answer every other question I ask you immediately and honestly?'

Pepito summoned his courage and spat at the man. Spittle ran down his still-smug face.

'And this is the thanks I get.' He reached over, turned the camera on, and wound an old-fashioned egg timer to fifteen minutes. 'I will ask my next question when the time expires.' He flipped back the cloth and picked up a thin-bladed knife. 'Most men are so wasteful,' he said. 'There are millions of nerve endings in just your little finger. *Si*, it is true! This is where I begin. I assure you, the next fifteen minutes will seem as long as years.'

He bent forward and placed the point of the blade just below the nail on the little finger of Pepito's left hand.

Outside, the two guards circling the house heard a sound like the howl of a coyote caught in a trap, and they shivered. A dusty wind carried this tormented sound for hundreds of yards, past sage, Joshua trees, and creosote bushes. The two continued their pacing.

When the timer finally went off, Pepito's face was covered in sweat. His head flopped to one side as the excruciating agony lessened. There would be no true relief from the deeper pain until his interrogator fired his weapon. Too much damage was done. With the unhurried pace of a man enjoying an evening stroll, the fingernail had been cut from the bed then slowly withdrawn with needle-nose pliers. A mere preliminary. The bones had been broken and then bits of finger removed until only a stump at the hand, cauterized with a propane torch, remained. Pepito's torturer had been probing this sensitive area with a needle when the timer went off. For a full ten minutes, during screams of pain, Pepito had begged him to stop. Had promised to tell him everything. But the man had shaken his head and pointed to the awful timer.

Pepito drew rasping breaths as the man reached for the timer. 'Now you know the rules. If I set this timer, not even God almighty will stop me until it expires. So, are we done?'

The absence of the urgent agony had strengthened the man's resolve and he shook his head weakly. 'Very well.' The man set the timer and drew out a hammer and a small bag of long nails from beneath the cloth.

'Wait! Mother of mercy, NO!'

'You know the rules,' the man said, positioning a nail above Pepito's left wrist.

Outside, the sharp rap of a hammer, four times repeated, rang out just before an unearthly howl of pain filled the empty night.

The time passed, the house filled with agonized screaming and begging; pleading to be allowed to talk. The alarm went off at last, and the interrogator smiled pleasantly. 'I believe you may be serious this time. If not …' He shrugged. 'There is the rest of the night. You should know, before you answer foolishly, that I will set the timer for half an hour next and I will proceed … as that time allows. So, shall we talk?'

'Y-yes,' Pepito croaked out. '*No mas, por favor.* Ask me what you will.'

'Excellent! Once again, a simple question—'

The creak of the door opening drew the man's attention and he turned with a scowl, the first emotion he had shown all evening. 'I told you I was not to be disturbed. What do you want, you fool?'

But his words faded and his annoyance became puzzlement. A hooded figure stood in the doorway, face hidden, clothes tugged by the rising wind.

'Who the hell are you?' the man asked uncertainly.

The figure entered noiselessly and threw the hood back. 'My name is Jesse Raynard.'

The man's eyes were wide and his mouth hung open loosely, his features a bizarre mixture of surprise and fear. 'The men outside, they will—'

'Never smoke another joint or fuck another woman. You needn't worry about them.'

'But I heard nothing.'

'Over the caterwauling of this fool? You wouldn't have heard an explosion.'

'How long have you been—'

'A while. I've been watching you work. I could offer you a few tips on improving your technique, but there'd be no point.'

The man began to recover his wits and saw that there was no weapon in the stranger's hand.

Raynard smiled. 'I'm unarmed.'

The man leaned towards his gun.

'Uh-uh-uh!' Raynard said, then whistled softly. An enormous grey animal with piercing blue eyes walked in, a deep rumbling growl filling the room.

Raynard stroked the animal's head. 'She's a hybrid. Part dog, part wolf. It's said they're hard to train and not to be trusted, but I disagree. Cherokee and I understand each other completely.' Raynard lifted one finger and pointed. A blur of grey like an eruption of smoke from a cannon's mouth arced across the room and terminated in a ruby explosion as Cherokee took the man's throat.

'Raynard, thank God!' Pepito cried.

Raynard turned. 'Pepito, Pepito, what are we to do with you? And you so ready to tell your secrets after a mere half hour. A whistle, and Cherokee's head snapped around, her eyes like glacial ice. Raynard smiled and pointed.

***

Carlos glared at his uninvited visitor. 'I didn't expect to see you again so soon, Raynard, though I'd be happier to see you without your dog.'

'She's not a dog. And I had no intention of being here at your … palatial residence … a second time. A disappointment for both of us. Have you heard from Pepito lately?'

'No,' Carlos said, dismissing Cherokee as quickly as Raynard had. 'I haven't heard from that dirty fool for weeks, which violates my explicit instructions. I've tried to contact him, but—'

'He's dead,' Jesse said casually, eyes fixed on the Viper's bodyguard, Ramón, and not on Carlos.

'What? How?'

'I killed him. Actually, Cherokee ripped his throat out at my command, which I suppose amounts to the same thing.'

The Viper's eyes narrowed and his jaw clenched. 'Careful, Raynard. The next words from your mouth had better be truthful and free of insolence.'

The momentary silence was obliterated by a deep growl.

'Don't threaten me, Viper,' Raynard said. 'It puts Cherokee on edge. I came here voluntarily, after all.'

Carlos laughed suddenly, and the tension fled like a startled hare. 'And you shouldn't be so touchy. I expect if you killed Pepito, he deserved killing. Sit. Tell me in your own way. Here, take a cigar.'

By the time Raynard finished relating recent events, fragrant blue smoke drifted lazily in the upper air of the room. 'My God,' Carlos said, 'you've done me a service. Twice. Snipping the stratagems of the Escondido Cartel in the bud and ridding me of a dubiously loyal man. A little discomfort and he offers to talk! To tell all! Ramón, you would not betray me so, would you?'

'Never, *patrón*,' he responded woodenly.

The stare Jesse gave Ramón was as penetrating and impersonal as an MRI. 'The man performing the interrogation was skilled, at a rudimentary level. Best hope your loyalty is never put to the test in the same way.'

'Enough of that,' Carlos said. 'This is a happy time! Ramón, contact Alejandro from the Escondido Cartel. The game is up. If he will accept me as *patrón*, he will be my valued lieutenant. My first. That should bring him around.' He rubbed his hands together. 'Bring the tequila, the very special Añejo. We will celebrate and you will join us, Ramón. And fetch a beefsteak for the dog.'

'She prefers to get her own food, though perhaps in this case, an exception.'

'There, you see, Raynard,' Carlos said, after Ramón had hurried off, 'all is well. But now, my friend, with the cartels all under one leader, I have thoughts.' He waggled his finger in the air, Cherokee watching the motion like a spiteful cat watching a mouse. 'The world opens before us.'

Raynard's expression never changed, though 'us' had nearly caused a burst of laughter.

'I believe it is time to expand our operations,' Carlos said pompously, 'and so, at your convenience, I would like you to contact Ms. Emma Lister, formerly Smythe-Montgomery's number one. If there is a remnant of his empire, she will control it. What do you say?'

'An excellent idea. Ah, thank you, Ramón,' Jesse said, accepting the offered tequila. 'A toast, then.'

The three clicked glasses and drank.

'Delicious,' Carlos said, holding the glass away from him and admiring the nearly clear contents. 'Another toast. To the world, and our rightful place in it!' He drank again.

Carlos was in a high state of inebriation, excitement, and delusional visions when Raynard rose to leave.

'You're not going, Raynard? The party is just beginning. Ramón, fetch another bottle!'

'Alas, duty calls.' But before leaving the room, Raynard turned. 'What do you plan to do with the ship? The one the CIA so graciously returned to you?'

'The *Saint Martin*. Ptah. I can't use her except for hauling vegetables now. Too recognizable. And it's not worth the fuel and maintenance. She sits in harbor and rusts.'

'If you'd like, perhaps I could work a little magic. A facelift—paint, superficial structural alterations—some new documents. It's possible you bought her from a bankrupt shipping company in Chile. Voila!'

A snap of fingers, and four aces suddenly appeared in Jesse's hand.

Carlos turned a drunken grin to Ramón. 'Did you see that?' He clapped vigorously and Ramón joined in. 'Ah, Raynard, you can always amuse me!'

Jesse smiled graciously. 'I'll see to it then. And perhaps, in the future, I might also make use of the ship? An enterprise we can discuss at another time.'

'My dear Raynard, if you can accomplish this miracle, she will be at your service when you need her!'

'Thank you.' Raynard withheld the subservient '*patrón,*' and left the room, thinking, *How easy it would be to kill that fool.*

***

Raynard eyed Charlotte greedily as she set two drinks down on a table between them, her ample breasts nearly tumbling from her dress.

'I'm told Emma Lister is quite beautiful—and talented,' Raynard said, reaching out to caress the smooth, amber skin of Charlotte's arm.

'I would expect both, as she was in such a prominent position with Sir Conrad. Talented,' she repeated, a flash of mischief in her eye showing she hadn't failed to detect Raynard's double entendre.

'And you've already contacted her. Well done! And how is Ms. Lister enduring the absence of her former employer and lover?'

'Well enough, though she had a certain anticipated windfall of cash stolen from her at the last moment. An extraordinarily sizable amount.'

'Poor thing. And yet ...'

'The wise woman had a third fallback position, untouched, that left her enough to discreetly leave England, establish herself in Morocco, and maintain a certain amount of luxury.'

'Morocco?'

'A temporary holding area, safe from extradition. Since those early days, her talented legal team has managed to erase any blemish on her character. The poor woman, it seems, was merely a tool, manipulated by the evil Smythe-Montgomery. She could walk the streets of London today with impunity.'

'So, she is in London?'

Charlotte shook her head, her golden hair brushing her shoulders. 'In the Caribbean. Working on her tan. Also, and more to the point'—she darted another glance at Raynard, who was smiling—'reestablishing contacts both at home and the Far East, primarily Indonesia. She has friends in MI5, which in part explains her complete freedom of movement in England.'

'Ah, the "talented" woman is gathering her remaining resources. And Iran?'

Charlotte laughed lightly. 'She prefers to have no further entanglements in the Middle East.'

'Wise, too. Once burned … And is she open to a discussion with representatives from the sole remaining cartel in the Americas?'

Charlotte walked over to a small table, put a slender hand into her purse, and pulled out a piece of paper. 'Our itinerary. Airline reservations and the governor's suite at the Hotel La Perle de la Mer in Antigua.'

Raynard stood and joined her, glancing at the slip of paper, then gently took her shoulders and kissed her deeply. A soft whisper, breathed onto her neck. 'Another talented woman.'

***

The sun had set fire to a low band of clouds over a sparkling sea. The delightful warmth of the day would soon give way to even more delightful wafts of cool air drifting across the sea. The private, well-guarded beach was remarkably quiet. Only three chaise lounges topped with rainbow-striped umbrellas broke the smooth surface of the sand that ran from the thin grass near the house to the water. Near the break between grass and sand stood a small outdoor bar, the discreet bartender watching for a raised hand or a crooked finger that indicated a request for a refill by one of the guests. The bartender occasionally polished an already gleaming glass or wiped nonexistent stains from the teakwood bar. The pay was outstanding, considering these three rarely needed his services. They had been out on the beach most of the day in various stages of undress—another benefit of this job—sometimes talking, at other times just sunning or sipping drinks. For the past half hour, they'd been still, taking an occasional glimpse out to sea.

As the sun slipped below the horizon, Emma Lister pushed her sunglasses to the top of her head. 'I have to admit, Raynard, you're not at all what I expected.'

Jesse smiled. 'I get that a lot.'

'Quite. And Charlotte, your girl Friday,' Lister said, turning to the other woman.

'Actually, she's my girl every day, aren't you, Char?'

'Of course I am.' She shrugged. 'But I'm not overly jealous.'

Lister glanced at first one and then the other. Her smile remained, but there was a tension in her look and more than a hint of desire. She shook her head and laughed, sure that she had inferred something that wasn't there. 'Not at all what I expected.' She raised her hand and the bartender was instantly at her side.

'What can I bring you?'

'One more round?' Emma looked from side to side. Smiles and nods. 'One more round, and then you can go. Please leave the bar as it is, we may visit it later.' She reached into a small purse and pulled out a hundred-dollar bill. 'Thank you, Salvatore.'

'Thank *you*, miss!'

Fresh margaritas with ice and salt appeared faster than a magician could produce a rabbit from a hat, and Salvatore withdrew, repeating his thanks.

'So,' Lister said, returning to business, 'you may reassure your employer—'

Raynard held up a peremptory hand. 'Emma, please be very clear. I perform certain services for Carlos Velasquez when it suits me. I receive remuneration. But I am free to accept ... or decline ... these assignments. For now, it pleases me to negotiate this arrangement with you.' Raynard's eyes slowly drifted over Lister's nearly naked body, eyeing the curves and the play of muscles beneath smooth skin. 'It very much pleases me. But I am *not* an employee.'

Emma smiled inwardly and felt a gentle stirring at Jesse's glance, as though a finger had run along the arch of her foot, up her leg, over her belly, and between her breasts. She put the sensual feeling aside with some effort. Raynard's status as an independent operator had been made clear much earlier in the day, but Lister had wanted to hear it again. 'Good,' she said, without elaborating. 'And we have negotiated the preliminaries of an arrangement beneficial to *each* of us. Sir Conrad had a truly stunning vision of world empire, but he was fatally flawed. What would you say were his flaws?'

Raynard smiled and motioned to Charlotte, who answered, 'Some would say megalomania combined with paranoia, but I'm inclined to disagree.'

'Really?' Lister said, amused. 'I suppose you've reached the same conclusion I have. His downfall was precipitated by a blind desire for revenge.'

Charlotte smiled tolerantly. 'That was the effect, produced by the underlying cause.'

'Really?' Emma repeated, though less amused now. 'I worked with Sir Conrad for many years. I also know the errand he was on the last time he left me. A quest to bring two fools—Diana Foster and Richard Crandall—to their rightful end. You think otherwise?'

'Not at all—regarding that violent expression of his anger.'

Emma turned to Raynard. 'A psychologist, perhaps?'

'Pffh. An actress whose true talents were wasted, finally having found her place in the world. Her place as my "girl Friday."'

Emma turned back to Charlotte. 'Please, enlighten me.'

'Sir Conrad Smythe-Montgomery suffered from pathological insecurity. The poor peasant who wanted to be a lord. The grubby commoner putting a knuckle to his forehead and saying "Yes, m'lord" or "Yes, m'lady" every time he was told to jump. Every bit of his life screams insecurity. Trace every action he took, and at the core of each one is that simple truth.'

Lister lay back in her chair. 'That's worthy of consideration. However—'

'Do you like tricks?' Raynard asked.

Lister's eyebrows shot up her forehead.

'Card tricks,' Raynard clarified.

'Not really,' Lister replied.

'Honesty!' Raynard cried, glancing at Charlotte. 'Well, perhaps you've never seen the right kind.'

As if anticipating this question, Charlotte passed Jesse a deck of cards, then, much to Lister's surprise, proceeded to remove her bikini top and slip out of her bottom before lying back onto the chaise lounge, stretching seductively. 'You'll see,' she said, with the ghost of a wink.'

Raynard went through a series of standard tricks, shuffling the deck and producing cards from nowhere.

Lister was impressed, though not overly so. She had seen magicians in England and the States perform similar sleight of hand.

Raynard, noting her reserve, fanned the cards, all facing towards Lister. 'Pick two.'

Lister gave a lopsided smile and took two cards from the deck.

'Hand them to Charlotte. Don't let me see.'

Raynard folded the deck and set it on a table. 'Difficult! Hmm. Hearts. Both of them. Why, Emma, are you sending some kind of subliminal signal? Charlotte, tear up the two cards.'

The bits fluttered to the ground.

'Sad,' Raynard said. 'Still, as the old saw goes, when one door closes, another opens. From one world into another. I believe I know where the ace—your first pick—has gone.'

Lister lay, breathing slowly, as Raynard reached over and lifted her bikini top. And there it was, the ace of hearts.

Lister's heart was racing now. She glanced over at Charlotte, whose face glowed with anticipation.

'And the queen of hearts, Emma. Where might that have gone?'

Lister took a quick shuddering breath as Raynard reached for the hidden card.

Salvatore watched from behind a dune, licking his lips as the trio of arms, legs, and bodies writhed in the failing light. When it was finally too dark to see, he sighed and headed homeward.

***

Despite the coolness of the evening, three bodies lay covered in sweat on the large beach blanket. The warmth of the sand continued to soak upward from beneath them, keeping them comfortable even as they slowly dried.

'So you're a magician?' Lister said, turning to Raynard with a smile.

'I'll take that as a compliment. I did enjoy some modest success in Sin City, oh, a number of years ago, but I found my greater talents lay elsewhere. Still, I do enjoy a good trick.'

'Amen,' Lister sighed. Her eyes held a mischievous sparkle as she added, 'I don't know any magic, but I take a certain pleasure in collecting unique toys, some of which produce rather magical effects. I wonder if you and Charlotte would care to spend the remainder of the night at the house. I find a combination of delicate white powder, my toy box, and a vivid imagination can produce spectacular results.'

Raynard rose immediately and extended one hand to Charlotte and one to Lister. 'Please, lead the way.'

The Reality of Illusion

'When I got older, he taught me how to play the big stand-up fiddle too.'

Chapter Four

Getting the Band Back Together

Even before Cathie entered the house, she heard the music. She didn't recognize the artist or the tune, but it caught her attention. Just piano and bass. The pianist was good, though subdued, but the bassist …! The beat was complex—a rapid-fire series of syncopated notes that literally flew up and down the scale. Not overplayed, not pounded out. Forceful but subtle, leaving quiet interludes where the piano came to the forefront, then bursting into wild, joyful recklessness. She opened the door and before even glancing up said, 'Logan, what band is that? And who the hell is playing bass? It's extraordinary. Almost like—'

The music suddenly stopped. Cathie's eyes followed the path to the now extinguished music and she was shocked to see Logan sitting at his piano, looking sheepish, and another man—a middle-aged African-American with a gleaming smile and a bass guitar slung over his shoulder with such natural ease that it seemed a part of his body. The guitar was an old Fender Jazz Bass, and the fabric strap was tattered and faded. The man's short-cropped hair was sprinkled with salt, as was his neat goatee. He was five foot ten or eleven and solidly built, with no hint of fat or excess anywhere. The smile remained on his face, both cheerful and amused as he saw Cathie's confusion.

'Cathie, this is Tyrone Morris, a longtime friend of Chuck's, and the new bassist for The Fourth Harmonics. That is, if he really wants to play with a bunch of amateurs like us. Tyrone, this is my wife, Cathie.'

Tyrone stepped forward and offered his hand. 'Pleased to meet you,' he said, his voice resonant, but softer and slower than she'd expected. It managed to express confidence without arrogance. 'I've read your novels with pleasure and I'm looking forward to reading your first venture into nonfiction, though considering the subject of your book, it may be hard to differentiate fact from fantasy. Smythe-Montgomery's life stretched credulity to the breaking point.'

'Wow,' she said. 'And a pleasure to meet you.' Her eyes went back to Logan. 'Mr. Morris's last comment exactly described my biggest dilemma in writing about Sir Conrad. A real life that dwarfs fiction.'

'Tyrone, please,' he said, in the same low rumble. 'And yet I believe he was never truly satisfied, let alone happy. The poor rich man.'

'And a philosopher, too!' Cathie exclaimed.

'Wait till you hear the rest of his résumé, darling,' Logan said. 'I blush for my own lack of accomplishment. But more to the point, his bass seems to have a soul of its own.'

'Too kind, really. I've played since I was a child, and I've always hung out with musicians, even while pursuing other studies.'

'C'mon,' Logan said. 'The sun has set. Tyrone, I've got a couple of steaks begging to be grilled, and there's one with your name on it. And a nice Cab to go with it. Why don't you join us for dinner and you can tell Cathie your life story?'

'Yes to the dinner, with thanks, and I'll at least tell you how I came to leave gloomy, damp Seattle for the warm, sunny Southwest. And that's a hint having to do with arthritis.'

***

The desert heat lingered, but the air was pleasantly dry as they sat down to dinner on the back patio. Tyrone ate the same way he spoke: slowly and with precision. It wasn't until the end of the meal, with coffee and cheesecake all around, that Cathie tried to focus the general thread of the conversation.

'I know I'm prying, but I'd like to hear this interesting story of a life that can humble my husband. Plus, you've barely mentioned how you happen to know Chuck Johnson. Wait— We've known him for a long time, and there was one person he's talked about who we've never met. You can't be the legendary T-bone, can you?'

Tyrone graciously bowed. 'The nickname of my misspent youth. I should warn you, though, whatever Chuck said about me is probably gross exaggeration or a full pack of lies. The incident of the sheep on the roof of the high school was'—he coughed—'well, mostly untrue.'

80

Cathie gaped. 'I'd like to hear the story from you. "Lamb chops" was how Chuck's story ended.'

Tyrone shook his head. 'You see? A complete lie. You don't get lamb chops from a fully grown sheep. Now, mutton ...'

'Wait, wait!' Logan said, with a laugh. 'You mean you knew Chuck in high school? Please, start at the beginning.'

'Ah, you mean "Chapter 1: I am Born,"' he said with a grin.

'Dickens,' Cathie said. 'So you appreciate fine literature.'

'I do, though I don't read as much as I should. I'll skip the part of my life that I only know because my momma told me. I knew Chuck long before high school. We both grew up in Philly, me on Poplar Street, Chuck near but not too near. For the uninitiated, the area Chuck grew up in was rough; mine was worse. The Projects. Run down. Nasty. Drugs. Crime.' He shrugged. 'Momma somehow kept me safe from all that. It's funny, even half a mile away was like a different world. I used to tell Chuck he lived in a mansion, though it was an apartment not much bigger than mine. Not as many bugs, though.

'By the time I was in high school, I could've written a book. Friends who took a wrong turn, who started dealing or stealing. I doubt a quarter of the kids I knew growin' up made it through high school. They'd get arrested, put in juvie, shot, or just dropped out and disappeared. Two were fished out of the Schuylkill River.'

Logan sat silent, while Cathie shook her head sadly.

'Oh, don't feel too sorry for me,' Tyrone said, sensing their concern. 'By the time I was a freshman, I had my head screwed on tight. Thanks, Momma,' he said, looking up to the sky with a smile. 'I studied hard, stayed out of trouble.' His smile widened. '*Serious* trouble. Chuck was younger than me, but had the gall to think he could take my starting spot on the basketball team. He had some game, he did. But old and wily won out. Senior year we were teammates. Two badass guards with moves like greased lightning. Finished second in state to a team with a seven-foot-tall center.

'Despite the occasional boyish indiscretions—like the sheep—I kept my head down. Finished high school top of my class. You should've have seen Momma bawlin' her eyes out. Then I managed to get into Temple. More tears.

'Not to be tedious, I ended up in med school, also at Temple. Practiced in Philly at the Temple U. Hospital for a while. I spent some time in Iraq—as a civilian—working communicable diseases and chemical exposure. Met up with my old buddy Chuck while I was there. Oops, I hope I haven't given anything away about his clandestine past.'

'Not to worry,' Logan said. 'I worked with Chuck during the same period; even provided him with a couple of useful toys, which is all *I* can say.'

Tyrone nodded. 'After that junket, I moved to Seattle. Spent some time at the Hutchinson Cancer Research Center before calling it a career and deciding to track Chuck down. Not much family left, so I figured I might as well adopt that little SOB.'

'An amazing life,' Logan said, refilling his wineglass. 'And now, here you are, destined to make the rest of The Fourth Harmonics look like the raw amateurs we are.'

'Not so,' Tyrone replied. 'Your piano is better than good. If the rest of the band is up to your talent, we'll be having some fun times. Oh, almost forgot. I give my momma the lion's share of the credit for keeping me out of the morgue—at least, until med school—but I've got to mention my uncle Zach. He's the one that put a bass guitar in my hand at an age when it was bigger than me. I tried giving it up a hundred times as a kid, but he never let me. "Son," he said, "your friends will come and go, your momma and me will depart this world for a better one, but this"—and he'd pat that old guitar like it was his lover's tushy—"will be with you till the day you die." When I got older, he taught me how to play the big stand-up fiddle too.' He lifted his glass. 'Here's to you, Uncle Zach.'

'To Uncle Zach,' Logan and Cathie echoed.

***

'I like him,' Cathie said, after Tyrone left.

'Why wouldn't you?' Logan quipped. 'He complimented your books.'

Cathie gave him a frown that lacked any real irritation. 'I'm serious. What a life he's had!'

Logan chuckled. 'Told you I felt inadequate. And a nice guy to boot. I imagine we'll be seeing a lot of him, and not just in the band.'

'Hmm,' Cathie replied, as she rummaged through some papers.

'What's that?'

She dropped the stack. 'Just some notes for the book tour in London—times, dates, locations, the usual dull but necessary logistics. I meant to go through them today, but just never did.'

'A little late now.'

'I suppose. Sure you don't want to come along?'

'What, and spoil your chances to pick up some doting English lord? Nah. Besides, you'll have Colin to help you at the London venues, and where Colin is, can Yvette be far away?'

'It was generous for him to volunteer. And you're right about Yvette. They seem close. Funny how they started out as bosom enemies.'

'That does happen, doesn't it? Not like you and me. Love at first sight!'

'I remember things differently.'

'Really? Well, given the lateness of the hour, we could cuddle up and you could remind me.'

'You old lecher!'

'Now that part I remember.'

***

Yvette and Crandall entered the Triple S London office, unoccupied except for Jason Stone, who folded the newspaper he was reading and rose to greet them.

'Yvette, Richard, good to see you. Back in civilian clothes, I see.'

Yvette was wearing jeans and a faded, oversize T-shirt. Crandall, though dressed less casually in a sport coat over a crisp white shirt, responded with enthusiasm. 'Yes, thank the gods. How men ever survived in the age of the choking cravat is a mystery to me.'

'You looked quite elegant, Richard,' Yvette said. 'Still, I do enjoy being comfortable. Any news of note, Jason?'

Stone tapped the newspaper. 'The entire sad tale of our existence, with maybe a unique tidbit or two. Later. First, what have you managed to come up with?'

'Ah,' Crandall said, 'you may find this interesting. We input the details of your investigations as well as the relevant points from your previous news searches—a primitive but useful approach. The information regarding Carlos Velasquez was also illuminating. I take it you canceled your trip to the Bahamas when you confirmed your hypothesis about the mechanic at Bahamian Sapphire Resort.'

'Postponed. But yes, Randy made the call the next day and we talked it over. Couple that with the cold shoulder we're getting from the CIA—and Chuck's son got the silent treatment as well—and I'm beginning to smell a rat.'

Yvette scanned the room. 'Surely not!'

Stone and Crandall laughed heartily. 'Figurative, my dear,' Crandall said.

'Well, naturally.' Her face settled briefly into a pout, but brightened instantly. 'Perhaps we've confirmed your "rat," Jason.' She pulled a laptop from a large satchel.

'I approve of your large projection screen,' Crandall remarked. 'Where might Yvette hook up?'

Stone saw the embarrassed blush streak across her face, but merely pointed to a computer station with numerous loose cables. 'Any of the HDMI cables will work.'

After twenty minutes of reviewing predictive data, Stone was at a loss. 'Sorry. But I must be missing something. A bunch of seemingly unconnected events that are, well, unconnected.'

Yvette grinned while Crandall clapped gently. 'Well done, Mr. Stone. A lesser mind would have missed it entirely. You are indeed a suitable consort for Luana Chu.'

'I love being brilliant, or at least being told I'm brilliant,' he said. 'What I hate is not knowing why.'

Crandall motioned to Yvette. 'Please explain.'

Yvette reset the model to a level that showed a variety of basic information: the death of the congressman and his family, the stonewalling by the CIA, the cartel wars, the capture of the *Saint Martin*, the rise to power of Carlos Velasquez, and a variety of other world events including, oddly, the break-in at the CDC. 'As you've rightly pointed out,' she said, 'these events are *seemingly* unconnected. However … they aren't. Think of it this way. Perhaps you're building a puzzle. You've lost the cover as well as many of the pieces. You manage to put some of the remaining pieces together, but the empty space exceeds what you've completed. However, the empty space is of a shape—'

'That reveals what's missing,' Stone said in amazement. 'And you're telling me that you know what's missing?'

'Alas, no, Mr. Stone,' said Crandall. But as Stone's face fell, Crandall grinned, a rare expression for him. 'However, the model can predict with 88 percent probability that these events are connected—are all part of the same puzzle!'

'Holy shit! Is there even any hint about the connective material?'

Crandall turned to Yvette. 'Another brilliant observation from Mr. Stone. Unfortunately, there's nothing conclusive—yet. But now, what of this new item of interest in today's news. I must admit, what we've brought is nearly forty-eight hours old.'

Stone lifted the paper. 'It's a brief article. You may be able to dig up more. Let me read it:

'"Rescuers arrived too late last week to save anyone in the remote village of Huata, Guatemala, finding only burned houses and charred remains. Reports of a plague-like epidemic had reached authorities a few days earlier. Doctors and medical staff found the entire village and all its people dead and burned. Interviews with residents of nearby villages were unsatisfactory and were quickly followed by open hostility, forcing the withdrawal of the humanitarian team. Information pieced together from multiple sources indicates that residents of surrounding villages, fearing the plague's spread, destroyed Huata and all who were living there."'

'Sounds horrible,' Yvette said. 'Jason, you were recently in Guatemala.'

'Yes, briefly. In Puerto Barrios. Maybe sixty or seventy miles from Huata.'

'May I?' Crandall asked, gesturing for the paper. 'Hmm, yes. We'll do a worldwide search for more information and have this event entered in the predictive chaos model by this time tomorrow. With all the activity in Mexico and Central America—including your madly heroic adventure—this can't be a coincidence.'

'Madly heroic?' Yvette said, turning from one to the other, settling on Crandall. 'Your description to me was rather more bland.'

'Impressionable young minds,' he said.

'You know the model's results depend on the precise input of all relevant data. I'll expect a full explanation later.'

'Yes. When you've completed your research on this plague-village. Be sure to check local news and any public reporting of—'

'I do know what I'm about, Richard,' Yvette said, giving him a venomous look.

'Maybe Richard is worried that Colin is proving a distraction,' Stone said, though his tone and a tiny wink indicated he was teasing.

'Colin has been very helpful, Jason. Testing algorithms, setting up simulations. Some of today's information was a direct result.'

'She's right,' Crandall said. 'He's become highly interested in predictive chaos modeling. You could almost say it's a passion.'

Yvette elbowed him gently but Stone noticed Crandall's only response was a proud smile.

'And he's offered to help when Ms. Fletcher returns to London for her book tour,' Yvette said. 'We both have. We know the city better than most, and her itinerary has three stops in areas we're quite familiar with. We also know popular pubs that would provide a break between or after book signings.'

'And an opportunity for Ms. Fletcher to meet crowds of other people informally. An even better way to boost her status,' Crandall commented.

'Have either of you seen a draft of her book?' Stone asked.

Yvette and Crandall glanced at each other and shook their heads. 'I'm not sure I could bear to revisit some of the events, even after all this time,' Yvette said.

'I hope she's devoted at least a chapter to the sword fight between Smythe-Montgomery and Diana,' Crandall said. 'And to the heroic actions of this young lady,' he added, turning to Yvette.

'Richard! I thought you'd died! It was awful. I certainly couldn't read that part.' She looked to Jason for support but was surprised to see him frowning slightly and focused inwardly. 'Why, Jason, what's the matter?'

'Hmm? Oh, nothing. Not much anyway, I hope. I've asked Cathie for a reading copy of her magnum opus for some time, but haven't gotten one. I was hoping you two had seen it.'

'Well, we haven't,' Crandall responded. 'What's your concern?'

Stone laughed, a startlingly false sound. 'I just hope Cathie has used … discretion. Some things are better left unsaid.'

***

'"Some things are better left unsaid,"' Yvette repeated later that evening. 'But he wouldn't elaborate.'

'Your Bond-like friend is very mysterious,' Colin said.

'No, no. He's John Steed and Luana is Emma Peel. You know, the Avengers.'

'Right. Still, what do you suppose he was getting at?'

'I'm not sure.'

Colin glanced at her uncertainly. 'What little I know, things were bloody awful. Diana has told me some.' He shrugged. 'She seems to trust me. Would it be too painful to tell me more?'

'We have work to do,' she said, though her uncertain tone almost begged him to insist.

'I'll help. You know I will. Please tell me. And not just what happened, but how you felt.'

It was exactly what Yvette hoped he'd say. For the next hour she shared the story of events leading up to the final horrific night.

'I shot a man, you know,' she said, and tears sprang into her eyes. 'I didn't know I could do it, but he forced his way into the house—this house—and threatened Richard. I acted calmly, I remember, but there was a fire burning inside me at the effrontery of the threat. At the insult.'

'Did you …?'

'No. I shot him in the knee. He went down screaming and passed out from the pain. Afterwards, I couldn't stop shaking, I was so terrified. Then, several days later, Diana and Richard argued, and I was forced to make a horrible decision. You see, Diana had shared a secret with me. Smythe-Montgomery and his father had taken her legs, but that wasn't all. He was a truly evil man, *Sir* Conrad.' She spat the word. 'Spawn of Satan. I can't tell you what she said. It wouldn't be right. Even Richard doesn't know, but it was awful. She was done hiding from Smythe-Montgomery. She wanted to fight. Richard wanted to take her away into hiding. I chose Diana's way. I had to, you see, because I knew.

'I felt awful for Richard, so sad and lonely when I left with Diana. I did help her, though. I pointed the gun at another man, Smythe-

Montgomery's driver, but didn't have to shoot. He came along peacefully because he'd heard about what I'd done before. I tied him up and was waiting, as I'd been instructed by Diana, until it was over. She was fighting Smythe-Montgomery. It was her plan.'

Yvette paused and a defiant smile crept onto her face. 'What a surprise it must have been to realize she had been a world-class swordswoman. Even with her lower legs gone, he never had a chance. In fact, all would have gone well but for Richard's eleventh-hour arrival, determined to rescue his friend. He showed no fear at all nor, unfortunately, any common sense. When he threw the door open to their private dueling room, Smythe-Montgomery was there, and that vindictive man stabbed Richard. I took care of him while Diana attended to Smythe-Montgomery. Richard was soaked in blood, and so was I, by the time help came. So much blood.' Her account faded to a stop. She gazed into her lap, where she had held and stroked Crandall's head before the ambulance arrived.

'I ... I'm so sorry. Which sounds pathetically inadequate because it is. My God, you're amazing.'

She looked up and smiled at that. 'Foolish, certainly. Bullheaded, obviously. Lucky? Well, here I am still. And now, maybe we should do a little work.'

***

Crandall had left his London home as soon as Colin arrived, his emotions a strange mixture of joy and apprehension, declaring that he needed to spend the evening at his country estate. Yvette and Colin began filtering news articles and running simulations, working in the study.

A software error—each playfully blaming the other—set them back several hours. After a successful test run at last, they ordered Chinese, and were now finishing a bottle of wine as they reached for the fortune cookies. Yvette flicked on a lamp, the study having grown too dark for them to read.

'You first,' Colin said.

Yvette broke her cookie. 'It says "Count on friends to get you through dark times." A bit late. I've had my dark times and my friends were with me. And now I've a new one. What does yours say?'

Colin unfolded his fortune and his eyes narrowed, his bright smile fading a bit until he forced it back. He set the fortune aside. 'I don't need that. I've a better one: *You've met the love of your life. Tell her now, you fool!*'

Even in the dim light, he could see the blush creep up Yvette's neck and face, leaving pink blooms on her cheeks. Before she could speak, he leaned forward and kissed her lightly. 'I'm lost, you know, without you. I sometimes wonder when and how it happened. I think it was the day you eradicated the malware from the school computer!'

Yvette pulled back and swatted his arm. 'You liar! You gave me such a look that day, and it wasn't love!'

'No,' he said, leaning back into the couch. 'I'm sure it was. Your beauty and brilliance conquered me completely.'

Yvette slipped off the couch and came around to face him. She kneeled back onto the couch, straddling his legs and holding his head between her hands. 'Say it again,' she whispered.

'Your beauty and brilliance conquered me completely. And they always will.'

Then her mouth was on his and he was breathing in her scent and tasting the lingering sweetness of the fortune cookie. His hands reached around to her shoulders then slid down to her hips as her fingers twined his thick hair. After what seemed only an instant she pulled back and stood. He gave her a puzzled look until she smiled and held out her hand. With a worldly bashfulness—a product of her unusual past—she said, 'It's late. Come to bed.'

***

July, 2007, Las Vegas

A street magician, sweltering in full costume, worked the crowded Vegas strip on an evening where as much heat poured from the sun-baked concrete and asphalt as was radiating from the setting sun. It was the start of the business day for the self-styled Illusion's Master, who would work the crowds until long past sunset, beginning here in front of the Bellagio's swaying fountains. 'Time To Say Goodbye' resonated across the huge pond while the jets of water pulsed and whirled in perfect synchronization with the music. Overheated pedestrians looked longingly at the spray of water as they passed, but only an occasional whiff of moisture survived to float across the sidewalk, not nearly enough to provide any refreshment.

89

Illusion's Master walked the pavement with the crowd, performing simple card tricks or pulling items from a raven-black top hat. When the crowd could be bothered to glance up from their determined, jostling stride, applause would compete briefly with the music and the splash of the fountains. Children in particular—though far outnumbered by adults—would stare in fascination while feats of real magic were performed by the magician in the black pants, ruffled white shirt, and flowing cape. Those who did were invariably rewarded with small trinkets and candy, raising the popularity of Illusion's Master another notch.

Tonight, there would be something special: a much more complicated illusion that had taken significant planning.

Larger groups were gathered near the bases of the many overhead walkways that crossed the strip and intersecting streets, designed to prevent distracted pedestrians and drivers from making intimate, deadly contact, which had happened often enough. Alcohol and bright lights, it seemed, lowered people's IQs. Before crossing the walkways, couples, families, or groups of friends would often stop and consider their options. Cross to Caesar's Palace? Head to New York, New York for a drink and dinner, or stop at another casino to try their luck?

At the corner of Las Vegas Blvd and Flamingo Rd, Illusion's Master pulled a segmented tube from beneath the cape. With a flick of the wrist, it became a small table, roughly waist high. A deck of cards materialized with a single snap of the fingers, and soon a small crowd gathered. The sun had finally set and the cool shadows made people more inclined to stop for some brief entertainment. After all, it was free.

The show was going well, and Illusion's Master moved to more spectacular magic, engaging the crowd and making small items move from one person in a group to another: car keys, a pocket comb, a cell phone. A dove flew from the top hat. Then a raven. More applause. But one person in the crowd refused to be impressed. An older man with a long, horsey face and an abrasive voice was belittling the show, pointing out how he'd seen much better at the Magic Castle in Los Angeles or at any of the casinos along the strip. His comments became louder and more offensive, and people glanced at the man, distracted.

Illusion's Master soldiered on, but began making mistakes. Shuffling the deck sent cards spilling in all directions. The heckler let out a braying laugh. At this, the magician stopped entirely and focused on the man. 'Who are you to mock Illusion's Master? You have the intelligence of a moth, and I'm inclined to turn you into one as punishment for your arrogance.'

The old man blew a loud raspberry at the magician, then beamed at the crowd, some of whom laughed and others who looked on in stony disapproval.

A voice suddenly boomed. 'So be it.' The magician whipped off the cape. It flew at the man like a striking serpent, while words of power thundered in the air. The cape landed squarely on the man's head and settled slowly, lazily to the ground while the onlookers gaped. A brilliant flash of light and a BOOM that faded to silence. A tiny rustle in the fabric of the cape caught their attention as Illusion's Master strode forward and lifted the cape from the ground. There was no sign of the loud-mouthed man, but a large monarch butterfly flew up and away, drifting towards the Paris casino on a light breeze.

Illusion's Master stared after it with a puzzled frown. 'Perhaps he was right and I should practice my magic. It was supposed to be a moth.'

Thunderous applause, cheers, people pointing. 'Did you see that?' 'Turned him into a butterfly?' 'Shut his stupid yap for him?' 'I want to see more?' 'Hey, what casino do you work at?'

Illusion's Master bowed gracefully and produced a small shower of candies for the nearby children. At last, the applause died and people moved away, with many a backward glance, until only one man remained. A tall man in a tan sport coat, his expensive silk shirt unbuttoned a third of the way down. He was still wearing dark glasses despite the sun's earlier exit.

'I've seen some interesting performances,' he said, extending a hand, 'but for sheer knockout punch, nothing ever beat this. I'd love to know how you did it.' He held up his hand to forestall the magicians' usual polite refusal to disclose the details of their art. 'But more than that, I'd like to offer you a job—contingent on seeing what you would do on an indoor stage.' He pulled off his glasses and Illusion's Master immediately recognized the man: owner of at least two huge casinos, one on the Strip. 'Ah,' he said, 'I see you know me. Come to my offices tomorrow.' He pointed across the road to a building blazing in neon extravagance. 'Let's say two o'clock. Ask anyone working there for directions. You can tell me what I might expect from you as a regular performer, three nights a week, and we can discuss a contract.'

Illusion's Master nodded and bowed again.

'Good.' The tall man replaced his glasses, walked off, and was soon lost in the crowd.

The ship's superstructure had been dramatically altered by a small army of men with cutting torches, sheet metal, and welding tools.

Chapter Five

Transformation

Jesse was tiring of this game, but at least in this instance Carlos was not controlling the terms of their meeting. The setting sun, sparkling the waters of the Pacific Ocean, had succeeded in making even the dismal Puerto Esperanza seem cheerful. A difficult task. The dock area was as squalid as any western seaport in El Salvador, Guatemala, or Costa Rica, or dozens of others that littered their eastern shores. Dogs with a bedraggled look rooted through garbage heaps. By dusk, the place would be alive with rats. A few pathetic prostitutes would try to lure drunken longshoremen into parting with their hard-earned coin.

Many of these hard men had been busily adding the last touches to the magically transformed *Saint Martin*. No longer the *Saint Martin*, of course, but the *Reina del Mar*, an aging, respectable cargo ship. The ship's superstructure had been dramatically altered by a small army of men with cutting torches, sheet metal, and welding tools. Grinders, shrieking like tormented souls, had removed superficial rust. Dull red primer and a bright new paint scheme had done the rest. It hadn't been trivial. No. Hours of noisy, backbreaking work with toxic fumes heavy in the air. Numerous injuries, but no fatalities. And now, to all but the most perceptive nautical eye, the *Saint Martin* was no more, replaced by the *Reina del Mar*. A metamorphosis worthy of Illusion's Master.

But the real magic had been in falsifying documents of construction and registry that completed the transformation of this ship from a well-known smuggling craft to a nearly respectable cargo ship, old but proud, with a long history, easily verifiable through the usual channels. A deeper scrutiny might reveal the truth, but who would waste the effort?

A trio of black SUVs pulled up on the dock alongside. Jesse scowled. Why must Carlos be so obvious? He might as well paint Drug Lord on the sides of the vehicles. After a few heavily armed goons got out, performed a quick examination of the dock, and nodded their approval, Carlos exited the second vehicle, smiling at the exhausted, disinterested workers.

'Well, Raynard, a job well done, I see,' he said, stepping onto the bridge. 'Even I wouldn't recognize her.'

Jesse forced a tight-lipped smile. Carlos couldn't tell a freighter from a rowboat. 'Let's step out onto the deck. The paint reek in here is piercing my skull.'

A small table and several chairs were set up outside near the bow, with glasses, ice, and tequila available.

'Yes, you've done well,' Carlos said, in a condescending tone.

'The ship's papers are, as you see, all in order.'

'Not now, Raynard,' Carlos said, pushing the offered documents to the side. 'You must learn to enjoy the moment.' He splashed tequila into two glasses. 'Come, a toast.'

Jesse reluctantly raised a glass and clicked it against Carlos's, but set it back on the table without drinking. Carlos didn't notice.

'Ah, the reward,' he said, eyeing the clear liquid. 'A fine Añejo. *Gracias*!' He threw the remains of the first glass back and poured another. As he set the bottle down, he glanced at a book lying on the table. He reached out and hefted it, making a great show of its size and weight. 'What's this, Raynard, a little light reading? Ha ha ha!'

Jesse's head had been pounding all day, partly from the fumes of paint and diesel exhaust, and partly from a sour anticipation of this meeting, a meeting which had so far been even more vexing than expected. The braying of this ignorant jackass was like a spike in the skull.

'I picked it up at the airport. You might want to read the title, at least.'

'Eh? Of course. *The Fall of an Empire: The Tragic End of the Family Croker / Smythe-Montgomery*. Ah, the sad tale of my one-time compadre. Pity, really. Still, we shall do quite well with his associate, Ms. Lister. And to what do you attribute the fall of his empire, eh, Raynard? Was he too greedy? No.' Carlos waggled a thick finger. 'Careless. That's it. He became careless. His organizations penetrated, his lieutenants identified. Careless, not like us.'

'Not like you, you mean. Still, you might want to look at the cast of characters Ms. Fletcher delineates at the start of the book. Page twelve, I believe. Oh, and be sure you check the organizational structure she's drawn on pages thirteen and fourteen. Oddly, those two pages are devoted not to Smythe-Montgomery's syndicate, which is much larger and is dealt with later, but to yours. It seems Ms. Fletcher has done her research and someone—or several someones—have provided her with interesting and accurate information. Careless.'

The smile, frozen on Carlos's face, turned to a grimace as he scanned the pages indicated.

'I perused it carefully,' Jesse remarked. 'It is all correct, isn't it? Well, you would know, but I found no flaws.'

Carlos's face had gone red and blotchy. He snatched the bottle, gulped down several mouthfuls, then slammed it to the table. 'Ramón!' he bellowed, though his ever-present bodyguard was only feet away.

'*Si, patrón!*'

'You will find the author of this abomination and deal with her, do you understand?'

'*Si, patrón!*'

Jesse waved a lazy hand at the book. 'Turn it over, Carlos.'

He did, to find Cathie Clark Fletcher grinning at him from the dust cover. 'Wow,' Jesse said with a smirk, 'I've solved the first critical identification problem. Another job well done. Oh, and in today's paper there was an article detailing the author's scheduled book tour. She'll be in London for a few weeks. And now I've solved the entire puzzle.'

Carlos glared at Raynard, then rounded on Ramón and snarled, 'You heard? Get busy.'

'*Si, patrón!*' Ramón withdrew quickly and pulled a cell phone from his pocket.

'You aren't really going to pursue this, are you?' Jesse asked. 'The damage is done, after all.'

Carlos took another heavy drink from the bottle, then pointed it at Jesse. 'Be careful, Raynard. Despite all you've done, I grow tired of your insolence. Know your place. And never, NEVER disrespect me in front of my men!'

Jesse merely shrugged, wondering when this fool would stop beating around the bush. An assassination attempt was long overdue, and Jesse preferred a counterstroke to an open assault on Carlos.

Carlos settled back into his seat and lost some of his fury. He decided to try logic. 'You see what she's printed in the book, that bitch. Fletcher. Where did she receive the information, eh? And why expose my organization in a book about Smythe-Montgomery?' This last complaint came out like a small child asking why the principal was picking on him when there were so many other naughty boys and girls who'd done worse.

'Who knows?' Raynard said. 'Maybe she just did it for completeness, because the information was available. My point is, why bother to kill her? The information is out and you'll have to make minor adjustments: reorganize some operations, replace a few less-than-discreet lieutenants. It changes nothing.'

'Ah,' said Carlos, waving the bottle once again, 'there you are mistaken. In my position, not to act would be seen as weakness. There must be consequences. As for the disloyal lieutenants—'

'I believe I said "less-than-discreet."'

'To allow such information to become known is disloyal. It is treachery! You, my friend,' Carlos said, suddenly smiling and patting Raynard's arm, 'will find these traitors for me, *sí*? Come, we should be allies and never quarrel. Let us drink to it.'

He poured two shots from the half empty bottle, tapped Jesse's glass and threw his own back, never noticing that Jesse, using an elementary bit of distraction, made the drink 'disappear' into the ship's scuppers. Carlos was nearly drunk now. It was time to remind him of his promise.

'I would like to use the ship in the near future, *my friend*,' Jesse parroted, 'as we agreed.'

Carlos waved this away. 'I have several valuable cargos for Europe. The *Saint Martin* will be perfect transport.'

Jesse groaned inwardly, amazed that this man could wipe his own ass without help.

'The *Saint Martin* is no more, yes? Cut up for scrap, I believe. Might you be referring to the *Reina del Mar*?'

'What? Oh, *sí, sí*! Ha ha ha! Amazing what a new coat of paint will do!'

At that moment, Jesse could only picture Carlos's neck being ripped open by Cherokee: the crimson gush of blood and the sparkle in

Cherokee's eyes like blue glaciers. And the end to the jackass braying of this idiot.

'So, the ship?'

'Be patient, my friend,' Carlos said, his breath as potent as the toxic fumes. 'One trip … perhaps two. Valuable cargo.'

Jesse nodded tersely. A delay of a month or more! Annoying but tolerable. It would help to camouflage Jesse's subsequent plans.

'There, you see? Cooperation among friends. And during the time, perhaps you can identify the traitors in my organization. With your skills, it shouldn't take long.' The smile slid from his face and he reached for the bottle again. 'Ah, but the delay. All the way around the Horn once again.'

There was no end to the foolishness of this man, and only the image of him lying in a pool of his own blood prevented Jesse from grabbing the bottle and dispatching him instantly.

'Carlos,' Jesse said, once again offering the papers he'd so carelessly rejected earlier, 'the *Reina del Mar* may sail through the Panama Canal. She is a perfectly legitimate freighter coming from a refit in Talcahuano, Chile. Nothing more normal.'

His eyes had become unfocused, and it took half a minute for him to grasp the concept. When he did, a huge grin split his face. 'My friend, another miracle.' He stood unsteadily and adopted the serious face of a powerful man, a man of business. 'Well done, Raynard. Rest, but not too long, eh? I need you.'

Jesse's grimace might have been confused for a smile. *A few days at the cabin with Cherokee and away from all this. And who knows, I might just stir things up in Carlos's organization. A minor illusion. It would be sad for him to find that some of his most loyal men were the source for Cathie Fletcher's ill-conceived tome. I'm certain he'll deal with them severely.* The thought brought a sincere smile to Jesse's face.

* * *

The flight to Atlanta was late. To make matters worse, Jesse's appointment wasn't in Atlanta, but in Dallas. Not in Texas, thankfully, but in Georgia; a small town miles to the north and west of the crowded Atlanta metro area. A bedroom community with the usual assortment of schools, strip malls, and restaurants. A quick phone call from the airport reassured Jesse. For a dying man, Carl Heskin was surprisingly patient and had promised to wait at their chosen rendezvous, Calliope.

Despite the garish name, Calliope was a quiet restaurant located at the crown of a tall hill, used during the Civil War as an artillery outpost for Sherman's troops. A few of the old guns had been preserved among the pines around the perimeter of the restaurant. They now shared the stunning perch with several telescopes, allowing patrons to stroll out and see far-off Atlanta, lights ablaze. The scene was as unlike what Sherman's scouts would have seen as present-day Manhattan Island would have appeared to the early settlers.

Heskin sat in a room that jutted from the main body of the restaurant. The other tables in this room were empty, and though the restaurant was far from crowded, Jesse wondered what magic or bribery Heskin had used to ensure their total privacy.

'Jesse, so good to—' A fit of coughing stopped him short. 'I beg your pardon,' he choked out after he'd gained control.

'Don't be ridiculous, Carl,' Jesse said, stretching out a hand.

Heskin nodded his thanks and took the offered hand, which Jesse noticed was trembling and clammy.

It was a stark realization for Raynard. *I have so few friends, and this man is one. Charlotte, of course. A friend, confidante, and lover. Any others?* The answer came back instantly. *I know hundreds and have only two friends.* Heskin watched these internal musings play across Raynard's face. 'How are you?' Jesse asked at last.

Heskin smiled weakly. 'As you see me. Between the medicines and the radiation, I'm pretty well ... but what's the point. You look healthy. A bit of a tan, or am I mistaken?'

Jesse smiled. Carl would deflect in this way, not wanting to share the burden of his not-so-distant destiny. A slow, painful death. Raynard's one small consolation was that the man had been given purpose, a reason to live and fight long enough to see the plan through to completion. Carl had been with Jesse from the beginning, the thought stirring distant memories.

Even a small feat of magic required intense preparation. A businessman had once told Jesse that the key to giving a good presentation—one that was easily understood and whose conclusions the audience believed they had reached on their own—was simple: practice,

practice, practice. Wise words that Jesse had adopted. Everything accomplished to date had been the result of planning, preparation, and practice, practice, practice. Jesse's grand scheme had been one of several conceived years ago. Finding someone like Carl had been the key to moving forward, tabling the other ideas and focusing on this one long-term objective.

Nearly three years earlier, rumors had led Jesse to Carl, drowning his sorrows in cheap liquor at a seedy bar in Atlanta.

'Leave me alone,' Carl said, without turning his head, as Jesse sat down next to him on a stool sticky from countless spilled drinks and drunken tears.

Jesse said nothing and bought another round. Twenty silent minutes went by before Carl turned to look at this persistent stranger. 'Since you won't go away, tell me what you want. I warn you in advance, I have nothing to give you. At least, nothing of value.'

'I've heard only parts of a story,' Jesse said. 'Your story. I'd like to hear it all, and before you ask, I don't work for the CDC. I'm also not a cop, lawyer, detective, newspaper reporter, or a member of any government agency.'

'Who are you, then?'

Jesse laughed. 'If I knew, I'd tell you, but that question has puzzled me since I was a kid. For now, let's just say I'm a concerned citizen who feels you've gotten a raw deal and may be entitled to some retribution. Let me add that, based on what I know, no one can help you with your medical problems. I'd be sorry for that except it's the only reason I'm here. It's a requirement, in order for you to help me.'

Carl laughed, then coughed dryly. 'Why should I help you? You just said you couldn't help me.'

'Carl, if you're going to be useful, I must ask you to listen more carefully. Words are the basis for successful communication or dismal misunderstandings. How much bloodshed has been caused by sloppy language? I choose my words carefully. I said I couldn't help you with your medical problems, but there is another area where I have some small expertise, and it's in that area where I can be of service.'

'And this area of expertise?' he said, his voice thick with sarcasm.

'Retribution.'

The smirk slid from Carl's face, replaced by the clenched jaw and daggering eyes of a younger, healthier man. 'I'm listening.'

Carl's defensive walls dropped as he accepted another drink. He had nothing to lose. He'd lost it all already.

This was a partial lie, and he knew it, but what he had left—a wife and two children to share his tears—would eventually suffer as well. Maybe this person could help in another way.

'I didn't catch your name,' Carl said.

'Jesse Raynard.'

'Well, Jesse Raynard, exactly what do you want to know?'

'A brief history, including how you took employment with the CDC. I may have other questions for you when you're done, but for now, the floor is yours and I won't interrupt.'

'Yes, my sad tale of woe. I'll start by saying I'm a fool. Not only a fool, but a brilliant fool. You should take that into account before engaging my services.' He glanced at Raynard. 'I see skepticism in your eyes. Well, perhaps when I've explained.

'I flew through college and medical school. I had very little money, so I wasn't able to start my education at a prestigious school like Harvard or Johns Hopkins. I gained some notoriety when I developed a faster, more reliable technique for detecting viral mutations in early stages. This was during my residency, when most doctors are too sleep-deprived to think straight. In those days, four hours of sleep charged me to full capacity. I wrote a few papers, presented at a few conferences, and suddenly found myself the darling of the medical profession, at least in the area of contagious diseases.

'I began working at NYU, with a research lab of my own and a growing staff of research assistants. Numerous papers followed and a few minor breakthroughs in the detection and treatment of various nasty diseases. During this time, I managed to fall in love with the finest woman on the planet. Not a doctor, thank God. A poet. She can weave a story with half a dozen words and produce a depth of emotional response that most novelists can't achieve in a thousand pages. She won my heart with a couplet! Am I boring you?'

Raynard said nothing, but sat patient and focused.

102

'So I fell in love and married. At about this time—oh, when was it? Spring. Cold and damp. Ninety-nine or 2000. Funny how the year escapes me, but the persistent rain does not. I was approached by a member of the CDC, or so I thought. In fact, the person in question was affiliated with the CDC but was really employed by another three-letter agency. It was an offer too tempting to turn down: My own lab at the premier agency for disease control. Two doctors and half a dozen technicians to assist me. Access to the best toys. Most tantalizing of all, the goal—or so I was told—was to study certain reported diseases that had cropped up in the Middle East. Suspected biological weapons, some traceable to research originating in China and North Korea. My assignment: Analyze these pathogens, determine their source, project their evolutionary path, and develop counteragents. Intriguing, yes?'

Heskin tapped his empty glass, and Raynard silently signaled for another round.

After taking a drink, Heskin turned to Jesse. 'I can see that your word means something. Not an interruption since I started. I begin to imagine you are not really here and I am only talking to myself, which is good. What I'm about to say—talking to myself—is at a level of classification best left to the imagination. If you happen to overhear me, why should I care? It was all a lie, you see. Good people were caught in the trap, including the fool you are now indulging with your patience.

'How to put it succinctly? The project evolved? No, that's a lie. The project was never one of detection and cure. It was about development.'

Raynard stiffened.

'Ah, I see I've piqued your interest, listening as you are while I talk to myself. The status of my lab was changed. We were moved to a new, separate facility. I signed many papers, and poof, we became a fiction. No outside collaboration, no publishing of papers. No talking to my wife! Did I say fiction? Not accurate. We became an illusion. The CDC's Extremely Hazardous Disease Response Group. We even had an official logo and some very fine polo shirts. Rubbish. Do you really understand the significance of what I'm saying? We were *developing biological weapons against all official treaties and in violation of all moral decency. I, of course, was no longer in charge. The EHDRG was managed by the other agency. Other doctors were brought in, some quite brilliant but colder than a dead moon.*

'I was merely on staff. I emphasize this because, in addition to being subject to a death sentence, I wouldn't have my pride wounded by being accused of leading the idiocy that followed. The doctor in charge was enamored of transformative mutations leading to previously unknown modes of transmission. Here I'll stop myself. The details fascinate me to this day, though I'm now a dead man. Our chief had hired assistants that were as clumsy as they were foolish. There was a breach and I am the result. Have no fear, I'm no longer contagious. And I'm alive. In that sense, our project was a failure. Three others died quickly. I'm still here.'

Heskin sighed. 'My tedious story comes to a close. I swore to expose them. They didn't bother to remind me of all the agreements I'd signed, they simply threatened my family, demoted me, wiped out my pension, and sent me back to work. If I cooperate and behave myself, they have promised to look after my family. Lies, of course. My wife and daughters will be alive, but with none of the future I'd hoped to provide. I may actually live a few years. Long enough to watch the slow destruction of my hopes.'

He turned back to his drink, and the small noises of the bar provided the epilogue to his story.

Raynard's jaw was clenched, eyes fierce. A long time passed.

'Well, Carl,' Raynard said at last, 'when I arrived, I offered my services in providing retribution, which is clearly your due, but I'm delighted to find I have one other service I can provide for your family: financial security.'

'Humph. I had hoped to send both of my children to medical school. Can you provide that and a lifetime income for my wife too?'

'A modest enough request.'

Carl's head popped up. 'I was joking.'

'I wasn't. How does $10 million guaranteed in an untraceable Caymans account strike you, plus, let's say 20 percent of any additional ... profits from my endeavor?'

'You have a deal,' he said, reaching out a hand.'
'Hadn't you better find out what I want from you?'
'No.'
They shook hands.

His grip had been stronger then. And not so damp.

'A tan? Maybe. I've been close to the equator for too long. I miss my mountains. But enough of that. Tell me what's happening at work.'

'Easy enough. The rumors from Huata, carried by the local villagers as well as the aid team that was driven off, have several of the doctors concerned. The symptoms described are inconclusive. Could be Ebola or bubonic plague. What to do? I still have a certain stature at the CDC, augmented oddly enough by my imminent demise, and I pointed out that no other villages have reported any illness, and the doctors and aid workers who were on the scene have been given a clean bill of health. The result is hesitation. Advocates for an immediate and thorough investigation are confronted with at least a dozen other instances of outbreaks worldwide that require the CDC's immediate intervention. Our resources are limited. Heated discussions have taken place, and naturally I listen without bias.'

'Very wise.'

A slight chuckle. 'I believe inertia and other more urgent events will result in no action being taken. As we agreed, there is nothing more to be gained in this case.'

'No. It's only the first demonstration of several, after all. Pictures and reports that I've released have caused a quiet stir among potential interested groups. This event has served its purpose.'

'So, you move on to other demonstrations?'

Raynard nodded. 'As we've planned. Is your team in place?'

'Yes. Large sums of money have changed hands, and in that part of the world, reality is what you can buy. For that matter, so is illusion. The right people will act when the time comes.'

'A respected doctor is on the team?'

'Two. Well known for their philanthropic work and unquestioned integrity. Their reward is the good works they achieve.'

Raynard smiled crookedly. 'Until enough money is offered. What could be better than good works and wealth combined?'

Heskin returned the smile. 'Actually, I will be making only modest demands on your wallet in the case of those two. As it turns out, staying out of a Bangladeshi prison is even better than wealth, and it's far better than good works.'

Raynard raised a questioning eyebrow.

A shrug. 'As you know, I'm quite familiar with that part of the world—Bangladesh in particular—from a contagious diseases point of view. There was an incident a few years ago where two careless young doctors were reusing an unsterile speculum to test the prostitutes for disease. They spread the disease the way the Santa Ana winds spread wildfire. I discovered their blunder, but kept quiet. The doctors have made amends through years of *good works*,' Heskin said, spitting out the words as though they left a sour taste in his mouth. 'A small amount of cash plus a promise to refrain from sending the incriminating evidence to a government prosecutor was sufficient motivation. A death sentence awaits the two if they are found out.'

'Blackmail! I'm impressed, Carl. I'm also surprised that a disease outbreak or even the death of large numbers of prostitutes would cause such retribution.'

'Pffh. It normally wouldn't. But a number of politicians, including the prosecutor, were heavily invested in the establishments affected. If you cause a politician pain, or worse yet, loss of revenue, you can expect swift, brutal justice.'

A discreet waiter stood nearby, waiting for a brief pause in the conversation. 'May I get you anything from the bar? Or would you like to order your dinner?'

Heskin gestured to Raynard, who said, 'I'd like a glass of wine—your Duckhorn Vineyards Cab. Then the prime rib, rare, some genuine horseradish, baked potato, and your house salad.'

'Ah, very good,' the waiter said, scribbling. 'And you sir?'

'Jack Daniels on the rocks. What's your soup?'

'Potato and broccoli tonight, sir.'

'The Jack, a big bowl of the soup, and some warm bread.'

When the waiter left, Jesse asked, 'Just soup?'

'And bread. I can tolerate both pretty well.'

'And the Jack?'

Heskin smiled widely. 'I tolerate that best of all. Don't be worried about my liver, I'll be dead long before I can damage it. Now,' he continued, dismissing the topic of his health, 'tell me about your other endeavor. How is the ship?'

Jesse grimaced. 'That fool Carlos the Worm wants to use it for a while. More human cargo.'

'That may work out in your favor,' Heskin said.

'It's funny you deduced that so quickly. I came to the same conclusion a bit slower, my logic clouded by blind fury. How can a moron like that become head of the largest cartel in Mexico and Central America?'

Carl grinned. 'With your help, all things are possible. Poof! The rabbit is pulled from the hat. Entertain me, Raynard. I'm sure you have a pack of cards on you.'

When the waiter returned, he saw Jesse performing simple card tricks for a man who, though pale and sickly, was smiling broadly and clapping his hands on occasion.

'Ah, you should have been a magician,' Heskin said, some fifteen minutes later, when the food arrived.

The cards were tucked away. 'I never had an audience as appreciative as you.'

'That's a lie,' Heskin said playfully. 'I do appreciate the occasional departure from reality.'

'It's my specialty, Carl. Sleight of hand. Illusion.'

'Magic. Yes, I know. I suppose we should combine a little planning with magic. Tell me what else I can do to prepare for your nautical demonstration.'

'Unfortunately, the execution date will depend on Carlos's whims. Unless …'

'Patience, Raynard. Hah,' he laughed, 'I never thought I'd be saying that to you! I'm the one who's on the clock.'

'We're both on the clock. These events—these demonstrations—must be perfectly timed and integrated with our release of information.'

'Still, killing Carlos outright—don't deny your inclination, I can see it on your face—won't help. I imagine you'll find it far more difficult to use the ship with his organization thrown into chaos. Right now, you have *his* commitment. If he's dead, you have nothing.'

'You're right again. We'll let that sleeping dog lie. Once I do get the ship, here's what I'll need from you …'

Nearly two hours passed before Raynard and Heskin rose to leave.

'A pleasure to see you, Carl,' Jesse said, once again taking his hand.

'And it's a pleasure to be seen,' he replied. 'For a while longer. For long enough.'

'Get some rest, my friend.'

'You've given me too much to do,' he said, coughing violently at his own feeble joke.

***

Jesse stood on the deserted patio of Calliope, a cigar in one hand and a cognac in the other, and stared out at the distant glow of Atlanta. If only there was some other help for Carl. But this was pointless sentimentality. There was none. Nearly half an hour later, a chilly rain shower brought an end to fruitless musing. Jesse crushed out the cigar, swallowed the last of the cognac, and left. There was much to be done.

The signing at the Tower went extremely well, and, though the crowd was formidable, Cathie managed to sign every book ...

Tourist boats and pleasure craft clustered on the banks in outcrops, and numerous freight haulers shared the waterway ...

Chapter Six

Book Tour

When Cathie called to say she and Joy would be getting dinner after their shopping day, Logan wasn't surprised. He was still sitting at the piano, playing melancholy chords at random, when the phone rang again.

'Logan, I heard you were batching it tonight. Wanna buy me a drink and talk about our imaginary relationship?'

'Becky Amhurst! It hasn't been a half hour since Cathie called. How the hell did you find out?'

'Your spouse—quite accurately—doesn't see me as any kind of threat, and she was feeling guilty about bailing on you, so she called. To be fair, she called Chuck first, who is otherwise occupied. He suggested me as a poor second choice.'

'My head is spinning, but I'd love to get together. I'm curious about how ARC is doing on the contract with—'

'Nope! No business or no deal.'

'That means I won't be buying you any drinks.'

'I'm hoping you'll see the light. There *are* other things to talk about that don't involve sex, my company's contracts, or sex.'

'Hmm. You left out sex. All right, you've convinced me. How about Sky Box—just for old time's sake—at 7:00?'

'Make it 6:00. I'm really tired of this place and your old friend Gary is driving me batshit.'

'Heard that,' said a distant voice.

'Excellent. I'll be wearing a white carnation in my lapel,' Logan added, in his best imitation of Bogart.

'And I'll be dressed in red. Blood red!'

Logan chuckled as he hung up the phone. He played a few chords, more cheerful, then went to get changed.

***

'Well, holy shit!' Logan said, as Becky approached his table, her incendiary red dress drawing numerous looks—some envious, some salacious, depending on the gender of the looker.

'Where's the carnation, Humphrey? Ah, the things I put up with.' She sat down across from Logan. 'It's good to see you too. How long's it been?'

'Too long. Your usual?' he asked, as the waiter hustled up.

'Nah. A warm glass of milk just doesn't seem right for this place. How about a nice Chardonnay?'

'Two,' Logan said.

It wasn't long before Becky leaned back from the table and said, 'OK, what gives? You agreed to see me, and I certainly didn't expect to be seduced, but you've hardly mumbled twenty words since I got here, and you've gone back to the weather three times.'

Logan faked a casual laugh, then frowned at his feeble attempt. 'Yeah, well, uh ...'

'Now see,' Becky said brightly, 'if you'd said that right up front it would have made everything crystal clear.'

'If I ... what?'

Becky threw her head back and laughed heartily. 'Still an easy mark. However, you're beginning to worry me. Has Elaya Andoori's husband risen from the grave, howling for revenge? Or maybe Chuck has turned out to be the deepest Soviet double-agent of all time. Or you have a hangnail. Or ... throw me a bone, here.'

Logan saw genuine concern in Becky's intelligent, expressive eyes. He took a drink. 'I could lie and tell you I'm just nervous about the band's upcoming gig, but what would be the point? You're coming, I hope.'

'Naturally.'

'And your "little friend"?'

'If I'm coming, I'm packing. Your gigs can be dangerous.'

Logan gave her a lopsided smile.

'So now you've told me what you're *not* going to tell me. Are you planning to get around to the truth?'

112

'The truth.' He tipped back the remainder of his drink and automatically motioned for another. When he spoke again, it did nothing to reduce Becky's anxiety.

'Remember when you were a kid? Sometimes you'd get a creepy feeling like … I don't know … something bad was going to happen. And then it did. Of course, for every fifty times you had that weird feeling, nothing happened. But once in a while something did.'

'And it made you certain those feelings really did predict the future. Yeah, I've felt that way. I'm not totally abnormal.'

'Thanks for not laughing,' Logan said, as the waiter placed another glass of wine in front of him. 'Ah, no,' he said. 'I need a double Jack.'

Becky reached across the table and took the glass. 'I'll drink his.' When the waiter left, she said, 'Go on.'

'Yeah. Been feeling something. Most of the time I think I'm being a stupid kid, but the rest of the time I'm scared shitless.'

'Any notion of what's coming?'

'You believe me?'

'More than you know, big fella.'

'As for a notion, no. Nada. Which means I can't do a thing about it.'

Becky reached a hand across the table and placed it over Logan's. 'Wrong. You can talk to a friend who won't laugh at you, and you can try to relax. Buy me some dinner and I'm yours for the duration. Now, tell me more.'

Logan smiled, a perceptible burden lifted from his shoulders. He was about to say 'Thanks' when Becky smiled and waggled her finger in front of his nose. 'Don't need that between friends.'

***

'I'm really glad you and Chuck moved to Tucson,' Cathie remarked, glancing at her friend before returning to a critical examination of two blouses. In the end, she put them both back on the rack. 'Now I'll get to see you more often than our once-a-year wine-tasting extravaganzas.'

'Chuck twisted my arm for weeks trying to convince me to move: cajoling, bribing, lying. In the end I decided I couldn't live without the old grump, but I didn't tell him that. First he sweetened the deal by saying I would be the office manager—the uncontested office queen were his words—here in Tucson. With an actual salary! We're building a thousand-square-foot extension on our house. A combined game room (of course) and office for Triple S with three dedicated terminals, a huge display, a conference table, and secure connectivity to London. Plus a *very* nice private office for *moi*. But do you think I caved to that?'

'No ma'am,' Cathie said, smiling conspiratorially. 'Your momma didn't raise no fool.'

'That's right. So, I pouted and groused until he finally said that, as the uncontested office queen, it would probably be necessary for me to make an annual trip to London to coordinate operations.'

'An "*annual*" trip"?'

'And that's what *I* said. In the end we settled on no fewer than quarterly trips, with others as needed to properly fulfill my role. Office queen!'

'I think that deserves a toast. So why are we still here?'

'I'm all shopped out, but the clink of fine china and a crystal glass filled to the brim with a Cosmo sounds appealing. Have you got a—'

'Jade. Just a little west on Sunrise. Cosmos to die for and the best Asian food in Arizona.'

'And yet, we're still here!'

'Not for long.'

***

'So what's with you?' Joy asked not much later. The two were seated at a candlelit table, and their first Cosmos had magically evaporated to half full. 'I've made two very witty remarks and barely gotten a grunt in return. Please don't tell me you're missing the boys.'

This brought a laugh. 'No, not that. Just nerves, I guess.'

'Nerves? Nerves about what?'

Cathie looked down into her drink with embarrassment. 'It's ridiculous. I've done book tours ever since I started selling well enough to make it worthwhile. I've always enjoyed them. They're flattering. But this thing in London is just … making me nervous.'

'Having never been in your situation, I have no idea what advice to give.'

'Oh, just tell me I'm being silly.'

'You're being silly.'

'You're right.' Cathie shook her head. 'Anyway, enough with the irrational butterflies. Are you going to the new band's debut?'

'Hell yes. I've heard the venue is amazing.'

'It is. I went with Logan when he and Tyrone talked to the manager. It's a converted old ranch on the western foothills of the Tucson Mountains. They gutted the main building, added a bar and a restaurant with a wall of glass facing west. The view is phenomenal.'

'Don't you get sun blasted?'

'They have twelve-foot-tall tinted panels on tracks that keep the place pleasant till sunset. Plus, the entire glass wall opens to an outside dining area. The band will set up outside and play three sets from 6:00 to 9:00.'

'Sounds great. What's the name again?'

'Jazz West.'

'Hmm. Sounds a little schizophrenic.'

'It is. The décor and menu are nouveau Western. The music is strictly jazz. You wouldn't think it would work, but it does. Reviews have been fabulous.'

'Not to put too fine a point on it, but how did the Fourth Harmonics manage to land a gig there?'

'Ah, their secret weapon, Tyrone Morris. An old buddy of his from his time in Iraq owns the place and knows Tyrone can play. Easy.'

'I'll bet Logan's working up a bag of anxiety.'

'Worse than me and this London trip. He turned white when he saw the place. Even tried talking Tyrone out of it. Fat chance. Anyway, the band'll do just fine.'

'You'll be there, right? You won't be off to London yet?'

'I leave a couple days after the concert.'

***

On the evening of their performance, Logan walked into the restaurant like a man walking to a funeral. Tyrone nudged him in the ribs and gave him a big grin. 'It's gonna be fun, Logan.'

'Yeah, so you say. How come you're not nervous? Oh, wait, it's because you're a pro.'

Tyrone's rumbling chuckle would have made Santa Claus proud. 'Listen,' he said, sotto voce, 'I still get butterflies. I always have. They disappear before the third bar.' He looked directly into Logan's eyes. 'The secret is, stay smooth.' He motioned with the flat of his hand as though stroking a glass surface.

The corners of Logan's mouth lifted in a tiny smile.

'That's my boy,' Tyrone said. 'Let's go have fun.'

***

Tyrone had taken off his bass guitar and switched to the 'big stand-up fiddle' for the final set of the evening. His solo improvisation had brought the crowd to a raucous ovation. Afterwards, the band members had slipped off the stage to join friends and family for a late dinner. Chuck had been unabashed in his praise.

'Dang, T-bone, you've still got it! You even made Logan's motley bunch sound fantastic.'

Tyrone smiled but shook his head. 'I got so far behind on my transitions that it's amazing these guys had the patience to let me catch up.'

'That was a lovely, creative, massive lie,' Logan said, raising his coffee cup. 'I think I saw smoke coming off your strings, Tyrone. I've never seen or heard anyone play a bass like it was a banjo. I tip my hat to a superior musician.'

'Oh, I learned a few tricks from Uncle Zach,' Tyrone said, digging into his cobbler.

'To Uncle Zach!' Becky said. She drank the last of her coffee and stood to leave. 'Thanks for letting me join the table of the two musical masters. I'm off. Some of us still have a day job.'

'And here's to not needing your little friend!' Logan said.

Cathie gave him a quizzical look, but Tyrone laughed. 'Part of a great line from *Scarface*, Cathie. "Say hello to my little friend." And what a delivery by Pacino! You'll have to check it out.'

Sated at last, everyone brushed the crumbs from their laps and headed for home. Three days later, neither having told the other of their inexplicable anxiety, Logan drove Cathie to the airport for her flight to London.

***

As she perused the map of London spread out on Diana's dining room table, Cathie couldn't help but notice the gentle, physical contact between Yvette and Colin; the touching and nudging as each would point out an

116

area of interest or one of the venues for Cathie's book tour. *Ah, young love*, she thought.

'The timing will never work,' Yvette said, putting her hand on Colin's shoulder. 'How will Cathie ever get from a ten-to-noon signing at the Tower Hotel in the City to a one o'clock engagement at Royal Booksellers in Chelsea, never mind having time for lunch?'

'Yvette's right,' Colin agreed, covering Yvette's hand with his own. 'I don't know what your London agent was thinking.'

'We couldn't drive? It looks so close.'

'Oh, Lord no!' Yvette and Colin said simultaneously, then laughed.

'You can't imagine the crush at that time of day. The tube?' Yvette offered doubtfully.

'Maybe, if every connection was spot on time,' Colin said, frowning.

'Well, hell,' Cathie said. 'It was my U.S. agent, Kyle, who set this up, the little weasel. Probably didn't even bother talking to anyone familiar with London.'

'It's a shame,' Yvette said. 'The second day's schedule is manageable, but this ...'

'I'll just have to cancel one or the other. Or maybe trim off a half hour from each.'

'I've got it!' Colin crowed, his triumphant tone cutting across Cathie's gloomy words. 'A private water taxi! Look.' He pointed to a small jetty near Tower Bridge Road. 'A brisk walk past the Royal Armouries takes us to Tower Pier. I know a friend whose father owns a service. We have lunch waiting on the boat, enjoy a pleasant cruise viewing the city, several historical H.M. ships docked along the north bank, past the London Eye, Westminster, and disembark here'—his finger moved to an even smaller jetty—'at the Albert Bridge. An easy walk to let lunch settle and we're at Royal Booksellers in Chelsea.'

'Brilliant,' Yvette said, beaming at Colin. 'I dub you Knight of City Logistics.'

'It sounds lovely,' Cathie said. 'And fun. You two are relieving a lot of anxiety, and Kyle may be able to keep his chestnuts. We can run through it again tomorrow, but tonight, I'd like to take the two of you out to dinner. Is there something nice nearby?'

Yvette and Colin exchanged a glance. 'Somersby Pub, not twenty minutes up the road, is excellent, though you really don't have to,' Colin said.

'Well, I insist. I've already twisted Diana's arm, but she has another engagement. With Richard Crandall, I believe.'

Yvette nodded. 'In that case, we'd be delighted,' Colin said. 'And perhaps you might share some of your adventures. I understand your writing has gotten you involved with all types of international intrigue, like Mr. Stone.'

Cathie gave an unladylike roar of laughter. 'My "adventures," though more than enough to suit me, can never compare to the escapades of Jason Stone. However, I'll tell you all about them if you promise to stop me when you get bored.'

'Not bloody likely!' Colin said, with a grin.

***

The interior courtyard of Diana's estate was dark but for the few decorative lights that glimmered like fireflies among the trees and bushes. Yvette and Colin sat alone in the huge banquet hall, sharing a final glass of wine.

'Good Lord, what a story,' Colin said. 'Kidnapped by terrorists and held in an ancient prison, then rescued—single-handedly—by Jason Stone! Cathie and her husband have certainly had their share of adventure.'

Yvette sipped her drink. 'Don't forget, those "terrorists" were just hired thugs of Smythe-Montgomery. Her story is only a fraction of what went on.'

'Oh, I know. The fight in Breckenridge and …' His boyish enthusiasm faded and his smile became tentative. He'd been about to mention Diana's sword duel with Smythe-Montgomery, a chaotic event where Richard Crandall had nearly been killed. 'Sorry,' he said, his eyes dropping to his wineglass. 'I know it upsets you.'

Yvette put a hand to his cheek, and his eyes rose to meet hers. 'Silly boy. Silly, kind, considerate boy. If you're not careful, I might just fall in love with you.'

'It's too late for me, I'm afraid,' he said. He leaned forward and kissed her.

118

'More wine?' she asked. 'Or bed?'

He pushed his glass back and smiled.

***

The signing at the Tower went extremely well, and, though the crowd was formidable, Cathie managed to sign every book and say a few words to everyone, despite Yvette fussing in the background and Colin tapping his watch with significance.

The three exited the hotel into a lovely London day, with temperatures in the mid-sixties and only a few clouds drifting lazily across a pale blue sky. Cathie gaped at the Tower Bridge like any other tourist as Colin set a brisk pace for the pier.

As they boarded the water taxi, Colin made introductions. 'Cathie, this is Tony, a school friend from many years back.'

'Well, I know that's a lie,' Cathie said, taking Tony's offered hand.

Tony's eyebrows shot up and he turned to Colin.

'I'm joking, Tony,' Cathie said. 'Neither of you is old enough to have a friend from "many years back."' She eyed the table and chairs set up under an awning at the aft end of the boat. There were place settings for three that were far too fine for a water taxi, along with several bottles of wine. 'You'll join us for lunch, won't you?'

'Oh, I really should—'

'Really, after my ham-fisted attempt at humor, I insist.'

***

Food was served as the boat pulled away from the pier.

'That's HMS Belfast, a World War II cruiser,' Colin said, pointing to the other bank of the river, 'and just back from the shoreline is London Bridge Station.'

'Are you going to give us a full guided tour all the way to Chelsea?' Yvette teased.

'You go right ahead, Colin,' Cathie said, with a smile. 'I've never seen London from the river.'

Colin recovered his enthusiasm quickly, and before the boat slipped under the low concrete arches of Waterloo Bridge, he was pointing out the sights with the eagerness of a child.

Tourist boats and pleasure craft clustered on the banks in outcrops, and numerous freight haulers shared the waterway with these smaller vessels.

'There's Waterloo Station off to the left—a bloody great barn of a place—and of course the London Eye is visible for miles.'

After completing a turn to the south, they were right alongside the Eye, which extended out over the muddy Thames. Another turn to the west took them under a large railroad bridge and then Chelsea Bridge.

'Almost there,' Colin announced, pointing to a pier up ahead. 'That next bridge is the Albert and we'll put ashore just before we get there.'

'You sound like a sea captain,' Yvette said. 'The Dread Pirate Colin! Yarr!'

'Oh, all right,' he said, shaking his head.

'You know,' Cathie remarked, 'it's never been more apparent that London is a river town. Naturally I've known that the Thames passes through the heart of the city, but from land, I've hardly given it a thought. Oh, I've crossed a bridge or two in a day of sightseeing or shopping, but by my count we've just passed under thirteen bridges since we left the City—auto, railroad, and pedestrian combined. It never really sunk in till now. An added benefit of traveling by boat!'

Colin smiled and Yvette gave him a peck on the cheek. 'Well done, Captain.'

As the boat hands were tying off at the pier, Cathie turned to Yvette. 'I'm embarrassed to ask whether it would be appropriate to offer any tip to the captain and crew.'

'Ah,' she said, 'that's not expected, but there is one thing ...'

Cathie smiled and nodded as Yvette whispered her one thing.

As she reached the gangway, Cathie stopped. 'Tony, thank you for a lovely trip.' She held out a copy of her book. 'This is for your mom. A little bird told me she might like a signed copy.'

'Thank you, Ms. Fletcher.' He flipped the book open to the title page. 'And I see the little bird told you my mother's name as well.' He smiled at Yvette.

'Off we go then,' Colin said briskly. 'We have twelve minutes to get to Royal Booksellers, which leaves us about two minutes to spare. Thanks, mate,' he said, shaking Tony's hand.

***

A row of three- and four-story buildings stood side by side, like old soldiers on parade, facing Cheyne Walk across neat enclosed courtyards. Royal Booksellers was part of this row, distinguishable from its neighbors by slightly darker brick and white awnings above the ground-floor windows. A low stone wall topped with a wrought iron fence flanked the fanciful double gate. A small crowd had already gathered in the store, which occupied the two lower floors, and spilled into the courtyard. Smiles and waves greeted Cathie as she climbed the three entryway stairs and entered the building.

'Sorry there was no back entrance, Cathie,' Colin muttered.

'Why? Everyone here is so nice and cheerful and polite. Not like getting mobbed by some of the crowds I've dealt with in the States.'

'Ah, Ms. Fletcher.' An elderly woman with shining silver hair fixed in tight curls hustled up to her and extended her hand. 'I'm Mrs. Tafferty, the store manager. We've spoken on the phone.' She took Cathie's hand in a firm grip that belied her years. 'And this must be Yvette and Colin. Welcome. I say, you've cut it a bit fine.' She glanced at her watch. 'Still, on time to the minute. This way, please.'

Mrs. Tafferty led the three to a back corner of the store's first floor where a table sat at a diagonal. She ushered Cathie to an old leather chair behind it. Several pens lay in the middle of the table, with stacks of books on either side. Colin and Yvette barely had time to join her, sitting on smaller chairs near the wall, when Tafferty announced, 'Ladies and gentlemen, I'm delighted to introduce our guest author, Ms. Cathie Clarke Fletcher. Her latest book is quite a departure from her previous novels. This first foray into nonfiction, *The Fall of an Empire: The Tragic End of the Family Croker / Smythe-Montgomery,* offers a tantalizing look into the life of the eccentric billionaire who would be emperor. As I understand it, Ms. Fletcher played an active role in some of the grittier events described in the book. I'm sure you'll all want to ask her questions, but please be considerate of your fellows and keep them brief.' She swept her arm towards Cathie. 'Ms. Fletcher.' Polite applause from the crowd, and it was on.

The hours slipped by. A few people, too shy to make conversation, simply slid their books across the table for Cathie to sign. Others claimed to know Smythe-Montgomery or to know someone who knew him. These individuals passed on interesting anecdotes of dubious reliability, one even offering to help her do research on a follow-on volume. Most were somewhere in the middle ground, asking a few questions or making polite comments on Cathie's previous works. The last person waiting, who sat down across from Cathie twenty minutes after the official close of the event, was one of these. She silently offered two copies of the Smythe-Montgomery history as well as a stack of well-worn paperbacks, all in pairs. Cathie caught the title of the first, *Address Unknown*, one of her earlier novels.

'Oh, I hope you don't mind, Ms. Fletcher. My aunt and I are such great fans. I waited till the end so as not to monopolize your time, but I realize you're already past schedule.'

'My pleasure, Ms. ...?'

'Just Gladys, Ms. Fletcher. And my aunt's name is Maude. Oh, this is so exciting. I think I'll return Maudie's books one at a time, just as a treat for her birthday or Christmas. Never have to buy her another present.'

Cathie laughed and both Yvette and Colin were smiling.

'Well, Gladys, first off, you should call me Cathie, and second, if you write your name and address on this paper, I'll be sure to send you and Maude signed copies of my next book—whatever that might be.'

'Oh, thank you Ms.—Cathie! You're too kind, too kind.' She gathered up her books in both arms and smiled as she left, unable to wave.

'Well, that was wonderful,' Yvette said, collecting pens and books.

'Just leave that to me, dear,' Mrs. Tafferty said, appearing from nowhere. 'A delightful event.'

'Thank you for hosting us,' Cathie replied. She rose from her chair and stretched with a soft groan. 'The time flies by, but my back counts every minute.'

'I know a lovely place for a massage,' Yvette offered. 'Walk-ins always welcome.'

'Now that sounds like a plan.'

'I think I'll pass,' Colin said. 'Don't forget. Dinner at Diana's at 7:00.'

'Plenty of time,' Yvette said.

Colin scanned the area quickly. 'I believe we have everything, so we're off.'

Mrs. Tafferty escorted them to the front door. As they were about to exit, Yvette cast an accusatory eye towards Colin. 'Everything except my green satchel, which you promised you'd help me remember.'

'Ah,' he said, 'it seems you've forgotten your green satchel.'

'Why thank you,' Yvette replied, with mock sincerity. 'What would I do without you? I won't be a minute.'

As she hurried back into the bookstore, she heard a sound like someone hammering nails. *An odd time to be doing construction*, she thought. Then came the scream.

Yvette flew back to the doorway and a scene of confusion.

Cathie lay on the steps, her body crumpled at an odd angle, a pool of deep red forming around her head. Mrs. Tafferty had her hands to her mouth, her eyes wide in terror, shaking in every limb.

Yvette knelt at Cathie's side, though she was fearful of moving her and too uncertain to do anything. *She seems so uncomfortable lying like that,* was her only coherent thought as time slipped past. A few people had followed her out of the bookstore, and Yvette finally managed to croak out, 'Call an ambulance.'

She glanced up and saw Colin standing, looking out towards Cheyne Walk. Just beyond him, she caught the rapid movement of a man ducking between two parked cars. The roar of an engine and he emerged onto the street on a flaming red BMW motorcycle, hidden previously by the cars. The man crossed the street, his rear wheel squealing and smoking, and forced the bike through a narrow gap in a dense wall of trees and bushes separating Cheyne from the larger, busier Chelsea Embankment. Honking horns and a background of screeching tires added to the roar of the bike. Though Yvette couldn't see, she could guess that he'd cut across all four lanes of traffic and was now moving west, probably on the paver walkway beside the bank of the Thames. It was a confused blur of sight and sound. Her eyes refocused on Colin.

'Colin, come help me!' she yelled.

He turned slowly, a smile forming on his lips as his eyes met hers. He held his hand to his chest, like an American saying the Pledge of Allegiance. From between his fingers, a torrent of thick red liquid flowed. He tried to speak, and Yvette thought she heard him whisper her name.

Then he collapsed onto the grass of the inner courtyard, as a horrible scream tore Yvette's throat.

She was at his side in an instant, leaving others to tend to Cathie.

'Colin, Colin, don't move. You'll be fine.' A distant siren wailed. 'Stay still, love, help is coming.'

His eyes fluttered open. 'I say, are you all right?'

'Hush, I'm fine, I'm fine.'

'Cathie?'

She put a finger to his lips and shushed him, cradling his head in her lap. 'Quiet now. You'll be fine.' But her pants were already crimson with his blood and she could see more throbbing from his chest.

'I saw him. Tried to stop, to ...'

'Oh, please just hush, dear.'

'"Dear." I do like the sound of that.'

He was silent for a moment, then glanced at the sky. 'Bloody chilly for such a sunny day.' He focused on her face again and drew a rattling breath. 'God what a fool I was not to fall in love with you sooner.' The tiny smile froze on his face.

'No, Colin, you can't go. You can't. I love you. What will I do? How can I ...'

The words were lost in choking sobs as she clutched his lifeless body. Then she sucked in a deep lungful of air and let out a scream. It wasn't a scream of loss, but of defiance. A threatening, bloodcurdling scream that would have made Jason Stone step back in shock. It was full of knives and broken glass. Pure hatred. Revenge.

***

Only moments later, Yvette realized she must take control. She laid Colin's head gently on the grass, stroking the hair from his eyes and memorizing the look of love on his face. A look of peace. It was precious, and she knew she'd never see it again. Then she stood, a stony façade covering her grief.

'Is she still breathing?' she asked Mrs. Tafferty, who knelt at Cathie's side.

'Aye. Weak and raspy, but still there.'

'When the ambulance arrives, please tell them what happened.'

'Your young man?' Tafferty asked.

'I'll speak to the police,' Yvette said, 'but first I have to make a call.'

'Colin?' Tafferty tried again.

Yvette already had her phone out. 'Hello, Richard? I need your help. Cathie has been shot. An ambulance is just arriving. Yes, I'm OK. What?' Yvette drew a ragged breath. 'No, he isn't. Just listen, please. I need you to let Diana know what happened so she can get a message to Logan, but call Jason first. We're all at Royal Booksellers in Chelsea. No, Richard, just listen to me. The shooter's gotten away. Call Jason and tell him what happened. Can you do that? I don't know what hospital, but I'll find out and call you back. Please, hurry.'

A glance towards Cathie showed EMTs swarming around her, and Mrs. Tafferty speaking with a local constable who, despite his attempt at stoicism, was ghostly white, beads of sweat on his brow. Tafferty pointed, and an EMT ran over to Colin and knelt down beside him in an ocean of blood.

How did he fit it all in his slim body? Yvette wondered.

The EMT spent very little time with Colin before rising and returning a moment later with a white blanket, with which he covered the body.

Goodbye, darling.

'Miss? I say, miss, what happened here?' Another officer, an older man with coarse, pocked skin and grizzled hair was staring at her, his face grim.

This one has seen blood before. 'Were you a soldier?' Yvette asked.

'What? Why yes, miss. Royal Marines. Let me help now. Do you need to sit?'

Yvette shook her head.

'Then—'

Yvette gave the man a concise account of all that had occurred, including a description of the shooter and his motorcycle.

'Excellent, miss,' he said. 'I need to call this in immediately. See if we can catch the bugger on the first hop. Was the young man your friend?'

'Yes.'

'Are you sure you won't sit down?'

'No, I'll be fine. Go ahead and make your call, sir.'

'I wasn't more than a colour sergeant in the Royal Marines, miss. Police sergeant now. Thank you for the information. I've never seen a tougher young woman.'

'Thank you, sergeant.'

The EMTs had stabilized Cathie to their satisfaction and were loading her into an ambulance. Another unit arrived to deal with Colin.

Yvette's phone rang. Jason Stone. He was able to say only a few words before she interrupted.

'I want to go to the hospital, Jason. They're about to leave.'

'You really should get back to Diana's.' He said it reflexively, knowing his suggestion would be ignored. 'Fine. I'll meet you there.'

***

An hour later, Stone spotted her in the lobby and hurried to her side.

'Thank you for coming,' she whispered.

In response, he wrapped her in a crushing embrace and waited. As the adrenaline dissipated, Yvette began to tremble. Here was help at last, and she wasn't alone.

'She's still in surgery,' Yvette murmured. 'No word from the doctors, no word of any kind.'

Stone gently escorted her outside. 'Let's get a little air.' They found a bench in the hospital courtyard and sat.

'I'm sorry,' he said. 'I wish …' But he wished for far too many things to complete his thought. He wished he'd read Cathie's book. Clearly, something she'd written had triggered this attack. He wished he'd accompanied her to her book signings. He wished he'd given Colin some defensive training. He wished Yvette hadn't been there at all.

If wishes were horses, beggars would ride. An old saying of his father's. 'Listen,' he said, 'I'd like you to tell me everything you remember. I know you told the officer, but I may be able to mobilize other resources. Maybe get to the shooter first.'

Yvette took a deep, quavering breath. 'I want the murderer dead. I want the bastard who hired him dead. It won't make up for what they've taken, but they deserve it.'

'No argument,' Stone replied.

She repeated everything she'd told the officer, plus a few other details she'd just remembered.

Stone left her in the courtyard and went inside to talk to the ER staff. When he returned, he said, 'Cathie'll be in surgery for hours, that much they'd tell me, and they promised to call you and me if there was any news. Her condition is critical, and that I discovered by leaning over the desk and reading some paperwork when the nurse was distracted. There really is nothing we can do here, unless ...'

Yvette shook her head. She had no desire to see Colin again, having already captured the last memory she would ever want.

'Come on, then,' he said, extending his hand, 'let's go to Diana's.'

***

After the long ordeal of ambulances, police interviews, and the hospital, Stone delivered Yvette to Diana's house. Luana and Crandall joined them. They'd all gathered in the small dining area of Diana's estate's west wing. Arthur Enfield, Diana's driver and general helper, hurriedly prepared some food, but most were drinking rather than eating. Yvette was a specter, clutching a cold cup of tea and staring blindly.

The first call from the hospital was terse, only saying that Cathie was out of surgery and in the ICU, but absolutely no visitors were allowed.

The exhausted friends somehow made it through the night, catching a nap in a chair or on a couch, until grey morning arrived at last.

Diana's house became the base of operations for Stone, who'd made contact with a few critical sources in London. His phone rang periodically and he'd listen with frozen features, asking crisp questions and giving instructions. Yvette would instantly accost him when he received a call, pressing him for information.

By a miracle of frantic activity and hideous travel, Logan arrived, accompanied by Chuck, roughly twenty-four hours after the shooting. Stone had briefed them when they landed, and they'd opted for going directly to the hospital.

Arthur, as shattered as the others, had set out the evening meal and, at Diana's insistence, had gone home. Luana talked quietly with Stone at one end of the table, while Richard and Diana stood at a sideboard putting a few items on a plate for Yvette, who sat alone, her face an impenetrable mask.

She mechanically accepted the food handed to her by Diana but subsequently ignored it. Luana nudged Stone and he nodded, moving over to sit at Yvette's side.

'You should eat something,' he said. 'You're no good to anyone if you pass out.'

She flashed him a threatening glance, then realized he'd deliberately said those words to provoke her, knowing only anger would jolt her out of her stupor.

She stabbed a piece of fish and brought it to her mouth, chewing slowly.

'Is it always this way?' she asked.

'Yes. The loss and the fury take turns twisting your guts till you want to vomit fire. Friends—good people—gone. Sometimes the guys who did it die in the same fight. It doesn't make you feel any better. Sometimes you never catch them, or you never know for sure.'

'What if you do catch them?'

Stone glanced at Yvette. She'd guessed the truth, but far from wanting to enforce it—certainly not to glorify it!—he wanted to bury it deep. But the question hung in the air. He couldn't hide from it.

'You make them pay.'

'That's what I want!' she said fiercely. 'To make them pay!'

He saw the hatred in her eyes, and took her hand gently. 'You can do that, but it won't make you feel any better. In fact, you'll feel worse. A lot worse. Trust me, I've been there.'

'It didn't stop you, though, from making them pay.'

'No. But I'm hoping—no, I'm certain—that you're a better person than I am.'

'I'm not.'

He laughed lightly. 'Of course you are. You don't really know me.'

Yvette tilted her had back defiantly. 'Luana does, and she loves you for all that.'

'Yes. What can I say? I'm the luckiest man alive.'

'You're a good man who's done ...'

'Terrible things. She says the same. Who knows?'

'I'll do terrible things.'

Stone's phone buzzed. He pulled it from his pocket and glanced at the screen. 'Let's hope you don't have to.'

He stepped away and put the phone to his ear, but his rough comments and slumping shoulders told the story. Yvette was at his side as he ended the call.

'Well?'

'Things just got harder. The man is a pro. Might as well tell everyone.'

He moved back to the table, drawing the attention of Crandall, Diana, and Luana.

'News?' Luana asked.

'Not good, I'm afraid. First, I'll tell you what both the police and my sources agree on. The shooter abandoned his motorcycle in the back alley of an industrial neighborhood where he had a car waiting. My contact found out the make and model by, um'—he glanced at Yvette— 'interviewing the owner of the warehouse where they found the bike. The police were given that information. The car was spotted heading for Heathrow, and the pursuit was on. A bad move. The shooter abandoned the car shortly after, but was spotted on surveillance cameras heading for the tube, this time for Gatwick. How that bastard must have laughed, sending us chasing our own tails.'

'Was anyone able to ID him?' Crandall asked.

'The bike and the car were both stolen within the last 48 hours. Like I said, a real pro.'

'What about the surveillance video?' Luana said.

'He was wearing a hoodie, but the cameras saw glasses, a bushy beard, and long dark hair.'

'I don't remember the glasses,' Yvette said, 'but the beard and hair match.'

Stone shook his head. 'I wouldn't trust either. They're perfect for hiding facial features and plenty easy to fake. The guy probably has blond hair or he's bald.'

'So, what about Gatwick?'

'He got on a nonstop to New York. We finally had him in a box.' Stone's laugh was hollow. 'I have a friend there …'

'You have friends everywhere,' Yvette commented.

'And enemies. My friend George was at the adjacent gate when the shooter's flight landed. George actually bought a ticket to Amsterdam to get in the terminal. Anyway, he told me it was a first-class operation. At least five non-uniformed FBI waiting to discreetly pick the guy up as he got off the plane. No fuss, no muss.' He laughed again. 'Care to guess what happened, 'cause this was a new one on me?'

No one offered a suggestion, so he continued. 'Francis Harbuckle couldn't have been more astonished when the FBI pounced. It seems Francis was on standby when a helpful airline employee convinced him a seat had become available, handed him a ticket, and told him to board.'

'This Harbuckle must have gotten a good look at the shooter, anyway,' Crandall offered.

Stone shook his head. 'The *young woman* who gave Mr. Harbuckle the ticket didn't work for the airline. She and the shooter disappeared with no leads—official or otherwise.'

'An accomplice!' Luana said.

'Yes. And an astonishingly well-planned hit.'

'So, a dead end,' Crandall said.

'For now. We were hoping for a quick grab and got played like fish.'

'There can't be too many people capable of this,' Yvette said, piercing Stone with her pale-blue eyes.

He shrugged noncommittally, but Yvette saw he was holding something back. 'I still have a few feelers out,' he said. 'By tomorrow … we'll see.'

Crandall ignored the stares and pressed on. He came to the entrance of a narrow garbage-strewn alley and turned in.

Chapter Seven

Yvette Regresses

Tomorrow came and went. Stone would occasionally get a phone call, and if Yvette was in earshot, she would harass him the moment he finished, hoping for some new information. But after several days, the trail went cold. Stone moved back into the official offices of Triple S, where he consulted strategy with Chuck. Logan remained at the hospital, sleeping in the waiting room, until Chuck and Stone finally convinced him to rent a hotel room nearby—Diana's estate was just too far away. Chuck visited with his friend often, Stone less frequently. He was still pursuing leads on the killer.

Logan's daughter, Kelly, had flown to London not long after her father, staying by his side until he insisted she return to the States. As he'd pointed out, she still had a job and a steady boyfriend, and London was only an airline flight away if any dramatic change occurred. When the doctors predicted an extended coma, she relented at last, insisting only on daily updates from Logan.

The next day, Cathie was moved from the ICU. She was still in a coma, though, and Logan had many hours of one-sided conversation with his wife. He'd even managed a small joke with Chuck one evening when Chuck had dragged him to the local pub for dinner and a beer.

'It's funny,' he'd said. 'I've never gotten the last word in a conversation this many times since I first met Cathie.' But his voice had cracked at the end, and he'd said no more that evening. After a hasty dinner, he went back to the hospital while Chuck returned to Diana's estate.

Yvette's behavior during this time had been puzzling. She'd be bubbly one moment, talking and even laughing, and stone-faced the next. Her eyes were red, though she was seldom seen crying, and her cheeks were sunken, her hair unkempt. She'd explode in anger at inanimate objects—a book she'd dropped, a plate still greasy after vigorous wiping, an error message on a computer simulation run—but was scrupulously polite with Diana and the others. Too formal; too much in control. She'd only been contrary and immovable in one thing: She refused to attend Colin's funeral. Whether the casket was open or closed made no difference. She had her precious last memory. There would be no others. Diana, Richard, Stone, Luana, and Chuck had all gone, Richard making the best explanation he could for Yvette's absence.

It was late one evening, and Diana had been searching the house for Yvette. She could call, of course, but how foolish it seemed to lose someone in one's own house. She had talked briefly with Stone in the Triple S headquarters and was now walking down the long hallway of her estate's east wing when she heard clinking and rustling coming from the great dining hall where they'd celebrated such a short time ago. At the far end of the dining table, Yvette stood with a rag, polishing one of a platoon of candlesticks standing in a crisp line like soldiers on parade. To her right, those she'd finished stood in equally strict ranks, to her left, those to be cleaned. There was no need. The sets were indistinguishable in their brassy brilliance.

'Yvette, whatever are you doing? It's after ten.'

'Why, polishing, of course. It's been so long since Colin and I gave them a proper scrub. And Jason has promised to stop in if there's any news.' She set one candlestick aside and reached for another.

Diana came up to her and laid a firm hand on hers.

A blazing, violent light filled Yvette's eyes, and her muscles tensed. An instant later, she collapsed in a chair, sobbing.

Diana put her hand on Yvette's shoulder. 'It's all right to cry. I cried for days ... weeks ... after the man I loved was killed. Sometimes, months later, I'd start up again out of the blue, and I'd feel the hurt fresh as the day it happened. It becomes bearable, after a time. An old, old wound. So, cry when you must. However, it's *not all right* to polish perfectly clean and sparkling candlesticks at this hour. You must go to bed.'

Yvette shook her head weakly.

'No, dear, I insist. And also ...' She hesitated, then coughed, searching for words. 'Tomorrow, well, tomorrow ... You should know that Richard

and I have discussed this and we are in rare agreement, which means ...
that is, we agree it would be best ...'

Yvette searched Diana's face, though Diana refused to meet her eyes.
Yvette reached out a tentative hand and touched the one that lay on her
shoulder.

Diana saw the hurt and emptiness that she knew only too well. She
looked away quickly. 'Oh, sod it,' she said harshly. 'Tomorrow you must
leave here and go home. This isn't a good place for you right now. And
soon—not, perhaps, this week—you must return to school. It's for your
own good.'

The last words sounded painfully harsh and clichéd. 'Oh, please say
something,' Diana begged. 'I feel like an old fool.'

Yvette stood and walked to the hallway, where she stopped. 'You've
been very good to me. Far better than I deserve. I'll leave in the morning.'
She hesitated, as though she might say more, then turned away. Diana
could hear her receding footfalls echoing down the hallway.

'Oh, haven't I just handled that well?' she muttered.

***

Diana's attempts to reopen a discussion with Yvette the next day were
met with polite, monosyllable responses. Yvette packed the things she'd
brought over to Diana's, declined a ride from Arthur, called a cab, and left,
leaving Diana hollow and depressed.

'Good morning,' Stone said, having located her in the study of her
west wing. 'I was hoping to catch you before I go out. By the way, where's
Yvette? I've been in the office since 6:00 and she hasn't stopped by even
once to ask for an update.'

'She left at 8:00.'

'She left? On an errand, or ...'

'She's gone back home—Richard's London home. He and I thought
it best, but now I feel like a fool.'

'Got any coffee?' he asked.

She pointed to a pot. 'A bad Yank habit I sometimes indulge in.'

He poured himself a cup and sat down. 'It might not have been a good
idea to press her so soon.'

'Oh, I know.'

'All the smiles bookending the boiling anger,' Stone mused. 'I've seen it before. She isn't close to accepting what's happened, and she's created a fiction that she can't accept it—can't be whole—till she's had her revenge. It never works. A little gentle handling might have set her right.'

'But the two old Brits tell her to buck up and carry on. Stiff upper lip and all that, wot? How could I have forgotten how long it took me to recover? Did I mention I feel like a fool?'

'Don't. In some cases, a soldier will respond to a crisp command calling him back to duty. You can overcome the loss of a comrade, maybe even a friend. But she's still so young, and she was in love.'

'What can I do?' Diana asked.

'Let me call Richard first, then I'll try talking to Yvette.'

'Yes. Please tell her ... No, I'll tell her myself when the time is right.'

Stone drank the last of his coffee and rose to leave.

'Jason,' Diana said, 'I should ask how your hunt for the murderer is coming.'

'Ah. There I might have some good news. Yvette was right. Not too many killers—even pros—could pull off such a clean hit and escape. I've narrowed the field, and a friend of mine in Scotland thinks he may have something.' He frowned. 'Yvette said I had friends everywhere. She never guessed I just use "friend" as a substitute for "acquaintance." I don't have many friends, but she's one.'

He walked to the doorway, then stopped. 'I've been assuming way too much lately. Not good. I assumed Arthur drove Yvette back to Crandall's.'

'No. She called a cab.'

'Shit!' Stone pulled the phone from his pocket. He was dialing before he asked Diana, 'When did you say she left?'

'Oh, an hour or so ago. Around 8:00.'

'How long would it take her to get to Richard's?'

'Perhaps another half hour.'

Diana faintly heard Richard's 'hello.'

'Richard, this is Stone. Yvette should be on her way to your house, but according to Diana she was pretty upset. No, Arthur didn't drive her. It may be nothing, but I'd appreciate it if you'd call me when she arrives. If I don't hear from you in an hour, we may have another problem. Yes, I'll stay around. I was planning to go to Scotland. Why? Fine fishing, I hear.

136

It can wait until Yvette is safe with you. Yes, I'm worried, but let's not panic. Just call me when she arrives, OK? Thanks.'

'Oh, Jason, what have we done?' Diana said, her hand to her mouth.

'Probably nothing at all. I'm just tired of assuming.'

***

The call never came, and as Stone had said, they had another problem.

***

The night arrived early, hurried on by a grey blanket of fog. Yvette's phone had been found hours ago, jammed into the backseat cushions of the cab she'd taken from Diana's estate. Since then, there had been no word.

'It's not your fault, darling,' Luana said. But her repeated use of that phrase had dulled its power to convince. Stone simply replied with another variation of the responses he'd been giving for hours.

'No. It's the killer's fault. But I could tell she wasn't dealing with it and was near a breaking point. They say justice delayed is justice denied. In my business, justice doesn't always come, or if it does, it's so delayed its almost unconnected with the crime. Of course, she doesn't understand that. To top things off, she has an overblown estimation of my capabilities.'

Unfortunately, Luana thought, *he's right about that last bit.*

'Damnation,' Stone continued, speaking more to himself, 'I should be chasing leads and going after the killer, but ...'

'Priorities,' Luana said. 'Catching the killer now or next week or never won't bring back Colin or help Cathie. We must find Yvette.'

He nodded, then brushed the hair back from his brow. 'Trouble is, my brain is mush. I can't seem to focus.'

'Since the shooting, how much sleep have you gotten?'

'You know I don't sleep much.'

'Which is a far cry from not at all. Rest is what you need, then talk to Richard in the morning.'

'Let me just make a few calls.'

Luana shook her head. Argument was futile.

At the rustle of covers and jostling of the bed she turned to the clock on the nightstand. Nearly 2:30 a.m. She rolled over and wrapped an arm around him, falling asleep again against his warmth. Stone stared at the ceiling, his mind racing, till grey morning light peered in around the curtains.

***

Yvette found that very little had changed in her old neighborhood. A few acquaintances were gone. Others greeted her like a returning prodigal. When they asked about her long absence, she shrugged. Once, when pressed by a particularly belligerent young man, she'd proceeded to knee him in the balls and brandish a knife. No one else questioned her further.

She found that her shoplifting skills were still good. By noon she'd stolen a jacket and enough food to satisfy her limited appetite. It felt good. Her years in the care of Richard Crandall were a dream, an illusion. This was home. The world was raw and full of deceit, but it was real. Sex was a commodity, violence a compelling persuader, friendship situational. Here you were alone, relying on your wits and skills to survive. The purity of the primitive.

One image haunted her return to the world of her childhood. Such a gentle face. Such a look of love.

She spent the afternoon reacquainting herself with the neighborhood and its denizens. The tailor shop was closed, the old man and his wife having died. One or two of her prior acquaintances had also died, poverty and violence being as deadly as old age. The bakery was still there. Yvette circled around to the narrow alley behind and secretly checked the barred half window into the cellar. Only Yvette knew the trick to releasing the latch from outside. A quirky smile flitted across her face. She'd sleep here tonight, but would have to rise before the dawn to avoid the outrageously early activities of the shopkeeper and his family. Most of their hard work was done before 8:00 a.m.

She continued walking the streets until a short, heavyset girl with a dark tangle of hair raised a hand in greeting. 'Well, if it ain't Maggie May. Haven't seen you in a while, love.'

'Hello, Doris. How's tricks?'

'*Comme ci, comme ça,* as them Frenchies say. Where you been keeping yourself?'

'Tried my luck across town.' She shrugged. 'Now I'm back.'

'You always was a windbag. Never could get you to stop talking. Say, got a smoke for your old pal?'

138

'Nah, but I've got the next best thing.' She pulled a few bills from her pocket.

'Nice!'

'C'mon, let's get some fish and chips, then we'll grab a pack of smokes.'

'This all your treat? Cause if it is, I want to know who you are and where you stashed the body of the real Maggie.'

'Is that a no?'

Doris hurried over and linked her arm with Yvette's. 'No, ma'am. I ain't about to look into no horse's mouth.'

'It's a gift horse, Doris.'

'Bought, gifted, or stolen makes no difference to me.'

'Is old Chauncy and his street cart still around?'

'Hell yes. He's out every day harassing the coppers and selling his wares.'

'He still at the end of the alley facing—'

'Ridley Street. You bet. Greasiest fish in London. I love it!'

The two continued to talk, and by the time they'd eaten and were on their third cigarette, the sun had set.

'Well,' Doris said, 'iss almost time to start my shift.' She eyed Yvette closely. 'Still got no meat on your bones. You freelancing or …'

Yvette had almost forgotten this side of street life, taken so much for granted by those who lived it.

'I'm just back, and I've still got a few things to work out. I promise not to cut in on your territory, Doris.'

'Well, them as like skin and bones won't be courting my services, anyway,' she said, with a laugh. 'Besides, I seem to remember your skinny fingers like dippin' into other's pockets. Am I right?'

'Right as rain. Good to see you, Doris.'

'Oh, aye, and I'm glad to still be seen.' She waved a hand and ambled off.

After Doris left, Yvette considered her options. For now, she had money, but it wouldn't last the week. After that? True, she had light fingers, but even that skill wouldn't keep her in tea and biscuits. There was only one sure way to that kind of money. She knew the risks and the rewards. She could handle herself. But that damned, blessed face kept intruding. She could go back to that life if it might someday guarantee her revenge. The smile on the face said no. But if she was to believe that, then what was she doing here? She walked the streets for hours, turning down generous offers and avoiding others where the threat was too apparent. At midnight, she had no answer.

She circled back to the alley behind the bakery and, releasing the window latch, lowered herself into the dark warmth below. She'd filled herself from the drinking fountain at the corner first. It was a foolproof alarm clock to wake her before the 4:30 rumblings began in the bakery above. She settled herself in a cozy corner, rearranging sacks of flour to form a serviceable bed and pillow, just as she'd done a hundred times before. In this quiet, dark womb, she slept, only one vision intruding into her dreams.

***

Stone was up at dawn, determined to find Yvette, though the previous day's efforts had all been in vain. He showered and shaved, forcing himself to think more clearly than he had earlier. A random search of London was pointless, and Richard had been too upset to be much use. But by the time Stone walked into the kitchen, he knew he'd need to start with a visit to Crandall. He could be there in half an hour if the Tube was on schedule. He glanced at his watch. *Too early*, he thought. *No point in waking him. Let him sleep if he can.*

Luana shuffled in, her bathrobe swirling around bare legs, and poured Stone a cup of coffee from a pot she'd put on a few minutes earlier. He gratefully accepted the cup.

'Thanks. I hope I didn't wake you.'

'Hmm. A vain hope, I'm afraid.'

'I'm sorry.'

She placed a hand on his shoulder. 'Don't be sorry. I know how upset you are. You'll think more clearly, though, if you do two things.'

He raised a questioning eyebrow.

'First, drink up.'

'Amen. And number two?'

'Stop blaming yourself. I mean that. You have a disciplined mind. A great strength. But you're letting guilt cloud your reasoning. The best way to find Yvette is to absolve yourself and focus that disciplined mind.' She

140

smiled. 'So, chew on that thought and drink your coffee while I take a shower. Then you can tell me your plan.'

***

When Luana returned, Stone was on his third cup of coffee, and his face had lost the tension of the previous day.

'I have an idea,' he said.

'How extraordinary!'

'I'd already planned to see Richard in person. I think I can calm him down using your clever wisdom. I have a hunch he knows where Yvette is, he just can't think clearly enough to realize it.'

'Guilt will do that.'

'Yes.' He wrapped her in his arms. 'Thank you.'

'I'll expect compensation,' she said, with a playful smile.

'With pleasure,' he replied. 'Now, I'm off.'

***

It took longer for Crandall to stop his pointless self-flagellation. Stone attributed it to the inferior quality of tea versus coffee and to his own inferior skills at persuasion. Crandall poured another cup of tea, his hands steady at last, and dropped into a chair.

'Well, I suppose I'm ready to think now.'

'Excellent,' Stone replied. 'How much do you know about Yvette's childhood, parents, places where she lived?'

'I'm ashamed to say, nothing. I tried, of course, at first. She never would talk about it. I finally learned her first name—first name only, mind you—last December. In the earlier days of our acquaintance her past was off-limits. To be honest, I lost interest quickly.' He shook his head. 'As I grew to know her better, I discovered she was intelligent and inquisitive. No. Far more than that. Considering her age and her previous environment, she showed signs of brilliance. As she became my apprentice, my curiosity resurfaced, so I tried again. She was still unwilling to discuss anything with me, but I deduced she'd been living alone—on the streets—for quite some time.'

'That's it, then,' Stone said. 'I'm glad I never got a concrete lead on the killer or his location, or I'd have bet money that's where I'd find her. As it is, I'm betting she went home.'

'Home?' Crandall said, his shoulders slumping. 'I'd hoped she thought of this as home.' He spread his arms to encompass the room and the house.

'I know she does,' Stone said gently. 'It's just, in times of extreme stress or loss, people do strange things. If it was home to her for a long time—as you seem to think—then I'd bet she went back.'

Crandall rose from his chair, his jaw set. 'I'll go at once.'

'I'm going with you.'

'Jason, if you're right, perhaps it would be best if I went alone.'

Stone considered. 'No dice. I've left too much to chance lately. But I'll tell you what, I'll hang back; give you plenty of space. If all goes well, I'll disappear. From what you've told me, though, this old neighborhood of hers is a little rough. No more chances.'

Crandall nodded.

***

Crandall hadn't been to the seedier parts of the East End in years. Not since he'd stopped looking for new companions to satisfy his sexual desires. He'd been on just such a quest in the Whitechapel district when he'd come upon Yvette, a quest that had transformed his life.

As promised, Crandall lost track of Stone once they'd left the Tube station. He'd stopped several times, his glance darting all around, but had never caught so much as a vanishing shadow. Crandall smiled. For a big man, Stone moved like a ghost.

Other eyes followed Crandall, some curious, some threatening. In clean trousers, shirt, and tailor-cut jacket he was woefully out of place. He'd been far grungier in years past. Another extraordinary change brought about by Yvette.

Crandall ignored the stares and pressed on. He came to the entrance of a narrow garbage-strewn alley and turned in. Not a half minute later, two lanky teens nodded to each other and followed.

Crandall walked past boxes, old crates, and trash bins, the stench of rotting garbage filling his nostrils. A stubby side alley split off to his left. There she was, a half-eaten bun in one hand and a cigarette in the other. Her head snapped up at the sound of his steps. She froze, her face a mask of pain and confusion.

Crandall stopped and stared, his eyes clouding. When he found his voice, the words that came out were identical to those he'd used in the past. 'Yvette, it looks like you could use a shower and a hot meal. Why don't you come with me?'

Memories, like rolling ocean waves, swept over her. This man, taking her off the streets. Her strange evolution from a sex object to a ward. Richard Crandall. *Sir* Richard Crandall. And there was Colin with his gentle smile, nodding his approval.

The bun and cigarette fell to the ground. Yvette held out her arms and Crandall embraced her, mumbling reassuring words. They stood that way for a long while. It was Yvette who heard the footsteps.

Two young men, barely more than boys, stood with an insolent attitude watching the scene. One still had a sore groin where Yvette's knee had struck the day before.

'Well, now, Ralphie,' the injured man said, 'I guess we know where Maggie's been this long while. Keepin' this old geezer warm at night is my guess. Then she run away, and he come to fetch her. Brings a tear to my eye, it does.'

'Look, lads,' Crandall said, 'we don't want any trouble.'

'Thass maybe so, but you found it anyway. And this little bitch,' he snarled, pointing a long, bony finger, 'owes me a little something. Maybe I'll just let you kiss it and make it all better. What do you say, Ralphie?'

'Hardly seems right, do it? There's two of us now.'

'By gor, that's a fact. Reckon you can give Ralphie some when I'm done with you.'

'I'm warning you gentlemen,' Crandall said, 'you're making a big mistake.'

'Shut your gob, arse wipe! And start emptyin' those fancy pockets of yours. You know the drill. Watches, rings, wallet. C'mon, snap to. If you're real lucky, you can have thirds.'

Yvette pushed Crandall back with one arm, and pulled a knife from her pants pocket, deftly snapping the blade open.

'Not gonna work this time, luv. Ralphie ...'

Ralphie pulled a small-caliber revolver from his waistband and tilted his head insolently. 'Set the knife down real slow-like or gramps gets one in the melon. Good girl. Now, come right over to your new best friend and kneel down. Ain't got all day.'

The first man chuckled and began to unzip his pants. Yvette took a slow step forward, then her eyes widened in surprise. Crandall followed her gaze.

A sudden blur of motion.

Ralphie's gun went flying to the side, he was spun around, and dropped with a grunt, clutching his solar plexus. The other, kicked from behind, dropped to his knees, a yelp of pain as they smacked the concrete, his pants around his ankles.

Stone retrieved the gun, emptied it, and smashed the hammer against the brick wall. He tossed the now-useless gun into a trash can. His eyes were blazing, his muscles rigid as he considered his next move. These two scumbags had insulted and threatened two of the people he cared for. He briefly considered breaking fingers, arms, necks. He glanced up, saw the perplexed look in Yvette's eyes, and hesitated. He could almost hear Luana's voice: *This is an opportunity, Jason. You know what to do.*

Unfortunately, he did.

He grabbed both men by their collars and hauled them upright.

'OK, assholes, here's the deal. I expect you to listen and do what you're told. If you don't, I'll let the young lady start carving you. Kick off your shoes and socks.'

'Look 'ere, mister, we—'

A blow to his ear knocked him sideways. He bounced off the wall and Stone caught him again by the collar.

'Did that clear your hearing, or do I need to do the other ear?'

The man clutched his ear, whimpering. 'No more, all right?'

'Fine. Shoes and socks, off and into that trash bin.'

This time, both men complied.

'Now, since dropping your pants was on your mind, do it. Both of you. Move!' he bellowed. 'Pants and unders into the trash, pronto.'

The two now stood, trying to cover their privates, while Crandall and Yvette stifled giggles.

'There. Now I think we're even. You march on out of here. What you do when you get to the street isn't our concern, but if I see you in this alley again, you *will* regret it. Understood?'

The two nodded.

'Off you go then.'

*'Why do you drag this thing?' one asked, pointing to the gleaming
mobile home attached to the Range Rover.*

Chapter Eight

Bad Decision

Jesse continued to fume at Carlos's stupidity in attempting to kill Cathie Fletcher. The warning had been made in the strongest terms, but he'd put on his macho act and ordered the hit. What was Jesse to do with such an imbecile? Kill him, of course. But when? Carl had been right. The agreement with Carlos the Idiot was the only path towards gaining access to the ship, and the ship was crucial.

At least Jesse was home. A funny concept, but the cabin high in the mountains of New Mexico was home now. Not Las Vegas with its glitter, not LA with its glamor, and not San Diego with its sparkling water and clouds of sails. This place was comfortable and self-sufficient for months at a time. A serious consideration since the only access—thirteen miles of dirt road—would be covered in at least a foot of snow by late December. A tracked ATV was an option, and an Argo Centaur sat fueled and ready in the storage building, but why bother? A freezer full of food, a huge tank of propane, a stack of cordwood, and a library—both physical and electronic—to kill for. Oh, and the company of a sure friend.

As if sensing she was the subject of thought, Cherokee raised her head, her blue eyes brilliant. Jesse smiled. 'Good girl. Go get us a deer, would you? Hamburger meat is starting to bore me.'

Cherokee stared hard at Jesse, then stood with a stretch and a growling grunt. The cabin was equipped with an extra-large dog door that led to a small vestibule with an equally large door opening to the outside world. The cold and wind were no joke in the Sangre de Cristo Mountains, and this arrangement allowed easy access for Cherokee while effectively sealing the cabin from winter's frigid bite. There were deer aplenty in the mountains, along with elk, rabbits, and squirrels, the latter barely a snack for Cherokee. What would it be tonight? She left the cabin noiselessly but for the slight slap of her personal door as it closed.

Just as Cherokee left the cabin, a text message tinged on Jesse's cell phone. Only two people had this number, and both their names began with C-a-r-l. Sadly, the 'o' and 's' established this as a call from the person Jesse wanted to kill.

Jesse read the message. A hint of a smile faded to a scowl. Carlos wanted to talk about the promised use of the ship—good so far—but wanted to meet in Puerto Peñasco. He made a great point of how inconvenient this was for him, being so far north, and hoped that Jesse would find it possible to meet him in three days' time. Sadly, no arrangement could be made for the dog. The Azure Palace did not accommodate pets. Jesse cursed softly. The fucking ship was hardly worth it.

Outside the cabin, dusk was deepening. Only the stars would lend a delicate light to the majesty of the mountains this night, the new moon having arrived. Jesse drew a deep breath. Chilly, bracing air, with just a hint of ice crystals. Tonight would dip to near freezing, and soon a blanket of pure white would cover every inch surrounding the cabin. By that time … But Jesse didn't want to think too far ahead. The meeting with Carlos would come first, then finalizing plans with Carl. The phlegmatic mountains would wait.

***

The usual flamboyant security precautions accompanied Carlos's visit to Puerto Peñasco. Multiple checkpoints, men armed with automatic weapons, a veritable caravan of armored black SUVs. Jesse sighed. It would be so much easier to meet at a small beach-bar in Zihuatanejo. Jesse could drive there in the Range Rover, and Carlos in a rented Lexus. No one would know or care. It was Carlos's ego far more than his caution that required him to arrive in state; a legend, as Clint Eastwood would say, in his own mind.

The projection of this same ego had been Cathie Fletcher's downfall. Not only was there nothing to gain by her assassination, there was far more to lose. International law enforcement was already digging deep, as was another more obscure group, whose name Jesse had already forgotten. A terse call from Emma Lister had mentioned the likelihood of this group becoming involved. Another meeting with Lister would be advisable. The corners of Jesse's mouth curled up ever so slightly. Memories of an erotic beach day with Lister and Charlotte haunted Jesse like a pleasant fragrance.

Jesse drove these thoughts away as two of Carlos's goons approached.

'Why do you drag this thing?' one asked, pointing to the gleaming mobile home attached to the Range Rover.

'I prefer to sleep here when I can.'

'Carlos says you will sleep in the hotel.'

'Carlos can kiss my pasty white ass,' Jesse responded. 'I sleep here or he can just go fuck himself.'

The man backed away and slid his hand under his sport coat. 'Out of the car. And I think I'll just have a look inside your mobile home, *si*? Pedro, tell the *patrón* I will bring Raynard shortly.' He turned back to Jesse as Pedro hurried towards the hotel. 'Now, open this thing up.'

'You're making a mistake,' Jesse said softly. 'The biggest in your life.'

'Open it or I shoot the lock off. Or maybe I miss and put one in your leg.'

'You're new in Carlos's organization,' Raynard said, moving easily to the rear of the trailer.

'*Si*. So?'

'You report to Ramón?'

'I work for Señor Carlos,' he snarled.

'Still, I imagine Ramón was assigned to explain your duties to you. What did he say about me?'

'That you are an arrogant *pila de estiércol* who talks too much.'

'Dung pile? How rude. But all my service to your boss, to the Viper, that counts for something, yes?'

'To him, maybe. Not to me.'

'I wonder how he'd weigh my *years* of extraordinary accomplishment against those of a newcomer. Someone from one of the cartels he swallowed up. Thanks to me!' The last words were loud and grating, stunning the man at first. He recovered quickly.

He grinned as he slid the gun from its holster and calmly pointed it at Jesse. 'Too much talk. Open the door.'

'Someone once said a fool and his money are soon parted. Now what could be more valuable than your money?'

Jesse turned the key in the lock, gave a piercing whistle, and opened the door.

The man never got a shot off. Cherokee's one hundred twenty pounds hit him in the throat, her teeth gripping and then tearing free from the force of her momentum. The man's head hit the asphalt with a sharp crack. An instant later, he was lying in a pool of blood, eyes staring blindly. Cherokee stood nearby, front legs splayed, hackles raised, growling thunderously. She spun, snarling, as two men approached: Pedro and Ramón.

'Steady, girl,' Jesse said. 'I think we've made our point.'

'*Madre de Dios!*' Ramón said, stopping a safe distance from Jesse and Cherokee. 'What happened?'

'I tried to explain to this man—this new man—that these were my private quarters, and I preferred to sleep here. He insisted I allow him to inspect them. Had the audacity to point a gun at me. Well, I warned him, but he was intransigent.'

'Intransigent! His throat is gone!'

'No. It's right there,' Jesse said, pointing. 'Cherokee isn't really hungry.'

Pedro glanced at the bloody mess that had once been his companion's throat, then bent double and vomited.

'More mess to clean up!' Ramón bellowed. 'How do I explain this to the *patrón*?'

'Easy,' Jesse said, reaching into the trailer for a towel, and calmly wiping the gore from Cherokee's muzzle. 'This man—Escondido cartel?'

'*Si.*'

'I was suspicious. I've heard rumors. I offered him money to kill Carlos. He said yes. He was a traitor, still angry at the debasement of his previous *patrón*, to whom he is—was—fiercely loyal. What luck I decided to let Cherokee travel with me.'

'My God, Raynard. Does life mean nothing to you?'

It was a peculiar question coming from a man like Ramón. A hired killer.

Raynard shrugged. 'I deal in illusion. Reality doesn't affect me all that much. So, is our story clear?'

Ramón turned to Pedro. 'Well?' he snarled.

'*Si, si*, Ramón. A traitor.'

'Fine,' Ramón said coldly. 'Raynard, please come with me. Pedro. Fetch Mateo and a couple mops. Move!'

***

'I suppose I owe you a debt of gratitude, Raynard, for ridding me of yet another man of questionable loyalty?' Carlos said, sounding anything but grateful.

'Oh, don't mention it,' Jesse said.

'Still, I wish you hadn't brought the dog.'

'Not a dog, Carlos.'

'The wolf-dog. Who cares? It's a vicious animal.'

Unlike humans? Jesse thought. *And that's why you're at the head of a drug cartel and order the disemboweling or beheading of rivals. So civilized.*

With difficulty, Carlos calmed himself. 'At any rate, keep her in her kennel. If she shows a nose, it might just get shot.'

Now Jesse boiled with rage. A half dozen objects in this room would crush Carlos's skull like a walnut. So easy!

Carlos eyed Raynard, waiting for the eruption. When it didn't occur, he shrugged and shifted to another topic. 'Fletcher has been dealt with, as I ordered, and the publicity will cow any fools who might resist or offer to expose my organization. As I knew it would. Well, what say you? You're unusually mute. Your clever tongue tied in a knot?'

Jesse drew a long, deep breath. 'Since you ask, I say what I said weeks ago. It was a pointless and foolish gesture. If she dies—and you know she's still alive—she's a martyr. Evidence of the evil she so bravely exposed. That's you, by the way. As for cowing anyone, only a blind idiot would believe that. By your actions you've proven yourself to be petulant and easily baited into an irrational act.'

Carlos wagged his finger at Jesse. 'You always choose to skate on thin ice.'

'Not much ice in Puerto Peñasco.'

Carlos laughed. 'Yet you never fail to amuse me, Raynard. But come, we have serious business to discuss. Rita!' he called, and a small woman instantly entered the room, her eyes downcast.

'*Si, señor?*'

'Dinner on the patio, as soon as it is ready. Bring tequila, plus shrimp, jalapenos, and *queso* for appetizers. Go, go!'

'*Si, señor.*'

'Come, Raynard, let us sit on the patio. A cool breeze off the water, yes?'

'Yes.'

When they were seated, Rita and three other nameless servants brought shrimp, melted cheese, tortillas, and roasted jalapenos.

Jesse took a jalapeno, bit off a third, and chewed silently.

Carlos watched intently, waiting for the reaction as the flaming pepper bit back hard. There was none.

'Bravo, Raynard! Those peppers are from my private garden, bred for their sting!'

'Delicious,' Jesse said, with sincerity.

'Ha ha ha, there you are! We are bound by our love of true Mexican delicacies. Come, some tequila. A toast.'

Jesse, sensing an opportunity to smooth relationships, took the offered tequila and drank. It wasn't bad. The idiot at least had some taste.

'Now, Raynard, as you know, I've only had one successful voyage with the *Saint Martin* since her metamorphosis to the *Reina del Mar.*'

'Two,' Jesse interjected, realizing it was important to nip this lie immediately. 'Maritime records are public, Carlos.'

'Oh, *si, si*, two. Ha ha. I had forgotten. Your very famous president said "Trust but verify." Bill Clinton, *si?*'

'Close enough.'

'So, *two* trips. Very successful, very profitable.'

'Congratulations.'

'*Si. Gracias.* No! Wait.' He motioned to Ramón who pulled a large envelope from inside his jacket and handed it to Jesse.

'You see, it is congratulations to both of us. A small token of appreciation for your efforts.'

'Thank you, Carlos. You're very kind.'

'Ah, you see, Ramón. My friend Jesse is gracious … and reasonable. There is another cargo, equally precious—'

'No,' Jesse said softly.

'What? No, you must understand—'

'We had a deal. The ship is mine, for one special voyage, after two business trips to England.'

'The profits will be splendid, my friend.' He motioned to the envelope. 'Twice that … at least.'

'Thank you, but you see, right now I have no need of more money. What I need is a ship. The ship you agreed to put at my disposal.'

'And so it shall be. One more trip. Perhaps a week or two.'

'No.'

Carlos stared at Jesse and lit a fat cigar. His eyes sparkled with suppressed rage. 'Yes, no, it is no matter. The ship sailed yesterday.'

'You dragged me down here to tell me you'd already broken our deal? My time wasted on—'

'I've shown you respect, my friend. We talk face to face, as equals. Circumstances, not my personal wishes, prevent me from granting your request as we'd previously discussed.'

'It wasn't a request. It was a deal.'

Carlos slapped a hand down on the table at his side. 'The deal has changed! I trust you will be appropriately grateful when your share of the profits, which you are so scornful of now, are in your hands.'

'And the ship?' Jesse said, with quiet venom.

Carlos made a dismissive motion with his hand. 'When it returns, it is yours for two weeks, no more! Are we clear?'

'Crystal,' Jesse said, rising and walking for the doorway.

'Raynard!' Carlos called. Jesse turned back to face him.

'When this is done, I think it will be time to reevaluate our relationship, *si?*'

Jesse nodded and walked out, thinking, *There's no need to have a relationship with a dead man.*

***

The others left Yvette pretty much to herself. She'd come back willingly, and she was home. That was the main thing.

153

Home, for now, was Diana's house. Stone took Yvette to the side for a quiet talk on her first evening back. They walked down the long drive bordered by ancient, and now dead, elm trees. The evening was calm, with a cool, dry breeze to rattle the old branches and set the tall grass that bordered the road to swaying.

'You feel OK now,' he said. 'I'm sorry to say it won't last.'

'Is there *any* word on the killer?'

'Here's the deal,' he said soberly, 'I'll be square with you and you be square with me.'

'I can't. You wouldn't understand. You're not a woman.'

He grinned and nearly clapped her on the back, as he would have one of his old fighting comrades.

'Now see, that's being square! It's all I ask. So, deal?'

'You're an enigma, Jason. Yes. Deal.'

'I've got a lead. A good lead. There's a high-end assassin who lives— sometimes—in Scotland.'

'Do you have a name?'

'I have several. All bullshit, naturally. But I have a lead on a small dingy town in the northeast. I'm planning a visit.'

'I want to—'

'No. You've got to understand, this man kills like you and I breathe, without giving it a second thought. Plus, he may not even be the guy.'

'What will you do?'

'Approach him like I would an animal I was hunting—slowly, patiently. It could be days or weeks. And if he bolts—'

'Jason!'

'You don't understand. Him bolting is good. It means two things. One, he's our guy, with high probability. And two, an animal that's on the run is far more vulnerable than one gone to ground.'

The tension in her face lessened. 'I understand.'

'I think you do.'

'If he is the killer, what will you do?'

'There are lots of possibilities ranging from "I kill him" to "he kills me." Ideally, I can bring him in—alive—and hand him over to MI5.' He shrugged. 'They may beat me to him. They're not stupid.'

'That isn't good enough.'

'We've talked about this. Revenge won't make you feel any better.'

'What about finding out who sent him? Once he's in custody, he'll get a lawyer and say nothing.'

'Maybe. Depends how much leverage they can apply. But look, he may not be the man. I'm not joking about that.'

They walked on, shadows of the leafless sentinels growing longer. The air grew cool and damp. Night birds began to stir. When they reached the main road, they turned back.

Yvette glanced at Stone occasionally. His eyes were thoughtful but distant, as though he were mulling something over. Before they were halfway back, he stopped and turned to her.

'Look, I think I can promise this. If I'm the one to find him, I'll do what I can to get him to give up his employer. I can be fairly persuasive. Sometimes even a real hard case will let a nugget of information drop without intending to. Triple S isn't officially involved in this investigation, and I'm sure as hell not bound by MI5's rules of engagement. No promises, but I'll do my best.'

Yvette nodded and then leaned forward and kissed his cheek.

'I'm so thankful for what you did today, protecting Richard and me. I truly am, even if it's taken me this long to say so. I'll be even more grateful if you can find out who's behind the shooting.'

Stone began walking again.

'There is one thing I'd like you to do,' he said, a short while later.

'Yes?'

'As you so accurately pointed out, I'm not a woman. But I happen to know a few who'd be happy to talk to you. Luana and Diana, for instance. However, I think there's someone else who might be better suited, given the circumstances. Know who I mean?'

'Yes. But she's seldom here, and is so busy ...'

'She'd be hurt if you didn't at least consider giving her a call, but all I'm asking is that you consider talking to someone, a woman you can trust.'

'You really don't make unreasonable demands, do you?'

He laughed. 'You can thank Luana for that. She's taken off most of my sharp edges.'

'But not all.'

'Definitely not all. They come in handy from time to time.'

***

Stone was working late and alone in the Triple S offices when Diana and Crandall came by.

'She's sleeping. Or, at least she's in her room and I haven't heard a sound,' Diana said. 'How did your talk go?'

'Well enough. You two need to understand that she's going to swing hot and cold on this for a long time. Best to give her as much leeway as possible.'

'Her schooling?'

'Schooling is one thing, school is another. You've taught her before, Richard. It might not hurt to do that for a while.'

Crandall rubbed the stubble on his chin. 'As much as I hate to admit it, she's grown beyond what I can easily teach her.'

'Oh, what nonsense, Richard,' Diana chided. 'You'll do well, and it's only temporary.'

'It will mean hitting the books again myself. Do you know how long it's been since I was a student?'

'Good lad,' Diana said, patting his shoulder. 'Other thoughts, Jason?'

'Keep her busy, naturally. Give her a challenge with the predictive chaos model. Her own algorithm to design, integrate, and test, for instance. I'll keep an eye on her whenever I can, but I have to do some traveling.'

'That's worrisome,' Diana said, 'considering the perfect cock-up Richard and I made of things before.'

'I suggested she talk to you, Luana, and especially Becky Amhurst.'

'Of course!' Diana said, smiling. 'That extraordinary woman. Yvette took to her immediately and they formed a bond.'

'Distance is a problem,' Stone commented, 'but I know Becky would ditch a board meeting to talk with Yvette. She's also a longtime friend of Logan's. I wonder if they've been in touch since the shooting.'

'I don't know,' Diana said. 'But long-distance commiserating isn't much more effective than long-distance mentoring.'

'We take what we can get,' Stone said, followed by a noisy yawn. 'Sorry. I just can't get by on three hours sleep like I used to.'

'Off to bed, then. Luana's still in your apartment, I take it?'

'Yes. Business of her own to attend to.'

The three left the Triple S offices in darkness and Stone closed the door.

'One last thing,' he said. 'Certain events are going to trip her circuit breakers.' He saw the blank looks on Diana and Crandall's faces. 'What I mean is, particular information about the killer or his boss may cause Yvette to react ... unpredictably. I've promised to share intel with her. It only seems fair. But if something comes in, I'll give you a heads-up. We'll all want to keep an extra sharp eye on her.'

Crandall nodded. 'I'm off to bed. I need to be thoroughly rested if I'm to teach differential equations.'

Diana hooked her arm in his. 'Bollocks, Richard!' she teased.

'Language, Lady Diana. Children are present.'

***

Yvette had prepared a carefully worded message, deferential and almost apologetic: she had promised Jason she'd call, she knew how busy Becky was, she was getting along much better after her appalling lack of judgment. When Becky's familiar voice said, 'Hello! I'm so, so sorry. I should have called ages ago,' Yvette could barely string three words together.

'It's OK. I know I'm busy ... I mean *you're* busy. I'm just, well, not busy.'

Yvette bit her lower lip until she could taste blood. She'd promised herself she wouldn't break down, not with Becky.

Becky sensed what was going on. 'My schedule has been pure hell for weeks. Don't ever let anyone tell you being CEO of a company is all parties and yachts. It's a bullshit excuse, but it's all I've got. I've only managed a quick call to Logan and I'm truly ashamed for not contacting you sooner.'

'It's fine, really.'

'It's not fine, but I'm going to try to make up for it. I've told Gary he's on his own for the next week. He's VP of engineering now, by the way. I figured if I flattered his ego, I could get him to slave away even harder. So far it's worked. Anyway, he's the boss man for a while. I'm pretty sure he's already moved into the corner office in Tucson. I know, I'm babbling. It's just ... what the hell can I say that will make any difference?'

'Someone murdered my Colin,' Yvette sobbed, her resolve gone. 'And I'm so full of hate. Jason tells me revenge won't make me feel better, but Colin's face was so pale and he had such a sad smile.'

Becky let her cry. When she stopped, Becky chose her words carefully. 'I don't absolutely agree with Jason. We'll talk when I get there, day after tomorrow. You and I will have plenty of time.'

'Logan is your friend, too.'

'Don't worry, there's enough of me to go around. You'll both be sick of me before I leave.'

After the call, Yvette was calmer. She gave considerable thought to what Becky had said, particularly her comment about disagreeing with Stone. What exactly did she mean?

***

Jesse relaxed as the miles went by. The twisting mountain road would soon turn to dirt, and it would be a slow, bumpy ride to the campsite. Jesse avoided more popular campgrounds. Most people were uncomfortable with an animal resembling a wolf lurking just beyond their campfires. Jesse had discovered this deserted backroad through the Chiricahuas years ago. It made a pleasant halfway stop when traveling from New Mexico to Los Angeles, or San Diego, where Charlotte stayed most of the year.

Thinking back on the encounter with Carlos set Jesse's blood to boiling. True, he had agreed to relinquish the ship. Maybe he would keep his word this time. But his threat was obvious. The relationship with Carlos the Viper, would-be drug lord of the Western Hemisphere, was coming to a close. He needed to die. His bodyguard, Ramón, would need to die as well, though Jesse felt a certain reluctance. For a hired killer, Ramón had some good qualities. Not so the Viper.

Cherokee was delighted to be back in the familiar mountains. When Jesse opened the back door of the camper, she leaped out eagerly, moving like mercury through the trees and scrub before disappearing entirely. A short while later, firelight danced on the trunks of nearby pines and along the sleek bark of the manzanita. A half-moon would soon shine down into the small clearing where Jesse had made camp, and the air would grow cold as the ground's warmth fled into the clear night sky.

After a light dinner, Jesse settled into bed. Cherokee would be back before dawn and would see to it that no one disturbed a much-needed sleep.

***

As darkness deepened, lights flared, and Jesse performed along the Strip in Vegas. The magic became ever more complex, ever more dazzling. The crowds grew huge, cheering wildly, but a frown never left Jesse's forehead. It wasn't enough. It was never enough. One grand illusion to stun a jaded world. People would be dumbstruck, stunned into admiration.

Ideas bloomed. Plans were made. There would never be such magic again. Hands ceased clapping and the crowd, as one, dropped to a knee. A suitable salute for the greatest illusionist of all time.

***

A chattering Mexican jay accompanied the first grey light of dawn, which trickled through the curtains of the trailer and caught the contours of the smile on Jesse's face.

***

The steady beeping of the monitor was as depressing as a death knell when Becky entered the hospital room. Chuck gave her a wan smile and stood, stretching his back. Logan glanced her way and raised a hand in greeting, then turned back to the bed and the incessant monitor. Chuck motioned to her and the two stepped out of the room.

'Christ, Chuck, how long has he been there?'

'Way too long. I drag him out when I can, but lately he's been refusing to come. Just sleeps in that damn chair.'

'He looks like shit. And not to be rude, but so do you. How long have you been sitting with him?'

Chuck just smiled and shrugged.

'Well, this is bullshit. Off you go. I've already checked on Cathie's status, and the doctors say they'll call if there's any change—which they don't expect.'

'What about ...?' He jerked a thumb towards the room.

'I'll get him out for some exercise and maybe a stiff drink or three, then some rest. He's no good to anyone like this. And "no" is an answer I won't accept.'

'You may be just what he needs, that stubborn old shit. Dang, I'm glad to see you.'

'Go on, Chuck. Take off.'

He nodded and began walking down the hallway.

'Oh, and Chuck …'

He turned back and gave her a questioning look.

'You should get a shower.'

'Hmph! Can't argue with that.'

Becky reentered the room and walked up behind Logan, placing a hand on his shoulder. He turned again, this time giving her a smile and a 'Hi.'

They stayed silent for the next ten minutes, then Becky said, 'It's time to take a walk. She's in good hands.'

'You go ahead.'

'I am. And so are you. This is not optional. So, get your sorry ass out of that chair, Fletcher. I'm going to buy you lunch'—she glanced at the clock—'or dinner. Jet lag sucks. We're going to need to find a pub with a few outdoor tables. You're even riper than Chuck.'

Logan hesitated, taking in the stony expression on her face.

'Well let's go, big fella,' she added forcefully.

Slowly, and with obvious pain, he rose from the chair.

They found a small pub a few blocks away with a handful of outdoor tables. A chilly breeze blew steadily, so Becky pointed to a table tucked between the brick pub wall and a trellis covered in thick foliage.

When the Guinness arrived, Logan took a sip and leaned back, a quick spasm of pain causing him to shift his position. 'I guess I've been sitting too long.'

'Yah think?'

'Where'd you come from?'

'The usual. Indonesia, Taiwan, Japan.'

'How's business?'

'Well, for a phony company set up by the CIA as a front to bring down Smythe-Montgomery, I've been pretty busy.'

Logan looked from side to side, and Becky laughed.

'No one's listening. Besides, who'd give a shit? Point is, we've won some legitimate business with Pacific-Indo-Asia Airlines. Some new business. Plus some leads to other airline work. And you'll never guess who's picked up the pieces of Smythe-Montgomery's legitimate business.'

Logan just shrugged.

'The lovely Ms. Emma Lister.'

'What?' The first interest Logan had shown in the conversation.

'That's right. She survived the scandal of Smythe-Montgomery's downfall, and when no one else stepped up, she flashed some legal documents giving her sole authority to a number of businesses, including the airlines.'

'She always had some impressive assets,' Logan said dryly.

Beaming, Becky reached a hand across the table and cupped his bristly cheek. 'There's my big teddy bear!'

'So, you're working with your former rival.'

'It's a mad, mad, mad, mad world,' Becky said. 'Reminds me, she left a curious voicemail the other day. Wanted to talk, but wouldn't say about what.'

'And you haven't called her?'

'Plenty of time. I've been flying for what seems like a hundred hours straight.' She raised a finger and waggled it from side to side. 'OK, step one is complete. Logan Fletcher is speaking again. Step two, nourishment.'

The waiter dropped off two plates with mounds of fish and chips.

'Step three,' she said, her mouth still half full of a chip, 'get the man to give me some information. First things first. How are you?'

Logan tried to smile but failed, reached for the Guinness, changed his mind, took a bite of fish instead.

'Stalling,' Becky said, drumming her nails on the table.

'Well, you could have started off with an easy one,' he grumbled. 'OK, I'm tired, dirty, my back hurts—'

'Stop! I said, how *are* you?'

A long silence. Logan took a deep breath that caught in his throat. 'I'm fucking lost, Becky. I've never felt so lost in my entire life. I just don't ...' He turned away, coughing, dug through a pocket, and produced a hanky that had seen plenty of use recently. When he turned back, his eyes were red and sunken.

'I'm pretty much useless without her. What am I supposed to do?'

'You're not alone. Never were. Lean on your friends, you stubborn man. I'm still mostly in the dark. Can you tell me what happened, from your perspective?'

'A lot of my perspective is actually Yvette's perspective. I was in the States. Shit, I never should have let her come here alone!'

'Step four. Stop useless self-condemnation. She's a big girl. No!' she commanded, holding up a hand. 'Not another word about it. She had plenty of support here, and everything should have gone fine, like dozens of other book signings.'

Logan slouched. 'Poor Colin, and poor Yvette. She's the one who needs you most.'

'Never you fret. I'll see her soon. Maybe later today. Tell me what you know, what you've heard.'

'I'm ashamed to say I'm not completely up to speed. Chuck tells me things and it goes in one ear and out the other. Stone has come by a few times too. I think he's got a lead on the shooter. Colin's killer. But I'll tell you, I haven't been too engaged.'

'Start at the beginning. When did you first hear?'

Logan took another deep breath and related everything he knew from the day of the awful call through his rushed trip to London and the blur of days in the hospital room. 'I can't even tell you how long it's been.'

'Did you know Yvette ran off? Back to her old haunts in the seedier part of London?'

'No. Wait. Maybe. But she came back, right?'

'Brought back by Richard and Jason. She's staying with Diana again. Which is where I'm headed after I see you to your hotel.'

'Becky, a million thanks, but I think I'll just check in at the hospital again.'

'Step five. Break your routine. You're not going back to the hospital today.'

'But—'

'For one thing, you stink, and you'd be doing everyone a favor. For another, you're about two weeks behind on sleep. So, you're going back to your hotel, taking a shower, and getting into bed.'

'How can you be sure I'll do what you say?' he said, with just a flicker of a smile.

'Ah! I've already bribed the duty nurse at the hospital and the staff of the hotel. Any deviation from the plan, and they call. I return, angry, and tuck you into bed like a little boy. Imagine the embarrassment!'

'So, I'm under house arrest?'

'Yeah, pretty much. Oh, you get a two-hour window tomorrow morning and another in the afternoon to visit Cathie. If you break parole, there will be consequences!'

A full smile finally forced its way onto Logan's face.

'Well, you're sure right about one thing. I've got friends.'

***

After the long flights and a difficult discussion with Logan, Becky was happy to accept Diana's generosity. Arthur, Diana's driver, had arrived at his promised time and was taking the quickest route to Diana's estate.

Becky leaned back into the soft leather and closed her eyes for a few minutes before realizing she was missing an opportunity to gather information. Her eyes still closed, she casually asked, 'How is Yvette reintegrating into the household?'

'Oh, quite well, I'm sure. A question better put to Diana.'

'Which is why I'm asking you,' Becky responded, her eyes popping open and showing a piercing glint.

Arthur smiled. 'I see. You'd like my unofficial opinion as a disinterested observer.'

'We understand each other. And you can rely on my discretion.'

'I do. Your reputation is well regarded at the estate.'

'So ...'

'Yvette came back willingly enough but is far from settled, though her more apparent behavior would indicate she is. I see her occasionally wandering the buildings or the grounds, often in the dining hall or ballroom. She talks to herself, though I'd be embarrassed to say I'd overheard her private thoughts. Mostly, I see the distress still fresh in her eyes.'

'The window to the soul.'

'Matthew 6.'

'You're a biblical scholar, I see.'

Arthur laughed. 'Taught to me by strict parents.'

'Any other observations?'

Arthur squirmed in his seat. 'I really shouldn't say.'

'For Yvette's sake?'

'Hmm. As you Yanks say, that's dirty pool. In your ear alone, I believe Richard and Diana misjudged Yvette's reaction to Colin's death. They'll be more watchful now, certainly, but I believe they still don't understand the depth of her distress.'

'And Jason Stone?'

'He understands the pain of loss. He was, after all, a soldier. But I doubt there were many young women under his command whose first loves were killed by the enemy.'

'How is it that you are blessed with these insights? If you don't mind my asking.'

'Three daughters,' he said, with a wry smile.

'Wisdom comes from unlikely places, doesn't it?'

Arthur just nodded as he turned onto the long driveway leading to Diana's house.

Becky gazed at the double line of dead elms bordering the drive. 'Why hasn't Diana had them removed, I wonder?'

The question was to herself, but she was pleased when Arthur responded.

'The expense, of course, though no doubt Richard Crandall would provide the funds. I believe it's a reminder of her childhood, her parents, and the glory days of the estate. Days made even more glorious as they fade from memory.'

'And you're a philosopher as well,' Becky said. 'Diana is so lucky to have you.'

'Here we are, then,' he said. 'I see Diana waiting on the stairs. I'll see to your luggage.'

Diana greeted her with a warm hug. 'You've come to the aid of your friends.'

'For what it's worth. So good to see you. You look well.'

'A façade, and a poor one. First the tragedy with Cathie and Colin, then Yvette's sudden disappearance.' She laughed humorlessly. 'I'd hoped my autumn years would be less traumatic.'

164

'I've seen Logan,' Becky said, with a shake of her head. 'He looks like shit and isn't doing well, despite his bravado.'

'Awful. Just awful.'

'But at least Yvette is home.'

'Yes,' Diana said, brightening. 'Richard and I hope the worst is behind her.'

The illusion Arthur feared, Becky thought. 'Arthur is a gem, you know.'

'Yes. But I'm an awful hostess. Come in, sit down, relax. Cynthia is helping out today,' she added, indicating a shy woman of about thirty who suddenly appeared. 'Cyn, this is Becky Amhurst. Please make her comfortable and show her to her room if she'd like to freshen up. Dinner will be at seven, drinks at any time you like.'

***

Dinner was a quiet affair, with only Diana, Richard, Yvette, and Becky present.

'Oh,' Richard said, seizing on a topic, 'Yvette is incorporating an entirely new behavioral analysis subroutine in the predictive chaos model. You should tell Becky about it.'

'I doubt it would interest her,' Yvette replied softly. 'And you needn't make so much of it. The mathematics are trivial.'

'But the psychological basis is not. You see, Becky, my modeling is based on large events, time spans, and populations. The smaller the numbers, the greater the uncertainty. When an anomalous individual—'

'Like Sir Conrad,' Yvette chimed in.

'Well, I was thinking generally, but I suppose we could use him as an example. In any case, the model has been woefully weak in the incorporation of individuals—even powerful ones—into the overall prediction. Conversely, the ability to *identify* an individual exerting influence on global events will also be enhanced when Yvette's algorithm is—.'

'Enough, Richard, please!' Yvette said, cutting him off again.

What doesn't she want me to hear? Becky thought.

Yvette's faux playful smile was frozen on her face as she saw the question in Becky's eyes. 'I'd like to hear how Becky's business is coming along,' she said.

Becky's amusing anecdotes could barely keep the conversation afloat for the remainder of the meal. When it was through, Richard and Diana excused themselves, knowing the real dialogue could only begin when they'd gone.

'Would you like a cup of tea?' Yvette asked.

'I'd like a stiff drink, but what I'd really kill for is a cup of strong, hot coffee. Any chance?'

'Cynthia prepared a pot, just in case. I might have some, too.'

'C'mon, let's grab some mugs and step outside. I need to stretch my legs.'

***

The two women walked slowly around the old fountain in the center of the circle drive, and by unspoken consent, began heading down the long elm-lined driveway. Moist, flower-scented air swirled gently, and the gravel crunched beneath their feet.

'You were kind of rude to Richard,' Becky said.

The accusatory tone took Yvette by surprise. Her first words of denial died on her lips. 'I was, and I'll apologize tomorrow. He does tend to bore guests with his talk of modeling.'

'That's not it,' Becky said. 'You didn't want him talking about your algorithm.'

Yvette didn't respond, and the two walked on in silence for a while.

'Let me guess,' Becky began. 'I'll bet after you returned, Richard offered you a challenge. Design and incorporate your own algorithm in the predictive chaos model. A tempting offer. But how does it help you achieve what you really want? To find Colin's killer.'

Yvette spun around to face Becky, her eyes blazing and her jaw clenched. Then she simply turned back and continued walking. Becky kept pace.

'If I'm right so far,' Becky pressed, 'you conceived a plan to do both. What did Richard say? "The ability to *identify* an individual exerting influence on global events will also be enhanced." You proposed the idea. He was delighted to see you re-engage and completely missed your deeper motive.'

'Becky, I don't know how you've reached this conclusion, but—'

'No, hang on. I'm on a roll here. Jason and Richard brought you home. Richard may not understand your pain, but Jason would. So, I'm going to guess you made a deal with him. You behave, he feeds you information for your model. How am I doing?'

'Shocking in your perception. Yes. All true, though I can't be sure Jason will be completely forthcoming with me.'

'You could offer to sleep with him,' Becky said slyly.

'Becky! How could you suggest—'

Becky burst into ebullient laughter. 'Sorry. I was just wondering how far you'd go to get information.'

'That was mean,' Yvette said. 'Not that far. Besides, he's quite attached to Luana.'

'Really? I hadn't noticed.'

Yvette laughed. 'John Steed and Emma Peel. The comparison only grows stronger over time.'

They'd reached the country road at the end of the drive.

'It really is getting chilly, and this coffee has done all it's going to do,' Becky said. 'To make matters worse, my hair feels like limp spaghetti with all the damp.'

'The walk was your idea,' Yvette said, with an impish smile.

'I've got another idea,' Becky said. 'We head on back and find something to warm us up before I collapse in a massive, jet-lagged heap.'

'Will you tell Diana and Richard?'

'Do I look like a snitch? Let me tell you something I've not told anyone, even Logan. I'm a military brat. My dad was a Marine. My brothers were Marines. It won't surprise you to learn that my first and only true love was a Marine. He was killed in Afghanistan. And do you know what I did? I went down to enlist. I wanted to kill the motherfuckers who'd killed him. My brothers stopped me, not just by hauling me back from the recruitment office, but by making me a promise that they'd kill the motherfuckers for me.'

'What are you saying?'

'I'm saying I'll help you. *If* you're totally straight with me. BS me and the deal's off. Richard and Diana won't know. Jason ...? He'll figure it out. He knows me pretty well. But he won't interfere if we color inside the lines. If my offer is of interest, then let's talk over the details. We'll both

167

be putting one over on Richard and Diana, and they're two of the most wonderful people in the universe.'

'They …' Yvette swallowed hard. 'They are. So are you. Much better than I deserve.'

'I doubt Colin would agree. Now let's walk.' She touched her head. 'Spaghetti hair.'

It was kind of you to invite me to your home in the mountains,' Carl said. He was sitting on a heavily padded chaise lounge behind the west-facing wall of Jesse's house.

Chapter Nine

Making Plans

It was kind of you to invite me to your home in the mountains,' Carl said. He was sitting on a heavily padded chaise lounge behind the west-facing wall of Jesse's house. The afternoon sun glistened through the dancing pine trees; the light breeze was cool, but pleasant.

'I'm glad you came,' Jesse replied, sitting down beside him. 'I wasn't sure how traveling would agree with you.'

'Oddly enough, my doctors thought a trip away from the city to the clear, brisk air of the Sangre de Cristo Mountains would be good for me. I agree.' He took a deep breath. 'My God, that's fresh. Faintly sweet. Ponderosa pine?'

Jesse nodded.

'I envy you. And I appreciate you driving me from the airport in your very comfortable vehicle.'

'The roads are rough. I wouldn't want you to arrive battered to bits.'

Cherokee came up and nuzzled Carl's free hand and he idly scratched her head. 'I'm amazed she tolerates me,' he said.

'Cherokee knows a friend, and so do I.'

'What about an enemy?'

'We know them too. I suspect the next time the Viper and I meet we'll be exchanging gunfire rather than words.'

'But he did give you the ship?'

'He did, which ironically means I no longer need him.'

'Once the demonstration is complete.'

Jesse nodded deferentially. 'As you say, once the demonstration is complete.'

'I'm surprised you haven't run out of patience,' Carl said. 'I know the man is a boil on your skin. He's not a partner, let alone an employer.

171

Certainly no intellectual peer. Simply a dull tool for you to wield while you prepare to make the space shuttle disappear or pull white tigers from your pocket.'

Jesse laughed. 'My parents always hated the idea of a magician in their family.'

'What? I'd have thought you'd say illusionist.'

'*I* would. *They* wouldn't. Card tricks or space shuttles, it made no difference to them. It was fake. There was always a trick.'

'They must have approved of your stint making movie magic in Hollywood. A real job with a very real salary.'

'You'd think so.'

Carl gazed at the sun as it slid behind the mountains. 'It's about that time. I'd appreciate a nice bourbon on the rocks or a single malt scotch if either is available.'

'Either or. Is it really such a good idea, though?'

'Are you one of my doctors now? I thought being away from their constant nagging was one of the advantages of this trip.' His laughter ended in a fit of coughing. When he was finished, he smiled and said, 'The bourbon, please. I doubt I'll die any sooner.'

'I was hoping you'd insist,' Jesse said, rising. 'I hate to drink alone.'

'Now that's a lie.'

When Jesse came back, Carl returned to the previous topic. 'So, you're telling me your parents were disappointed in your movie career too? Kind of hard to please, those two.'

'But consistent. They'd have been prouder, I think, if I'd been making porno movies in Reseda. My cinematic illusions—costumes, prosthetics, special effects, CGI—were all just fakery.'

Carl stared long and hard at Jesse before saying, 'My friend, please don't tell me you're doing all this to impress your parents?'

'Hardly. They're both dead, and I don't miss them. To use a pun, I'm under no illusion that anything I do would have impressed them.'

'Siblings?'

'Let's just say I've lost touch over the years. Don't shed any tears for me, Carl. I've got Charlotte, Cherokee … and you!'

'Two out of three,' he said, with a laugh.

'Enough of this horseshit, anyway. I need to fire up the grill or dinner will be after your bedtime.'

'What's on the menu?'

'You have two choices. Ribeye steak, courtesy of the grocer, or venison, courtesy of Cherokee.'

Cherokee, hearing her name, lifted her head and looked from one to the other.

'Fresh venison, huh? Tempting, but I believe I'll stick with the cow.'

'Plus baked potatoes, a salad, and a nice Cab.'

'Sounds great.'

'We have some planning to do, plus I might need you to take another trip. But I never said that before dinner.'

'Mixing business with pleasure. Whatever happened to polite society? Oh well. As long as there's pleasure!'

***

As dinner began, Cherokee drifted off as silently as the smoke from the grill. Jesse watched her go. 'We won't see her again until morning. I hope she doesn't overreach this time.'

Carl raised an eyebrow. 'Overreach?'

'She's a born hunter, but she sometimes misjudges size—at least in the wild. A two-hundred-pound man doesn't stand a chance. She's stronger and faster.'

'What about a one-hundred-fifty-pound bear?' Carl asked.

'Ah, you nailed it! I was out wandering the woods when I came across her. She'd pinned a full-grown black bear in a tree. How the bear came to believe Cherokee could take him down is a mystery. He'd have run out of patience eventually, and there'd have been one hell of a scrap. I'd put money on the bear.'

'You called her off, I take it.'

'Yes. I've never seen her so close to disobeying, but she came at last.'

'If she gets another appetite for bear?'

'Her problem. I can only hope I see a deer or some rabbit fur on the porch tomorrow. I swear, if there's a dead bear, you'll see its skin in front of my fireplace next time you visit.'

Carl laughed heartily.

'Come on,' Jesse said, 'let's grab the steaks and head inside. Food's ready.'

'And this,' Carl said, holding up his glass.

'Fresh bottle at the bar.'

***

After dinner, Jesse brewed a pot of coffee, cleared the table, and spread out a map of Central America.

'On to business,' Carl noted. 'Ah, you're not planning to sail from Puerto Barrios, are you?'

Raynard grinned. 'Is that a problem?'

'Wasn't that the port where you encountered—some difficulties.'

'The *Saint Martin* was boarded, overrun, and turned over to the CIA during a detestable human smuggling operation.'

'As I said, some difficulties.'

'There are three very good reasons to sail from there,' Jesse said. 'First, Carlos the Superstitious has avoided it ever since. Second, the *Reina del Mar* is not the *Saint Martin* and has never docked there. Third, we can load up with legitimate cargo. Fruit and so on.'

'You mentioned using a new crew.'

'Yes, and that could qualify as a fourth advantage for Puerto Barrios. Sailors move from ship to ship. No questions are asked. To ensure no complaints, I've paid the old crew, through a third party, to crew for other vessels sailing much sooner.'

'Clever, Raynard. And the *Reina del Mar*'s destination?'

'Very mysterious, though the smart money is on South Africa, where she'll load up with blood diamonds. Or perhaps that's a ruse and she'll make port in Kolkata. Drugs or more human cargo has been mentioned.'

'Rumors! There's just no controlling them.'

'Now here's where I'll need your help.' Jesse pointed to a town on the coast of Belize. 'I'll bring the cargo—the real cargo—here. Be sure to buy a decent boat with a serviceable refrigeration unit. Nothing ostentatious, but no need to be too subtle. That is, with the ship.'

'I'm dying, Raynard, not mentally handicapped.'

'And you won't mind being me?'

174

'It was all part of the plan when I signed on. No, I don't mind. I just never thought when I agreed to impersonate you that I'd do so as your friend.'

Raynard slipped into a reverie, staring into the fireplace.

'Something bothering you?' Carl asked.

'What? No. Maybe. It bothers me … how this has to end.'

'We live, we die. It's really that simple.'

'And you've accepted that? No tears? No rage?'

'Now you've put me in mind of the Welsh poet Dylan Thomas.' Carl sighed. 'Oh, I suppose I'll rage when the time comes. I'm not proud.'

'I hope … Never mind.'

Raynard went to the bar and poured a glass of cognac. 'Nightcap?'

'Why not?'

Carl gave Jesse a nod as he accepted the cognac.

Jesse clicked his glass. 'Here's to our next successful demonstration.'

Carl swirled the cognac and gave it a tentative sip. 'Good stuff.'

A distant howl rose over the noise of a rising wind, and they listened intently.

'Cherokee?' Carl asked.

'Probably. At least she hasn't been eaten by a bear just yet.'

Carl set his glass on a side table and said, 'It was my idea originally, you know. Not to create it, but to prepare for it.'

'Our devil's brew?' Raynard asked seriously.

Carl nodded. 'It seemed so obvious. Why not combine the characteristics of some of the worst—as you say—devils that have plagued man. Deadly as bubonic plague, more contagious than the flu. Everything we at the CDC have feared for years. As I said, my chief in the illusional EHDRG loved the idea, but was too incompetent to safeguard his workers.'

'We'll use our disease for a better purpose, Carl. For one thing, it's already provided your family with the future you wanted. Though when we sell it, your children's children will be free from any want, even if they live to be a hundred.'

'And where are we, to that end?'

'Interest has waned slightly since the village. Time will do that. I believe scrutiny will intensify when word of our next demo gets out.'

'I like your showmanship, Raynard.'

'What good is a product—in this case, a deadly plague that will make world powers tremble—without advertising? Our next demonstration will draw the serious buyers out.' Jesse thought for a moment. 'You know, it should have a name. Something worthy for when the bidding starts. You mentioned transformative mutations. How many of those did you research?'

'Umm, forty-seven, I think.'

'DP-47. Sounds clinical and deadly … and a little psychotic.'

'I get the "47." What's the DP?'

Raynard's smile grew hard. 'Devil's Pathogen.'

***

Raynard suffered one setback before the *Reina del Mar* set sail: the captain and first mate insisted on making the voyage. It was awkward, but not unanticipated. These two were fiercely loyal to the Viper, and why not? They'd profited greatly from the previous voyages of the *Reina del Mar* and had had their pick of the young women during the crossing. As ruthless and brutal as their predecessors, they'd murdered when necessary, raped at will, and collected a fat paycheck at the end.

Once it was clear they'd be in command, Raynard had communicated their destination: first Buenos Aires, then Cape Town. Peculiar enough, at least with an original cargo of vegetables and fruit. Even more extraordinary was their first stop. Montego Bay! Raynard had made it clear they would receive additional instructions—and cargo—at all three ports. The captain had read the instructions several times, then called for the mate.

'What do you say to this?' the captain asked. 'This Raynard is a mysterious one.'

'Have you met Raynard?'

'Me? No. I take orders from the Viper.'

The first mate spit over the side. 'Not on this trip, eh?'

'We humor this gringo for one trip. Those are my orders from Carlos himself. But—and I say this only for your ears, amigo—this Jesse Raynard may be having health issues. Serious health issues, understand?'

'Like what? Cancer or something?'

'No, idiot! Like the kind of health issues that come from displeasing the Viper.'

The first mate gave his captain a dull stare, then his mouth widened into a gap-toothed grin. 'Oh, *si, si*! A bad case of lead poisoning.'

'*Si* ... but stay quiet. I don't trust this new crew. But we'—he patted his first mate's shoulder—'get a special bonus for our loyal service.'

'Just as well,' said the mate, slipping instantly into a morose state, 'no ladies on this trip. A dull voyage.'

This time, the captain smacked the back of his first mate's head. 'Idiot. Montego Bay.' He made the curved outlines of a female body with his hands. 'The women there are *muy* beautiful.'

'You expect a cargo?'

'Of course. There and perhaps Buenos Aires also. For the South African trade.'

'Ah,' the mate said. But refusing to give up entirely on his gloominess, he pointed to another part of the orders. 'Why do we heave to at 17 degrees N 87 degrees W? We're to hold there from 2:00 a.m. till 4:00 a.m. There's nothing there! Just ocean.'

'Read the next line.'

'Special cargo? Two containers to be immediately placed in cold storage. I don't understand.'

The captain stabbed himself in the chest with a fat finger. 'That's why I'm captain. All you need to know is the Viper said to humor Raynard. Then the big bonus.'

'*Si*. And the beautiful *señoritas*?'

'First pick to the captain, second to you. Not too bad, eh?'

***

At least Belize was relatively civilized. Carl had scoured the docks and finally purchased a seaworthy commercial fishing vessel with a refrigerated storage area sufficient to hold his cargo. He pulled the bandana from his neck and wiped the sweat from his forehead. Heat was one thing. He loved the desert Southwest with its dry, one-hundred-plus days, but humidity made him grateful that he was only mortal. He smiled and slipped into a fitful coughing spell.

'Señor Raynard? The papers?'

'What? Oh, yes. Of course.'

177

He signed several pages that made him the legal owner of the *Manta Ray*.

'Is there anything else, Señor?'

The sun burned ocher in the western sky. Traffic noise and the chatter of human life assaulted his ears. How he longed to die.

'Señor?'

'*Si*. A taxi to the Christo, *por favor*.'

'The Christo, *si!*'

The Christo was one of the newest, most decadent hotels in Belize City. Twenty-three floors overlooking the sea. After he checked in, Carl collapsed in his room, struggling for breath. But after an hour inhaling the cool, blissfully dry air, he felt much better, and his spirits revived. He still had work to do this day. He reached for the phone.

'Room service,' came the brisk response.

'Yes, I'd like a large bowl of soup and some warm bread.' He glanced over at the mini fridge. 'Do you have any Jack Daniels?'

'There isn't any in your bar area?' the woman asked, shocked.

'Just a moment. Why, yes there is, thank you.'

'There are glasses in the cabinet over the bar and ice in the freezer section of the fridge,' the woman added. Apparently, this guest needed to have everything explained.

'Yes, I've got it now, thanks.'

'If you need anything else, don't hesitate—'

Carl hung up. 'Condescending bitch,' he grumbled.

The steaming soup and bread arrived in less than five minutes, improving his mood immensely.

He slid the glass door open and stepped out onto the patio. Bearable now that the merciless sun had drifted behind the hotel. He could see most of the harbor from here, including his newly acquired fishing boat.

He reached for his cell phone and dialed a familiar number.

'Hello, Carl,' Jesse said. 'All is well, I hope?'

'I'm sorry, but my name is Raynard. Jesse Raynard. And I've just purchased a lovely fishing vessel, now riding at her moorings in Belize City's commercial port.'

Raynard laughed. 'Well played, old friend. I'm about two hours out, with the cargo.'

'You are driving carefully, I hope?'

'Running stop signs, blasting along thirty over the limit, engine howling and tires squealing.'

Carl ignored Raynard's rapier wit. 'I wish to God you didn't need to be here.'

'Grown tired of my company?'

'I'm serious. Having you board the ship is risky.'

'You know I'm the only one who can manage this.'

Silence. 'I still don't like it.'

'How's the hotel?'

'They have bourbon.'

'I'll join you for one. This time in two days. When does the *Reina Del Mar* sail?'

'Noon tomorrow. They'll have plenty of time to make the rendezvous.'

'And the ...'

'The *Manta Ray*. Berth 28. The skipper I hired was bursting with questions, which he elected not to ask once I showed him an envelope of cash and the title to the boat, transferred to him in four days' time.'

'We're giving him the boat?' Raynard asked.

'Why not? Were you planning to go into the fishing business?'

Raynard laughed. 'No more than a few trout from a mountain stream. Really, Carl, you've become a master of international crime.'

'I'll take that as an insult,' Carl said. 'So, you'll be arriving ...'

'After sunset. Despite my bravado, I'd rather load the cargo after dark. Once it's secure, I believe we'll sail.'

'Tonight? You'll be early.'

'Ah, you know, I may just wet a line near the Caymans. There are rumors of enormous sailfish packed so close you can walk to Jamaica across their backs.'

'You're not serious?'

'No. But a little asynchrony in our sailing times can't hurt. Plus I'll need time to prepare.'

'Why not let me come along? I could help and you know it.'

Raynard hesitated. The help and expertise would be welcome. 'I didn't want to impose.'

'I'm offering. Going once … Going twice …'

'Fine. Do you get seasick?'

'Only when I'm sober.'

'Meet me at the dock at nine. Oh, and there's one more thing, if you're willing. Do you know a Dr. Shukhov?'

Carl smiled crookedly. 'Constantin? Oh yes.'

'There may be an opportunity to take advantage of his presence in Jamaica at this critical time. In fact, *Jesse Raynard's* presence in Jamaica could be doubly useful. I'll explain on the boat.'

***

At 10:00 p.m. the *Manta Ray* put to sea. In exactly fourteen hours, the *Reina del Mar* would leave Puerto Barrios for a rendezvous unlike any other in maritime history.

Despite the storied history of St. Andrews and the 18th century dignity of the Old Course Clubhouse, Stone found the place dull.

Chapter Ten

St. Andrews

Stone stood on the walkway just at the point where it met The Links, an appropriate name for the narrow road bordering St. Andrews' famous Old Course. Bright green fencing with a repeated X pattern ran both along the road and down the walkway towards the first tee. Across the walkway from the starter's shed stood the Old Course Clubhouse, and beyond, the sparkling waters of the North Sea washed along a deserted beach that pointed like a long tan finger to the north. Tattered clouds hurried across the sky, driven by a brisk breeze that kept golfers in jackets or heavy sweaters.

Despite the storied history of St. Andrews and the 18th century dignity of the Old Course Clubhouse, Stone found the place dull. Acres of grass, without a tree or shrub to break the monotony, reminded him of the huge lot around his childhood home. By the age of eight, he'd been assigned to mount the old riding lawnmower and keep the grass at a respectable level. With the summer rains in Albany, Georgia, this meant once a week. Despite the tedium of the work, he'd enjoyed the feeling of accomplishment as the shaggy green lawn was transformed to one of smooth, emerald perfection. And his yard had been bordered by many trees and thick brush. There was no ocean view, but at least the grass wasn't this resentful, drab green with tan bleeding through like a carpet worn past its prime.

Stone's thoughts returned to the task at hand as four men emerged from the starter's clubhouse and sauntered over towards the first tee to meet with their caddies. Though Stone had considered following this group while playing a round himself, his real interest was in a particular man in the foursome: the fishing he'd cryptically mentioned to Crandall. Also, he hadn't played in years. No time. He grinned at the notion he'd do

183

better shooting the ball with the H&K handgun tucked neatly under his arm than striking at it with a club.

He'd promised to keep Yvette informed of his progress tracking Colin's killer, and he had—to a degree. After the police and Stone had been played for fools, he'd thought long and hard before acting. Yvette's intuition—that few men could do what this man had done and escape—was correct, and even before he'd brought her back to Diana's home he'd been considering a handful of professional assassins as suspects in Colin's murder. He'd shared the information with Yvette as part of their deal. Since then, he'd been patiently gathering threads of information. When a name, Caldwell Simms, had finally popped, he'd decided to make this trip. He'd failed to share the name or his travel plans with Yvette, and he wondered if he was breaking his word. He shrugged inwardly; this could be a complete dead-end. Self-delusion. Stone's gut told him he was on the right scent.

The wind tugged at his jacket as he unzipped it and pulled out a powerful pair of binoculars. The tiny men sprang to nearly life-sized. As the caddies organized clubs and bags, Stone focused carefully and examined each player. Two had the greasy look of financiers whose primary business was illegal. Low-born men who'd become wealthy by using their brains to manage the coffers of drug lords, Mafia dons, or Russian oligarchs. Both held cheap, fat cigars and were talking nonstop. A third man, the oldest of the group, seemed unamused by the first two. His grim expression cracked enough to support a small smile when the fourth man nudged him and pointed towards the pin.

The fourth man was Caldwell Simms. He wore a jaunty plaid cap on his nearly bald head. Stone studied him. Six feet tall, or thereabouts, possibly thin beneath his jacket. Certainly not stocky. An eagle's nose and hard jaw beneath pale-blue eyes. When he smiled, Stone saw no humor, and the glances he threw at the first two men communicated an indifference bordering on animosity. If they burst into flames, Simms wouldn't waste piss to put them out. He was more cordial to the older man who was similar enough in appearance to be related. *An uncle?* Stone wondered.

He tracked Simms until each player had hit his tee shot and the group began moving towards the creek that bisected both the first and eighteenth hole. Stone made the best assessment he could. Simms carried himself with confidence, moved easily and with purpose, but didn't have the look of a soldier or even, with the exception of that jaw, a tough street fighter. And despite the fatal results at the bookstore, Stone had no admiration for the man's marksmanship. Cathie was still alive and Colin had died of a body shot. Admittedly, Colin had leaped in at the last second: a distraction as well as a necessary second target. Stone frowned. If the man wasn't a crack shot or a skilled hand-to-hand fighter, how had he become a top assassin? Stone's conclusion—reinforced by Simms' remarkable disappearing act after killing Colin—was that the man was intelligent. No. Perhaps not that, but clever. A fox who killed and disappeared. After all, the second most impressive item on an assassin's résumé was never being apprehended. Stone smiled. The most impressive, of course ... being alive.

Stone checked his watch. *Should have plenty of time to chat with the lads at the Dunvegan Hotel's tavern, find out what I can about Mr. Simms, then enjoy an easy walk towards the Old Course Hotel. If I'm not mistaken, there's a nice bar nearby with a view of the 17th and 18th fairways.*

***

The Dunvegan's tavern was a favorite haunt of the caddies, being two short blocks due south of the clubhouse, and Stone was able to strike up conversations with several for the cost of a round. It turned out Simms *was* the older man's nephew and they were, if not quite regulars, not unknown. The older man was taciturn, but made up for his lack of charm with better tips than the young man.

'They say the old fellow was a bomb maker for the IRA when he was still wet behind the ears,' said one of the caddies who'd accepted Stone's offer of a dram, 'but you never heard that from me. Fair golfer, though not as good as his nephew. Tips aside, I'd rather caddie for the young one. Don't know what he does for a living and don't plan to ask, but I've heard them talking. Younger fella has a place ... oh, off up in the mountains, northwest of here. Likes his privacy, apparently. Ah, no thank you,' he added, holding up a hand as Stone pointed to his empty glass. 'I've another customer in ten. Best if I can see straight. But thanks for this one.'

The caddie strolled out with a wave, leaving Stone at least an hour to process the information and plan. Despite the clink of glasses and chatter of golfers reliving their best shots of the day—some of them imagined—

Stone was able to think clearly, relaxing in the mellow atmosphere of the old tavern. Pictures of famous golfers had been hung in every conceivable place on the walls and support posts. When vertical space was exhausted, the owners, not thwarted for an instant, had screwed wood frames to the ceiling, so it now had the look of an upside-down chess board extracted from Lewis Carroll's bizarre imagination. The polished wood of the bar gleamed almost as brightly as the tubular brass railing surrounding it, and the afternoon sun sparkled off bottles and glasses.

Stone nursed his drink while considering his options. He knew where Simms had parked. Following him to his house in the mountains shouldn't be too difficult. At the hour's end, he slid from his seat and exited Dunvegan's, his plan fully formed.

***

After a ten-minute walk, Stone entered the Jigger Inn, a quaint restaurant and pub appended to the Old Course Hotel, where he was staying. The maître d' gave him a peculiar look when he asked to be seated outside—it was a chilly day—but smiled pleasantly at the vagaries of Yanks. With the patio to himself and an unobstructed view of the Old Course's 17th and 18th holes, Stone sipped a Lagavulin whisky and relaxed. As each new foursome walked the fairway, he casually lifted his binoculars. Another group came and went as he ordered a second scotch. A half hour later, Simms and the other three passed by. Stone pulled out some bills and, with a nod to the bartender, sauntered out to the hotel parking lot.

While waiting, he'd sent a text to Crandall, informing him that the fishing was excellent and he wouldn't be returning to the office for a week or so. He hoped his final words, 'Keep a sharp eye on our mutual friend until my return,' would be sufficient warning to keep a close watch on Yvette.

***

The grey and damp of the Grampian Mountains had become familiar to Stone over the past five days, the air so thick with moisture he could sweep his arm around him and find water droplets rolling off his jacket. What Simms might see in a place like this, other than a guarantee of privacy, escaped Stone. True, Simms could drive to Aberdeen, Edinburgh,

186

or Glasgow in several hours, and St. Andrews was within easy reach. Apparently, the gloom didn't bother him.

Stone had followed Simms from St. Andrews at a discreet distance until he knew the intel he'd gathered at the pro shop was accurate, then taken a long, circling route. He'd found a rundown B&B, paid for a week's lodgings in advance, and hiked off into heather-covered mountains to his present location. Clusters of primrose and bogbean broke the monotony of the Highland scene. Stone had been fortunate to find a cluster of willows tucked behind a ridge that gave him a clear line of sight to Simms' house plus plenty of cover. Being wetter than a swamp was the downside to this otherwise excellent location.

For three days he'd watched, returning to the B&B only for fresh clothes and a hasty meal. Simms' sole visitor had been his uncle, who'd stopped by the day after their golf outing, stayed through lunch, and left around 2:00. Stone was glad he'd decided to surveil the location before making a move. A large mastiff, unseen the first day, patrolled the grounds, and he'd seen Simms checking cameras and alarm systems both at and around his house.

Taking days to prepare was risky, though. Simms might get another job, leave, and not return for weeks or months. But Stone's luck held. The afternoon of the fifth day, he checked his supplies, not least of which was a string of bangers: thick, fatty sausages he'd bought from the owner of the B&B. Now he was ready.

Simms was clever, but nearly all his safety measures (the mastiff being the exception) ran on electricity. Stone's first inclination—cut the power, deal with the dog, and break into the cabin—had been modified when he saw the backup generator, a serious machine well-hidden behind a small outbuilding. The generator itself was covered by motion sensors and cameras, but a junction box near the house was in a blind spot. His plan was complete.

Deep dusk sucked the remaining light from the day, and Stone made his way down the hillside using night vision gear. The mastiff lay on its side, unconscious, after consuming three bangers and enough tranquilizer to sedate an elephant. Simms, following his usual routine, left the house and whistled shrilly. 'Hamish, you bloody hound, where are ye? Got some nice beef bones for ye tonight.' He whistled again. 'Well, rot my soul, where've you gotten to, you son of a bitch?'

Grumbling and cursing, Simms walked around to the rear of the house. 'I'll beat you bloody, you useless—' He stopped, stunned, as he saw the vague shape of the dog, lying on its side and wheezing softly. Before he could regain his wits or make any move, Stone pressed the button on a modified garage door opener in his jacket pocket. A small charge went off in an electrical box near the access road, and the house went black. An instant later, the generator rumbled to life, but blue, arcing light melted the cover of the junction box as smoke poured from the electronics of the generator. It ground on for a while with a sound like stones tossed into a gear box, then was silent.

Simms was fast. He'd pulled a light from his pocket and was just reaching for the small semiautomatic at his hip when Stone said, 'Don't.'

Inside the house, Stone used zip ties to secure Simms to a heavy chair.

'Being so remote does have its disadvantages,' Stone said, as he jerked the wire from a table lamp. 'You can yell if you want, but no one will hear you. And I'd appreciate it if you'd just tell me what I need to know.'

'Fuck you! You're fuckin' dead, you know that?'

'Oh, wow, I don't know if I've ever been threatened before.' He began stripping off insulation from the electrical cord.

'Not by me, you ain't. Do you know who I am?'

Stone stopped what he was doing and stared intently at the ceiling. 'You know, I really don't! So that'll be my first question. Who the fuck are you—really?'

'Go bugger a sheep!'

'An interesting concept. Don't think I'll try it. And after tonight, you won't be able to.'

Stone unzipped the man's pants and pulled them down.

'What are you, some kind of fuckin' perv? Go on, then, give it a blow.'

Stone fished in a pocket and pulled out a large alligator clip. He attached one of the lamp-cord wires and held it up. 'This goes onto your tiny dick.' He made a biting motion with the clip. 'Feel like talking?'

Beads of perspiration were running down Simms' face now, but he tilted his head back defiantly. 'Sod off.'

'Suit yourself.' Stone opened the alligator clip and released it on Simms' penis.

'Aaaarrrggh, you mother-humping pile of shit!' he bellowed. 'I'll fuckin' murder you, your wife, your family!'

Stone's fist sliced through the air, striking Simms' jaw with a gut-churning crunch.

'No, you won't. Ready to talk?'

This time, Simms said nothing, grinding his teeth in pain.

'Well, aren't you a tough mother.' Stone struck him again, then hooked his fingers in the front of Simms' button-down shirt, ripping it open. Fishing in his pocket, he produced another alligator clip. Smaller. He attached it to the other wire, and without a word, clamped it to the man's nipple.

'Shiiittttt!'

'Ready to talk now?'

Simms breathed heavily, face contorted in pain. Then a thin smile crossed his pale lips. 'Fuckin' dumbass,' he growled. 'You cut the fuckin' power.'

Stone feigned surprise, and Simms threw his head back, laughing hysterically. 'Bloody idiot!'

But when Stone returned his gaze, Simms grew silent. There was death in this man's eyes.

'This your phone?' Stone asked casually, lifting a cell phone from the table.

Simms said nothing, and Stone flashed him a grin. The grin of a skeleton. As he began to dial, he thought, *OK, Yvette. Would you be willing to go this far?* He hadn't finished entering the numbers before he knew the answer. He stepped out the front door and closed it. Simms' bellowing was mere background noise added to the falling rain.

'Hello. Yes, this is Mr. Simms. My electricity's gone out, and I have a cake in the oven. How soon do you think you could restore power? Why, yes, there was a flash at the post near the house. Really? Splendid.'

'Good news,' Stone said, as he reentered the house. 'A crew will be out in less than half an hour.' He tossed the phone onto the table and the façade of playfulness slid from his face, replaced by a hellish indifference.

189

'So that's how long you have to tell me what I want to know. Ready to talk *now*?' The 'bitch' was silent.

***

Yvette met Stone at the door, a cold, accusatory expression clouding her face.

'You promised,' she said through clenched teeth.

'Well, hello to you, too. And I'll keep my promise. I don't suppose I could take a shower before I debrief?'

Yvette's scowl deepened.

'You're a tough nut. Fine. Meet me in the Triple S office and see if Diana wants to join us.'

'Richard and Logan are here as well.'

'Good. Round them all up, would you?'

An icy stare.

'Please?'

Yvette nodded tightly and hurried off.

Within minutes, all five were seated around a small conference table. Stone noticed Logan fiddling nervously with a copy of Cathie's book. To Stone's silent question, Logan replied, 'No change. But you have news?'

'Yes. Where to begin?'

After a moment's hesitation, he told them of the leads that had finally yielded a name, and how he had tracked the man Simms to his home in the Grampian Mountains. He avoided many details of Simms' capture and glossed over his interrogation. Yvette eyed him grimly but remained silent.

'Not to be tedious,' Stone said, with a horribly affected laugh, 'I got all the information I could from him.'

'Are you certain?' Yvette asked harshly.

Crandall and Diana exchanged an anxious glance, as, with glacial slowness, Stone turned to face Yvette. His eyes locked with hers for a long time. It wasn't until she dropped her gaze to the tabletop that he said, 'Positive.'

'And what did you get, exactly?' Logan said, his calm words diffusing the explosive situation.

Stone shrugged and leaned back in his chair. 'Maybe not as much as you might hope. Confirmation that he was the shooter. The name of the woman who assisted him in his escape. An acknowledgement that he was hired to do the job by an overseas employer.'

'Who?' Yvette asked, though more softly than her previous question.

'What you have to understand is that Simms is no fool. It's the only way he's managed to stay alive in his profession. He never met his actual employer. He worked through an intermediary and only knew the man's first name. Ramón. If he'd known more, he'd have told me, and you can believe that. Now, I have several friends working leads on Ramón, and I'm pretty sure—'

'It's him,' Logan blurted out, flipping Cathie's book open to the organization chart for Carlos the Viper's cartel, the one intimately involved in Smythe-Montgomery's worldwide network of drug trafficking.

Stone examined the graphic. 'It's likely. My sources should be able to confirm this easily.'

'Carlos the *Viper*,' Yvette said, with a sneer in her voice. 'He's responsible.'

'It looks that way,' Stone said. 'It won't take long to trace back if this Ramón'—he tapped the page of the book—'was Simms' contact.'

'Now look, Yvette …' Crandall began.

Yvette's eyes blazed as she rounded on Stone, a thought exploding in her mind. Her question cut across Crandall's cautionary comment.

'What happened to Simms?' she asked, a broken-glass edge returning to her voice.

'I let him go. I'd gotten the information I wanted.'

'But he killed Colin! He tried to kill Cathie.' She leaped up and her chair toppled behind her. 'You bastard! I'll kill him myself!'

'Yvette, *please*,' Diana said.

'No!' She stabbed a trembling finger at Stone. 'He promised! And now … And now …'

'Sit down,' Stone said quietly, though the tone of command got everyone's attention. 'I've had patience with you because of your loss, but now I've run out.' He pointed to Logan. 'His loss may be as great as yours, but you don't see him acting like a foolish child. You said you'd trust me but you don't. It shows you really don't know me at all, and I guess I don't know you. Fine. But we had a deal, so sit down and shut up. I'm not a complete idiot.'

Yvette was trembling in every limb at this sudden rebuke, though a tiny voice inside her said she'd earned it.

Crandall looked at her, his eyes wet. 'Please, Yvette. Oh, I hate to see you hurting so!'

Logan retrieved her chair and Yvette crumpled into it, her eyes vacant, her chest heaving.

'Simms won't live out the week,' Stone said. 'You can take that to the bank.' He ran his hand along a bristly chin. 'So you'll fully understand, realize that I broke about fifty laws in capturing the man, and my interrogation technique was … medieval. If I'd reported him to the law *before* I questioned him, he'd have gotten a good lawyer and weaseled out. There was no proof. And I couldn't report him after I'd questioned him. Nothing he'd said was admissible in court and, oh, I'd be behind bars for a very long time. I could have killed him.'

The way he spoke the words sent a shiver through everyone in the room. No boast. No hyperbole. Only the stark, emotionless truth.

'I almost did, because, believe it or not, I hate him almost as much as you do. I decided not to give him the easy way out.'

Only Logan appeared to understand, as Diana, Yvette, and Crandall exchanged puzzled glances.

'I've outed him. If Ramón is who we think he is, he and others from the Viper's organization will track Simms down for giving them up. He'll die in a way that will make my questioning seem tame. When the body is found—and it will be, 'cause the Viper will want to send a message—the police's attention will be drawn to the cartels, not us. And you won't want to see a picture of the body. Now do you understand?'

Yvette rose from her chair, nodded, and left the room without another word.

Diana and Crandall left soon after, Diana giving Stone's shoulder a quick squeeze on the way out.

'Have you had anything to eat?' Logan asked, when the two were alone.

'What day is it?'

Logan stood and motioned Stone to follow. 'C'mon. Let's see what we can rustle up.'

It turned out, there wasn't much to rustle up in this wing of Diana's home. But a refrigerator in a service room just off the dining hall yielded a hunk of roast beef and a jar of mustard. A bag of fresh rolls, and their feast was complete. More importantly, Logan opened a bottle of Merlot. He and Stone sat ludicrously at the lower end of the great table, washing down the cold roast beef sandwiches with fine wine.

'Best meal ever,' Stone said. 'I only wish you had better company.'

'I wish Cathie was here,' Logan said. He managed a smile. 'But I'll settle for you. Want to talk about it?'

'I thought I had.'

'Not what I meant,' Logan said, crumbs spluttering from his mouth.

Stone gave him an appraising glance, swirled the wine in his glass, then drained it. He held the empty glass out to Logan. 'Refill?'

Logan poured and waited, the silence stretching.

'I'm tired of being me,' Stone said at last. 'You know my background. The things I've done. I wasn't joking with Yvette. A bullet in Simms' brain would have been merciful.' He glanced at Logan, his eyes haunted with the past. 'But that's just not me, is it?'

Logan said nothing, so Stone continued.

'Funny thing is, even me at my most brutal didn't satisfy her.'

'She's heartbroken and confused, Stone. She'll come around.'

'Will she? Will she come back around to idolizing me as a modern-day John Steed? I've seen the old TV series. Never a drop of blood spilled on that show, but my hands are soaked in it. So what does she want? The sterile cartoon hero or the butcher?'

'She doesn't know, but I'm afraid ...'

Stone held his gaze. 'Me too. She won't be satisfied till she deals out some lethal justice to Colin's killer, and when she does, it'll be too late. She'll have lost herself. I've tried to explain, but she won't believe me.'

'Maybe,' Logan said cautiously, 'she doesn't believe you because she knows you're lying. She knows what you've done, and she still sees a good man.'

'Nicest thing anyone's ever said to me.'

Logan raised a skeptical eyebrow.

'OK, Luana says it all the time, but she's different.'

'That she is,' Logan said, tapping his glass to Stone's before taking a drink. 'What do you think Yvette will do?'

'If you're right, she won't be satisfied till she gets some very personal revenge. Until she sees blood.'

'Is that so bad?'

Stone considered for a moment. 'No, as long as it isn't her own.'

***

'Yvette! To what do I owe the honor?'

'I'm … I mean, hi. Do you have a minute to talk?'

'Give me a sec,' Becky said. The sound of ice tinkling into a glass followed by a muted sloshing. 'Sorry. That sounded serious. What's up?'

'Now I've got you on the phone, I'm not sure where to begin.'

'A wise man, Lewis Carroll I believe, had a character with a similar problem. The solution was, "Begin at the beginning and go on till you come to the end: then stop."'

'I need your help. Jason found Colin's killer but let him go.'

'Wait, what? That's not the beginning. Go back further.'

Yvette gathered her thoughts and slowly recited everything she knew, guessed, or felt. 'The worst thing is,' she said, as she finished the last painful scene with Stone, 'I think Jason was right.'

Only sloshing this time.

'Jason *is* right,' Becky said at last.

Yvette sighed loudly.

'But he's also wrong.'

'Wh-what?'

'Think about it. He's never loved someone like you have.'

'Luana?'

'As a woman. Look, what do you want to do?'

'I want to track down the man who took away my Colin and destroy him.'

'Will it bring you peace?'

'Of course not. I believe Jason about that. But it will bring some justice.' She thought back to the day she had inserted Crandall's aggressive anti-malware software onto her school's computer and to the destruction it had wreaked on the perpetrators. 'Yes. Some small justice.'

'Honesty. That's good. Let's see if I can figure out a way to help.'

***

An hour later, Becky was finally satisfied. She rubbed her eyes, which had suddenly refused to focus. 'Summarize.'

'You are military, aren't you?'

'I've only kept the good habits. So …'

'I'll continue with my modeling, trying to find a pattern with Carlos's movements. You'll contact—I still can't believe it—Emma Lister. How do you know that the reason she wanted to talk to you is connected to the shooting?'

'I don't. Call it intuition. Continue.'

Yvette sighed. 'I'll apologize to Jason, and I'll mean every word. And not to get back on his good side so he'll keep sharing information.'

'Though that won't hurt!'

'No. But that won't be the reason. I've been blind with anger and I truly forgot who he is and what he's done for me. Now I've remembered and I'll tell him.'

'Good girl. And …?'

'The puzzle with the missing pieces that Richard and I discussed with Jason. I'll work on that. There's something bigger going on here. Richard and I agree. But again, I can't see a connection to the shooting.'

Becky took a long time before saying, 'There may be none, but even if there isn't, you'll be helping Triple S solve another mystery connected with human trafficking, unexplained deaths, and the sudden rise to power of Carlos the Viper. A worthy effort.'

'Yes.'

'Now don't forget, you can call me at any time. Find out what you can, and don't ever lie to Jason Stone. But …'

Yvette smiled. 'I don't need to tell him *all* our plans.'

Just beyond their port quarter—almost, it seemed, within touching distance—was the dark hull of a ship ...

Chapter Eleven

The Dutchman

Becky was astonished when she heard a familiar, sultry voice on the other end of the line. She'd expected an answering machine or, more likely, a flunky hired to screen calls.

'Hello, Ms. Lister,' Becky said, trying to recover from her surprise by adopting a serious, businesslike tone.

'Is it Rebecca? Rebecca Amhurst? Do you mind if I call you Rebecca? You must certainly call me Emma. After all, we've shared more than a business interest.'

Becky laughed. They certainly had. Both had been physically involved (there was no question of romance) with Lister's onetime employer, Sir Conrad. That involvement had been expressed in bizarre fantasies and long nights of drug-enhanced sexual activity. Yes. They had *that* in common.

'Emma it is, and you should call me Becky.'

'Becky. Very good. I've been looking forward to this conversation. Since I hope we're to be friends, tell me … did you find Conrad to be a satisfactory lover?'

Another bout of laughter. 'Since you ask, he certainly had stamina, though that fine white powder might have had something to do with it. But you know, I think he got most of his thrill from the role playing.'

'Exactly! The captured damsel at his mercy. Taking his archenemy's wife … or daughter.'

'Ooh, we never did those. But I did have him handcuffed to a bed once when he thought I was an Interpol agent.'

'No! And he believed it?'

'At first. He promised me a slow, painful death once he was free. His description of the torture was quite graphic.'

'Please, tell me more.'

For the next half hour, the women shared their memories of Smythe-Montgomery's perverse sexual scenarios.

'Ah,' Emma said, when they'd finished, 'I almost miss him. Still, it's gratifying to be one's own boss.'

'It is,' Becky agreed. 'Which, unfortunately brings us to the real purpose of my call. Or actually, your purpose, since I'm calling at your request. If it is business, as I guess, we might want to arrange a time when my VP of engineering, Gary Walkin, could join. I think he'd enjoy a three-way with two lovely women.'

'If you've never indulged in a private threesome, I'd highly recommend it. Surprised Conrad never thought of it.' She paused to let a sudden fantasy blossom before adding, 'Yes. Perhaps you and I and Conrad. Hmm. Shame we'll never get the chance.'

'There are other worthy men out there, I'm sure.'

'There, you see!' Emma said triumphantly. 'Not only friends but kindred spirits.'

'You mentioned Conrad's association with the Viper,' Becky said, trying to redirect the conversation.

'Indeed,' Emma replied. 'Bloody fool, the Viper. What Conrad saw in him ... well I'm sure I don't know.'

'He was part of the network, wasn't he?'

Emma appreciated Becky's discretion in not explicitly mentioning the drug trade that was at the heart of Smythe-Montgomery's plot to form a new world empire.

'Yes. And in fact, I do know what Conrad saw in him. A convenient resource, risen to sudden high authority in the Mexican and Central American cartels, mostly by the brilliant efforts of Jesse Raynard.'

'And who is this Jesse Raynard?'

Visions of sweating bodies and prolonged ecstasy clouded Lister's thoughts for a moment. 'Oh, someone you should meet someday. Crucial to the rise of the Viper, though not currently in his good graces.'

'The enemy of my enemy ...'

'Yes, precisely. And so you know, or have guessed, that Carlos was involved in the shooting of Cathie Fletcher and the murder of that poor young man.'

'That poor young man, as you put it, was deeply in love with a close personal friend.'

'The heir to that eccentric fellow, Richard Crandall.'

'Your intel is excellent,' Becky growled.

'Please don't take offense. I've met the Fletchers. Cathie Fletcher's book—her extremely ill-advised but accurate history of Sir Conrad and his associates—was the trigger for this sad event. Murdering Fletcher was a stupid attempt to salve the Viper's bruised ego. Raynard argued for Carlos to show some restraint, but the man is a fool. A puppy who thinks he's a full-grown Doberman.'

'A grass snake who thinks he's a pit viper.'

'Yes. Such pests are meant to be exterminated.'

'I couldn't agree more. What did you have in mind?'

'A simple exchange of information. We both have resources. Perhaps the right word in the right ear could lead to the elimination of a man whose irrational viciousness is not welcome.'

Becky's first thoughts were of Stone, but then a tight smile without a trace of humor crossed her face. Yvette. She took a deep breath. 'I'm in.'

'Outstanding. Let me pass on a few more tidbits ...'

***

The sun had set in a blaze of liquid fire long ago. The passengers of the hired fishing vessel *Reverie* were three sheets to the wind as the boat plowed a leisurely furrow in the Caribbean Sea, heading towards its home port of George Town on Grand Cayman. The four men who'd hired the boat, Chicago lawyers whose clients had considerable sums in the Cayman banks, lounged on the fantail telling the classic fisherman's lies of the one that got away. They still had four more hours of casual cruising and heavy drinking before their boat would dock. Paid for in advance, by the way! Services—meaning alcohol—all included. And they intended to make the most of it. The unusual haze that had closed in soon after sunset didn't bother them in the least.

The crew, however, was keeping a weather eye. If the fog thickened, they'd have to hurry back to port. Their navigation gear was primitive, and they had no desire to be picked up by a Cuban patrol boat.

The dusk had nearly gone, and the greenish tinge to the west had been swallowed in grey, when the skipper reluctantly strode to the fantail to suggest they increase speed. Reluctant since he knew that if he irritated this foursome, they'd cut his tip to the bone, or even argue for a refund.

The mist had become so thick that the ship's cheerful lights, designed to brighten the spirits of the passengers and loosen their purses, were encompassed in glowing orbs of reflected light like cloud-draped suns. He walked aft in gloomy silence, stopping and waiting for his passengers to take notice of him. At long last, his presence disturbed their drunken chatter, and one said, 'Well?'

His head hung low, the skipper said, 'Sorry to disturb you gentlemen, but …' He glanced up and his words froze in his mouth. When he recovered, he bellowed, 'Mother of God!' He turned away from his passengers and screamed to his mate, 'Jerry, hard a-starboard, full power.'

The lawyers followed his frozen stare, their arrogant complaints dying on their lips. One screamed and threw himself to the deck as the others stared in horror.

Just beyond their port quarter—almost, it seemed, within touching distance—was the dark hull of a ship, terrifying in itself at such a close proximity. But that wasn't what had stoked panic in the *Reverie*'s crew and passengers. Hanging over the ship's starboard rail were two grinning sailors, as grey and cold as the mist. Worse yet, their lips were drawn back, their eye sockets empty; bloody, putrefying sores covered their arms and faces.

The sobering effect was astonishing. One of the men yelled 'The *Dutchman*!' and followed his companion's example, flopping face down on the deck and trembling violently.

'Jerry!' the captain shrieked. But the ships engines were already roaring, and the scene of horror was fading into the mist.

***

Back at port, the four fishermen, shocked into sobriety, decided being sober was *not* a good idea right now. They left the boat in a blinding hurry, never leaving the smallest tip for the captain and first mate.

'You should've seen it,' slurred one of the lawyers, a short hour and four gin and tonics later, 'a big honking boat with a dead crew.'

His loud voice had drawn a crowd at the Mermaid, most of whom looked skeptically at the four drunken Chicago loudmouths.

'What color was the ship?' one asked.

200

'How many crewmen did you see?' another said.

'Were you already drunk as skunks?' a third commented, to general nods and chuckles.

'I've seen it,' another voice said, and silence fell like a dropped brick.

The speaker, an older local man, had been sitting quietly at the end of the bar nursing a beer, his first of the night. There was no question of him being drunk. He had been frequenting this watering hole for nearly twenty years and operated a small charter boat, though he often went out after dusk to fish alone.

'What d'you mean, Smitty? You saw what?'

'Yesterday ... no, the night before, I was out. I ain't tellin' you guys where, but it was a good spot. Let's just say southwest of here a ways. I was moving slow, trawling, and the motor was purring. Then I hear a deeper note. A low throbbing. A big ship, you know. No running lights, which is peculiar. So I swing my spotlight around, and there, on the starboard bow is a wall of steel bearing down. I sheer off to port, my heart in my mouth, but I got one look at their rail—just a glimpse as the spotlight caught it—and there, I thought, are two mad lunatics, grinning at me. One seemed to wave, but it must have been the wind or the roll of the ship.'

'Oh, go on! Maybe he did wave. Maybe the dang fool was running without lights. It happens.'

'True,' Smitty said, nodding slowly, 'but that sailor must've been waving for the fun of it, 'cause he never saw my boat.'

'And how the hell do you know that?'

'Because he had no eyes.'

That unsettling comment silenced the room. Then the first speaker, the drunken lawyer, roared, 'I told you! I told you!' He sloshed the contents out of his cup as he thrust it towards the bartender. 'Another!'

A steady rumble filled the bar. Men called their friends, and within half an hour the bar was filled to bursting. Only its owner, a man known as Easy Ronnie, was relaxed and happy. He never fished.

Smitty had been coaxed from his barstool to a small table in an alcove overlooking the harbor. Three other charter boat captains were pressing him for more details.

'We've heard rumors from other drunken vacationers. Started a couple days ago. About the time you first saw … it. C'mon. No bullshit now. What the hell was it?'

Smitty stared around the table, meeting the eyes of the other captains in turn. 'I know what I saw. Men, it was the *Dutchman*.'

Silence, followed by a whispered, 'Bullshit!'

'No skin off my nose if you don't believe me,' Smitty said. 'But you've known me for a long time. I'm not lookin' for publicity let alone fame. So why the hell would I lie to you?'

'To get a free drink?' one answered, though his joking tone was tinged with fear.

Smitty held up his empty glass. 'Ain't working so far, is it?'

When another round arrived, the man who'd paid asked the obvious question, 'So what do we do?'

'Ah,' Smitty said, 'as for me, I plan on business as usual … except if I run afoul of fog. In that case, I'll be heading back to port as fast as the *Grouper*'s engine will take me. I tell you fair and square, there're only dead on that boat.'

'What boat?' one asked. 'I doubt *Flying Dutchman* was painted on her hull.'

Smitty raised his glass in salute. 'That's the only intelligent question I've heard tonight, though I appreciate the suds.'

'And …?'

'Hard to make out, you know, with the fog and all. 'Sides, my eyes were more focused on them poor dead fellows.'

The others exhaled, disappointed.

'But,' Smitty continued, 'the words were new painted. A ship fresh from a refit. Looked like … I could be mistaken … *Reina del Mar*.'

***

The next two nights found the Mermaid overflowing with drunken sailors, swapping lies about having seen the *Dutchman* or knowing someone who had. Late night had turned to early morning, and some of the crowd had begun to shuffle out when a tall burly man and his skinny first mate—known by the locals as the Skipper and Gilligan—shoved their way up to the bar, both men pale as a salmon's underbelly.

'Kind of a late night, Skipper,' the owner said, giving the bar a cursory swipe with a damp rag before tossing down two coasters featuring a huge-breasted mermaid with long golden locks and ruby lips. 'The usual?'

'Shot of Jack. Now.'

The Skipper's usual was a mug of India Pale Ale, and Ronnie eyed him suspiciously. But there was something in the Skipper's eyes that made him bite back an amusing quip. He turned to Gilligan, who nodded. Two shots of Jack were produced and thrown back with no seeming effect. Without waiting for another request, Ronnie poured two more, leaning forward and whispering, 'What the hell is it, Skipper?'

The Skipper threw back the second shot. When the third disappeared, he finally met Ronnie's eyes, his own still round and full of sober fear. 'I've seen her. The *Dutchman*!'

Ronnie looked around, then smiled indulgently. 'C'mon, Skip, every man in this bar has seen her. It's been the talk for the last two nights.'

The Skipper's heavy hand shot across the bar and grabbed Ronnie by his shirt, dragging him forward. Heads turned at the ruckus.

'I tell you I've seen her!' the Skipper said, his deep voice reverberating. Half the people in the bar were now staring. 'And ... we got pictures!'

'What? Let go of my shirt, you big ox. Pictures of what?'

The Skipper released the shirt and grabbed his drink, draining the glass in an instant. 'Another! Show 'im, Gill.'

Gilligan produced a cell phone, his hands trembling, and pulled up the first photo, turning it towards Ronnie.

Ronnie just stared for a long time, then brought the bottle of Jack to his lips and took a swig. 'Mother of God!'

'Swipe it,' was all Gilligan said, grabbing the bottle from the distracted barkeep and helping himself.

Men crowded around the bar now, trying to get a good look as Ronnie swiped to subsequent photos in the sequence.

The pictures had been shot late in the evening, with just enough light for the phone's camera to capture a decent image. The first two showed gulls circling a freighter, two of the crew leaning over the starboard rail, like Smitty had said the other night, only there were birds perched on the men, like trained parrots. But these birds weren't interested in crackers.

'We moved in closer and ... well, see for yourself.'

Ronnie stared at the images. The skulls of two men, picked nearly clean, and on the flying bridge, another man hanging over the rail, dead birds cluttering the deck near his feet.

A man who wasn't close enough to see the photos let out a loud guffaw. 'Oh, hell, don't believe them pictures. My son can use Photoshop and make it look like Hitler is having dinner with Kennedy.'

'Is that so, Harvey?' Ronnie sneered. 'Let him up here, guys.'

A lane cleared and the loudmouthed Harvey pushed forward.

'Take a good look, Harv'. Can your kid do that?'

Harvey stared at the first photo and the color drained from his face. Ronnie ran through the subsequent images. Before he was halfway through, Harvey turned away, making it back to his table before vomiting up the night's indulgence of beer, pretzels, and pickled eggs.

'Yeah, thanks Harv', you a-hole,' Ronnie yelled.

The focus of the group turned back to the Skipper.

'Where'd you come across her, Skip?' one man asked.

'Maybe forty, fifty miles west-southwest of Jamaica.'

'You were out a long way.'

'Aye.'

Another man asked, 'What was her bearing, Skipper?'

The Skipper shrugged and returned to his glass, but Gilligan said, 'Her course was east-nor'east. For Kingston maybe.'

'Holy fuck!' the man said. 'Hadn't we better tell someone, Ronnie?'

'Tell a priest,' Gilligan said. He was hunched over, his face inches from his drink, and he didn't look up when he added, 'You guys don't get it. She's a ghost ship with a crew of dead. Better she sails straight to hell.'

***

Jamaican patrol boats went out—reluctantly—and scoured the sea west of Jamaica. Nothing. Local officials cursed the drunken bastards from Grand Cayman. Stupid fools spreading rumors of mysterious ships manned by the dead.

What none realized was that, deprived of human guidance, the *Reina del Mar* was making great loops as she moved, generally, to the east. Her course, when spotted off the western tip of Jamaica by a random patrol boat, was northwest.

'Unknown ship, heave to and identify yourself,' a young, nervous lieutenant called through a bullhorn.

No response.

The captain, a tall man with skin the color of polished jet, stuck his chin out aggressively. 'Move in closer,' he said. He'd seen many unusual things in the Caribbean, and he was certain this was another one.

'Closer, I said!' he repeated.

'Aye, sir.'

The helmsman gingerly steered the patrol boat towards the unknown vessel, wishing the whole time he'd taken the job as an office clerk for his uncle in Kingston. Long before any visual identification was possible, a devilish stench of putrefaction wafted across the sparkling waters.

The helmsman gave his captain a nervous look.

'Binoculars!' the captain barked. A subservient sailor passed them silently, and the captain strode onto the foredeck, cursing. There was something about this ship that wasn't right, and he'd lost much of his bluster. The offer of a land job was now crossing his mind as well.

He focused carefully, scanning the bridge, the foredeck, and finally the rail. 'Mary, Jesus, and Joseph,' he muttered, handing the binoculars back and crossing himself three times rapidly.

'What do we do, captain? Board her?'

The captain rounded on him with a snarl. 'Are you mad? It's the *Dutchman*, man! Take us about! Get upwind. Now!'

When the patrol boat was a good quarter-mile upwind of the ship, the captain said. 'Take our position. What would you say her bearing is?' he asked, pointing.

'Hard to be sure at this range,' the helmsman replied tentatively. The captain's menacing glare brought a quick addition. 'Nor nor-west, maybe four knots.'

'Report it,' said the captain, 'then set a course for Kingston.'

The helmsman looked puzzled.

'Did you hear me?' the captain thundered. 'And give that death ship a wide berth heading home. Understand? We let the medicos handle this.'

***

By a stroke of good fortune, a respected epidemiologist, recently with the CDC, was vacationing in Jamaica. The commodore of the small fleet

205

of patrol boats harbored in Kingston requested his help, and he grudgingly agreed.

Dr. Constantin Pavlovich Shukhov had emigrated from Russia as a young man. His wealthy parents had supplied him with tuition money to satisfy his whim of becoming a doctor, only to be truly amazed when he applied himself with a will, receiving his MD from Georgetown and taking postgrad training at NYU. In addition to being heir to massive wealth, Constantin could trace his lineage back to Russian royalty in the days of the czars. No longer an advantage in modern Russia, his aristocratic lineage still drove his behavior in America. After all, there had never been royalty in America! His abrasive resistance to authority proved to be a major impediment in his otherwise stellar career.

An argument with the CDC's director resulted in an early retirement, Constantin barely fifty years old. Having inexhaustible financial resources allowed him to snatch up his ball and go home. An extended vacation in Jamaica seemed a nice way to pass some time.

The young lieutenant who'd known Constantin was visiting—none other than the officer who'd seen the ghost ship—was heartily congratulated by the commodore. The awkward situation of needing to investigate a potentially infected ship had left him puzzled, and his own small medical staff had shaken their heads and balked at any investigation. They weren't trained; they hadn't the equipment.

Constantin organized things quickly. Being given full authority, he raided local hospitals for hazmat gear, finding a full suit for himself and another for a nervous medic assigned to the patrol boats. Two other sailors would have adequate gear for a close approach to the ship. They wouldn't be going aboard.

Within thirty-six hours, their boat was scouring the sea northwest of Jamaica, a commercial airliner and a search helicopter having spotted what they believed might be the ship. It was nearly dusk when the patrol boat's skipper called to Constantin.

'There. Three miles or so to the north. Is that her?'

'Well,' Constantin said, sarcasm thick in his words, 'I can see the dead crew from here, steering for their unholy port. Yes, *Flying Dutchman* is stenciled on her forward quarter.' He scowled. 'Idiot! Bring us closer!'

The lieutenant in command muttered something under his breath about 'Czarist aristocratic bastard' and altered course. Within minutes, there could be no doubt.

'*Reina del Mar*,' he said, 'as reported several days ago by a Cayman fisherman.'

'My God, Captain, you can read! You'd best suit up, then come alongside. Felipe, let's get our gear. We're going to board.'

The young sailor followed Constantin up the hastily rigged boarding ladder, though he kept looking back towards the relative safety of the patrol boat as though it were a vision of heaven. Constantin was already on deck.

'Hurry up with the equipment, you fool,' he shouted.

Constantin's first stop was the forward quarter, where the putrefying remains of two sailors lay. A few dead gulls littered the ground around them, but no living gull would approach, their instinct or sense of smell enough to warn them away from the bodies.

'Interesting,' Constantin said, prodding one of the bodies with a metal rod. Decay, naturally, but preceded by an obvious necrosis. See these lesions? Here … and here.' He turned to the sailor, who had spun away from the gory scene and was hunched over, hands on knees, trying not to be sick inside his suit.

'Useless,' Constantin grumbled. He activated his recording device and began a terse clinical description. 'Gross lesions, with bleeding and tissue discoloration. Difficult to be certain with all this decay and after the birds had their fill. The disease was apparently transmitted to the birds, their bodies also showing damage similar to the men's. The blood and secretions from the men are similar to that seen with Ebola.' He pulled back some of the men's tattered clothing. 'Although certain aspects more resemble bubonic plague. Hopefully, the bodies of the men on the bridge or below decks will be less disturbed and easier to diagnose.

'Felipe, are you able to accompany me?'

'No! Please no, Doctor. I c-can't.'

Constantin's frustration evaporated in an instant. Very few men were cut out for this type of work. 'Very well. Stay. Better yet, return to the patrol boat for disinfection. Tell your shipmates to do a thorough job. I

207

believe we're dealing with a virulent and highly contagious disease, means of transmission unknown. Oh, and leave the camera.'

Felipe rose shakily and handed the doctor a camera before nodding his gratitude and heading back to the ladder.

Men are so easily manipulated, Constantin thought, as he climbed the short stairway to the bridge. *A little kindness from a known bastard causes them to go blind. So much the better.*

There was only one man on the bridge, the captain. He was slumped over the wheel, his body partially jammed between it and the forward bulkhead, accounting for the ship's heading: long sweeping loops to port on a sea steadily in motion with current and tides. His face was contorted in agony, with festering sores on his cheeks and neck. Areas of his clothes, blackened and sticky, testified to numerous additional lesions beneath his clothing. At his feet, a pool of nearly black goo that had flowed down his body, filled his shoes, and spilled onto the deck. This had been several days ago. His eye sockets were empty and black, though nothing had entered the cabin to feast on dead tissue. In fact, the eyes seemed to have ruptured outward, lines of bloody pus tracing a clown's face of suffering.

Constantin took pictures, then collected tissue and blood samples—a necessary waste of effort.

Three other crewmen were found below. Two had died in their bunks, another on the floor of the head. Clenched jaws and fisted hands spoke to the excruciating pain that had accompanied their final moments. The other physical signs were similar to what he'd seen with the captain.

When Constantin was satisfied there was no more to be learned, he went back on deck and hailed the patrol boat.

'Ahoy, Captain. We need to remove these bodies for more detailed study.'

'No, sir. Those are not my orders. Have you completed your examination?'

'Yes, but you don't understand. What we have here is an extraordinarily deadly disease, clearly transmitted from one man to the other. And to the seagulls who've eaten the flesh.'

'Which is why I have been ordered to allow no material to be brought back to Jamaica.'

'Surely my samples?' Constantin held up a case.

'Leave it.'

'What! What was the purpose of coming here?'

'You have photos? You have a record of your examination?'

'Yes, but—'

'It will have to do.'

'This is nonsense. I'm coming aboard.'

Constantin swung a leg over the railing, but a sharp order from the captain froze him mid-motion. When he looked down, the boat had pushed back from the side of the *Reina del Mar* and two sailors were pointing rifles up at him.

'Please,' the captain said, 'do not put my orders to the test. Leave the case. Others can deal with this. Then come aboard to be disinfected. I will not repeat myself.'

With great care, Constantin place the case of samples on the deck and began his climb down as the patrol boat once again nudged the *Reina del Mar*'s side.

No one saw the tiny, twisted smile that flickered across Constantin's lips.

So easily manipulated.

***

Back in port, the doctor's audio record was quickly transcribed and his photos integrated into a package that was reviewed by a joint military panel, the Prime Minister, and key members of his cabinet.

Constantin spoke eloquently about the need to retrieve the bodies, if not actually sail the ship to a Jamaican port. He spoke of the horrible effects of the disease. The 100 percent mortality rate, he argued, might be grossly exaggerated. The ship was a small, enclosed community. No disease killed every infected individual. The death rate might be as low as 90 or even 80 percent in a general population.

The panel listened in horror to the graphic details then turned to the Prime Minister, who shook his head sadly. Jamaica was not a wealthy country, nor one with the medical facilities needed to contain and study the disease. Both the Cuban military and the American commander at Guantanamo had vowed to fire on the ship if it entered territorial waters. And with the ship's course so uncertain, what would become of his own people if it grounded on a Jamaican beach? Had the doctor been able to set a new course … But sadly, he wasn't a sailor.

Constantin became louder and more abusive until he was finally removed from the room, where the Prime Minister gave the order that was most welcome to the others assembled there.

***

A little past 3:00 a.m., explosive charges set at the waterline of the *Reina del Mar* by Jamaican commandos erupted in crimson glory. With the slight headway, the ship plowed its way beneath the waves as cabin after cabin flooded. The sailors watched until her stern rose into the air, the screw still turning, and she vanished beneath the waves. With a collective sigh of relief, the patrol boat headed back to port.

Twelve minutes later, the *Reina del Mar*, still carrying her crew of dead, nosed into the thick sand at the bottom of the Cayman Trench, all her secrets lost in the eternal frigid blackness of the abyss.

***

The following evening, two men sat at a table on the second-floor patio of The Quarterdeck, an upscale restaurant and bar in Montego Bay with clientele far superior to that found in the Mermaid. Certainly more wealthy.

A pleasant breeze wafted in the fresh saltwater-and-seaweed fragrance of the ocean, as though the decay and stench aboard the *Reina del Mar* had never existed. Constantin was relaxed as he sipped his dirty martini, made exactly to his taste, but his companion was nervous, fiddling with a bottle of Dos Equis that seemed sadly out of place.

'Relax, Lieutenant,' Constantin said. 'In addition to your being away from a nagging wife and squalling children—you do have a nagging wife and squalling children, don't you?—this is your big payday.'

The lieutenant thought to argue, but the arrogant Russian had a point. He tipped back his bottle, draining it, and called for another.

'There you are,' Constantin said, with a smirk. 'Live the high life while you can.'

The two sat silently for only a minute or two when a light cough announced the arrival of another man. Constantin smiled, but the lieutenant leaped up and said, 'Mr. Raynard. Please join us.'

210

Constantin lifted an eyebrow and caught the glint in the eye of the new arrival. 'Of course he'll join us. Why the hell else would he be here?'

'Thank you,' the man said, with mock formality. He ordered a drink, and as soon as the waiter had left, he reached into the pocket of his sport coat and pulled out an envelope, which he handed to the lieutenant. 'Please don't fiddle with that here,' he said, as the younger man lifted the flap and peered in. 'It contains what we agreed to—plus a 20 percent bonus. And now, if you don't mind, I need a little private time with Constantin.'

Once again, the lieutenant did his best impression of a jack-in-the-box, brought his hand up in an awkward salute, and turned to leave.

Another gentle cough brought his attention back to his employer. 'Just a last reminder,' the man said. 'If you speak a word of our association to anyone, including your family, you'll be found in the harbor with no tongue, no eyes, and no balls. Have a nice evening.'

The lieutenant's features were still frozen in terror as he turned away and hurried towards the exit.

'Really, *Raynard*,' Constantin said, with an evil grin, 'such drama. The poor young man will need to change his shorts. Even I almost believed you.'

'Almost?'

***

News of the sinking of the *Reina del Mar* slowly traveled the world, to be followed at light speed by a far more interesting story of a modern-day *Flying Dutchman*, a ship crewed by the dead.

Stone read the story with extreme skepticism, but flipped to page fourteen of *The Times* to finish the article. He sat up with a jolt as he eyed a photo of the ship taken from a helicopter and shuffled back to page two, where the article had begun.

'*Reina del Mar*,' he muttered, verifying the name of the ship. He turned back and stared at the low resolution black and white photo. But what he saw was not the *Reina del Mar*. Stripped of the color that had effectively camouflaged her, and ignoring a few minor details, he was looking at the *Saint Martin*, a ship with which he and Randy were all too familiar.

'What the fuck?'

***

On another continent across the Atlantic, the words were repeated by a furious Carlos the Viper. He turned to the flunky who had innocently handed him the morning paper and a cup of coffee.

'What is this?' he bellowed, bringing his fist down on the table with such force that coffee sloshed out.

'What? I don't understand, *patrón*,' the horrified man said. 'Today's newspaper. You always read the newspaper with your morning coffee.'

Carlos crushed one end of the paper and swatted the man across the face.

'Fool! Send for Ramón, then make yourself useful. I want every online article about this ship printed and on this table in fifteen minutes, or you'll be spitting teeth and eating through a straw for the rest of your miserable days. Go!'

When Ramón arrived, Carlos shoved the newspaper at him.

Too frightened to comment, Ramón read mutely, his eyes widening.

'Is it true? A ship of the dead?'

'Idiot! Dead or alive, what matters is she's sunk. MY SHIP! SUNK! Someone will pay for this!'

'Wasn't the ship being used by Raynard?'

The volcano that had erupted in Carlos was suddenly extinguished, replaced by an even more threatening glacial calm.

'It was. This is all Raynard's fault, mark my words. Some bullshit, underhanded scheme.'

Carlos sat in silence while Ramón reread the entire article. When the young man returned with a stack of papers, Carlos flipped through them, verifying the essence of the story: Jamaican commandos had sunk the ship carrying a dead crew, their demise a result of some unknown disease. He set the papers down and turned a steely visage to Ramón.

'It's time for Jesse Raynard to die.'

Randy was nursing his second drink at a seedy bar near the harbor, wondering whether quitting the CIA had been such a good idea.

Chapter Twelve

Trying to Solve the Puzzle

The Quarterdeck Tavern and Restaurant, Montego Bay, Jamaica

'Peace at last and a quiet dinner,' Constantin said, though his focus was on the contents of his wineglass, recently poured from a bottle of Cabernet that would cost Carl nearly four hundred dollars.

'You should drink that and not just stare at it,' Carl remarked. 'Ten dollars is lost to evaporation every minute.'

'Pfh! Drink it? I'm *enjoying* it. The lovely color, the delicate nose. I certainly *plan* to drink it, but slowly, like making love to a beautiful woman. If your only wish is to become intoxicated, that swill you're drinking will do.'

'Ah, my friend, Jack and I have been acquainted these long years, and we've shared many a strange story.' He coughed. 'Sadly, we all know how the story ends. I have less time than you to savor life or make love to a glass of wine.'

Constantin gave him a sour look and took a delicate sip before saying, 'So you're Jesse Raynard. Imagine my surprise.'

This brought a soft chuckle and a smile from Carl. 'You played along rather well.'

'Seemed like the right thing to do at the time. Besides, I instantly realized you'd owe me a favor.'

'You may be overstating the value of your extraordinary impromptu acting, Constantin.'

The waiter arrived at that moment, placing French fried lobster and a tub of seasoned melted butter in front of Carl. A side dish of asparagus brought a scowl to his face.

'I thought I asked you to skip the greenery,' Carl said.

Before the embarrassed waiter could get more than a few apologetic words out, Constantin darted out with a fork, stabbed an asparagus, and plunged it into his mouth. He finished chewing and pointed with his fork to the table in front of him. 'Leave that. It's not bad. Ah,' he said, eyeing his main course. 'Manta ray steaks seared over a charcoal fire then baked in olive oil with capers and mushrooms. Only a fool would order any other main course.'

The stunned waiter finished placing fresh bread and hurried off. The Russian had been here before—sadly, many times—and the waiters fought to *not* serve him. He was just as likely to throw a plate of undercooked linguini as to leave a huge tip.

'You're still as big of an arrogant ass as you were, my friend,' Carl said.

'I would not want to disappoint you by growing soft and tolerant over the years. Have you forgotten our time together at the CDC?'

'One of the few times I've seen a department head cornered by a raving lunatic brandishing a beaker full of urine. What was her name? Gabriella Ramstein, something like that. You were screaming at her in Russian, as I recall.'

'Ah, yes. She was an idiot, gone in three months. You should have gotten the appointment.' He savored a piece of ray. 'It was Gatorade in the beaker.'

'It was urine!'

Constantin laughed. 'Oh, all right, it was.' The smile slid from his face. 'Had you gotten the spiteful German's position, what a difference it might have made.'

'I was far too junior.'

'Age and capability,' Constantin said, waving a piece of ray, 'are seldom correlated. Yes. You should have been head. Perhaps then you wouldn't have become involved with the Extremely Hazardous Dirt Group—'

'Disease Research Group. The *EHDRG.*'

'Yes, certainly. Ah, my friend, I would have ridden your coattails to glory.'

Carl laughed so hard he went into a coughing fit. When he recovered, he said, 'You would have stabbed me in the back, had my coat patched and laundered—tails and all—and taken my place.'

'That is what I meant,' Constantin said, with a flourish.

Both were silent for a while. They knew Carl's life would be short and would end in pain. A decision had been made and payment was nearly due.

Towards the end of the meal, Constantin, recalling an earlier part of their conversation, glanced up and caught Carl's eye. 'What did you mean when you said "You may be overstating the value of your extraordinary impromptu acting"?'

'Verbatim! Your memory hasn't been dulled by that expensive soured-grape water.'

'Yes. My memory is intact, and you're dodging. As an aside, I'd love to meet this Jesse Raynard someday.'

'I hope you will. Quite an extraordinary individual—'

'Dodging.'

'No, not really. You see, my not-entirely-perceptive friend, Raynard is an exquisite planner. Had it been important for you to play along, I would have informed you in advance.'

Constantin gave him a puzzled look.

'Either reaction—playing along, or challenging the assertion that I was Raynard—would have suited our purpose. Your acting has earned you nothing,' he concluded.

Constantin continued to stare at Carl, his mouth hanging open.

'Oh,' Carl said, as an afterthought, 'if Raynard ever asks you to play poker ... run!'

***

With Yvette's help, Stone had been searching for articles on the mysterious sinking of the '*Flying Dutchman*,' hoping for more photos or perhaps a description of the ship. But their searching had been in vain. The few low-res pictures from the helicopter were all he had. He pushed back from the computer terminal and rubbed his eyes just as the phone rang.

'Jason Stone,' he answered brusquely, then added, 'uh, of Stone Security Services.'

'And this is Randy O'Neil, also of Stone Security Services. A vice president, in fact, though I still seem to get all the shit work.'

In the background, Stone could hear Chuck growling, '*Junior* vice presidents are a dime a dozen. Now get me a coffee.'

'I'm talking to Stone.'

The noise of another phone connecting.

'Hey, Stone,' Chuck said. 'I didn't think Randy'd get through. It's ... what time is it there, anyway?'

'Kinda late, I guess. It's been dark for a while.'

'Hell, it could be noon with the kind of fog you get in London.'

'It may be twelve-something, but it sure as hell isn't noon. What have you guys got?'

'Not much,' Randy said, his voice turning sullen. 'As for photos of the ship ... what the hell was her name?'

'*Reina del Mar*,' Chuck said, 'aka the *Flying Dutchman*.'

'Anyway, those helo photos you already found were the only ones. You'd think if any of the locals had gotten a snap they'd have run to the nearest newspaper office holding out their hand for cash, but nothing.'

'Which means no other photos,' Stone said.

'Actually, some guy had a few cell phone pics of a ship—too far away—and a closer shot of dead bodies that was *too* close. Sold them to a local rag in the Caymans.'

'So no *useful* pictures,' Stone amended.

'However,' Chuck said, 'I did get a few pictures of the *Saint Martin* when you guys were crawling around rescuing the human cargo and, incidentally, having all the fun.'

'Night photos?' Stone's voice was thick with skepticism.

'OK, so they're not much better than the helicopter pics, but I did manage to identify six distinct features of the *Saint Martin* that, give or take a coat of paint, are identical to those of the *Reina del Mar*. Unusual structural features—modifications or repairs. It would threaten credibility if two ships had those same mods.'

'To be fair, boss, there were fourteen differences that weren't just paintwork, but heavy metal.'

'You want some heavy metal? Try Led Zeppelin. I'm guessing she's the same boat.'

'Lead who? Anyway, I say it's not conclusive.'

'And I grudgingly agree,' Chuck said, 'though a little positivity wouldn't hurt.'

'Hang on a second, guys.' Stone's voice became muted. 'What have you got, Yvette?'

A brief, unintelligible conversation was followed by, 'This is great. Go to bed now, OK? I absolutely promise not to solve this mystery till morning.'

'Yvette is a computer wizard,' Stone said. 'She found a record of transit through the Panama Canal for the *Reina del Mar*. Prior to her transit, she apparently put into Talcahuano, Chile, for a refit.'

'But no photos?' Chuck asked.

'You haven't heard the best part yet,' Stone said. 'It's what Yvette didn't find.'

'What she *didn't* find?' Randy asked.

'Yeah. She didn't find any records of previous ports for the *Reina*.'

'Bad record keeping?' Chuck mused.

'There's more,' Stone said. 'The *Saint Martin*, as you know, was operating out of Puerto Barrios, Guatemala, when we found her. Had been for a while.'

'So?' Chuck and Randy together.

'Well, she rounded the Horn sometime later, after the CIA generously returned her to "her rightful owners."'

'An idiotic move,' Chuck grumbled. 'Wait. Are you saying—'

'Yvette couldn't find any other record of the *Saint Martin* after that trip. The timing, coincidentally, is within a month of the magical appearance of the *Reina del Mar*.'

There was silence on the other end of the line.

'Now comes the tricky part,' Stone said, 'the part Yvette is still unsure about. Turns out there isn't any evidence—dockyard records, et cetera—of *Reina del Mar*'s refit in Chile. However, her last stop prior to passing through the canal was a long one, in Puerto Esperanza. She entered port at night, or maybe she didn't, the reports are confusing. The other confusing thing is that her documents of construction and registry seem weird.'

'Weird?' Chuck asked.

'Too new. Supposedly recovered from archived data after a fire in some records office in some shipyard in some country ...'

'Wait a minute,' Randy said. 'I'm getting confused. Give me the dumb person's version.'

Stone took a deep breath. 'Remember, Yvette said this is speculation and I agree. The *Saint Martin* was a well-known ship, and the Agency was undoubtedly keeping tabs on her. The Viper, or a more intelligent person in his organization, says "Let's make a new ship from the old." They sail her around the Horn, never to be heard from again. A dozen plausible reasons why, the most believable being she was cut up for scrap. Another ship, the *Reina del Mar*, appears out of nowhere. Documents of her refit in Chile and of her very existence are dodgy. A mysterious stop in Puerto Esperanza, and the shiny *Reina* sails for Panama.'

Stone could hear the rasp of Chuck's hand across his whiskers before he spoke. 'That explains a hell of a lot. Paint is paint, but the physical structure of the ship could have been modified. It solves the mystery of why some features of the two ships are identical and some aren't. Faking the documents couldn't have been an easy task, either.'

'True,' Stone said. 'So, here's the deal. We can adopt a working hypothesis, subject to confirmation, that the *Saint Martin* was transformed into the *Reina del Mar*. A neat piece of magic. 'But that leaves us with a bigger mystery. How did she become the *Dutchman*? Or maybe a better question is "why?"'

***

'You see, Randy, when Stone asked "Anyone feel like an all-expenses-paid visit to Central America?" my response was no,' Chuck said. 'You didn't say anything, which means you volunteered. Silence gives consent, get it?'

Chuck had been patiently explaining to Randy why his new assignment involved a trip to the garden spot of Puerto Esperanza. Explaining in the same way a cat would explain to a canary that it was about to be eaten.

'Doesn't seem right ... or fair,' Randy grumbled. 'You'd think a warm climate would suit your old bones.'

'Too humid!' Chuck countered, with an annoyingly wide grin. 'You're young and spry. A quick trip, a little sleuthing, and presto, you've solved the mystery of the *Saint Martin / Reina del Mar / Flying Dutchman*.

You should be thanking me for the opportunity to be a hero. The Sherlock Holmes of Triple S.'

'Oh, Lord, enough already, Chuck. I might just puke. Well, since I'm stuck, I'm gonna hold you to that whole "hero" thing.'

***

It certainly was humid in Puerto Esperanza, plus unseasonably hot. Randy was nursing his second drink at a seedy bar near the harbor, wondering whether quitting the CIA had been such a good idea. He'd been sitting long enough for the stink of stale beer and cigar smoke to become less noticeable, and he could only hope the new odor of unwashed human wasn't his own.

He'd been carrying on a halting conversation with the tavern keeper, using his hard-earned Spanish. Gail was fluent and had encouraged him to learn, making a reasonable case that it would be valuable in a border state like Arizona. Unfortunately, his growing capability had been cited by Chuck as another reason for Randy to travel to Central America to investigate the miraculous transforming freighter. He took another pull of warm beer and silently cursed Chuck for being a sadist.

He was startled out of vengeful musings when the bartender prodded him and pointed to a table tucked under a flickering, muted television. A soccer game occasionally caught a glance from the few patrons, though most ignored it. The newcomers, two worn but rough-looking men, clearly had no interest in the game, but were motioning impatiently to the bartender.

'That is them,' the bartender said. 'Jesus and Octavio, I think. These are the men who work on the far side of the harbor, mostly cutting metal for scrap. They may have seen your ship.'

'Armando,' one called to the bartender, 'tequila. Now.'

Randy also heard some choice words about the bartender's ancestry and sexual habits, words never used by Gail. The meaning was clear enough. After a brutal day of heat, noise, and fumes, they planned to drink themselves into oblivion before heading home, and the sooner the better.

The bartender gave Randy a questioning look. Randy nodded and threw a few bills on the counter in exchange for a bottle of tequila and two glasses. He grinned nervously and headed for the table.

The two men looked up at Randy balefully as he approached.

'Go away. We didn't order a bottle. Especially añejo. Only a rich gringo can afford añejo.'

'Not that we would mind drinking it,' said the less surly of the two. He looked pointedly past Randy and called out, 'Armando, who's your new gringo waiter? Is he stupid? Send over two shots of the usual.'

'You say you wouldn't mind drinking this,' Randy said, holding up the bottle. 'Would you mind drinking it with me if I was buying?'

The friendlier man turned to his companion. 'What do you say?'

'Look here,' the first one said, 'nobody gives away tequila. *Good* tequila. You must want something, so spell it out or fuck off.'

Another word Randy hadn't learned from Gail. He smiled inwardly. A formal education in Spanish was hardly useful. 'You're correct. I want something. Information. But I'm not the police, an underling of your employer, or a reporter. Tomorrow I'll be gone and you won't see me again. However, if I like the information, if it's useful, another bottle of this will be waiting for you tomorrow.'

At this, both men looked towards Armando, who nodded.

'Well, a generous gringo. Fine. Sit. We are full of useful information.'

The old wooden chair creaked under Randy's weight as he sat. He unstoppered the bottle and poured two shots.

'What, you won't join us in a drink?' the first man said. 'How rude. No one expects you to keep pace, gringo, but it would be better if you drank.'

Randy turned and raised a hand, but Armando was already on the way with a third shot glass. The friendlier man, who introduced himself as Octavio, poured Randy's shot. 'First we drink, like fine amigos.' Randy joined the other two, who tossed their shots back like experts.

'Oh, *si!*' Octavio said. 'Very fine.' He splashed the three glasses full again. 'Now, ask your questions.'

Randy began with simple questions about the men, their families, the type of work they did. He did this both to put them at their ease and to allow the soothing effects of alcohol to dull the edges of their natural suspicion. Unfortunately, these men were hard drinkers, and he'd barely gotten his first hint of a smile from the grim Jesus before he'd run out of preliminaries. And though he'd been drinking cautiously, either Jesus or Octavio would invariably top up his glass when he'd sipped it half empty.

He cleared his throat. 'Um, so you're both metal workers, though most of your jobs are scrapping.'

Jesus raised a suspicious eyebrow. '*Si*, we told you this.'

Randy tried a casual laugh. No good. 'Umm, have you ever done any work on a ship named *Saint Martin*?'

Both men froze, drinks to their lips. They exchanged a glance. Octavio drank, but Jesus lowered his glass carefully to the sticky table. 'What do we care what a ship's name is? If she's metal and they tell us to cut, we cut.'

'Oh, I was just—' Randy began.

Jesus stopped him with a motion of his hand. 'Why do you care? You are with the insurers, no?'

'What? No.'

The two men gave him a hard stare. Randy had anticipated this, knowing he might have to give information to get information.

He leaned forward and lowered his voice. 'Look,' he said, 'the *Saint Martin* was used for human trafficking.'

Both men seemed startled. They didn't know. In fact, they might even have friends or family in towns where traffickers had taken people. Good. They were no allies to modern-day slavers. Randy pressed on. 'The ship was stopped by ... U.S. federal agents. I'm working for a humanitarian group to make sure she isn't being used that way again.'

Jesus reclaimed his drink and tossed it down. 'Filthy bastards, selling humans. Not like a good whorehouse. Those women work and get a share. But these. Women, children, even men, just as you say. Slaves. May the slavers rot in hell.'

Randy was shocked to see the bottle emptied as Jesus refilled his glass. He motioned to Armando. 'Another.'

'Not to worry,' he added more quietly. 'Whatever you don't finish tonight *plus* a fresh bottle will be waiting for you tomorrow. Now, the *Saint Martin* ...?'

'She came in late one rough night,' Octavio said. 'Raining to choke the frogs. Me and Jesus were finishing up a double shift, chopping up an old trawler, when Socorro—'

'Socorro is the night shift foreman,' Jesus interrupted. Randy was pleased to hear a slight slurring of his words. *At last!* he thought.

'I was getting to that!' Octavio grumbled. 'Where the hell was I? Socorro, he says, "You two men leave that. Go home and get some rest. For the next week, maybe two, you work on that." He pointed to the freighter.

'"What?" I said. "Scrap a ship that size? Here?"'

'"I didn't say scrap, did I, you fool."'

'No,' Jesus chimed in, grinning ear to ear. 'He didn't say fool. He say "idiot." Oh, ha ha ha!'

'Shut up! And you thought the same as me at the time, you drunken son of a whore.'

Jesus shrugged. '*Si*. That is true.'

Octavio waved his hand at Jesus in disgust. 'Socorro, he says, "You just cut where I say cut, weld where I say weld, and grind where I say grind. Do that, work twelve-hour shifts, and keep your mouths shut and you get double pay for the duration. *Si*, idiot, double!"'

'I told you,' Jesus remarked. 'He say "idiot."'

'But the ship,' Randy said quickly, 'was she the *Saint Martin*?'

'I thought I said?' Octavio looked puzzled. 'I didn't say?'

Randy fought back the urge to reach across the table and slap the confused look from his face, though there seemed to be two Octavios now, and he wasn't sure which one to hit. Jesus saved him the bother.

'*Si*. The *Saint Martin* when she came in, but not when she left.' He began to giggle.

'Who is the idiot now?' Octavio asked. '*Si*. We cut, welded, and ground, while others painted. The stench! By the time the big boss arrive, the *Saint Martin* is pfff, and she is ...' He nudged his friend. 'What did they paint on her?'

'The *Ray*? *Manta Ray*? No, no. *Ray del Mar*!'

'Not *Ray*, *Reina*,' Octavio said. '*Reina del Mar*, that was it.'

Randy smiled. Confirmation! But he had forgotten something. Something important. Octavio had made a passing comment that Randy was certain was crucial. He focused, his head throbbing. Ah!

'Big boss. You said by the time the big boss arrived. What big boss?'

'Oh, we're not supposed to tell,' Jesus said, with a shrug. 'But for you, our amigo.' He reached out a hand and patted Randy's cheek. 'His name is ... I don't know his name! But to everyone he is just the Viper.'

***

A light rain had done nothing to relieve the day's heat as the three men stood outside the tavern. Barely half a bottle of tequila had been reclaimed by the bartender, to be offered up tomorrow along with another full one. Octavio and Jesus had each insisted on giving Randy a long, drawn-out hug, while singing his praises as a fine amigo and hoping he'd catch the evil slavers.

If only they knew, Randy thought, but then realized even thinking hurt his head. *I hate tequila*. At last, the two ironworkers staggered off, and Randy spent a tense few minutes trying to remember where his hotel was. It came to him at last, and he moved off on tiptoe, the impact of his feet on the ground threatening to explode his cranium. His last coherent thought as he staggered towards the hotel was, *Shit, it's hot*.

Despite the buzz of angry hornets that filled his head, he could hear Robin Williams voice from *Good Morning Vietnam*. 'It's hot. Damn hot. Real hot ...'

***

Snow was falling steadily as Raynard tossed a log into the fireplace. At least three inches had fallen already, with the promise of another six by morning. This was why Raynard loved the mountains. The beautiful silence and solitude, the covering of old sins with a blanket of white. True, the calm wouldn't last. There was nothing so dramatic as a spray of blood across fresh snow. The Viper's men were surely on the way by now. Raynard swirled cognac in a large snifter. Preparations were complete, and Jesse Raynard loved a good show.

***

October, 2012

Everyone liked a scary Halloween movie. At least, teenage boys did, and they spent good money to see them. Sometimes as a group, sometimes with a date they hoped would cuddle up close during the gory scenes. Many of these movies were pablum. Lots of chainsaws, knives, and meat hooks dripping a gooey liquid that could never be mistaken for blood. Rated PG-13, they relied on hokey scenarios and blaring musical stingers to coax out the requisite jumps from the audience. Classic tales of horror like *Alien* would include at least one

225

high-definition scene so distasteful and graphically gory that later scenes need only *imply* violence to keep an audience terrified. It was a clever touch and avoided the repetition that dulled exposed nerves. A typical zombie movie, for instance, became boring after the third or fourth shotgun blast to the head. But there was a third type of horror movie. Cinéma vérité! A movie that delivered hideous scenes of agony at a pace that took the exposed nerves, attached them to electrodes, and applied power again and again.

After working on several monster movies, slasher flicks, and zombie funfests, a relative newcomer to the City of Angels known only as I. M. collaborated on just such a movie. The title was innocuous enough: *Inquisition*. Based on the brutal period of the Church's history, it followed the fate of a noble English family captured in Spain, tried, convicted, and slowly destroyed while futile attempts at rescue failed. The scenes were so grisly, and drawn out over such long intervals, that even the most hardcore viewers found themselves wishing a swift end for the unfortunates. The deaths of the children precipitated threats of an X rating until the producers made cuts, much protested by the director and the special effects creator. It was rumored that, in the pursuit of absolute realism, I. M. had rejected the use of pig bones for sound effects, and had actually purchased corpses, including those of children, to correctly represent the gruesome snapping as the torturer did his work.

Religious groups, assured that they were witnessing a high-budget snuff film, protested vigorously outside theaters and the well-guarded estates of the producers. Only pitchforks and torches were lacking.

For the young master of special effects, both the movie and the reaction were delightful.

I. M. loved a good show!

***

Raynard's fire cast dancing shadows across the hearth and floor. Cherokee was out hunting, though Raynard expected her back soon. When she arrived, it would be time to move. Now was a time for introspection. Plans had been going well, and soon the situation with Carlos the Viper would be resolved. He'd been nothing more than a sideshow for several years—useful in some ways, even mildly entertaining, but now an irritant. The main act was underway and would need constant supervision. One never knew, in a live performance, what could go wrong. The key to success was meticulous planning and preparation, but Raynard had seen many a performer fail when a minor glitch occurred. Given enough shows, it was bound to happen. Then, only the truly superior actor, magician, or musician, with wits as sharp as broken glass, could still dazzle an audience.

Introspection. It rankled a bit. The inevitable question surfaced as Raynard considered the breathtaking enterprise now underway. One word. One syllable. Why?

There was satisfaction, naturally, in doing a job well. Every worker in every profession from janitor to astronaut could feel the warmth from accomplishing an assigned task; warmth like the heat from the pale embers of a dying fire. But these feelings were mundane. Commonplace.

At another level, one might achieve admiration for accomplishing what few others could. An Olympic gymnast sticking a landing, a naval aviator sticking a landing of another kind, a painter or sculptor creating a flawless facial expression in a work of art. That was nearer the mark for Raynard. Not embers, but a tumbling fire like the one in Raynard's fireplace. Logs crackled and flames leapt. Heat and light aplenty.

There was only one additional step. Supreme achievement. Becoming Caesar or Stalin. A person either feared, admired, or hated by the entire world. The flames became an inferno that blazed in glory or infamy, too hot and brilliant to be endured, and then vanished, leaving only echoes that reverberated over centuries.

When Rogelio forced himself around the last corner of the house, all he saw was a smear of scarlet against the pure white of the snow, leading from the base of the steps through snow-covered brush and into the woods.

Chapter Thirteen

Confrontation

Ramón had accepted the assignment to kill Jesse Raynard with trepidation. He had no choice, of course, but that didn't mean he was eager to take on the Viper's mysterious associate. And he wasn't a fool. Without asking permission, he'd recruited four of the Viper's best men. In this case, asking would have been a time-wasting formality. Ramón had never seen the Viper so livid and so eager for a life to be extinguished. There had been no suggestions of a slow death, let alone of bringing Raynard back alive. No. Jesse Raynard's death was the one thing the Viper demanded.

Just as well, Ramón thought, as he entered the tavern in Albuquerque where his four assassins had gathered, waiting for instruction. Three of the men were large, hard-eyed killers, their numerous scars a reminder that their adversaries had fared worse. The fourth man seemed out of place in this group. Smaller, with undamaged skin and nervous eyes that darted behind his glasses, he had the look of a cartel bookkeeper, not an assassin. In this case, a deception. Ángel had earned the reputation as 'the quiet killer' and earned it well. He had never engaged in a fair fight. Men and women had fallen to a knife between the shoulder blades or a razor swept across their throats as he grabbed their hair from behind. In this cadre of killers, he was feared but not respected. Ramón had chosen him because he had a brain as well as complete indifference to murder.

Ramón pulled up a chair and passed a large envelope to Ángel. 'Here are your U.S. IDs, cash, and directions to Raynard's home in the mountains. Approach cautiously. Raynard is a trickster. I'll wait for your return.'

No one commented on the fact that Ramón would be the field marshal for this expedition, but would not be joining the group for the kill.

One of the large men asked, 'What about the dog?'

'Not a dog,' another said. 'A wolf.'

'Half dog, half wolf. What do you say, Ángel?'

Ángel shrugged. 'Dog or wolf, we kill it. There are four of us. From what you've told me, Raynard is not a fighter. Two men deal with the dog. José and I kill Raynard. Take pictures. Lots of pictures.'

Ramón considered. 'Take Raynard's head and bring it with you. Better than pictures, *si*?'

The three big men laughed, while Ángel smiled a death's-head grin.

***

Ramón paced his hotel room, gnawing at his fingernails. The four men had left the day before, piled into a well-equipped off-road Jeep, and had checked in when they'd set up camp five miles from the cabin. The snow was an inconvenience, and the men weren't used to it, but Ángel had insisted they approach on foot and strike during daylight hours to give no advantage to the wolf-hound.

But despite his cleverness, Ángel was no intellectual match for Jesse Raynard. In this battle of wits, it was fair to say Jesse had already won.

***

'We've seen no wolf,' José whispered. 'Only Raynard walking around the cabin. It's big. Bigger than most houses. And there are no tracks of the animal either.'

Ángel held out a hand, collecting snowflakes, then slapped José abruptly. 'Idiot! Of course you see no tracks! Have you heard of snow?'

The slap hadn't been nearly hard enough to muzzle José. He was cold and they'd been waiting for hours. 'I say we go in, do the job, and get the hell out of here. The sun is already setting.'

This last point was valid. It was after 3:00, and fall shadows were already creeping like vines across the landscape. Mountains to the west would hide the sun in less than an hour. Ángel nodded tersely. 'Rogelio, you and Esteban watch the exits. If you don't hear from me after ten minutes, follow us into the house. Keep an eye out for the wolf.'

'You and José?'

Ángel grinned. 'We go through the front door, like civilized men.'

José was already reaching for a small explosive that would shatter the door when Ángel felt his first warning twinge. The smile slid from his face. The door was unlocked. He hesitated only a moment before pulling his gun and signaling for José to do the same. He glanced back to Rogelio's position (Esteban had already moved to a rocky spur overlooking the other side of the house).

'This Raynard is a trusting soul, leaving a door unlocked,' Ángel said. He shrugged. 'Let's go.'

A soft pressure on his arm stopped him. 'What if the dog is inside, Ángel?'

'Shoot it. *Madre de Dios*!'

Nevertheless, Ángel opened the door slowly, feeling a slight resistance, until José, positioned to his right, had a clear view into the corridor and whispered, 'Clear.'

A nagging thought gnawed at Ángel as the door, still gently resisting his push, opened into the hallway. José followed quickly. The hydraulic mechanism above the door whose resistance Ángel had felt closed the door behind them. There was a muffled but distinct sound of a bolt sliding home. Both men turned. Only then did they notice that the door, which had a rustic wooden façade outside, was smooth steel. José's small explosive charge wouldn't have made a dent.

Ángel nodded and José reached for the knob. 'Locked.'

A voice from an unseen speaker said, 'If you want the key, you'll have to earn it.'

Both men started, but the hallway was empty, stretching fifteen feet or so ahead, where it opened into a large room.

Ángel recovered first, and with his best bravado he replied, 'So, the clever Jesse Raynard is now trapped in a house with two professional killers. Brilliant.'

A low laugh built up to an almost insane cackling. 'Yes! Now you have me! Oh, what to do? Ha ha ha!'

'Call the boys,' Ángel said. 'Have them come down. Tell them to force the door or find another way in.'

José pulled his phone and began dialing, but was soon tugging on Ángel's sleeve like a five-year-old. 'No signal, boss.'

'What? There was plenty outside.'

Another burst of laughter. 'You men must be familiar with cages. Ever hear of a Faraday cage? Well, you're in one. It's a little like a Roach Motel. You know, roaches check in but nothing checks out? Your cell phone signal included. Still, all you have to do is find me and kill me. The key is in my pocket. Good luck.'

Silence except for heavy breathing. Then, unexpectedly, the sound of a violin playing a melancholy tune like a dirge.

'My own composition,' Raynard said, 'though I prefer jazz. Enjoy.'

'This Raynard is loco!' José said, when the tension finally overcame him. 'Did you know this? And Ramón did not come with us. Ángel, what the hell is going on?'

'Shut up, you fool. Raynard can obviously hear us.'

'Ángel,' he said, unsubdued, 'what do we do?'

Ángel raised his voice. 'We kill the motherfucker, roast the mutt over a slow fire, and drink all the good tequila. Now let's go.'

***

Jesse had overseen the house's construction, employing only highly qualified but vulnerable individuals—men subject to threats or blackmail—to complete all the rough work, discretion being almost as valuable as mechanical skill. The finishing touches had been applied by I. M. personally. *Never send a boy to do a man's job.* Raynard had laughed at the irony.

The house had been designed primarily for defense. A simple heavy-steel box would accomplish as much. Dull and efficient. Efficiency was certainly a trademark of Raynard, but dullness? Never! This house embodied creativity and flair.

***

Ángel and José moved forward towards the unknown room ahead. There was no other option. With a suddenness made even more terrifying by the eerie tune that haunted them, the floor beneath them dropped away, and both tumbled into the dark below. Stunned, Ángel searched for his gun, lost in the fall. José sat massaging a twisted ankle.

The corridor they had fallen into was dimly lit by a spectral green-tinged light coming from the same direction as the well-lit room above. Ángel was the first to recover his wits.

'Get up,' he ordered.

'My ankle ...'

'It'll be your head if you don't get up. Use the light on your phone and let's see where we are.'

José struggled to his feet and lit the corridor. The path behind them ended in a solid steel wall and the grey walls on either side had no openings.

A sudden jolt left both men staggering to regain their balance.

'God have mercy, Ángel! What's happening?'

The floor beneath them was slowly sliding back, creating a dark opening. When the two approached, they could see a drop of no less than fifteen feet. Worse, the room below was studded with steel spikes protruding a foot or two from the floor.

'Fuck this,' Ángel growled. 'Give me a boost, we'll go back up and wait for the boys.'

But as he pointed to the ceiling, the panel that had dropped beneath them swung back into position.

José was crossing himself rapidly and muttering an Our Father.

Ángel cuffed him with the butt of his gun. 'Stop that superstitious nonsense. It won't help and we—'

His back hit the wall behind him. 'Damn it!'

The opening to the pit below was growing larger as the floor beneath them slid back. Soon it would disappear beneath the dead-end wall, and they would both fall onto the spikes.

Ángel considered his only remaining option. 'We can still jump the opening, get to the other side.'

'Ángel, my ankle!'

'I'll go first, then you jump and grab my arm. If you don't, you're skewered.'

Without waiting for a response, Ángel took two short steps and leapt over the gap, clearing the opening by almost a foot.

'Easy, see? Now jump.'

The remaining platform barely gave José one long step before he pushed off with his good foot. The sole of his other foot came down on the edge of the gap, the force translating through his injured ankle.

'Aiee!' he screamed, as he teetered on the edge. 'Ángel!'

With the quickness of a lizard, Ángel braced himself and grabbed José's arm. He gave a tremendous heave and José landed face first on the floor at his feet.

'There,' Ángel said, pulling him upright. 'You see. Raynard isn't infallible. We must keep our heads and—'

A deep bass growl like the sound of an avalanche reverberated in the hallway. Neither man said a word, but faced the green light. Ángel rubbed his eyes. There was something strange about the room ahead that prevented his eyes from focusing.

An even louder growl, and then Cherokee's massive head blocked the passage ahead. She froze as she caught sight of the two men. In a blur of motion, she leaped.

José's scream as he staggered backward was drowned by three sharp cracks as Ángel fired.

José stepped back into empty air, then toppled into the pit. A thud like bread dough hitting a table was followed by a long, gurgling sigh and the sound of the floor sliding back into place.

Ángel was in a shooter's crouch, but his head was down, his eyes screwed shut as he waited for the agonizing pain of the wolf's first bite. Time passed, and he was still alive, still breathing. He looked up slowly and saw ... nothing. Nothing, that is, except the vague green of the room ahead, three neat black holes in a respectable grouping now marring its surface.

'Oops,' Raynard's voice said. 'Sorry, that was just a home movie. Maybe a bit too realistic?'

Ángel barely understood the words. He was still hearing the echoes of the wolf-hound, the wet thud, and that last gurgling sigh. He rose to his feet, his gun quivering in his hand, and approached the green wall. He pushed the muzzle of his gun into one of the holes and it tore slightly. A projection screen of some kind.

Raynard could see the fear in Ángel's eyes. He knew he was outmatched. It was time to make the offer.

'If you want to leave, you can. I make this offer once, conditional on you taking your two remaining friends with you.'

'Where are you?' Ángel yelled.

'That would be telling. So, will you leave? I don't need you dead, I need you gone.'

'José died like a pig! Why should I trust you?'

'Because your alternative is dying. A clever man like you should be able to make a choice between those two alternatives.'

But Raynard knew there was another factor involved, and Ángel soon stated it. 'If I leave, if I let you live, the Viper will cut out my beating heart and shove it into my mouth.'

'He won't be alive much longer. I hear Brazil is nice. Why not take a nice vacation until you hear the word: the king of the Mexican and Central American cartels is dead!'

For a moment, Ángel teetered on the edge of uncertainty, then his lips drew back in a snarl as anger overcame fear. 'Fuck you! Your overconfidence will be your death! Think of my reward when I bring the *patrón* your head.'

Silence for a heartbeat. Two. Three. 'So be it. I assume you have a cell phone?'

Ángel didn't answer. He'd worked himself into a state of bravado and there was no backing down. He pulled a switchblade from his pocket. The blade flew out with a reassuring snap, and he sliced an opening in the screen. Beyond, another murky hallway. He carefully inspected the walls, ceiling, and, especially, the floor. A soft yellow light spilled from a room at the hallway's end. He saw a chair, a table. There was also a faint buzz.

He stepped through the opening.

***

'Ten minutes,' Esteban said over the phone. 'Ángel said—'

'I know what he said!' Rogelio snarled. 'When Ángel is gone, I'm in charge. Wait!'

It was a full fifteen minutes before Rogelio spoke again. 'Move in. Check doors and windows at your corner of the house, I'll check my side. And watch out for the damned dog!'

The house was built on a slight slope, with outdoor steps leading from the lower level to a deck on the main. Esteban checked the windows of the lower level first. Seemingly flimsy, he brought the butt of his gun against one of the panes. A dull thud. He struck harder. There was no cracking. Closer examination of the framing revealed steel members supporting what he now assumed was high-impact glass. Even if a gunshot would shatter the glass—which he doubted—he could never fit through the opening of a single pane, and he was convinced he couldn't bend or break the frame. That left the stairs to the next level.

'Any luck?' Rogelio asked.

'No. You?'

'These windows and doors aren't what they seem.'

'I know. I'm about to try the next level on my side.'

'I'll work my way around. Be careful.'

Rogelio's voice was replaced by a low rumble.

Esteban looked to the sky, the blue dimming to a deeper sapphire already, but the few puffy clouds weren't the source of this sound. It couldn't be thunder.

A repeat of the sound—louder—was followed by an animal snort of indrawn breath.

Esteban spun around and saw Cherokee, not twenty paces away, hackles raised, blue eyes like ice, ready to charge.

Fear overcame logic. Esteban never even pointed his gun, but turned and scampered up the icy stairs, fast as a squirrel. He was almost at the patio deck, and was thinking of turning to face the animal, when the stairs folded like Venetian blinds, becoming a slick incline of forty-five degrees. At the bottom, Cherokee waited.

An ungodly scream pierced the evening air, turning Rogelio's blood to ice. There were more screams, cries for help, fading into the distance. When Rogelio forced himself around the last corner of the house, all he saw was a smear of scarlet against the pure white of the snow, leading from the base of the steps through snow-covered brush and into the woods.

***

'Good girl,' Raynard said, ruffling the thick fur over Cherokee's shoulders. 'You're as intelligent as you are beautiful—and deadly. Now help me move the body back into the storage shed. We're coming to the finale.'

***

Rogelio was bent over, breathing hard. He'd emptied every last bit of undigested food and bile from his stomach, and was once again thinking clearly enough to pose this simple question: run or stay?

A speaker alongside the house crackled to life, and Raynard replied as though the words had been spoken aloud. 'I'd run. But then again, Cherokee is still out in the woods. She isn't really hungry, but she does enjoy a good hunt. Your chances of making it back to your vehicle aren't good. Like drawing to an inside straight. Three cards. If you stay …' A door on the ground floor popped open. 'You might as well come in out of the cold. Ángel is still inside. Alive. The two of you might still win, though the odds aren't much better than running. Still, I'd hate to die in the cold. I can promise it will be warm inside.'

Rogelio looked at the darkening sky and the bloody smear turning black as light trickled away. He moved cautiously to the door, kicked it fully open with his foot, and bellowed, 'Ángel? Are you there? Ángel?'

A voice that sounded like it came from the end of a long, twisting tunnel answered. 'Ro. Rogelio, is that you?'

'*Si*, I am just outside.'

'Esteban?'

'Dead. The wolf.'

A string of curses. 'I'm in some kind of fucking maze. Just hallways that keep changing. Prop the door open and get in here. Follow my voice.'

Rogelio shoved an ice-covered rock into the gap between the door and the frame, then wondered if this was such a good idea. The door seemed to be steel, and the wolf was outside. He scanned the snow-covered terrain nervously. 'Son of a bitch,' he muttered, and kicked the rock aside. He closed and opened the door several times then shut it. 'No wolf is going to get me from behind.' He stared down the dimly lit hallway. 'Ángel, I'm coming.'

At first, Ángel's voice grew stronger as Rogelio pressed forward, but after a few minutes, it began to fade. He stopped to backtrack, turned a corner, and nearly ran into a solid wall that hadn't been there a minute ago. 'What the hell? Ángel, the walls are moving!'

Ángel had just reached the same conclusion. Though he never saw it happening, he was certain steel panels were opening and closing, running the two of them in circles. 'Raynard, you coward!' he yelled. 'I'm getting tired of your games. Face me!'

'Why, so you can shoot me? I suppose I owe you a chance. Fine.'

A panel on the left wall slid open, revealing another hallway that vanished into darkness.

'Follow it.'

'I'll fall into one of your pits.'

'No more pits. I promise.'

'I spit on your promise!'

An indeterminate way down the hall, a faint light began to glow. 'Do you see me?'

A vaguely human form waved a hand.

'Your friend Rogelio is coming from the other direction.'

'Rogelio, are you there?'

'*Si*, Ángel,' he answered, unmuffled, maybe forty or fifty feet down the hallway. 'I can see Raynard.'

'Move forward. Slowly.'

Both men approached from either side of the faint specter, who was now smiling.

'Close enough,' Jesse snapped out. Ángel and Rogelio froze and scanned the floor, the ceiling, the walls. Nothing.

'Rogelio,' Raynard said calmly, 'I made an offer to Ángel that he rejected earlier. Unaccustomed as I am to repeating myself, I'll include him in the offer I now extend to you. Leave. Swear you'll never trouble me again, and just leave. I'll call off Cherokee. I lied. There's no sport in killing you. We've all had our little game, and it ended the only way it could.'

'Why should I—'

'Silence!' Raynard commanded, effortlessly cutting across Rogelio's words. 'Listen carefully. You men came here to kill me, and your deaths won't cause me to lose a minute's sleep. But … it's not necessary.'

'No,' Ángel said. 'But your death is.' He saw his companion's hand begin to lower. 'Think, Rogelio, of the reward we will receive from the Viper. Just the two of us now. But if we fail, nowhere will be safe. Not for you. Not for your family.'

Rogelio's gun rose again and his grip tightened.

'Shoot and you'll never leave this house alive,' Raynard said. 'Take my offer. There are ways to keep you and your family safe from the Viper. A dead snake can't bite.'

'Lies!' Ángel shrieked. 'Fire, Ro!'

Both men raised their guns and shots echoed in the corridor. A piercing hot pain scored Ángel's ribs. He continued firing, then felt a shove to the center of his chest, followed by another. His magazine empty, the suddenly leaden gun slipped from his fingers and he dabbed at the hot, sticky fluid pulsing from his body. He slipped to his knees just as Rogelio collapsed in a boneless heap.

The flickering hologram of Raynard seemed to look from one to the other. 'Damn fools.'

Another wall panel slid open and Raynard stepped into the hall, the simulacrum vanishing.

'Raynard,' Ángel whispered. 'Are you a ghost?'

'No. But you, my friend, are now among the angels. Or devils. There's irony for you.'

Ángel let out a long sigh and fell face first to the floor.

***

What the hell was I thinking? Randy asked himself, for about the millionth time. He'd been sitting in a dusty jail cell in the town of Pina, southeast of the crushing mass of Mexico City, reviewing every mistake he'd made since leaving Puerto Esperanza. The first, and most obvious, was in not going straight home after completing his mission. Christ, an ex-CIA man ought to know that! You don't get extra credit for doing more sleuthing. He'd found out the truth about the *Saint Martin* and the *Reina Del Mar*, and he knew Carlos the Viper was involved. But there were things that just didn't add up. His two fine amigos from the tavern—he involuntarily brought a hand to his temple recalling the insane tequila hangover he'd suffered the next day—identified the big boss as the Viper. However, Octavio had mentioned another person there, and he and Jesus had argued about who really controlled the ship. Had that been in the bar or during the fond farewell outside? Randy was amazed he could remember anything.

But that wasn't all. The men had assumed that, under her new guise, the ship would resume her slave trade. Logical. Yvette confirmed the *Reina del Mar*'s transit through the Panama Canal. Time had passed. Enough for several Atlantic crossings. And then she'd become the modern-day *Dutchman*. A ship crewed by the dead. That left several new mysteries. What had she been doing, and how had she become a death ship? These questions were bad enough, but in a quiet part of Randy's mind, there was a barely formed question he didn't want to ask. It was the CIA who'd returned the ship to Carlos. Why in the hell hadn't they been tracking her? Or were they?

These questions had led him on his extracurricular journey to Mexico. He had good intel on where the Viper was staying—a huge villa southeast of Mexico City near the town of Pina. Full of enthusiasm, he'd decided to come here and ask a few questions. Maybe he'd get lucky. But he'd forgotten a fundamental truth: there are two kinds of luck.

Everyone in Pina knew he didn't belong there. It was obvious because of his clothes and his execrable Spanish. And asking questions? About the Viper, for the love of God! The grounds of the villa were just visible from the small hill at the town's center, where a dusty church stood, but no one spoke of the villa, no one glanced in that direction. It was a tumor come to their vicinity, and the townsfolk hoped and prayed it would vanish on its own if they only ignored it long enough.

Randy grew unpopular quickly and decided to take another tack. An enterprising street urchin wearing sandals and a sombrero that must have been handed down from an older sibling offered him a packet of Chiclets, and Randy struck up a conversation. The hat kept flopping down over the boy's eyes, but he pushed it back with determination and gave Randy a few answers, some possibly truthful, others—trained bulls patrolled the grounds of the estate—blatant invention. A shout from down the street cut the boy's chatter short.

'I have to go now,' he'd said. 'Papá is calling and he sounds angry.'

'Oh, I hope we can talk more later. What does your poppa do?'

The boy drew himself up proudly. 'He is the sheriff!'

***

That had been two days ago. Randy knew that word of his arrest had been sent to the estate. The young boy had happily told him so when he delivered meals. Apparently, the Viper hadn't yet made time to interrogate a nosy gringo. It wouldn't be long, however. Once they confirmed his name and his status as ex-CIA, Randy expected a long, unpleasant discussion.

Talks with Julio, the Chiclet entrepreneur, were Randy's only distraction from lonely hours revisiting his many bad decisions. It was fruitless, he knew, but his mind would torment him, logically pointing out where his logic had failed. On the second night, he found he couldn't sleep at all, thinking of Gail and his son, alone after his death. He had no illusions of ever returning from the mysterious, green-shrouded villa.

He had tested every aspect of his cell, usually three or four times a day, but it was solidly built, though old. The bars of the small window were well set in the surrounding block with no sign of rust or other weakness. The cell door was equally sturdy, with heavy vertical iron bars and a massive lock. Just across the small, dusty room, a ring of keys hung on a wooden peg behind the sheriff's desk. A total of three keys dangled there, one for each of the three cells, the other two cells empty. A picture of jailed pirates waving a bone and trying to coax a reluctant dog, keys in mouth, to come just a bit closer to their cell—a *Pirates of the Caribbean* image—brought a tiny smile to his lips. But there was no bone, no dog, and no chance to get the keys.

Julio cheerfully delivered lunch, sliding a tray through a gap beneath the door, and chatted through the bars. Randy listened with half an ear.

'My mother and father, they fight over you. *Si*, it is true! Mamá says Papá was a fool to tell men from the evil place about you. Mamá says he should let you go.'

Randy snapped to attention. 'And your poppa, what does he say?'

'Oh, he is wise, so he agrees with Mamá. Two nights ago, she refused to feed him. She say there is no food in our house for fools!' Julio laughed heartily. 'Then last night, she serves him burned tortillas. Burned! From Mamá!' The absurdity of it set him off again, till tears ran from his eyes. He would occasionally say 'b-burned, tortillas, oh ha ha ha!'

Randy tried to hide his impatience, even attempting a faux chuckle at the ridiculous impossibility of Julio's momma *accidentally* burning a tortilla. When Julio finally wiped a sleeve over his eyes, Randy ventured, 'So your poppa agrees that he should let me go?'

'Oh, yes, yes. He will have a full belly tonight. Not … burned! Ha ha ha, burned!'

'Yes, yes, very funny. When will your father release me?'

'Ho ho … what? No, no, he agree with Mamá that he was a fool to tell the bad men, and he agree he *should* let you go. But he can't. The bad men would know. Mamá sent me to bed then. All I heard was her asking, "What if he was dead?" then, shush, they go outside. I try to listen, but they were in the front and my bedroom was in back. Señor? What's the matter?'

Randy, his hopeful bubble burst, had flopped back onto his bed. 'Oh, nothing. I'd just rather not be dead.'

Julio crossed himself. '*Si*, to die so young is not good. Maybe better, though, than a visit with the bad men?'

'Maybe,' Randy said. He sat back up. 'You know, if I got out of here, I'd buy every Chiclet you have. In fact, you could have all my money, except for what I need to get home, which is very little. Do you think you could just, you know, sort of drop the keys outside my door? Like an accident.'

Julio shook his head solemnly. 'I would be walloped by Papá. "Wallop," is that the right word? Like spanked, but with a leather belt.'

'Yes, "wallop" is the right word. And we wouldn't want that.'

'Papá is very strong, though he mostly *says* he will wallop me, then I apologize and promise to do good and he doesn't. He is a fair man.'

The jail door swung open and Julio's father entered, his proud smile, impossible to conceal, indicating he'd heard Julio's last words.

'Julio, run along home now. Mamá wants your help. She's making carnitas enchiladas tonight.'

Julio leaped to his feet. 'I would like to sell you my Chiclets, I have so many, but my mother's enchiladas are the best. Maybe she makes enough for your dinner too.'

'I'm sure she will,' his father said, waving his hand, 'so run along and help.'

Julio was gone an instant later, dust swirling in the early-afternoon sun.

'My son is a good boy,' the sheriff said, 'but such a talker. I'm sure he told you of our family quarrel.'

'Burned tortillas,' Randy said, with a wry smile.

'*Si*. Horrible. Perhaps I made a mistake telling the men belonging to the villa, but I truly had no choice. There was one standing outside the cantina, talking to the waitress there, but watching you asking your questions. Foolish. In fact, it was safer arresting you than letting him or perhaps a few others grab you later. My wife disagreed.

'I would release you if there was any possible way to avoid retribution, and not just for me but for my family.'

'I understand,' Randy said. 'I have a family too. A wife and a little boy.'

The man nodded. 'I'm glad you understand. But still, to let you go to that place is death, perhaps after much torture. I cannot abide that ... or burned tortillas for the rest of my days.'

Randy grew tense. 'What are you suggesting?'

'It was Maria's idea. My wife. If you were dead, the men could not have you. I don't understand why they haven't come yet, but there are rumors of trouble for the Viper. But, as I say, this delay means we would have an opportunity to bury the body. It is quite warm, and the stink!'

Thoughts of his body decomposing and causing an offensive odor really didn't concern Randy. 'Your only solution involves my death?'

The man chuckled. 'No.' He pointed to Randy's cot. 'Those blankets might make a good noose, tied to the beam above your head.' He pulled a cell phone. 'I take photos. Proof. The priest comes, performs the last rites, and we put you in the ground. He hates the Viper, as do all the people of this village.'

'Still,' Randy said, 'the one little problem of me being dead.'

'Pictures can be made to show many things. I will explain how to support your weight. There may be some discomfort. Maybe even a bruise. But you will most definitely be alive.'

'How in the name of God can I ever thank you?'

The man smiled. 'Please, never return here. Oh, and I think I heard talk of buying many, many Chiclets.'

Randy grinned. 'And you're sure you and your family will be safe?'

'*Si*. Had the Viper not delayed, you would be lost. Now, there is a possibility. We even have a poor man who died of an accident several days ago. Perhaps I might have an item or two of your belongings to throw into the grave.'

'Uh, I'm not quite as tan as you all.'

'True, but the odor is quite real. I doubt the Viper's men will dig too deeply, if you know what I mean.'

'And the new grave?'

'Being prepared by Julio, his mother, and a neighbor.'

'So, no carnitas tonight?'

'No. But *mañana* we feast!'

***

Dusk was fading to twilight as a lone figure, dressed in the cotton shirt and pants of a farmer, exited the jail, his dusty head bowed with fatigue. He shambled his way out of town, ignored by the few people who even glanced in his direction.

***

'I even managed to recover my duffel bag after I escaped,' Randy said, as Gail stepped near the filthy object resting on a dining room chair.

He'd just finished a story of excitement and bravery, starring himself, in which he'd surveilled the Viper, been accosted by two heavily armed men, used his martial arts skills to disarm and disable them both, and made his way through Mexico, blending into the countryside like a native.

Chuck and Gail had listened to this account with growing suspicion, his miraculous return having brought Chuck to Randy's house on the double. The earlier events—what Randy had done in Puerto Esperanza— had the ring of truth, particularly since they confirmed previous guesses, but this last bit of derring-do …

Randy edged closer to the duffel but was too late. Gail unzipped it, then turned to him with an accusatory scowl. 'Maybe you'd better start over,' she said, the scowl changing to a grin, 'and this time you can explain where all these Chiclets came from.'

***

An hour later, Randy was on the third telling of this story—a command performance for Joy, who'd insisted on hearing both versions, claiming her position as Queen of Triple S, Tucson, required full disclosure. By the time he finished, Randy's face had returned to ripe-apple red (as it had been when Gail had forced his confession) and Joy was in tears, alternately staring at Randy and the bag full of Chiclets.

When she finally finished laughing, Chuck rubbed the stubble on his chin, a sure sign he was concerned.

'We've had our fun at Randy's expense,' he said quietly, and all eyes turned to him, smiles melting like snow in a skillet. 'Well deserved, I might add. But I suppose being the grumpy old guy requires me to drag this group back to reality. First, though it grieves me to say it, you really fucked up, Randy.'

'Oh, c'mon …' Joy began.

'No, he's right,' Randy said. 'I got all pleased with myself and went off script.'

Chuck nodded. 'Everything went to shit from that point. Bad decision after bad decision. It's only by pure dumb luck and the intervention of a benevolent God that you're even sitting here. You and I are gonna talk in private, but if you don't see the error of your ways, I'll never work with you again.'

These were probably the harshest words Chuck could have thrown at Randy, doubly painful because he knew they were true. 'I'm not looking forward to that talk, but I promise I'll listen,' Randy said.

'Good man. That's a start.'

'And what else have you to share, oh tactful husband of mine?' Joy asked.

'Ah, well, chewing on Randy was the easy part. The intel he did get was excellent, including the backhanded news about an operation taking so much of Carlos Velasquez's attention that he didn't have time to question our wayward hero. Lucky, but disturbing. There's been no news of cartel wars, major shipments, or other disasters in the world of the Viper.'

'It was personal,' Randy said.

Chuck turned to him with a sharp eye, and Randy shrugged. 'It's just an impression from talking to Julio and his father. There were no orders to bring me to the villa because Carlos wasn't giving them, meaning he was personally involved. Distracted.'

'Thank goodness,' Gail muttered.

'Maybe,' Chuck said. 'Unfortunately, the information you got on your actual assignment to Puerto Esperanza is equally confusing. I want to do a timeline with Stone and Yvette on the *Reina del Mar*. Try to find out what the hell she'd been doing before she became a death ship.'

'And what her previous ports of call were,' Joy added. 'Pray to God we don't find a trail of dead bodies.'

'Right. We may need to head to London, Randy.'

Randy said nothing. At least Chuck wasn't threatening to leave him behind.

'So,' Chuck continued, 'that leaves me with just two questions. One of them Randy already mentioned. Where the hell was the Agency in all this? They return the *Saint Martin* to the Viper after Triple S snatches her, lose track of her, and allow a miraculous transition to occur. Voila, the *Reina*. If the *Reina* was being used for human smuggling, that was a major fuckup. Then she becomes a death ship. What the hell is up with that? Still, no Agency involvement.'

'You don't know that for sure, boss,' Randy said, falling back into the deferential behavior that had been natural when Chuck had been his superior back at the CIA.

'True enough, Randolph. I'll contact Marcus. Something stinks. Maybe he can help with that part of the mystery.'

'You mentioned two questions, Chuck,' Gail said.

'Something else Randy thought about while lazing away in the town jail. At first glance it's not important, but there's a missing piece in this puzzle.'

'Can't say I remember what my other brilliant observation was,' Randy said.

'Someone else was at the transformation of the *Saint Martin* to the *Reina del Mar*. Your drunken compadres argued about who was actually in charge.'

'They were pretty drunk, boss, and so was I.'

Chuck shook his head. 'That won't wash. They knew something unusual was going on. A struggle over authority. That makes no sense if one of the strugglers is the Viper. In terms of the cartels, he has no peers left in this hemisphere. The alcohol didn't cause them to make up the story, only to loosen their tongues enough to tell you. Drunk or not, you heard it, true?'

'True as my epic headache the next day.'

'What are you thinking?' Joy said.

'I'd rather not say,' Chuck answered.

'But you're gonna,' she countered. 'If you end up being wrong, we all get to laugh at you like we laughed at Randy.'

Chuck looked from Joy to Randy, Randy to Gail. 'It's just this. Someone important struggled with the Viper for control of the *Reina*, then something important and personal vexes the Viper enough for him to disregard Randy. Sounds like two big events. What if it was only one?'

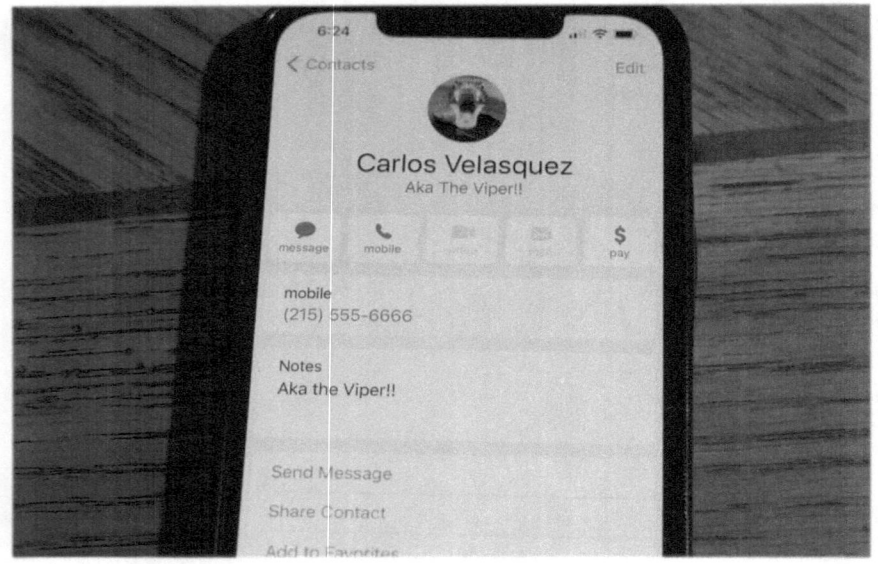

He glared at the cell phone on the end table, daring it to ring.

Chapter Fourteen

Ramifications of Bad Decisions

Raynard still had work to do before calling Carlos. José's ankle had been wrapped and the punctures and lacerations on Esteban's legs stitched and bandaged. Both were seated now in Raynard's living room, logs crackling in the fireplace and Cherokee curled up comfortably at Raynard's feet, though both icy-blue eyes were open and focused on the two.

After a long period of silence, José exchanged a glance with Esteban, who nodded. 'I accept your offer,' José said.

'*Si*, I too prefer to live,' Esteban said, 'though two things puzzle me.'

'Just two? We have time for two. Ask away.'

'It is simple. How and why?'

'Good questions,' Jesse said. 'By "how" I guess you mean how did I capture you. As for José, the pit was filled with long iron spikes … or so it seemed. With poor lighting and excellent paintwork, rubber can be made to resemble anything. The fall knocked you senseless till the floor panel slid closed and I gave you a sedative. I'm afraid you slept through most of the action.

'As for you,' Raynard continued, pointing to Esteban, 'I was counting on Cherokee obeying my command to fetch only and not to kill. She's extremely intelligent. I am sorry about the leg, but not too sorry. As it turned out, the track of blood was very convincing when combined with your screams. I expected Rogelio to turn back. It would have saved his life. I imagine you were surprised to see me in the woods.' Raynard shrugged. 'I drugged you and dragged you into the shed, where you also slept through the finale.

'If it makes it any easier, both Ángel and Rogelio were offered the same pardon you are both getting. They chose poorly and ended up shooting each other in the confusion of their final moments. That confusion … will remain my secret. There is your "how." The answer to "why" is both simpler and more complex.'

Raynard rose and added a log to the fire. 'Despite what you may think, I don't enjoy killing people. However, I can kill when I have to or when the death is deserved, and I never lose a minute's sleep afterward. If that sounds cruel, I suppose it is, though you two'—the fireplace poker pointed to each in turn—'can be grateful for the first part. There is your "why."'

'I am grateful,' Esteban said, slowly shaking his head, 'but it seems like magic.'

Jesse brightened. 'Exactly like magic. Now, you two know the terms. Off you go to South America. There's cash and an airline ticket in each envelope.'

Four identical envelopes sat on a coffee table. Raynard checked the printed names and handed one to each man, tapping the last two. 'A shame. It's also a shame, though unavoidable, that you two mustn't contact your families until you hear of Carlos's death.'

'You really plan to kill the Viper?' José asked. 'It will be most difficult.'

'I could have killed him a dozen times already and walked away. He'll be angrier now, which should make it even easier. Anger and clear thinking don't mix. However …'

Raynard pulled the cash from the two remaining envelopes and gave each man a new bundle. 'If two months pass and you haven't gotten the word, it means that Carlos has somehow survived and I'm probably dead. Use the cash to get your families out and bring them to you. I believe that covers everything.'

The men rose, watched with great focus by Cherokee. At the doorway, both turned.

'Goodbye, Raynard, and good luck,' José said. 'Do not be captured alive by the Viper.'

'Good advice,' Jesse agreed.

'*Si*. Good luck. I doubt I will see you again,' Esteban said, 'but I am in your debt, and if the future finds you in need of help, I will do what I can.'

'*Si*. I too,' José said.

Raynard watched them trudge down the snow-covered road, Esteban limping noticeably. 'Time to finish up, Cherokee. Still lots to do.'

***

Carlos paced the room like a big cat in a cage and gnawed his cold, lifeless cigar. He glared at the cell phone on the end table, daring it to ring. Filthy bastards! No word from Ramón. No word from Ángel. How long did it take to wring the neck of that skinny Raynard!

'I could have gone myself,' he muttered.

Immediately, his substitute 'Number One,' Ricardo, hurried to his side. '*Patrón*?'

Carlos rounded on him, eyes ablaze, then his expression softened and he patted Ricardo's cheek. 'You are a good man.'

Carlos removed the cigar from his mouth, spitting out a bit of tobacco, and hurled it at the blazing logs in the fireplace. 'Get me a fresh cigar and one for yourself.'

Ricardo hurried over to the bar and grabbed two fat Cubans. He reached for the tequila bottle, turning back and raising a questioning eyebrow as he did so.

'No tequila. Cognac. Take whatever you like and join me by the fire.' Carlos flopped into the leather chair.

Ricardo was at his side an instant later, offering the snifter and lighting the cigar. Carlos motioned to a chair across from him and Ricardo sat, cradling a very small tequila in his hand. He was still learning his boss's moods.

Carlos sent a lazy curl of smoke towards the ceiling and leaned back, relaxing. 'Someday I would like to retire.' He turned to Ricardo with a grin. '*Si*! Even with all the wealth and power I now possess, I would like to retire to a quiet hacienda near the sea. Ha ha! Yes, that has been my dream since long before I became *patrón* to so many. Maybe a few fat children running about causing chaos. You know, I've even thought about—'

Ángel's annoying 'La Cucaracha' ringtone, chosen by Carlos as appropriate for the man he thought of as a useful cockroach, destroyed Carlos's bucolic reflections. With glacial slowness he took the cigar from his mouth and hurled it into the fire.

Ricardo stiffened and willed himself to invisibility.

Carlos punched Accept, and Ángel's face appeared, wearing an insufferably insipid expression.

Struggling to control his fury, Carlos commanded, 'Report!'

Still, the ridiculous, tight-lipped smirk.

'Ángel, report or I will feed your testicles to—'

'A wolf?'

That voice. Not Ángel's, but familiar.

Ángel's image grew smaller as the phone was pulled back, his head barely filling the screen, then …

There was nothing below his raggedly torn neck.

'I'm afraid Ángel is not available at the moment. Bad sore throat.' The voice became stony. 'Bad *permanent* sore throat. His companions, too, are unavailable.'

The phone spun and there was Raynard, wearing a hard smile. 'I'm surprised you'd send fools like this to kill me. For one thing, the scrawny son of a bitch won't be more than a snack for Cherokee.'

'Raynard,' Carlos snarled, 'why won't you just die?'

'You first, asshole!'

'What have you done with Ramón?'

'Who?'

'My man, Ramón!'

'Ramón!' Raynard said, with a sneer. 'God, you're a fool, "Viper."'

'What do you mean?'

'I mean, Ramón hasn't been your man for ages. You have to be the biggest moron on the planet. Here, I'll send you a short video of your man, Ramón.'

The recording was blurry, the words muffled, but Ramón's voice— and his laugh!—were clear enough. As were the images and voices of Raynard and Emma Lister.

'It's simple,' Lister spoke, in her aristocratic English. 'You continue to "work" for that idiot. Send us useful intelligence when you can. No pressure! When the time comes …'

'You'll have no trouble cutting his throat, will you?' Raynard asked.

Ramón laughed. 'My reward?'

'His empire,' Lister cooed.

'Easy!' Ramón said.

'Your loyalty?' Raynard questioned.

'To us. To the enterprise.'

'Oh, that's enough,' Raynard said, appearing again on Carlos's screen. 'So, now who's your loyal man, you dickless wonder?'

'I'll kill you, Raynard!'

'Tried. Failed. There's nothing left for you, Carlos the Viper, but to count the minutes till your death. I hope you trust your "man." If not, it hardly matters. Death comes on quiet feet, like my Cherokee. Good Lord, you couldn't even kill a middle-aged author. Did you really think you could kill me?'

'I'll skin you alive!' he bellowed. 'And as for Fletcher, watch the news! Just watch the news! But you, I'll rip your eyes from their sockets, break every bone in your body …' He stared at the phone, but the call was disconnected.

'Aaaaah!' he shrieked, flinging the phone into the back of the fireplace, where it shattered. He spun back to Ricardo and pointed a trembling finger. 'You are my number one now. I will contact Ramón and order him to return here. You will prepare a special reception.'

'*Si, patrón!*'

***

Raynard set Ángel's phone down and whispered, 'Cut. Print everything.'

There had rarely been an easier bit of special effects and film editing in Jesse's career.

'Well, Cherokee. That's over. Time for a drink and dinner. Or maybe a drink and an early breakfast.'

Cherokee nuzzled up against Raynard, and a low, deep growl vibrated into Jesse's bones. 'I agree, girl. I couldn't have done it without you. Go on and grab yourself a nice fat rabbit or deer. Go.'

Cherokee shot out of the house.

Raynard poured a drink but made no move to prepare food. There was still a lot of blood in the rooms below the living quarters that would need cleaning, but Jesse had no heart for it, instead flopping into an old leather chair and murmuring, 'I wish you were here, Carl.'

***

Ramón had known there was something wrong. Ángel never missed a check-in, and now he'd missed three. Was it possible he'd somehow failed? Four killers versus one geeky purveyor of card tricks. Even as he thought this, a deeper, more sober part of his mind spoke the truth. Jesse Raynard was brilliant. Never conceding to employee status under Carlos, it was Raynard who'd rescued him, set him up as a principal player among the cartels, and relentlessly removed his rivals, effectively crowning him king of the narcotics trade in the Western Hemisphere.

Raynard selected which of the Viper's jobs to accept, forcefully declining others. Carlos could only fume privately. Raynard had been too important to kill. Until that stunt with the ship. That had been the snapping point, Ramón knew, but the analytical part of his mind had to wonder who had really run the cartel. Carlos was full of bluster and violence, but Raynard always had an edge. Perhaps still did.

The phone rang, making Ramón jump like a ten-year-old schoolgirl who's had her pigtails yanked. He pulled himself together, thankful no one had seen him, and picked up the phone in a firm hand. That bastard Ángel would get an earful!

His confidence evaporated faster than a puddle in the desert when he saw who was calling. The Viper! What could Ramón tell him? Best to blame the lack of progress and inexplicable silence on Ángel. Ángel was a good man—usually—but he would need to take the fall.

'*Patrón*,' Ramón began, with a shockingly false note of enthusiasm, 'I was just about to call. That braying jackass, Ángel—'

'Will bray no longer. He is dead. All your men are dead, yet you are still alive. It is strange, no?'

'Dead! What? It can't be.' As the words left his mouth, Ramón knew instinctively that it was the only possible reason for the lack of contact. Ángel, Rogelio, Esteban, José. All dead! Still, he could hardly bring himself to accept it. With a surprising lack of tact, he blurted out, 'How do you know? Who told you?'

The wilder Ramón became, the steelier Carlos grew. In a voice of ice, he said, 'Who could possibly know that all four were dead? Only one person on the planet.'

'No!'

'Raynard. You send four butchers, four fools, to murder one spindly trickster, and the trickster wins.'

'But, Carlos—'

'I saw Ángel's head, you imbecile, and three other bodies. Do not speak to me like an underling.' He said nothing of the video incriminating Ramón as a traitor, but drew a slow breath. 'Return immediately and we will discuss ... future plans.'

'Yes, of course, *patrón*, I am so ... I will kill Raynard myself! *Patrón*? *Patrón*?'

CALL ENDED.

***

Ramón had plenty of time to think about the bellicose nature of his one-time *patrón* as he made his way back to Mexico. The 'one-time' he had concluded early. He had observed the Viper for many years. A loyal employee would become a favorite and be given increasingly difficult (and rewarding) assignments, while the *patrón* lauded his accomplishments and held him up as a shining example. Then—always—some disappointment and a souring of the relationship. Difficult assignments became impossible ones. Failure followed failure. In the end, a summons to discuss 'future plans.' He'd seen it often enough.

Ramón stared at his hands. They had sometimes been the instruments of the removal of disappointing personnel. Failures. There had been one exception. Jesse Raynard had never failed the Viper. Often, it had been the other way around. This, too, he had seen. The order for Raynard's death had not been precipitated by failure, but by a long string of successes and the growing independence and arrogance of someone the Viper considered an employee. In the end, there was the loss of the *Reina del Mar*. But that

255

had merely been a catalyst. Ramón had known for many months that the kill order was coming. Another success would have triggered it as surely as the sinking of the ship. The Viper hadn't even bothered to try to determine why the ship had been sunk. Raynard might be blameless. It didn't matter. Jesse Raynard's time was up.

Or so it had seemed. How ...? Ramón shook his head in frustration. 'How' didn't matter anymore. Four dead. Four seasoned killers snuffed out by one bookish conjurer. Now Ramón was in the crosshairs of the Viper's vengeance. Failure—any failure—was dealt with harshly. Failure of this magnitude? He shuddered at what might be his fate. Days of torture, with never a question being asked. This would not be an interrogation, but a punishment suitable to the scope of his failure.

He considered running but dismissed the notion. It would be expected, for one thing, and the Viper's reach was long. He'd thought about Raynard and realized, as dangerous as the game might be, Raynard's only hope for survival lay in the death of the Viper. Yes, that was certainly true. A duel of titans. One of brute strength, one of remarkable intellect. Digesting this thought had led him to pursue his own risky option.

So, here he was, on his way back to the Viper to play a dangerous and necessarily short-lived game of chicken. His only hope was identical to Jesse's. The Viper needed to die. It was possible, if Ramón could maintain enough bluster and bravado to get an audience. He fingered the needle-sharp ceramic rod stitched into the seam of his pants. It would set off no alarms. A thorough pat-down, such as many he'd given, *might* catch such an item, but if not ... It was short, but long enough for the job. Slipping between ribs, probing up to pierce a beating heart.

His own heart pounded in his chest as he approached the first checkpoint on the road to the Viper's lair. Now the gamble began. He gave the guard an arrogant grin, befitting his status as the Viper's loyal number one, as he rolled down his window.

'Emilio, you old goat fucker, pulled guard duty again, I see.'

The wheel of chance spun. Would he be taken immediately, or had the Viper withheld the news of his disgrace from the lower help?

'Ah, Ramón,' Emilio replied. 'I'd watch my step if I were you. The boss is angry—furious—about something.'

'Probably some poor bastard he wants me to kill by morning.' He faked a yawn.

Emilio waved him through. 'Just mind what I told you,' he yelled at the receding car.

Ramón's hands were shaking, but a tight smile formed on his lips.

'I'm still in the game.'

***

It might have been Ramón's imagination, fueled as it was by growing anxiety, but the guards at the next checkpoint seemed to eye him more coldly, speak to him more disrespectfully. He kept up his façade to the best of his ability, but his confidence was crumbling like rotten wood in a chipper.

At the house, he was stopped again and searched. He'd brought no gun, so there was none to find, and the careless pat-down missed his tiny weapon.

It was a cool night, and he was escorted into a room where a fire blazed in the stone fireplace. Carlos stood on the hearth, prodding the logs with a heavy iron poker. He turned and glanced at Ramón with calculated disdain, grunted to the guard, who hustled away, and returned to the fire.

After what seemed minutes, he buried the poker in the angry yellow embers at the fire's heart and faced Ramón.

'You have much to explain.'

Ramón opened his mouth to speak, but Carlos raised an imperious hand. 'I will speak first.' He took a chair and reached for a glass of tequila, never inviting Ramón to sit or offering him a drink.

'You have been my strong right arm for a long time,' Carlos began, 'and have done well. Moderately well. But in your most important assignment, you fail me. You had four excellent men at your command. Had you chosen to participate, it would have been five against one, and that *one* is no fighter. The planning I left to you. You see my trust? How did you repay this trust? What is the outcome?

'A call from Jesse Raynard, the person you were sent to kill, informing me that your plan—which did *not* involve your direct participation—has resulted in four of my men dead and Raynard as healthy as an ox! Raynard, without a scratch. Not even a drop of perspiration!

'And I begin to wonder how this could be. Is my number one a coward? Was his plan idiotic? But then the mystery is solved.'

Carlos held up a tablet and played the recorded video of Ramón talking to Raynard and Lister.

Ramón's jaw went slack and he moved closer. Despite his plans, he began to assert his innocence.

'It's a lie! That isn't me! I swear it!'

'It looks like you,' Carlos purred. 'And it sounds like you. But we will have much time to discuss your treachery.' He cocked his head thoughtfully and narrowed his eyes, a delightful notion occurring to him. 'Perhaps you and Raynard together. We will see who is most responsive to … persuasion. Yes, perhaps I will let you two suggest techniques to be tried on the other. The most creative receives a quick death. Fair, no?'

Ramón abandoned the last hope he had of swaying Carlos. He was back to Plan A.

'Play it again,' Ramón said, edging closer and slipping the ceramic needle into his grasp. 'It is not me; I will show you. The man is an imposter. There is a scar …'

He moved up alongside Carlos's chair. The angle would be wrong. He'd expected Carlos to be standing. No choice. He summoned the most offended tone he could produce and pointed to the tablet with his left hand. 'You see, right there!'

He lunged the last several feet and brought his right hand down in a stabbing motion, but Carlos blocked with his left arm, the needle piercing between his two lower-arm bones near the wrist. The force of the blow drove the needle completely through Carlos's arm, the bloody point appearing on the other side.

Carlos howled in agony. In less than a second, Ricardo was there, clubbing Ramón to the ground with a lead-filled leather blackjack.

When Ramón regained consciousness, he found he was still in the living room, bound to a heavy chair facing the fireplace.

Carlos, a clean white bandage around his lower left arm, was talking with Ricardo. Both had glasses filled with tequila and both seemed relaxed.

'Ricardo, my brother,' Ramón rasped.

'He's awake,' Carlos said. 'I hope you had a pleasant nap, Ramón. Don't you hope so too, Ricardo?'

'*Si, patrón.*'

'Brother?' Carlos chided. 'No, no, no. My new number one is no brother to a traitor. A traitor who tried to kill me, with this.'

He held up the deadly needle, wiped clean of blood.

'Not metal. Clever.' He pointed to his arm with the tip. 'And very sharp, *si*? Ha ha ha.'

Still holding the needle, Carlos approached Ramón until the point of the needle was inches from his face.

'How easy it would be to pierce an eye.' He made a false lunge.

Ramón cried out and turned his head.

'Coward,' Carlos said. 'Yes, I could take an eye.'

He stared at Ramón then broke into a grin. 'But only one. You will need to see what I do to Raynard.' He lunged again, but stopped short once more.

Ramón was babbling now, pleading, begging.

Carlos walked away and placed the needle on a table. 'Maybe later.'

'*Gracias, patrón!* Let me serve you. My life is yours!'

'True,' Carlos said, his look now stony. He held up his left arm. 'But you hurt me. First by your failures, then by your traitorous behavior, and then physically. You hurt me.'

Carlos pulled the poker from the depth of the fire, its tip nearly white hot.

'Pain for pain.'

***

Ramón had been taken away for the evening—the first of many—and the mess had been cleaned up, all but for a few stubborn blood splatters on the chair and floor. Perhaps a useful reminder.

The fire had been stoked and Carlos now sat smoking a fresh cigar and sipping his tequila. Ricardo sat on the other side of the fireplace, pretending to drink and trying not to look as anxious as he was. To see Ramón treated so cruelly was a shock. Carlos the Viper had a reputation for brutality, and Ricardo had seen a demonstration. Failure was not an option. He would have to tread more carefully than a lynx if he was to avoid the same punishment.

The Viper seemed to read his mind, and grinned, though his eyes were icy. 'You have no need to fear, my friend. I know you will not fail me like that traitor Ramón. But there is much to be done. We have missed an opportunity to interrogate a nosy gringo, which is sad, but not as important as other things. My operations have experienced setbacks of late, and you, my number one, must visit my other lieutenants in Mexico, Guatemala, and Honduras. They must be made aware of my displeasure and guided back to the path of efficiency and unwavering dedication. However, this must wait.'

Carlos took a lazy pull on his cigar and let a thoughtful stream of blue-grey smoke trickle past his lips. 'A leader must not show weakness. A leader must have respect. But two obstacles stand in the way. Cathie Fletcher and Jesse Raynard.' He narrowed his eyes in thought. 'Both must die, naturally. It is the "how" and "when" I struggle with.'

Ricardo remained silent. The thought that his next assignment might be to eliminate Jesse Raynard froze his tongue behind his teeth. Ramón had failed (Ricardo refused to believe he was a traitor, though he wasn't foolish enough to say so) and would pay for his failure.

'Yes!' Carlos said sharply, causing Ricardo to jump. 'Fletcher first. Take a man or two to London. She is still in a hospital there. May even be dead by now. If not, kill her any way you can. No, wait. It must be spectacular enough to make the news. The famous author dead in a pool of her own blood. Raynard must know. You will then return, ready for the more difficult challenge. Jesse Raynard must be brought here, alive. Then we have some fun with Ramón and Raynard, as I promised.'

Ricardo was about to speak, but Carlos motioned him to silence. 'Never fear. It is a difficult assignment. You will take ... ten men. The wolf-hound you will kill. I want the pelt right there.' He waved his arm at a bare space in front of the fireplace. 'Soft on the feet, no?' Carlos's dreamy expression as he imagined this satisfying future dropped from his face like a sheet of snow sliding off a steep roof. 'Go now. You have much to do. I want Fletcher dead and Raynard groveling at my feet in ten days' time. Go!'

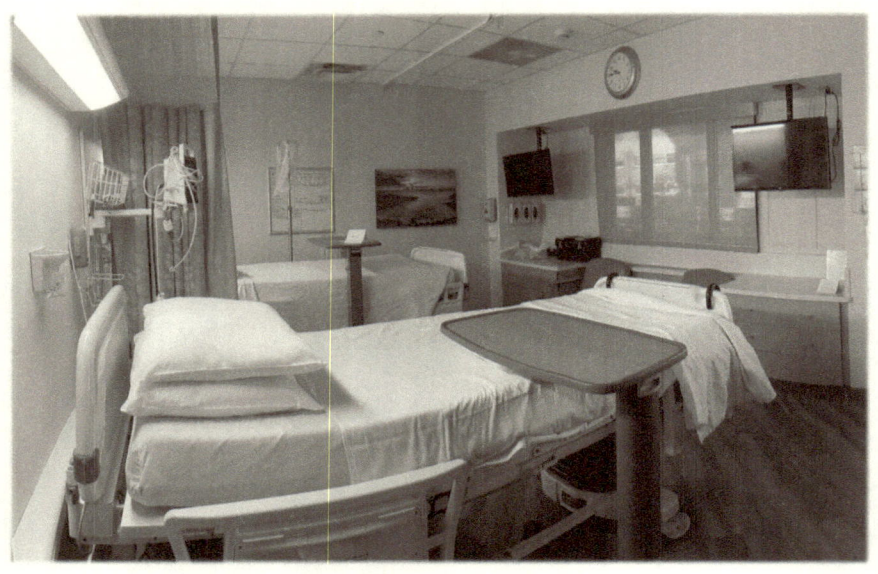

Cathie had been moved into a room of the hospital's convalescent wing.

Chapter Fifteen

She's Awake

T hirsty.'
   The inhuman croak was barely audible, but Logan heard.

He leaped from his chair, the book he'd been reading catapulting to the floor.

'Cathie, babe, it's me! It's Logan!' He grabbed her hand. 'I'm here, babe. Talk to me.'

Cathie's mouth moved, but only a low grating sound escaped.

Logan snatched the call button at her side and crushed it between his thumb and forefinger. Without waiting, he dashed into the hallway.

'Someone help! She's awake!'

Cathie had been moved into a room of the hospital's convalescent wing. There were seldom emergencies here, only slow healing or death. Two nurses at a station down the hall raised their heads.

'She's awake,' Logan shouted, then dashed back into the room.

'Cathie,' he said. 'The doctor's coming. What can I do?'

'Water.'

This time he heard. He scanned the room, but Cathie's rolling table was empty, pushed to one side. Water wasn't necessary for a woman who'd been unconscious for months and had what most assumed was a permanent IV providing fluids till she no longer needed them. Logan grabbed his own water from the tiny side table and was fumbling with it, trying to bring the glass to her lips, when a doctor and nurse entered and gently brushed him aside.

'Water,' Cathie whispered again.

The doctor nodded and the nurse dashed off.

'Well, Sleeping Beauty,' the doctor said, in a voice calm as a cat's purr. 'Awake at last. Water is on the way. Let's just check a few things, shall we?'

The doctor scanned the monitors and was listening to her heart when the nurse returned, giving him a questioning look.

'Just a little,' he said, indicating the water. 'Then we'll see. Here, I'll take it. Please call Dr. McAlister. Tell him he has a very lively patient who'd like a visit.'

He put the straw to Cathie's lips and she managed a few drops before coughing.

'That's terrific,' he said, in the same quiet rumble. 'You'll be playing tennis in no time.' He turned to Logan. 'Talk to her while I continue to check vitals.'

For the next fifteen minutes Logan talked, sputtering through his tears. Nonsensical jabber, nothing in sequence, nothing related to the shooting. Stories of Tucson barbecues past and future, friends, family, the weather. The doctor was pleased. Then Dr. McAlister and several others entered and he was whisked away.

When McAlister emerged, some forty-five minutes later, he took Logan by the elbow, and in a soft Scottish burr said, 'It's something of a miracle. I've seen it happen, but not often. A blood vessel moves a titch or finally shrinks away from the brain. Removing the pressure is like flicking on a light. We'll send her back to the ICU, just for a day or two, to monitor her progress. All her vitals are strong and, of course, her other injuries have healed long ago. You can stay a wee while longer, but you mustn't wear her out. She can talk, but she shouldn't. Rest is the order of the day. I've given her a mild sedative, and I've no doubt she'll be out soon. Well, go on, lad. You have five minutes to tell her you love her.'

Logan crushed the doctor's hand in his own, but no words would come. He reentered Cathie's room.

'I love you, babe.'

***

Two days later, after an astonishing recovery, Cathie was allowed to leave the hospital. As the doctor had speculated, a slight reduction in pressure on the brain had brought about the change. An MRI was conclusive, showing a small but significant change, and the medical staff agreed that a recurrence of symptoms was unlikely. Two weeks of additional rest interspersed with physical therapy were prescribed to restore function to dormant muscles.

In the excitement of the moment, as preparations were made to move Cathie to Diana's estate, everyone forgot one vital thing.

***

George Ellis was a small, nervous man, with thick glasses and frizzy gray hair that fought a losing battle with his balding crown. His eyes danced around the hospital lobby until he found the information desk. 'I'd like to visit Cathie Fletcher, please,' he said.

'Cathie Fletcher? The author?'

'Yes. I was an associate, a local agent you might say, for some of her earlier works.'

The woman went to her keyboard. 'I'll check, but I'm quite certain … Yes, you've just missed her. A miraculous recovery after her long coma. She left the hospital just this morning.'

She turned to the man with a grin and was surprised to find no answering delight in any of his features.

'I see,' he said at last, forcing a smile onto his face. 'What wonderful news. I, uh … you wouldn't happen to know where she's gone?'

The woman began to grow uneasy. 'She left. I couldn't say where she's gone. The hospital doesn't release any additional information.'

'I see,' he repeated. He turned without another word and headed outside, fingering the now useless straight razor in his pocket.

A day late, he thought. *Damn my luck! There goes my easy payday.*

A few minutes later, he slid his phone back into a pocket, a sour look on his face. Job not done, no pay. There was no reward for trying.

***

Ricardo stared out the window of his hotel room, desperately trying to suppress the only emotion he was feeling: fear. He had traveled to London to accomplish the first assignment—the easier assignment—for Carlos, and he'd failed.

You didn't fail, a lonely part of his mind argued. *She wasn't there. The intel was bad.*

You failed.

It had taken time, one precious day, to make contact with Ellis and plan for today's execution. How was he to know that some guardian angel would strike Cathie Fletcher on the head and she'd walk out of the hospital—walk out, for the love of God!—after months of coma.

'A few more days, you useless *puta!*' he snarled.

You failed, and you know how Carlos deals with failure.

No. There must be some other way.

But in his heart, Ricardo knew the truth. For days, weeks, she'd be surrounded by friends and family. He'd done his research. She'd be staying with Diana Foster on her secluded estate. A man with a sniper rifle *might* get a shot. It would be beyond difficult. Still, there was one man he knew who might pull it off. It would mean delay, but Ricardo didn't dare return to the Viper and report the one event for which there was no forgiveness.

Failure.

***

Tears, confusion, gentle hugs as though she were made of glass. Despite Ricardo's angry words, Cathie had not walked out of the hospital. She was seated in a wheelchair surrounded by Logan, Diana, Crandall, and Luana. Arthur, Diana's chauffer, butler, and manservant, was gently nudged aside by Logan, who insisted on wheeling Cathie into the west wing of Diana's sprawling home. The wheelchair caused no difficulty, her home having been fitted with ramps long ago to accommodate Diana's personal needs.

Arthur yielded the chair, then moved off to address a grinning Jason Stone, who had a fat cigar jutting from his mouth.

'Sir, she needs to be told.'

Stone turned a beaming face to Arthur, who was usually silent and invisible in the execution of his duties. In the general benevolence of the day, Stone reached into his jacket pocket. 'Arthur, have a cigar. Celebrate!'

Arthur stood mutely and made no move to accept the cigar.

Stone's smile quivered on the edge of dissolving. 'What did you say?'

'She needs to be told, sir. Yvette is inside. Ms. Fletcher will certainly ask.'

266

'Shit,' Stone said, dropping the barely touched Monte Cristo to the pavement and grinding it with his shoe. 'Help me.'

Arthur nodded, and the two caught up with Logan. 'I need a word,' Stone whispered. 'Now.'

Logan caught the urgency in Stone's voice and yielded the chair back to Arthur, who made a great fuss of checking the wheels. No one seemed to notice, busy with multiple competing conversations.

'What's up, Stone?' Logan asked.

'Colin.'

'What? I ... oh, God! She doesn't know! Oh, shit!'

'Listen, I've got a tactical plan. Unfortunately, it sucks for you. I'll get the others to back off. It's a nice day for this time of year. You suggest Cathie needs a little air. Take her for a walk around the fountain. You're the right man to tell her. No one else.'

Logan glanced back to Cathie, surrounded by bubbling, enthusiastic friends, then over to the house. Framed in a small side doorway, Yvette stood, arms at her side, her expression hollow.

'Let's do it now, before she sees Yvette,' Stone said.

Cathie was surprised but accepted the sudden change in plans. Truth be told, the excitement had worn her out. Logan gave Stone a quick look, his face a picture of despair.

'Everyone inside, please,' Arthur said, 'and I'll make a fresh pot of tea.'

'Arthur?' Diana asked.

Stone pointed to Yvette, and Diana's hand flew to her mouth. She marched straight to Yvette and crushed her in a hug. The others followed.

Stone turned back once to see Logan and Cathie near the dry fountain. He was kneeling at her side and her head was pressed against his shoulder.

***

The pleasant midday weather had worsened dramatically as a storm blew in from the Channel and smothered the remaining daylight in grey swaths of rain. A roaring fire had drawn the group back together. It had been a bipolar day, euphoria displaced by anguish. Everyone had suffered the guilt of having forgotten. It was Yvette who finally freed them from their shackles.

'We've all had time to adjust to Colin's absence.' A partial lie. 'And Cathie's recovery is nothing short of a miracle. We should all be celebrating. Colin would want us to.'

'Hear, hear,' Crandall said.

'Arthur,' Diana said, 'would you be so kind as to fetch—'

A faint smile lit his face as he advanced with a tray holding a bottle of cognac and snifters.

'He reads my mind.'

'Where would I be if I didn't?'

Diana counted the glasses. 'Good man. Now sit and join us.'

As the first snifters magically emptied, Arthur refilled. When a general buzz of conversation resumed, Stone rose and motioned to Yvette. 'Feel like a short walk, and maybe a little good news?'

'We've had plenty today, with Cathie's return, but I'd gladly accept more. Not very keen on a walk, though.'

Stone smiled. 'Not outside. Just down the hallway to the Triple S office.'

'You've piqued my interest, Jason,' she said, snatching her drink. 'Lead on.'

The wind-driven rain spattered the window panes of the hallway, while the relics of an older time, a medieval time, watched the two pass down the dim corridor just as they'd watched generations pass before them.

Stone led the way into a high-tech oasis, the room crammed with computers, monitors, notepads, and thumb drives. He bypassed all the modern apparatus and snatched up the one artifact of bygone days, a newspaper. He handed it to her, already opened to a page towards the back, where she read:

'A gruesome discovery. The mutilated body of a man was found washed up on the shore near St. Andrews Golf Club two days ago. Forensic analysis indicated he had been brutally tortured for several days. The cause of death is uncertain due to the mangled condition of the body. The man, identified by ID in his wallet and confirmed by dental records, was Caldwell Simms, a regular at St. Andrews, though there is reason to believe he had several aliases.

'This brutal murder was apparently in retaliation for a drug deal gone bad. Simms was suspected of ties to the Mexican drug cartel headed by the notorious Carlos "the Viper" Velasquez.'

Stone scrutinized Yvette while she read, but there was no apparent reaction. When she finished, she said, 'You were quite right, Jason, and I apologize once again for my previous behavior.'

'It doesn't really help, though, does it?'

'And again, you are quite right. But you know,' she added, gazing at him through teary eyes and squeezing his arm gently, 'it is some small justice, isn't it?'

'It is. Let's get back to the others.'

Yvette nodded, though she hung on to the newspaper.

When the Viper is dead, she thought, *Colin will have a little bit more justice.*

***

Ricardo stared at the newspaper in disbelief. The one man who might have been able to finish the job on Cathie Fletcher, though he had botched the first attempt, was dead. Murdered by the Viper for his failure.

Failure.

Madre de Dios, Ricardo thought. *What do I do now?*

***

'Nice of you to come to Atlanta, Raynard,' Carl Heskin said. A short burst of coughing truncated his words of gratitude.

'It makes a change from sitting at home waiting for the Viper to send more men to kill me.'

'You don't think they've heard of air travel?' Carl said, with a wry smile. 'And what about your home? Is it safe while you're gone?'

'My being gone is one of the things that makes it safe. They don't want to kill my house. The heavy snow—it's been a good season—is another safety feature. Cherokee is the most important one, though. I imagine news has spread of what happened there. It would discourage most rational people. There's also my phone,' Jesse said. 'I can see what's going on and take measures if I need to.'

Eight camera views in and around the house were displayed on the screen.

'Very efficient. That just leaves my original question about your personal safety—here.'

'I'm working on a permanent solution to that problem.'

'You mean to eliminate the Viper?'

'At last. I have work to do and he's too much of a distraction.'

'Supremely confident. Or is it arrogant? Hard to tell by your expression.'

'If I succeed, you can call me what you like, and if I fail ... well I won't care in that case either.'

Raynard flagged their waiter. The Calliope restaurant was busy, but they were seated once again in the quiet room away from the bustle, and whatever magic Carl had worked guaranteed both privacy and swift service. 'Another round, and we'd like to order.'

'Another round *is* my order,' Carl said.

'Not mine. I'll have the prime rib and all the sides. And you'd better at least have some soup, Carl. It's cold out there.' Jesse nodded towards the window, streaked by a sleety rain that beat down, buffeted by gusts of wind. 'Seriously, Carl, how are you?'

'I'm dying a bit more rapidly than I was the last time we met.' He shrugged. 'If we don't get on with your plan, you may need to act alone.'

'We're ready for Phase Three. Contact your two doctor friends in Bangladesh.'

'If I waited for your obvious instructions, where would I be? They've been alerted. The product?'

'I can see I'm the one holding up progress. It will ship soon.'

'Shouldn't you be going too?'

'Soon,' Raynard repeated. 'How is your colleague Constantin?'

'The man finds life to be no more than a farce. With all the buffoonery the world has to offer, he's happy enough, though he's intrigued by the evil genius of one Jesse Raynard, and he's eager to help.'

'Evil? I'm hurt!' Raynard said, smirking.

'You? Not likely.'

'He was a lucky find, your friend,' Raynard said, the smirk replaced by a stony seriousness.

'Yes. Another disaffected CDC employee, though not a dying one. How much should we tell him?'

'Only enough to satisfy his need for comedy. When we execute Phase Three, you're certain he'll be sent to Bangladesh?'

'Absolutely. There will be sufficient evidence to connect the disease outbreak on the *Reina del Mar* to what will be found there. I may even help to connect a few dots if the Director is a little slow on the uptake.'

'Now who's the evil genius?'

'Still you. By the way, have you received any inquiries regarding the sale of an asymmetric bioweapon?'

'Now you're poaching on my preserve!' Jesse said, with a laugh. 'There are numerous rumors on dark sites around the world, some of them started by me! It seems the events in Huata, Guatemala, and aboard the *Reina* may be connected and may not be a natural occurrence. The Chinese are suspected.'

'The Chinese! There's irony for you.'

'Yes. However, other rumors, also started by me, indicate otherwise. Would it be too cliché to identify the source as an evil genius intent on world domination?'

'I'm going to regret that comment, aren't I?'

'Yes you are. But don't worry. I've created an untraceable address, and I've received serious inquiries.'

'Have you responded?'

'Only with a tease to keep their eyes open.'

The food arrived, and Jesse and Carl ate quietly for a while. As Carl finished his soup, he said, as though no time had passed, 'I sincerely hope you manage to stay alive, Raynard.'

'I made it through this meal.' Jesse eyed Carl suspiciously. 'What's really bothering you, my friend?'

'Oh, I like having a friend.' He shrugged. 'I'd miss you on that level.'

'That level?'

Heskin coughed into his napkin, then fixed Raynard with a penetrating stare. 'When I first agreed to help you—you remember?—I was doing it for my family. My family, held hostage by unscrupulous people at the CDC. I never for an instant believed you could pull this off, but the money was good.'

'And now?'

'Don't laugh, but over time, God help me, I've bought in. I want to see this mad enterprise succeed. For that to happen, however, you need to live. Can you do that for your old friend Carl? Provide for my family and pull off the greatest—'

'I can.' Jesse turned from Carl and stared out the window. A few flakes of snow mixed with the icy slop of an hour before. Bushes and trees whipped in the wind. 'Part of my mind has been working on the problem of staying alive—background processing, I guess you'd say—and I think I've come up with a solution. At least, the beginning of a solution.'

'An elegant solution?' Carl asked, his eyes eager.

'Is there any other kind?'

Carl leaned forward in his seat. 'Tell me.'

***

The next morning, while walking through a dismal, sodden park north of Atlanta, Jesse Raynard placed a call.

Emma Lister sounded genuinely delighted. 'Jesse, what a wonderful surprise. Though if I had to guess, this isn't a pleasure call. Business?'

'In a way. We've talked before about the idiot associated with your former employer and his tendency to solve problems using extreme violence.'

'Yes ...'

'I've become one of his problems.'

'What! Are you all right?'

'I'm fine, thank you, though several of his hired thugs aren't. A recent attack on my New Mexico home left two dead and two others with a sudden change of heart.'

'Good for you! But surely he won't stop trying to kill you.'

'No. And that's more of a distraction than I can tolerate right now.'

'Distraction! Well, I hope never to be similarly distracted. Truth be told, he's been a terrible associate. I soon came to realize he'd be an awful business partner. Also ... in your ear alone ... I've been considering my options of late. The legitimate businesses I control have done quite well. Embarrassingly well. I can enjoy every luxury I desire without any subsidiary activities. And unlike Conrad, I have no desire to acquire a lordly title. So where does that leave me? With thoughts of a respectable future as a businesswoman and international playgirl.'

272

'I like the sound of that,' Jesse said.

'So you see, I no longer have any interest in maintaining a relationship with that boor Velasquez.'

'I trust his sudden demise wouldn't break your heart?'

Bubbling laughter. 'No,' Emma said. 'In fact, it would solve the thorny dilemma of dissolving our embryonic business relationship. But do you really mean to tell me you have a plan to ... disenfranchise the Viper?'

'Yes, several, though none are fully baked, if you'll pardon the colloquialism.'

'Ah. In that case, I may be of some service. I've had discussions with a close friend of the young woman whose love was murdered when Cathie Fletcher was attacked. We've been sharing information. The young woman, you see, is rather hell-bent on revenge.'

'An ally.'

'Perhaps even more. Let me make a discreet inquiry. But first, tell me some of your half-baked plans.'

***

'Now this is a Thanksgiving to celebrate,' Logan said.

'Maybe a little dreary?' Cathie commented, glancing out the windows of Diana's formal dining hall at the steady rain and overwhelming greyness.

'Not with you here,' Logan replied, with a grin.

'Really, how long can you keep this up?'

'Oh, don't throw cold water on it just yet.'

'And where's our beloved daughter to help you set this enormous table for tomorrow's feast?'

'Kelly's still jet-lagged. Yvette wanted to help, but I said I'd do it. She insisted on helping with the cooking, though, and I couldn't say no. Preparing food for fourteen guests isn't easy.'

'I'm surprised we're using the hall. I'd think it would bring back painful memories of Colin.'

'It was Yvette's idea. Said her memories here were pleasant. Do you remember that party?'

'How could I not? The food, the music, the dancing. I just wish ...'

'Don't we all.'

'Diana is such a gracious hostess, even with the extra company.'

Logan chuckled. 'It took her a while to adjust to the notion of a Thanksgiving turkey and all the fixings. She hinted at also having a goose and Yorkshire pudding, just so the poor British palates wouldn't be too confused. Of course, I told her I had no idea of how to cook either, so Arthur offered his services. The man is remarkable. Thinks of most everything.'

'OK, the table looks great. How about lending me an arm so we can join the others? What a treat to have both Marcus and Kelly here.'

'Lucky they were both able to tear themselves away from work.'

'Tell Kelly she can have jet lag later. I'm awake now and I want to talk to her.'

'Your wish is my—'

'Less talking. More moving.'

***

It was another memorable feast, though lower key than the previous dinner with its costumes and entertainment. Though the dining hall was far from full, there were more than enough guests to produce a steady rumble of conversation and laughter.

Cathie, Logan, and Kelly traded stories with Joy, Chuck, and Marcus, who were seated opposite. Richard and Diana made sure Yvette stayed engaged in conversation, as did Becky Amhurst who had brought Gary Walkin with her. Diana had also insisted Arthur join this group. Luana, enthusiastic and friendly, enjoyed everyone's company, laughing and conversing all around.

Only Stone seemed withdrawn. He would smile and laugh with the others when appropriate, then slip back into silence. To a discreet inquiry from Diana, Luana merely said, 'He's been that way lately. Something's bothering him. Maybe several things. But I've learned it's best not to push too hard when he's in this mood.'

Logan, Arthur, and Yvette insisted on serving the meal, though Crandall had hired a small crew to clear the table and wash dishes. When the main meal was finally complete and several well-picked bird carcasses removed, Diana eyed her guests. 'I propose a short break before dessert is served—several pies, I believe.'

A chorus of sated groans provided affirmation. 'Very good. There are drinks and cigars in the study, and the fire is lit.'

Arthur nodded.

'You mean we have to move?' Logan said.

'Don't be a boor, dear,' Cathie said, squeezing his arm. 'Besides, I need your steady support to walk down the hall.'

'We're both in trouble,' he muttered.

The study was another seldom-used room in the estate, just a short walk towards the main entrance. It had benefitted from the steady attention of Yvette when she felt a need to be active, and it was now more than suitable for company. Like the dining room, a bank of windows looked out to the inner courtyard, dark and gloomy tonight. But a roaring fire crackled and cast enough warmth to drive away any chill. Flanking the fireplace were floor-to-ceiling bookshelves crowded with a collection that would take a lifetime to read. Small tables and leather armchairs were carelessly scattered around the room on thick rugs that begged to be trodden barefoot. Two other tables, one rectangular and intended for study, one round and intended for cards, dominated the far end of the room. Cognac, brandy, and other whiskies were set on a sideboard, along with glasses and an ice bucket.

After a few minutes of chaotic shuffling, everyone had a drink, a cigar, or both, and had organized into loose groups. Chuck was just finishing an amusing retelling of Randy's time in a Mexican jail to a chorus of chuckles. Logan, expecting a sarcastic comment or two from Stone, noticed he wasn't in the room.

'Excuse me for a minute,' Logan said.

'Going to powder your nose?' Cathie asked.

'What? Sure,' he replied absently.

Chuck rose with him, guiding him first to the sideboard for a refill, then walking with him out into the hallway. An instant later, Marcus joined them. 'You left me badly outnumbered by ladies,' he said. 'Looked like time for a strategic retreat.'

'That's my boy,' Chuck said, slapping his shoulder. 'Now I don't suppose you had the foresight to bring—'

Marcus drew three cigars from the inner pocket of his sport coat. 'My daddy didn't raise no fool.'

'He didn't,' Chuck agreed. 'Light me up.'

275

Chuck savored the heady aroma, then turned to Logan. 'Where's Stone?'

'My question exactly. I've got a guess. Let's go down the hall to the luxurious Triple S London headquarters.'

The door was open, the white light of LED bulbs spilling out into the hallway. A cold, sterile light compared to the warm glow in the study.

'Hey,' Stone said, glancing up as they entered, but then immediately lowering his head to his computer screen and the disorganized stacks of papers surrounding it.

'Hey yourself,' Chuck said. 'I hear there's a party going on just down the hall. Some Yankee holiday. Oh, that's right, Thanksgiving. Care to join?'

'Don't take this wrong, Chuck, but no. I will take one of those, though,' he added, pointing to Chuck's cigar.

Marcus fished inside his coat and pulled out another, tossing it to Stone. 'Emergency backup cigar. Dad taught me to always be prepared.'

'Damn, I raised a smart kid,' Chuck said, lighting Stone's cigar. 'So, now you gonna tell us why you don't want to party?'

'I didn't say I didn't want to. I just need maybe an hour to finish digesting this shit'—he waved a hand at his desk—'then I'll be ready as hell.'

'I'm busy digesting turkey. Or was it goose?' Chuck said. 'Can you at least take five and tell us what's in *your* gut?'

Stone's expression softened and he leaned back in his chair, taking a long pull from his cigar and emitting a thin blue stream of smoke. 'It's a puzzle,' he said.

Blank looks.

'It was months ago, after the last big gala. I was having an interesting discussion with Yvette and Crandall regarding puzzles. They were using their predictive chaos model, plugging in apparently unrelated events: the death of a congressman, the cartel wars, our capture of the *Saint Martin*, the CIA's inexplicable behavior, the rise to power of Carlos Velasquez, and a break-in at the CDC. I added my little bit of intel from *The Times*. The story of a mysterious disease wiping out the entire village of Huata in Guatemala.

'Crandall and Yvette were convinced these events were connected and that, like a puzzle, if you fill in enough of the pieces, you can deduce the shape of what's missing. At the time, there still wasn't enough information, but boy have we added to it since. The rebirth of the *Saint Martin* as the *Reina del Mar*, and her continued use for human trafficking. The CIA ignored that little transgression, though they had insisted the *Saint Martin* be returned to its "rightful owners."'

Marcus chewed nervously on his cigar and drummed his fingers on a desk—a motion caught by Stone's practiced eye—but said nothing.

'Then,' Stone continued, shifting his eyes back to Chuck, 'think about the intel Randy dug up. At the time, we thought the most important information was confirming the transformation of the ship. But there was one other tidbit. During the transformation, there was another person, arguing with the Viper. An argument that cast some doubt on who was really in control. Does that make any sense? Who the hell can argue with the Viper? Not another cartel leader. He'd end up conveniently dead. An outsider? Or was it a powerful insider, someone who had leverage with the Viper?

'Now consider that the *Reina* makes three trans-Atlantic trips, presumably delivering human cargo to the great profit of the Viper, then turns up in the Caribbean Sea crewed by dead people. Sailors who died of some bizarre disease resembling the plague. Jamaican authorities do the logical but chicken-shit thing and sink the *Dutchman* into a trench so deep no one would ever try to recover anything. Hell no! Not from a human trafficking boat. Good riddance!

'Then tonight, before dinner, Becky and I were talking and she mentioned her budding business relationship with Emma Lister. Talk about strange bedfellows! Turns out Carlos Velasquez had more than a little help becoming Carlos the Viper, head of the Mexican and Central American cartels. Help from a brilliant person; a powerful insider. Emma Lister dropped a name: Jesse Raynard.'

'Never heard of him,' Chuck said. 'You think he's a piece of this puzzle?'

'I think he may be the entire missing section that completes the picture. At least it's a possibility. And that wasn't the only intel Lister handed to Becky. Turns out there's at least one rotten apple in MI5 who

277

was working with Smythe-Montgomery and who may have shifted allegiance to the Viper.'

'Holy shit!' Logan said.

'Still sounds like a lot of loose pieces to me,' Chuck said. 'And what about the CIA's strange actions?'

'I think I can add something there,' Marcus said.

Every head turned to him.

'I've been keeping my ear to the ground, Dad, like you told me, and there's still a lot I don't know. In fact, a lot of this is speculation …'

'No one's going to jump the gun or hold you to your guesses, Marcus,' Stone said. 'Make it short and simple. We can let it percolate and talk more tomorrow.'

'Phew. Thanks. OK, someone is blocking intel regarding that ship, and he's good at it. Someone pretty high up. Nothing so obvious that it'd get the Director's attention. And it's not a block like a solid wall, more like a padded cell. You can beat on it, but nothing gives. The idea to hand the boat back in the first place came from a meeting of a half-dozen ranking agents. A group decision to surveil the ship and try to link it to the big boss. Bullshit! One guy with a phony but compelling argument swayed that meeting. That's how it usually goes. And everybody else gets back to their day jobs. I know the guys who attended that meeting, but haven't been able to penetrate to the man calling the shots. When I tried talking to lower-level people, they got spooked. Asking around was a bad idea. That's pretty clear now. No one wants that booger on their finger.'

'The names of the guys you talked to would be useful,' Stone said.

'I'll give you the list.'

'Do your old man a favor, will you? It's good to see you occasionally. Maybe you could get yourself a job as liaison to, say, MI5. Just a thought. I'd get to see you in London, anyway.'

Logan nodded. 'I get it. Look for the connection with MI5. You figure there may be some cooperative activities going on.'

'Makes sense,' Stone said. 'Remember, this goes back to the days of Smythe-Montgomery, and his playground was the world. How handy would it be to have connections in major intelligence agencies around the globe?'

'Now,' Chuck said, looking at the stump of his dead cigar, 'how 'bout we go back to the party. I'm high and dry.'

'I just want to spend some time searching for this Jesse Raynard,' said Stone. 'That's what I was about to do when you three guys interrupted.'

'Put Yvette on the job,' Logan said. 'She's smarter, better looking, and smarter than you. Plus, obviously better on a computer, 'cause she's smarter.'

'Ah, shit,' Stone said. 'You forgot the fact that she's smarter than me. OK, I give. But I think we've made some progress on this puzzle.'

'Tomorrow,' Chuck said.

***

The next morning, Yvette was unavailable. According to Arthur, she'd bundled up in a heavy sweatshirt and raincoat and gone for an early walk with Becky. Stone had grunted his acknowledgement and poured a third cup of coffee. Turkey stuffing and goose drippings were still making his mind sluggish. He'd spent more than a few minutes on the computer and gotten exactly what he expected. Zero information on a Jesse Raynard, as though the man didn't exist. Stone had run across this phenomenon before—a man with no past. In fact, Jason Stone had been that man. Born James Kulwicki, he'd adopted his current identity after faking his own death. The freedom of being unknown had allowed him to complete a multi-year mission to find a missing Russian nuke. A mission given him by Chuck Johnson. What was Jesse Raynard up to?

He eyed the computer display balefully, then decided against continuing to hunt for a man who might not exist. Even if he was capable of digging as deeply as Yvette, he knew his mind wasn't up to the task. Why? There was more to it than a full belly. As he pushed his chair back, he realized the problem. He was puzzled by Yvette and Becky's unexpected disappearance. He knew they'd become close in the chaotic times of Smythe-Montgomery's downfall. They'd become even closer after Colin's death. That was the problem. Stone knew Yvette's frame of mind. She wasn't satisfied with the death of Caldwell Simms. She wanted the big fish, the force behind Colin's murder, Carlos Velasquez. He also knew Becky Amhurst. She'd coolly shot an assassin at a Fourth Harmonics concert, and she'd risked torture and death to steal information from

Smythe-Montgomery. Bottom line: Becky was brave and unpredictable, and Yvette was obsessed with thoughts of revenge. A volatile mix.

What to do about it? Direct questioning of either was pointless, and he didn't have the heart to spy on two of the few people he considered friends. 'Let that dog lie for now,' he muttered to himself. He shook his head, trying to clear the cobwebs, but they clung to his mind. He drank the last of his coffee and left the office.

***

Halfway down Diana's long driveway, her collar turned up against the wind and sputtering rain, Becky was saying, 'I met Emma Lister at a program review not long after our conversation. She has another friend interested in eliminating the Viper.'

'Who?' Yvette asked.

'She was a bit dodgy on that, naturally, considering the risks. It may be someone she's mentioned before and it may not. The important thing is we have an ally. And not just a well-wisher. Someone with intel and resources.'

'Yes?'

'First, the intel. It seems Carlos is leaving his home—one of his fortified homes—for a meeting with subordinates. A gated mansion on the beach near Puerto Peñasco, a four hours' drive from Tucson.'

'It will be guarded, certainly,' Yvette said.

'Of course. No way in by foot, auto, or even ship I'm told.'

'So how does this help us?'

'Let me ask you something,' Becky said. 'What do you see when you look up in the sky at night?'

'What? Stars, I suppose, although around here'—she indicated the gloomy sky—'nothing at night.'

'And how often do you even look up?'

Yvette shrugged. 'Almost never.'

'Most people don't. It's the weak point of Carlos's security.'

'If your goal was to confuse me, you've succeeded admirably.'

'Did you know Carlos likes to walk outside and smoke a cigar after dinner?'

'More intel? Who's the source? Must be someone very close to him.'

'Let me tell you one other thing. I mentioned that this mysterious helper has resources. Now let me explain how the resources and intel come together.'

Yvette's jaw dropped and her eyes widened as Becky explained. When she'd finished, Yvette could only manage, 'You've got to be bloody joking!'

Becky laughed. 'No. And I should have mentioned that Puerto Peñasco is a resort town. Caters to visitors from California and Arizona. We can easily get close enough without being too close.'

'We?'

'I think I deserve a short vacation in a warm climate,' Becky said. 'Visit friends in Tucson, take a little trip south of the border. Enjoy a margarita or two.'

'When might this vacation happen?'

'Not settled yet. Weeks, maybe months, depending.'

'This mysterious source knows all this? And we trust him?'

'Emma Lister does. Also, she would genuinely like to see the last of the Viper. I'm convinced she's become a legitimate business woman. Men like the Viper cluttering your past have a tendency to be inconvenient.'

'I'd be happier knowing the identity of this enigmatic person.'

'I told you she mentioned a name once. A powerful, shadowy individual deep in the Viper's organization. I passed on his name to Jason: Jesse Raynard. Might be worth your time to track him down.'

Yvette didn't reply. She was already considering search parameters.

A creamy orange glow in the west transitioned to a pale green before passing through a spectrum of blues that darkened to black in the east as the last of twilight fled the crowded streets of Dhaka, Bangladesh.

Chapter Sixteen

Phase Three

A creamy orange glow in the west transitioned to a pale green before passing through a spectrum of blues that darkened to black in the east as the last of twilight fled the crowded streets of Dhaka, Bangladesh. It was hot. The day's heat, trapped in the tightly packed buildings and streets, rose up through the humid air making even the night uncomfortable, though at least the merciless sun was no longer beating on the sheet-metal roof of the brothel.

Business had begun to pick up, as it always did this time of day. Visitors wandered into the dim vestibule past metal gates that had opened not long after sunrise. Beyond this area of bare concrete, two narrow hallways, lit by bare fluorescent tubes, were filling with customers and the women soliciting them. A few ragged signs and posters hung on the walls, adding to the air of decay. Doors opened off both hallways; doors with heavy bolts that locked from the outside and gave the appearance of a prison more than a brothel.

Splashes of color from the women's dresses and the bedspreads in every room broke the monotony of grey. In addition to the beds, which dominated each tiny living area, several rooms also boasted brightly colored cloths or posters on the walls. A few shelves, perhaps a small table, might also find their way into the rooms, but each room was a workplace, with a comfortable horizontal surface its primary equipment.

The doors to most of the rooms were open, prostitutes still chattering with customers, trying to entice them inside. A few doors were closed, an agreement already having been reached. But one door, the last at the end of one hallway, had been shut for far too long. The woman who ran the house frowned. She had talked to this individual before. Either she must increase her clientele or leave. The old woman marched to the end of the hall and threw the door open wide, then let out a terrified shriek.

***

By dawn the next day, chaos. Three other brothels in the same area had been locked down, though most of the women had already fled. There was fear of an epidemic sweeping through the poorer sections of the city. Two doctors, known for their philanthropic work among the prostitutes, braved the scene, entering first one locked brothel then the others. A total of eight women and three of their clients were found dead inside, all exhibiting lesions alarmingly similar to plague or Ebola.

At the end of six hours, Doctors Denpo Hoque and Hardeep Chakma came out of the fourth building exhausted. Standing under umbrellas in a steady rain that left the hot air saturated, they reported to a sparse press corps.

Dr. Hoque spoke first. 'My colleague and I have examined the bodies and concluded that we have an unknown pathogen capable of human-to-human transmission. We cannot speculate on the method of transmission at this time. The lesions, bleeding, and skin discoloration are not consistent with any known disease, though there are similarities to other highly contagious and lethal diseases. Dr. Chakma, please add any comments or observations.'

'We recommend securing these buildings and allowing no one inside until a fully equipped epidemiological team arrives. We appeal to the world community for support. The symptoms we observed are similar to those reported by the CDC and by a doctor named ...' He turned to his colleague.

'Dr. Constantin Pavlovich Shukhov,' Hoque said.

'Yes. Dr. Shukhov described a similar pathology aboard a cargo ship in the Caribbean. An outbreak in a Central American village has been documented, though in that case, the village was destroyed by fire before any qualified medical examinations could be made.'

As the doctors spoke, the few reporters who'd come out exchanged nervous glances and backed away. A disease outbreak in the cramped, unsanitary brothels was hardly news, which explained the small number of reporters. A contagious and deadly plague was another thing altogether.

Still, a journalism award—even a Pulitzer—was a small consolation if you died getting it.

'Please,' Chakma said, appealing to the newsmen, 'come take pictures. The world must know. The world must help! Please!'

But the reporters had scattered, leaping into cars or onto motorcycles and driving off. The two doctors stood forlornly, staring out into the empty street. The sound of rain drumming on roofs and splashing from downspouts filled the silence.

From under the eaves of a nearby building, an individual in a hooded rain jacket stepped forward. 'I'll take a few pictures, if you like. This story wouldn't be complete without them.'

The doctors stepped forward and Hoque nodded. 'Heskin said you would be here. Come take your pictures.'

Chakma slid back the folding gate.

As the three stepped under the shelter of the corrugated roof, the stranger's hood slid down. The doctors froze and exchanged a look of uncertainty. 'You are Raynard?' Chakma asked.

'Names really aren't important here, are they? Let's just say I am here on Raynard's behalf.'

The doctors entered the narrow hallway, but before they'd gone three steps, the stranger's hand shot out and grabbed the arm of Chakma. 'Let me remind you of your arrangement with Carl Heskin. Your discretion has been purchased at what is certainly a reasonable price. Your lives. Break this trust, and payment becomes due. Understand?'

'We do,' Chakma said. 'Take your photographs.'

***

Old grievances put aside, the CDC requested the services of the one brilliant doctor and researcher known to have examined victims of a similar disease, Constantin Shukhov. The bureaucracy moved at its ponderous pace. Constantin resisted this assignment, claiming he was no field researcher, but Dr. Carl Heskin made a compelling case. At the outcome of these discussions, a not-too-surprising conclusion: Constantin agreed to travel to Bangladesh if accompanied by Heskin. Administrative sluggishness was replaced by frantic activity. They were to pick their teams and be airborne before another day passed. Constantin could barely suppress a smirk.

285

***

Carl Heskin coughed, scarlet phlegm staining his white napkin.

Constantin eyed his friend critically. 'Why did you come on this trip?' he said, with surprising sincerity.

'I believe it was you who suggested it,' Carl replied.

'Pfah! You could have refused.'

'And miss this delightful eight-hour flight to Kolkata? Don't be ridiculous. Besides, this was the plan.'

Constantin considered this. 'You have a high respect for this Jesse Raynard, don't you?'

'Yes. For many reasons. Some you know. Raynard bought my services with a promise to care for my family. That promise was already kept, or the bank is lying to me.'

'Precisely what services has he bought?'

Carl chuckled. 'I'm a man of many talents, Constantin. I laid the groundwork for this demonstration in Bangladesh, for instance.'

'What nonsense.'

'I'm serious. Plus, I've told you of my involvement in the matter of the *Reina del Mar* and the village of Huata.'

A stewardess leaned over their seats and smiled. 'Roughly three hours to go, gentlemen. Can I get you anything?'

'A bottle of Jack and a glass of ice,' Carl said.

'A black coffee for me. As dark and strong as you can manage,' Constantin replied.

When the stewardess had gone, he said, 'You do know what time it is, don't you?'

Carl slid the screen up on his window. 'It's still dark outside. If it's dark, I can drink Jack.' He shrugged. 'The only exception I make is if it's light outside.'

Constantin shook his head. Later, as he sampled his coffee, he returned to their previous conversation, saying, 'You're not going to tell me the real reason Raynard hired you, are you?'

Carl smiled, but his eyes were distant. 'You're a clever man, Constantin. You'll figure it out eventually.'

***

The flight from Kolkata to Dhaka on an old turboprop was bumpy, hot, and humid. The air conditioning had failed, and the recirculated air—far too warm and damp—smelled faintly of old goat. As they disembarked, Constantin flashed a smile to the stewardess at the door and said pleasantly, 'Your airplane is a piece of shit.'

The stewardess feigned a hurt expression. 'It's not *my* plane.'

'Never mind the grumpy old Russki aristocrat, miss,' Carl said. 'He hasn't had a chance to beat his peasants yet today.'

'Come along, peasant,' Constantin said, with a smile and wink to the stewardess.

At the luggage carousel, Constantin assigned their team to collect everything, including the equipment from the cargo bay, and meet them at the hotel. 'So how do we play this?' he asked, once he and Carl were comfortably seated in a Mercedes limousine. Hotel shuttles were for those who carried the luggage.

'We're the pros from Dover. At least, you are. We get a good night's sleep—'

'No, no, this is a crisis. A crisis, I say!'

'Fine,' Carl grumbled. 'A quick stop at the hotel. Contact the local authorities and our two friendly doctors—'

'Yes! Captain Hook and Doctor Chocolate!'

'Would you shut up and listen? Doctors Hoque and Chakma will meet us at the first brothel. We'll get in our bunny suits and make an examination.'

'Photos have already hit the press.'

Carl shrugged. 'Raynard is precise and efficient. We'll take more, plus blood samples, tissue.'

'No bodies?'

'Of course not. The authorities have insisted we not remove them.'

'You're right. Precise and efficient. I'd like to see the marketplace.'

Carl glanced towards Constantin. 'Why not? It will be an education for you, though you have two PhDs and an MD.'

'It is fascinating. A deadly new disease, the plague of the twenty-first century, for sale to the highest bidder on the dark web. Spooky! I never even knew how to market my genius literary work on the obvious connection between Karl and Groucho Marx!'

Carl groaned. 'You can be a tiresome old son of bitch, Constantin. Did you know that?'

***

Diana's house was alive with a spirit of holiday. Christmas was only a week away, and Cathie had been given the green light to travel. A massive party in Tucson had already been laid on.

Becky, who had left a few days earlier, had promised to be there. Chuck and Joy would accompany Logan and Cathie back; Logan and Chuck were already in deep discussions of the wines to be served. Diana and Crandall had declined the invitation, pleading old age and a need to rest up for the coming year. To everyone's delight, Yvette had said she would come along.

'I've always wanted to see America. And the Wild West! I suppose if there is any Wild West left, it would be in Tucson.'

'Can't get any wilder,' Logan had assured her.

So people hustled and bustled, packed and repacked, all in a spirit of hopefulness.

Among these, only Jason Stone was as gloomy as the London sky. Something wasn't right. In fact, something was *far* from right.

'Why not join your friends?' Luana asked. 'Even though I can't be in Tucson for Christmas, we could meet in Breckenridge for New Year's Eve.'

'I'd love that, darling ...'

'But?'

He took her hands. 'I'll meet you in Breck for New Year's Eve and we'll celebrate both holidays together.'

'Can you tell me what's bothering you?'

'I would if I could. It's like a two-headed coin when I've picked tails. OK, that doesn't make sense. What I mean is, there are two problems. This business with the CIA and MI5 is one.'

'And the other?'

'That's the one that's really bugging me.'

She lifted a questioning eyebrow.

'I don't know what it is.'

***

Logan's house was decorated to the hilt. Even his grand piano was strewn with Christmas cards and paraphernalia, though the keyboard was clear. It was rumored the Fourth Harmonics would be jamming Christmas tunes during this Welcome Home / Pre-Christmas party on the 23rd. Cookies were scattered in decorative plates all over the house, bowls of nuts were everywhere, Dean Martin was crooning on the outdoor speakers, and the bar was open.

Guests had been arriving all afternoon and, as at all good parties, clumps of people would form and talk of things relevant and trivial, then break apart to form other clusters and begin again. The day was cloudy and cool, so the fireplace in the family room was a popular gathering spot, as was the kitchen, where both a turkey and a beef Wellington were roasting. Outside, a few hearty souls sat around the chimenea and smoked cigars.

Cathie, naturally, had been the focal point. Seated near the fireplace, she'd told her story many times to friends who'd only heard what the news had to offer. And being good friends, they never pressed when she grew silent. They knew a young man had been killed and they'd been discreetly told that the thin, blond Englishwoman had been in love with him. Still, there was much to discuss of a far more pleasant nature.

Logan and Cathie's daughter, Kelly, had been unable to come, having used every bit of her discretionary time with her mother in London when Cathie had come out of the coma. But Chuck's son, Marcus, was there. Marcus, Randy, and Logan were currently guarding the chimenea, each enjoying a cigar.

'Man, that guy Stone is a hard dude,' Marcus said.

Randy gave him a crooked grin. 'If you mean it would be a bad idea to cross him, I agree. Did you know he shot my wife?'

'What the—aww, you're jerking my chain!'

'Not so,' Logan said. He proceeded to give a detailed description of the first time Randy, Gail, and he had met Jason Stone in an aircraft hangar at Davis-Monthan Air Force Base. When he finished, he added, 'Surprised your dad never mentioned it.'

'He did,' Marcus said, running his hand across the stubble on his chin, a mannerism of his father's, 'just not all the details. So, Stone *grazed* her arm, surrounded by frickin' terrorists, just to keep control of the situation?'

'Yep,' Logan said, wondering how Marcus would react. Marcus didn't disappoint him. He took a deep draw on his cigar and blew out a cloud of blue-grey smoke.

'Whew! When I shoot, I go for center of mass, just like my momma taught me! The CIA agreed.'

'Stone's an interesting character,' Randy said, his deadpan delivery driving home the understatement.

'Complex, if you get my drift,' Logan added. 'Also, when it comes to a gunfight, he's got the speed and accuracy of a mongoose on cocaine.'

'Yeah,' Marcus said thoughtfully, 'I think I'll refrain from crossing him.'

'Good lad,' Logan commented, patting his shoulder.

'I'm kind of surprised he and Luana aren't here,' Marcus said.

'Me too,' Logan replied. 'I talked to him before we left London. Something's bugging him, that's for sure.'

'Logan, you crusty old SOB,' Tyrone called as he exited the house. 'Let's smoke a cigar, then we've got to light up some Christmas music! Hand me a smoke and introduce me.'

The conversation became more general when Tyrone joined the group, concerns about Jason Stone temporarily put aside.

'Where's the rest of the band?' Logan asked.

'Setting up inside. They had to move your Christmas tree and dining room table to make room. Joking!' he added, seeing the shock on Logan's face. 'You're an easy mark.'

'Too true. What have you been up to?'

'Just practicing my licks and enjoying the low humidity. And I try to keep track of what's going on in the world of medicine. Part of the old epidemiologist that just won't die.'

'You're a doctor?' Marcus asked.

'No longer in practice,' Tyrone rumbled, 'so don't bother tellin' me about your aches and pains. I still like to stay in touch with the community, though.'

'What's the latest?' Randy said.

Tyrone blew a stream of smoke and grew serious. 'Some disease outbreak in Bangladesh. In the brothel district of Dhaka. The news is sketchy, but the symptoms don't match those of a venereal disease like the one that struck there a few years back. Bad medicine caused that one. This'—he looked sheepishly at the others—'well, you'll think I'm being an alarmist, but from what I've heard it sounds a little like bubonic plague.'

'Plague?' Randy repeated, his voice tense.

'Yeah, but not quite,' Tyrone replied. 'I need to talk to Martha Zanders, see what she thinks.'

To the blank looks, he responded, 'Colleague of mine back in Seattle. Had a gift for diagnosis that left me in her rearview mirror.'

'Pretty high praise,' Logan said.

'Maybe, but true.'

'When you talk to her, there are a couple other incidents you might want her to consider,' Randy said.

'Really?'

'One involved a ship and another a village in Guatemala.'

'I remember something about the ship, but there was never a follow-up.'

'There wouldn't be,' Randy said, 'unless you fancied a trip to the bottom of the Cayman Trench to examine the bodies.'

Tyrone snapped his fingers. 'That's right! The ship was sunk by the Jamaicans. There was something else I remember. A doctor from the CDC made an examination. Conrad ... no, Constantin Shukhov.'

'You know him?' Marcus asked, surprised.

'More like I know *of* him. Another question for Martha.' He took a final puff of his cigar, then grinned. 'Now, how 'bout some music?'

***

Logan cracked his fingers and stared at the sheet music. He'd been practicing this tune since last Christmas and didn't want to blow it. Tyrone gave him a thumbs-up and Logan launched off into the Vince Guaraldi classic 'Christmas Time is Here.'

The next time Logan surfaced from his total absorption in the music, he heard the applause from his guests, and Tyrone was pointing at him with the bow of the big 'upright fiddle.' Becky whistled, then whispered something into Yvette's ear. The two had been together talking for most of the evening.

Jeez, Fletcher, what's wrong with that? he asked himself.

291

Before he could give it much thought, Tyrone gave them the beat for the next song. Soon, the room was filled with his sonorous version of 'Christmas Blues.' More applause at the conclusion, with Tyrone laughing and bowing low.

Logan had only an instant to glance in the direction of Becky and Yvette. They were gone. Not that unusual. People were wandering in and out, grabbing snacks, freshening drinks. Still, he couldn't shake the feeling of discomfort. He made himself a promise to share a drink with Becky and ply her for information.

Just as the band finished their last song, Cathie gave a cry of delight. Their friend and guest singer from the band's concert at DeSalvo's Vineyard and Winery, Judy Lewis, walked in, adding her own applause to the group's.

'And who is this lovely woman?' Tyrone asked.

'A friend of ours, and a singer with some serious pipes,' Logan replied. 'Our last bass player was killed the only time she ever sang with the band. I think I've mentioned it.'

'Holy shit!' Tyrone said. 'Ms. Lewis, I'd be honored if you'd join us for a finale.'

Logan was shocked as Tyrone took her hand and kissed it. 'Logan has sung your praises, if you'll pardon the pun, and I'd truly love to hear your rendition of "White Christmas," provided I'm still alive at the end.' Judy gave a start, and Tyrone gave Logan a sheepish look. 'Too soon?'

Randy interceded. 'We gave Steve a rousing sendoff. But Becky should be here. She certainly saved us the trouble of a lengthy investigation and trial. I'll go find her.'

As he moved off, Logan tapped his shoulder and whispered, 'See if you can bring Yvette in too, would you? The two of them have been thick as thieves tonight, and I don't mean that in an entirely figurative sense.'

'Worried about the silverware?' The playful smile slid off Randy's face as he saw no corresponding levity. 'What's wrong?'

'Oh, nothing. It's just …'

'I'll find 'em both. We'll talk later.'

As Randy moved off, the band began a jazz version of 'White Christmas.' At the conclusion, they repeated the final chorus, motioning for the audience to join in, reminiscent of the last scene of the classic movie. Loud applause, whistles, and toasts as the last chords faded.

'This lady almost makes us legit,' Tyrone said to Logan. 'Let me buy you a drink,' he added, grinning at Judy like a boy. The two moved off, already talking music, and Logan was left to wonder how he could have been so clumsy with women all his life, while Tyrone was so damn smooth.

He didn't have much time to sulk before Randy approached. 'Becky and Yvette are over there. I've got a foolproof way to draw Yvette off if you want a minute alone with Becky.'

Logan gave him a quizzical look.

'My kid—and Gail's—has a PhD in cuteness. Better than a puppy. Watch for your chance.'

Logan went to the bar and poured two glasses of the best Cab he had in the house. A minute later, he saw Gail passing little James Charles O'Neil to Yvette. Logan casually strolled over and offered a glass to Becky. 'Care to spend a minute with the old piano player?'

'Naw.' She took the wine. 'But I'd love to hang out with *you.*'

He led Becky out onto the patio and tossed another log into the chimenea.

'I have to admit,' Becky said, 'when you were finishing that song, I was getting nervous. Actually had my hand in my purse.'

'You didn't?'

She opened her purse, revealing a compact Glock. 'Always.'

'Got rid of the wheel gun and switched to a semiautomatic, I see.'

'Puhlease. More rounds mean more dead bad guys. Glad no one took a shot at Tyrone, who, by the way, plays a mean bass.'

'That he does. So, uh, how are you?'

Becky gave him a sharp look. 'Logan, that was biggest bullshit, uninterested, insulting question you've ever damaged my ears with.'

'You're right.' He shook his head. 'I suck at being a spy.'

Becky's features softened. 'How 'bout a friend?'

'I used to be OK with that. Have a seat, would you, and let me explain.'

'It'd better start with an apology.'

'It will. Also …' He held up the rest of the bottle of Cab. 'Snuck it out here right before I accosted you.'

'Wow! I like having you at a disadvantage.'

'Our eternal state.' He clicked his glass with hers. 'I'm sorry. Truth is, I've had a bad feeling that you and Yvette are cooking up some mayhem. I know she isn't over Colin. Hell, everybody knows. But his killer's dead. What else is there for her to do?'

Becky's eyes were an amalgam of respect, concern, and a lingering desire. 'Honesty is your strong suit, big boy. I'll always love you for it. No, shush. Let me tell you, you're right. She's not over Colin and she hasn't had her revenge.'

'Wait … what? I'm confused.'

'Top me up,' she said, holding out her glass. 'What I tell you now is under the condition you tell no one and take no action whatsoever, agreed?'

'Becky—'

'I'm not joking around, Logan.'

'I'm just trying to help. Don't you get that?'

'I do, but this time you have to trust me. Now, is it a deal?'

A sharp snap drew their attention to the chimenea for an instant. Sparks flew up as a log settled lower into the embers. When their eyes met again, a line of communication flashed between them like a lightning bolt.

'No.'

Becky covered her shock by draining the contents of her glass. 'Then thanks for the drink.' She got up and headed back towards the house, but turned back abruptly and said, 'Don't interfere.'

'Or?'

'No "or." Just don't be an idiot. If you get involved, it won't go well.' She spun around and disappeared. When Logan finally returned to the house, Gary told him Becky had left right after coming back into the house, Yvette going with her.

Too late, he thought. *I* am *an idiot*.

***

'He wouldn't agree?' Yvette asked.

'No,' Becky said, pounding through the gears of her Porsche Boxster and hitting ninety on the empty road south of Logan's house before getting control of herself. She double-clutched back into third and let the RPMs drop until she was going a sedate forty-five. 'I shouldn't have opened my stupid mouth, but ...'

'You trust him.'

'I do. Besides which, he isn't an idiot, though I accused him of being one. He knows we're up to something, and it seemed better to bring him in than to let him speculate and keep nosing around. Guess I was wrong.'

Yvette tentatively reached out and squeezed Becky's arm. 'You were right to try. How long until we're ready?'

Yvette's question was paramount. Time was everything, and Logan only had suspicions. He'd tell Randy and Stone, of course, but what could they really do? According to Yvette, Stone was still in London trying to solve the riddle of the *Flying Dutchman*. That meant first understanding how the CIA and MI5 were involved with the operation of the *Saint Martin / Reina del Mar* and who was pulling the strings. Chuck Johnson would help, as would his son, Marcus, but it was a formidable challenge. No, the only way Stone could interfere would be if he abandoned his current mystery for another. Not his style. Becky smiled. She could throw him a few additional tidbits of information to keep him occupied.

Yvette had noticed Becky's frustration slip away, to be replaced by calm confidence. 'You've thought of something, haven't you?'

'You know, having Emma Lister as an ally is proving invaluable,' Becky answered. 'Yes, I believe I can use her information to keep Stone busy until our plan is a fait accompli. Which shouldn't take more than a few weeks.'

'That soon? Outstanding!'

'I'll talk to Emma tonight. I've had Gary working on algorithms. I'm hoping we can have the hardware delivered in a day or two. Naturally, Gary doesn't know our true purpose. It wouldn't be fair to him. I'll modify the code myself. Then ... Are you up for a Mexican holiday?'

***

Despite the happy reunion, a knot had settled in Logan's stomach. A considerate host, he did his best to hide his anxiety. The party wound down early, as everyone could see Cathie was exhausted. Tyrone and Judy performed a dazzling version of 'Peace on Earth / Little Drummer Boy,' and the last guests prepared to leave. Randy put a hand on Logan's arm. 'You OK? You may be able to fool most people, but to me it looks like you swallowed a sour habanero. I take it the discussion with Becky was a bust.'

'What was your first clue?' Logan asked wryly. 'My sour puss or Becky and Yvette's sudden departure?'

Ignoring Logan's question, Randy said, 'Care to talk about it?'

'Yeah, but not tonight. Got to get Cathie off to bed.'

'Call me tomorrow?'

Logan nodded.

Soon afterward, the house was blanketed in the surreal hush that only occurs after a lively get-together. The Christmas tree and decorations blazed away in all their glory, filling empty rooms with multi-colored light, and candles sent the heady fragrance of pine and cinnamon into the stillness. Dean Martin's 'Marshmallow World' whispered from the sound system.

Logan had insisted Cathie leave the cleaning up to him. Lacking the strength and motivation to argue, she'd kissed him goodnight and curled up beneath the covers. He'd heard the regular breathing of deep sleep only moments later. Closing the bedroom door, he wandered off to the kitchen where, despite the help his friends had given collecting plates, bottles, and glasses, a considerable task awaited him. He moved to the sink but turned away, retreating to the bar where he poured himself a cognac. After adding a log to the fire, he flopped down in his favorite leather recliner. Dean Martin had moved on to 'I'll be Home for Christmas.'

Staring into the fire, Logan pondered his course of action. He'd talk to Randy tomorrow, of course, but it seemed his next move would be to call Jason Stone. What to tell him? A vague concern wasn't actionable intel, yet it was all Logan had.

For at least a half hour Logan sat, realizing all along that he didn't give a shit whether his intel was good, bad, or indifferent. Surprisingly, he also realized he didn't care whether Becky and Yvette were up to something. OK, he did care, but it wasn't what was causing the knot in his stomach. While Martin crooned 'I've Got My Love to Keep Me Warm,' Logan finally understood. He'd gotten crosswise with Becky. Seriously crosswise. Maybe even enough to destroy their long-standing relationship.

'Shit!' he muttered. Knowing the cause of his upset also meant knowing the answer. He reached for his phone just as it dinged.

The message from Becky read simply, 'I'm sorry.'

Logan quickly responded, 'Not as sorry as I am. Please be careful.'

Not thirty seconds passed before a second ding preceded the message 'We will. Say hi to Stone. I told him you'd be calling.'

'Now what the hell does that mean?' A puzzle. But the knot in Logan's stomach had miraculously untied itself. He hadn't destroyed his friendship. He would contact Stone. And Becky had already talked to him. The lights seemed cheerier, the pile of glasses and dishes seemed smaller. He poured himself another cognac and set to work.

Christmas music from the '50s, '60s, and '70s saw him through the cleaning up. His cognac had mysteriously evaporated in the process, and the clock had snuck around past midnight. He checked on Cathie—still breathing the steady pace of the pleasantly exhausted. Calculating the time difference between Tucson and London, Logan decided it might be possible to catch Stone.

The third ring proved him right, Stone betraying his tiredness only by the confused, 'This is Stone of Stone … umm … Triple S Security … ah, shit, who is this?'

'It's Logan. I know I didn't wake you up 'cause you answered your office phone, but you sound like you haven't had your coffee yet.'

'Wasted precious time searching for the filters,' Stone grumbled. 'Never could find 'em, so I used a paper towel. Worked OK. And no, you didn't wake me up, Becky did. Gave me some tantalizing intelligence then said you'd be calling. Now, how the hell is that after four hours of sleep?'

'Sucks to be you,' Logan said, without sympathy, 'but you could have been here. *Should* have been here.'

'Couldn't have. Still can't. There's something mighty fishy going on.'

'Still chasing the *Dutchman*?'

'Yeah, and Becky gave me a hot lead courtesy of Emma Lister, if you can believe it. I have to follow up pronto or I miss the chance. I can only guess Becky is doing herself a bigger favor than she's doing for me, and hence the purpose of your call.'

'Not bad for a half-asleep guy. Becky and Yvette are up to something, and when I tried to find out what, Becky slammed the door in my face. My nose is still bleeding.'

'I knew Yvette wouldn't let things rest, even though Colin's killer is dead. Leave it to Becky to egg her on.'

'It's worse than that. More like co-conspirators at this point. Well, since you're occupied, is there anything I should do?'

'You already did it. You asked. If I could come ...' He faded to a frustrated silence.

'How about Chuck or Randy?'

'I need Chuck out here ASAP. There's a CIA connection to manage. Randy's working some angles back in your town. Besides, he's had a couple too many adventures recently and needs to spend the holidays with his family.'

'So?'

'I'm wearing out my vocal cords telling people to be careful, but I think I'll toss that solid-gold advice in Becky and Yvette's direction one last time. Otherwise, they're on their own.'

'Becky managed Smythe-Montgomery.'

'She did, though she had plenty of backup. Do me a favor and get a hold of Chuck. Tell him to get his butt to Morocco. I'll text details.'

'Uh, Stone, you do know what tomorrow is, don't you?'

'Here in London, we call it the day after today. This shit can't wait. Johnson knows the score. Oh, and tell him to have Marcus lie low but keep his ears open.'

'Merry Christmas, Stone.'

'Maybe next year.'

In a deserted hollow surrounded by sand dunes, propellers spun up to speed and a drone—twin to the one used by Carlos to poison the fields of his rivals—rose into the dark sky.

Chapter Seventeen

Yvette's Revenge

Constantin Pavlovich Shukhov was annoyingly flashy, though in this case, it suited Raynard's purpose. Appearing in a grubby local TV studio, Constantin wore his three-thousand-dollar suit with the ease and carelessness a normal human might wear a sweatshirt and jeans. Hair slicked back, with not a lock out of place, he held the remote with recently manicured hands.

The first image seemed grossly out of context: A woman's body, naked, with deep subcutaneous bruising and odd bulbous swelling in multiple locations. Congealed blood traced a lurid path to eyes, ears, and mouth.

'As you can see, this individual shows conflicting symptoms that resemble both bubonic plague and Ebola. Other bodily fluids have been cleared away: urine, thin soupy feces. As for—'

'Stop!' The voice of the executive producer. 'You cannot show these images nor can you make such statements.'

Constantin turned with glacial slowness to face the man. 'Then why am I here? Eh? I enter those hell holes, do my examinations. The Minister of Health himself has asked me to go on television and report what I've seen. None of your local doctors, with two bold exceptions, would venture near the place. Do you realize'—his voice had risen an octave and doubled in volume—'this may be the same disease that's broken out twice already? Once in Guatemala and once on the damned ship in the Caribbean that I had the misfortune to investigate. This disease exhibits some of the more grotesque elements of the plague and is apparently more deadly, with a means of transmission unknown! What the hell do you want me to say? The victims died of boredom? I demand to see the minister!'

'Calm yourself.' The voice of a small, casually dressed man as he stepped forward from the rear of the room. His bald head, round face, and emotionless eyes and mouth reminded Constantin of a less-well-fed Buddha. 'I am the minister. Begin again and Nahrem will record everything. Then you and I will sit like civilized men and discuss what is to be broadcast and what shall remain, for now, in the hands of scientists. It is better that way. No need to cause a panic.'

'Very well,' Constantin said, 'but I reserve the right to protest any unnecessary censorship.'

The Buddha nodded. 'That is your right.'

In an isolated corner of his mind, Constantin smiled nastily. *These fools are even easier to manipulate than Raynard implied. Using people's fears to suit your own purpose is more than genius. What power! Perhaps I'll become a U.S. citizen and run for political office. A sheep dog has a harder job!*

Fifteen minutes of recording and two hours of faux negotiations and both Buddha and Constantin left the studio with exactly what they wanted. And just in time. A nationwide broadcast was about to begin, plus a release to the BBC, AP, and other major news outlets on every continent but Antarctica.

The news spread around the world like tree pollen in a gale. A newspaper in London described it in this way:

'A witness to both the outbreak aboard a ship in the Caribbean and now in the city of Dhaka, Bangladesh, the renowned CDC staff member Dr. Constantin Shukhov has observed with his own eyes the tragic consequences of this new plague upon humanity. "Though similar to other scourges of the past," he said, "there is no doubt it is more virulent. Transmissibility seems extraordinarily high. Death rates cannot be estimated, though—" And here the doctor hesitated, his demeanor under control, but his eyes shaded with fear. He set his jaw and showed the stoicism a Cossack would have admired. "Courage! The resources of the world, once focused, cannot fail. For now, exercise extreme caution, report all instances of similar symptoms."

'We can only give thanks for medical heroes like Dr. Constantin.'

302

Constantin was barely able to regain his breath. His tumbling laughter finally subsided. Then he read the words 'stoicism a Cossack would have admired' again, and he laughed until tears came and his sides ached.

'Are you done admiring yourself?' Carl asked.

'C-C-C-Cossack!' Constantin bellowed. 'The irony! My ancestors would have scorned a Cossack. Filthy peasants with swords. They had more fleas than their horses. Cossack! Oh, ha ha ha.'

'Calm down, people are staring.'

In one of the few upscale restaurants in Dhaka, it was unusual for a man to lose his composure in this manner. A few people shook their heads, others exchanged quiet remarks. Could this be the famous man, the great CDC doctor? The poor man must be turning to alcohol to relieve his stress. They turned back to their lobster and filets.

'Fine,' Constantin said, sniffing his rice pilaf with disgust. 'Good Lord, for a decent meal. Are we almost done here, Carl?'

Carl Heskin smiled. 'More than that. *Raynard* is almost done.'

***

Like others across the globe, Jason Stone read the news of the new plague, albeit from an English newspaper printed in Morocco. Only half his mind had really followed the story, but even half was enough to register a mental 'tilt.' Three instances of this new disease: one in Guatemala, one on board a ship known for human smuggling, and one in a brothel in Bangladesh. And this doctor—what the hell was his name?—a witness to two. Coincidence? A coldly analytical part of Stone's mind cried 'Bullshit!'

He abandoned his frustrated musings as he saw Chuck Johnson, a grimace on his face, exiting the Rabat-Salé Airport terminal. Stone motioned to the cabbie, and a minute later, Chuck was seated next to him, his luggage loaded and the cab heading for the hotel.

'Jeez, Johnson, smile or something. It looks like you ate a piece of raw meat loaded with maggots.'

'You mean instead of Christmas turkey with my wife's famous bacon stuffing?' he grumbled. 'Well excuse *me*.'

There was no point trying to dull Chuck's knife-edged mood. It would disappear over time. Best get to work. 'What does Marcus have to say?'

Part of Chuck's scowl slid away at the mention of his son. 'Your hunch was right. One of the four or five agents Marcus was keeping tabs on decided a trip to Africa was urgently needed. Marcus got a hold of his itinerary.'

'No shit? Way to go Marcus!'

'Guy's name is Doug Greenville. He'll arrive on the 5:00 a.m. flight tomorrow and he's staying at the Royale. Gives us time to prepare.'

'Becky's intel was spot on too. Greenville's counterpart in MI5, Danny Ivers, got here early this morning. Also staying at the Royale.'

'What really stinks is how today's agents get to stay at the shit-hottest hotel in Rabat. What fleabag dump are we staying at?'

'Johnson, you're not a CIA agent anymore. Nothing but the best for the executives of Triple S. Adjacent suites at the Royale.'

Chuck grinned. 'Screw the turkey. Do we get room service?'

'That's the spirit. Tonight, you can order anything you want on the hotel menu. Tomorrow, we dine at la Marrakesh. Five-ish star restaurant overlooking the harbor. Entrees start at $300 American. Turns out Danny made reservations for two.'

'That's one hell of a per diem for MI5. Could he be wining and dining a lady?'

Stone shrugged. 'Could be, but my guess is we'll find agent Greenville there.'

'How'd you get all this intel?'

'C'mon, Johnson, American money spends pretty well at hotel lobbies and with maître d's. If it's a bust, we'll have a great dinner. I hear the swordfish is pretty good.'

'And if it's not a bust?'

'Ah, then I think we'll have a nice, private conversation with Ivers and Greenville. So, drink heavily tonight. You'll want to see straight enough to aim tomorrow.'

'Aim what?'

'Don't be a hick from the sticks. I have friends in Morocco. Friends in low places.'

***

Chuck felt fully clothed with the comfortable weight of a compact Sig Sauer tucked inside his sport coat. As Stone had predicted, the swordfish was excellent. They were finishing up their main course when a tall sandy-haired man with nervous eyes was seated at a table for two near the windows overlooking the harbor.

'Ivers,' Stone muttered.

A few minutes later, a stocky man with a crooked nose and short dark hair wandered up to the table and took a seat. Stone could feel Chuck grow tense.

'I recognize him,' Chuck whispered. 'Didn't know him well, but saw him at a few meetings. His nickname is Pit Bull.'

'And?'

'He was a giant, prevaricating son of a bitch. You know how you get a feeling about a guy? Hope he's never assigned to watch your back?'

Stone gave a terse nod.

'How do you want to play this?' Chuck asked.

'After dinner, why don't you just go over and say hello?'

'And you'll be ...?'

'Outside, with a cab waiting.'

***

Greenville and Ivers were rising from the table when Chuck strolled up, a shit-eating grin on his face. 'Pit Bull? Haven't seen you in forever.'

Chuck's hand shot forward and he registered the quick motion of the others towards their jackets—carrying without a doubt—until they regained their composure. Ivers shot his companion a daggered glance, while Greenville shook Chuck's hand.

'Chuck Johnson,' Chuck said. 'Don't you remember me? It was 2008—no, 2009—in Oakland.'

'Johnson, sure,' Greenville said, in a deep, gravelly voice. 'This is my friend Danny.' He pretended to check his watch. 'Shit, I'd love to catch up on old times, but I'm afraid we have to go. See you around, OK?'

'I understand. I was just leaving too. After you, gents.'

Chuck tucked in close behind. At the bottom of a short flight of stairs, a cab waited, the door open. Chuck jammed the Sig up against Greenville's spine. 'Get in the cab, both of you. Let's not have a fuss.'

Danny was reaching under his jacket when Stone appeared silently at his side. 'Easy, Danny. I've got hollow-points in my H&K. Make a real mess of that nice suit.'

'You guys are making a big fucking mistake,' Greenville snarled. 'Do you have any idea who we are?'

'Oh, let me see,' Stone said casually, as he relieved the men of their firearms. 'You're a scumbag traitorous CIA puke and Danny here is an equally dirty member of MI5. We dropped a dime on both of you before you got to your soup course, and your more respectable colleagues are on their way to pick you up. You boys are looking at some hard time. Luckily, Chuck and I just want a little information, then you can be on your way.'

'Pier four, warehouse six,' Stone said, when they'd all slipped into the cab.

The cabbie gave a nervous twitch and drove off along the seaside road. In twenty minutes, he was driving out along a disused pier, the embedded railroad tracks rusty, the warehouses to either side lifeless. Number six was the last one still standing, the others crumbling heaps of steel, wood, and glass. Stone shoved a wad of bills into the cabbie's hands, and in his broken Arabic said, 'Your name is Otorro Utumbe, your cab number is 1432, and you had no fare at 8:30 this evening. If I hear otherwise, you're a dead man. Understand?'

The man nodded vigorously.

'Good man. Let's go inside,' he said to Ivers and Greenville, as the cab made a hasty retreat along the deserted pier.

Once inside the building, Chuck and Stone drew their weapons, their two captives in the line of a crossing fire. 'I know what you're thinking,' Stone said, 'but if we wanted you dead, you'd be dead. We want nothing more than information.' He smiled like a cougar facing a deer. 'And now you're thinking we'll kill you once we have what we need. I give you my word you'll walk out of here alive if you don't do anything stupid.'

'Why should we believe you?' Greenville asked.

'Why not, since you have no choice? We know you were working for Smythe-Montgomery, and since his sudden disappearance—for which you can thank Chuck and me—you've transferred your dubious allegiance to Carlos Velasquez. OK, first question. What do you know about the *Saint Martin*?'

Silence.

Stone shrugged. 'Fine. The hard way.' He pulled a pair of heavy-duty wire cutters from his pants pocket. 'Who wants to lose an ear first? Or would you rather take a chance on our magnanimity?'

'I'm not getting carved up for the filthy Viper,' Ivers said. 'I say we take a chance.'

Greenville nodded.

'The *Saint Martin* was a gold mine,' Ivers said. 'You know the cargo. We got a fat cut. Just a business proposition, mate.'

'You gave false leads, discouraged investigations, that sort of thing?' Stone asked.

'Yeah. How'd you—'

'Because I've done it myself. Next question. What do you know about the *Reina del Mar*?'

Greenville answered. 'The *Saint Martin* was snagged by some motherfuckers and turned over to the CIA. I was the one ... wait. You guys?'

'We are the motherfuckers to whom you refer,' Chuck said, grinning like a shark.

'Son of a bitch! Stone Security Services.' He turned towards Stone. 'So you must be—'

'No one. If you remember that, you might live to be an old man. Continue. You were the one ... what?'

'I was the one who got the Agency to release the boat. Supposedly to be surveilled. I already knew the Viper and Raynard had something else in mind.'

Stone pointed his gun at Greenville's forehead. 'Raynard? Jesse Raynard? What do you know about him? Think before you answer.'

'Easy,' Ivers said. 'We're cooperating, ain't we?'

'Hang on, Stone,' Chuck muttered. 'Let's hear them out.'

Stone's gun crawled from a head shot to Greenville's heart. 'The *Reina*. What do you know?'

'The *Saint Martin* disappeared. Some cutting. Some welding. A coat of paint. And some new papers. Poof. The *Saint Martin* is the *Reina*, and we're back in business. The next two runs were better than all the others combined.'

'What about the disease outbreak?' Chuck asked.

Greenville and Ivers glanced at each other, genuinely surprised.

'What of it?' Ivers said. 'Worst bit of luck ever. Our gold mine collapses.'

'You know nothing about that?' Stone asked.

'Course we know about it. Some damn plague takes the crew, and the Jamaicans sink the boat.'

The look Chuck gave Stone communicated his opinion. *They honestly don't know.*

A long ten seconds that seemed like minutes passed before Stone asked, 'Who the fuck is Jesse Raynard?'

'We don't know, other than he's high up in the Viper's organization,' Ivers said. 'Maybe had something to do with the ship being transformed, and that's it.'

'You're lying,' Stone growled.

'I swear, we're not!' Ivers pleaded. 'Here, wait a minute, didn't we get a photo of him, talking to that Russian doctor. In the Caymans. C'mon, Doug, you remember, you took some snaps.'

Greenville pointed to the pocket of his jacket. 'My phone?'

Stone motioned with his gun. 'Slowly.'

'There,' said Greenville a few minutes later. 'I got two pics at a pretty long range, but that one is the Russki doc. The other, I presume, is Raynard.'

'Is this the latest iPhone?' Stone asked.

'Yeah.'

'Nice. And the password?'

Stone verified it. 'Yours too, Danny.'

Stone pocketed the phones and, his eyes never leaving the two agents, asked Chuck, 'Anything else?'

'Nope.'

Greenville and Ivers tensed, but Stone motioned them towards the door of the warehouse. 'Off you go.'

'You're not going to kill us?'

'Gave you my word,' Stone said. 'We'll walk out with you, see you to the end of the pier where you can catch a cab and start your new life of disappearing off the face of the earth. We weren't lying about giving your names to the CIA and MI5, plus descriptions to local authorities. But you're smart. I give you a fifty-fifty shot.'

'Sixty-forty against,' Chuck said. 'Not too bad.'

Minutes later, Stone turned to Chuck. 'We should get these photos to Randy.'

'I'll send 'em, then head back myself. Gotta get home before the wife replaces me. You know, a little down time wouldn't kill you either.'

'Can't. I've got a few loose ends to tie up.'

***

Chuck walked through the crowded Dallas airport terminal towards the gate for his flight to Tucson. He'd managed to get an early flight out of Morocco. From there to Lisbon and a direct flight to Dallas. He felt like warmed-over garbage at this point, and was eager to get on the short two-hour flight back to Tucson. Unfortunately, he still had a couple hours to kill, so he settled onto a barstool at a busy restaurant called High Sierra, where he ordered a burger and fries. He'd changed his mind about a black coffee, and was now drinking a passable glass of house Merlot. Thoughts about what a gigantic pain international traveling had become were dispelled in an instant as he caught the news crawl on a TV behind the bar. He sat up straighter and rubbed his tired eyes until the focus improved.

'Holy shit!' he muttered. 'I wonder if Stone has seen this?' He grabbed his phone and began dialing.

***

The weather was unusually warm, which made sitting out on the rental house's balcony pleasant for Yvette and Becky. Located on a small hill, it was far enough from the beach to be quite inexpensive despite the recent updates to the kitchen and bathrooms and the fresh paint in every room. The realtor who'd shown them the property, while happy enough to find renters, had been inexplicably nervous. When the women had commented on the view of the ocean and the massive homes right on the beach, he'd grown dour.

'*Si*, it's a beautiful view from the balcony, but those mansions are on a private beach. You must never go there. There is a public beach a short … a moderate drive down the road.'

'Oh, but the beach is so close from here,' Becky said, with an unnoticed wink to Yvette.

'Please, no!' the realtor said. 'You must promise not to attempt to access the beach here. It is in the rental agreement. Those homes belong to … umm, powerful members of government who insist on privacy. You may even see security guards.'

'Ah, I understand,' Becky said.

The man's shoulders slumped. 'I suppose you ladies will prefer to look elsewhere.'

Yvette and Becky exchanged a glance. 'As it turns out,' Becky said, 'we're really not all that interested in the beach. My friend here is from England, and she'd burn within minutes. Her skin is better suited to fog. A quiet vacation spot through New Year's Eve with access to a few shops is what we had in mind. We'll take the house for two weeks and we promise not to set foot anywhere near the beach. OK?'

'Oh, *si*! OK. I'll just get the papers from the car.'

'You do that.'

'Did you really have to fluster the poor man?' Yvette asked.

Becky shrugged. 'He made it far too tempting. "Powerful members of government." What rubbish.'

'You're certain Carlos will be here?'

'In three days, according to Emma Lister. Time to troubleshoot the latest software update from Gary.'

'He really has no idea what the code is for?'

'For its true purpose? Not at all. I doubt he'd help if he did.'

'Becky, I'm … nervous. Will this really work?'

Becky gave her a solemn stare, though her eyes were gentle. 'This is your call, Yvette. We can stay here for a few days, drink margaritas, buy matching souvenir sombreros, and head back to Tucson. It might be for the best. Will our plan work? I'm confident. Plus, Emma Lister will be grateful, as I'm sure others will be when they get off their high horses.' She was thinking primarily of Logan. 'But none of that matters. So, Yvette Crandall, what do you say?'

Yvette drew a slow, deep breath. 'I say we do it. For Colin.'

***

Three days later, a caravan of SUVs arrived at the compound. Guards with automatic weapons scattered along the perimeter facing the land. A half mile offshore, a small unmarked boat began regular sweeps.

'Hand weapons—Uzis, I think—and a poorly concealed .50-caliber mounted on the rear deck of the boat.'

Becky passed the binoculars to Yvette, who studied the boat and the grounds. 'My God, it's an army,' she whispered.

'And a navy,' Becky added, with a wry smile. 'But no air force.'

***

Gary Walkin, Becky's VP of engineering at ARC Avionics, had been shocked when Becky had told him to take a week off after Christmas.

She'd laughed at his startled expression and said, 'What? You don't deserve it? Take two weeks. I'll be going on a quiet decompression trip to Mexico with Yvette Crandall. You're free to visit your girlfriend in Indonesia, if you want.'

'Can't,' he'd replied glumly. 'She burned her vacation last time I was there.'

'Oh, well. Get some rest. Look up old buddies. See you in two weeks.'

Three days later found him sitting with Logan Fletcher in the Skybox, a sports bar a short drive from Logan's house and one of his favorite haunts.

'Can you believe that shit?' Gary asked. 'Two weeks off. I mean, don't get me wrong, Becky's a great boss ... in much the same way Attila the Hun was a great motivator of men. But this!'

'I wouldn't get too enthused, buddy. I think this is more about *her* getting two weeks off.' *Her and Yvette*, he thought. *With Stone out of the picture.*

'Yeah, well, she could have ordered me to mind the shop. That'd be more typical. Especially if we're trying to break into the drone business.'

'Oh, I wouldn't worry about Becky. She'll be back to her usual— What'd you just say?'

'I said, I think she wants to expand into the drone business. Shit, if Amazon is gonna deliver packages that way, why shouldn't ARC be building them? Or at least providing the avionics software.'

'The drone business! Sounds like pure bullshit.'

'Oh really? Then why have I been busting my balls *after work hours* modifying flight code for Becky for some gadget she got hold of?'

'I give up. Why?'

'Wouldn't you like to know?' He motioned for another round. 'So would I. She dumped this load of shit on me personally and told me not to get any help. Said it would do me good to do some C++ coding again.'

'What old-ass piece of shit uses C++?'

'Some sort of farmer drone, I think. Believe me when I say she wasn't telling me much.'

'What kind of code?'

'The usual: platform stabilization, automatic course correction for atmospheric effects—turbulence, rain. Oh, and she wanted to be able to automatically lock the platform z-axis to an on-board camera.'

'In English, please.'

'She wanted the platform to point at whatever is in the crosshairs of the camera, got it?'

'Yeah, thanks. You want another drink?'

Gary pointed to the fresh drinks, just delivered. 'You OK, Logan?'

***

'Looks like another group arriving,' Yvette said. 'Two, three ... I count four more large vehicles.'

'That'll be the other former cartel bosses, I presume, now lieutenants of the Viper. And that should be it, according to Emma Lister's intel. She also provided us with the private phone number of our favorite criminal.'

Yvette studied Becky's face, where a half-smirk had replaced her thoughtful expression. 'What *are* you thinking?' Yvette asked.

'We need the Viper outside. Maybe we can encourage him to take some fresh air.' Becky pulled a cell phone from her pocket. 'Burner phone. I'll route the signal through the Indonesia phone exchange for good measure. Let's wait till after dinner. Then we'll send Carlos a little text.'

***

Shortly after 8:00 p.m., Yvette and Becky sat on their balcony and crafted a message. It read:

To Carlos the Fool,
Hope you enjoyed your dinner. Is it chilly where you are? I imagine things will warm up soon. No one likes a cold house. You'll burn here before you burn in hell!

312

After sending the message, Yvette said, 'Are you sure that was wise? Alerting him that way?'

'Just watch,' Becky said.

Within minutes, the largest estate resembled a beehive struck with a stick. Men swarmed out of the building, checking windows, doors, and autos before running back inside.

'Imagine the chaos!' Becky said. 'It shouldn't be long before—There! Walking along the shoreline. See the glow?'

'A cigar,' Yvette said.

'Yes. While his minions scour the house and the grounds for a bomb or incendiary device, the coward has wandered off to the safety of an empty beach.' She faced Yvette, her eyes sparkling. 'It's time.'

In a deserted hollow surrounded by sand dunes, propellers spun up to speed and a drone—twin to the one used by Carlos to poison the fields of his rivals—rose into the dark sky. Becky manned the controls, glancing at the IR camera view on a laptop as she commanded the drone to rise vertically to an altitude of two hundred feet, then proceed towards the beach.

Yvette sat staring at the display on a second laptop, another joystick untouched for now. Her view was different. It was nearly vertical, with a circle enclosing fine crosshairs.

Both had to remind themselves to breathe as the drone devoured the distance to the beach in minutes. Neither spoke. They were confident the subtle whine of the rotors would be masked by the wash of waves and by the louder rumble of the patrol boat, ordered closer to shore after Carlos received the threatening text.

Yvette stared unblinking at the screen, and then a distinctive glow appeared within the targeting circle. Becky throttled back and the scene below swelled.

'Last chance for a change of mind,' Becky said.

'Not bloody likely.'

'Thought you'd say that. Remember, once you get him in the crosshairs, push Lock. Gary's tracker will steer the drone and keep the firing axis as close as possible to the target. Descending to fifty feet. Passing control to you.'

Carlos still hadn't looked up. The patrol boat's engine noise was clearly overwhelming the buzz of the drone.

'Locked,' Yvette growled. 'Time to die, you bastard.'

Unlike the drone provided to Carlos by Jesse Raynard, this particular model carried neither trees to be planted nor capsules of poison. Each projectile was tipped with a hunting arrowhead: crossed V's of steel, sharp as a shaving razor. Within the projectile, four ounces of lead.

Yvette squeezed the joystick's trigger and a projectile daggered earthward, striking Carlos on the back of his left shoulder before thudding into the sand. A shriek from Carlos as his cigar tumbled away and his right hand flew to the sudden agony of his shoulder. Before he could pull it back, Yvette fired again, impaling the hand and piercing the shoulder again.

Disoriented and in pain, Carlos turned all around, looking for a ground-based attacker. A third shot sliced through his scalp, eyebrow, and cheek, blinding him in one eye. Blood flowed across his face and onto his shirt as he finally tipped his head skyward. With the bellow of bull, he began running along the beach, the sand hindering his pace.

The fourth shot pierced his calf, bringing him down with scream. He tried to pluck the projectile away, but the arrowhead had fully penetrated the muscle. He began to crawl. A shot into his opposite thigh brought his crawling to a halt. In the distance, shouts could be heard. Too late. Too far away.

Yvette fired three shots in rapid succession, two piercing his back, one his neck just below the skull. Carlos's body spasmed and he tossed onto his back, driving the blades deeper. Yvette closed her eyes and fired the remaining projectiles at his head. A glancing blow to the neck opened an artery, and black blood poured onto the thirsty sand. Another penetrated his throat and his bellowing ceased.

Death rained all around him until a shot through his eye and deep into his skull silenced him completely.

'It's done,' Becky said. 'Release control of the drone.'

Heavy breathing and sobs.

'Yvette? Release control. Yvette?'

Becky reached across her and pressed the release key, then commanded the drone to climb as it headed out to sea. The drone would fly for at least twenty more minutes before it fell and vanished beneath the waves. There was no chance it would ever be found.

Becky wrapped an arm around Yvette, who collapsed into her embrace, her body shaking uncontrollably.

'It's OK,' Becky said. 'It's all over. Time to go home.'

***

Chuck had actually surprised Stone with the news of Carlos the Viper's gruesome death. When he'd finished delivering the basics, which is all he'd gotten, though he'd twisted the bartender's arm to switch from the soccer match to a news station, he asked, 'You don't suppose …?'

'Yes. I do.' Stone's voice was weary. 'I just hope to God they were careful.'

'When I get home, I'll check in.'

'I doubt if either of our friends will linger so you can interrogate them. Talk to Logan. He may have heard something.'

'Will do. You and Luana haven't been to Breck recently. Why not take a break? Stop by Tucson first, then go rest. You do know what rest is, don't you?'

'Never heard of it,' Stone said. 'Look, this shit with the Viper is—and I hope remains—a sideshow. God, I hope they were careful! And who's that guy you used to know? The bass-playing doctor?'

'Tyrone.'

'Show him the pics we got from Greenville.'

'Why?'

'Just a hunch. He might be able to give us some intel on this Constantin guy.'

'What's got you wound up?'

There was a long silence before Stone answered. 'Something I meant to tell you when you arrived in Morocco. There've been three outbreaks of what seems to be the same deadly disease. Dr. Russki happens to show up in the neighborhood for two of them.'

'So what?'

'I can't say for sure, though the idea of a brand-new plague is damn disturbing. Something else is going on, and I'm thinking—especially with the Viper conveniently removed from the scene—that Raynard is involved, and maybe Constantin Shukhov as well.'

'I'll talk to Tyrone. And you? How about that trip to the U.S.?'

'I'm assuming Yvette will be back in London soon. I need her skills on the predictive chaos model to help solve this puzzle. I hope she's up to it.'

He didn't need to say more. Both knew that if she'd been involved in the Viper's death, there might be more on her mind than an arcane puzzle.

'Yeah, well,' Chuck said, 'I'd tell you to get some rest, but what would be the point? Just don't keel over and croak. I'd be out of a job.'

'No promises.'

***

Tyrone wrapped Martha in a bear hug near Tucson airport's baggage carousels. 'Thanks for coming down!'

'Do you know what it's like in Seattle this time of year?'

'Uh, yeah. I used to live there, remember?'

'Yes, I do, and I miss your mellow, offbeat wit.' She looked around at the few dozen people picking up luggage. 'Is this it?'

'Tucson!' he said. 'Biggest little city in the West. C'mon, I'll bet your bag is already circling around.'

In fifteen minutes, they were out of the airport, heading north.

'Where are you taking me?'

'Logan Fletcher's house. He absolutely insisted I bring you over for a barbecue. He promised some very tasty burnt cow, as I recall.'

'I see the sunny Southwest has turned you into an even bigger smartass. Never believed it was possible.'

Tyrone grunted as he turned east on Valencia. 'The warm, dry air is good for my bones. So is hanging out with my old high school buddy again, after … too many years to count.'

'I don't know how long it's been since I haven't seen a single cloud in the sky.'

'You know what we call that here in Tucson?'

Martha gave him a twisted smile, suspecting the punchline to an obvious setup. 'What?'

'Yesterday! Ha ha ha!'

'God, you're awful,' she said, leaning over and squeezing his arm. 'I've missed you.'

***

'Can I get you more burnt cow?' Logan asked.

'You and Tyrone are like a comedy act,' Martha said. 'Thank you and Cathie for being such gracious hosts. And it's really OK for me to spend the night?'

'Cathie and I insist. A friend of Tyrone's, et cetera. And the cow?'

'A tiny bit, if you have some of that wonderful Cab to wash it down.'

'I just might.' Logan headed for the wine cellar.

'I love the 75 degrees and 2 percent humidity, Tyrone,' Martha said, when the two were momentarily alone on the back patio. 'And your friends are wonderful.'

'Oh, just wait.'

***

When dinner dishes were finally cleared, Chuck and Joy helped Cathie bring out dessert and coffee.

Chuck lifted a pouch from under the table and waved a cigar in Tyrone's direction. Tyrone nodded, as did Logan. He offered one to Martha, who grinned and said, 'Absolutely.'

The four lit up. With a mischievous curl of her lip, Martha said, 'Cigar is just a tad dry, Chuck. Maybe a bit more moisture in your humidor.'

'A connoisseur! And you're right. Too long in the pouch.'

'A damp sponge in a Tupperware container and they'll be good as new.'

'Amen,' Tyrone said, in his deep rumble.

Logan produced a bottle of cognac like a conjurer.

'This is wonderful,' Martha said. 'I may consider retiring to Tucson.'

'You'd be welcome,' Joy said.

'Hey, T-bone, mind taking a gander at this?' Chuck asked. He pulled a photo from his wallet. 'It's the Russki doc who's seen the new plague. I think you know him.'

Tyrone examined the picture. 'I know *who* he is. Didn't actually know him. Martha?'

She took a glance. 'Same arrogant smirk I grew to hate.'

'Uh-oh,' Chuck said, 'I'm sensing a backstory here.'

'Oh, don't mind me,' Martha said, with a forced laugh. 'I know him well enough to dislike him intensely. Clever, certainly. Brilliant? Maybe. Arrogant, egotistical, and thievish? No doubt. He and I worked together

317

for the better part of a year on a virus identification algorithm. That is, I worked and he critiqued. In the end, he wrote a paper behind my back and stole the credit. That's what we call, in medical parlance, being a dick.'

'Didn't know,' Chuck said. 'Sorry.'

He went to retrieve the photo.

'Funny to see him having dinner with just the opposite sort of man,' Martha remarked, as she handed it back.

'You know Jesse Raynard?' Chuck asked.

'What? No. I don't know any Jesse Raynard. The other man is Carl Heskin. A truly brilliant scientist. Extremely sick now, I believe. Terminally ill. Shame. The arrogant asshole is healthy enough.'

No one noticed Chuck's look of shock, and he hid it quickly. 'Excuse me for a minute, folks,' he said. 'Nature calls.'

'TMI, darling,' Joy said, as he hurried away.

In the Fletcher's guest bathroom, Chuck placed a call.

'You do know what time it is here, don't you?' Stone grumbled.

'No. Don't care. Listen up, the second guy in the photo isn't Jesse Raynard, according to a friend of Tyrone's who knows Constantin Shukhov all too well.'

'That sounds like a long story.'

'For later,' Chuck said. 'Did you hear the important part?'

'All of it is important.'

'The other guy is someone named Carl Heskin! Dr. Carl Heskin.'

'Got it.'

There was such a long silence that Chuck finally asked, 'Stone, you still there?'

'I am, and I'm wondering. Who the fuck is Jesse Raynard?'

January in the Sangre de Cristo Mountains was cold, the snow deep and heavy around Jesse's cabin.

Chapter Eighteen

Who is Jesse Raynard?

Photographs taken before and after the onset of the plague, plus predictions as to what events were to occur and when, had validated the claims on Jesse Raynard's website and discredited other crackpots and pretenders who'd claimed responsibility for the horrible disease that had struck three times. Governments and terrorist organizations were now taking Raynard's claims regarding DP-47 seriously.

The website gave no explanation for the name DP-47. Raynard and Heskin were the only people who would ever know they had jokingly called this new disease Devil's Pathogen. The 47 related to the number of transformative mutations Heskin had at one time researched. The name DP-47 was coldly clinical and aroused more fear than any Hollywoodesque description, especially when associated with projected infection rates and the observed fatality rate—100 percent. Gruesome photos of the victims added to the visceral dread.

The entire village of Huata, Guatemala, had been wiped out. Only vague descriptions of the disease had come from Raynard's first demonstration, since terrified people from nearby villages had, upon discovering the carnage, burned the village and the plague's victims to ashes. Raynard's website had predicted the timing of the outbreak and had shown photos taken before the inferno. Bodies in houses or on streets with bruises, strange swelling, putrid lesions, and blood weeping from eyes, nose, ears. No other medical institution or news organization could produce this evidence.

A Raynard prediction regarding the *Reina del Mar* had come *after* the ship had sailed from its final port of call but *before* its reappearance in the Caribbean, crewed by dead men. A famous CDC doctor had verified the same pathology and brought back photographs. His samples had been lost when the ship was sunk by Jamaican commandos, a guarantee that she'd never make port and infect others. Raynard had implied that the ship's loss was part of a plan. The disease was for sale, and not being given away.

***

January in the Sangre de Cristo Mountains was cold, the snow deep and heavy around Jesse's cabin. It provided protection and isolation from the outside world, though the death of Carlos the Viper had been the greatest guarantee of safety.

Raynard rose, added a log to the fire, and topped up a snifter of cognac.

'Yes, please,' Charlotte said, before the offer could be made. She was using a computer on a small desk off to the side, analyzing the latest messages. She took a sip of cognac and held out her glass. 'It seems strange to have so much uninterrupted time to focus on your project.'

'Fortuitous,' Raynard replied. 'Having Carlos the Pig eliminated and the cartels tossed into chaos has removed the distraction of being hunted. I have to thank Emma Lister and her friends. Using the seed-planter to kill him was genius. Her business associate, Becky Amhurst, must have skilled engineers. Perhaps when the dust is settled, we'll throw a party.'

'At that nice beach again, I hope,' Charlotte replied, tossing a lascivious glance at Raynard.

'A fitting reward, once the job is done. We'll invite Amhurst as well.'

'A foursome! Better and better!'

Raynard's hands were on Charlotte's shoulders, massaging gently. 'For now, business. What have you found?'

'We're down to three potential buyers. I've blocked the other pretenders, including crude efforts by the CIA and MI6 to impersonate terrorist organizations or rogue regimes.'

'The fact that they keep trying proves we're the genuine broker. You *have* let the legitimate bidders know about these attempts, yes?'

Charlotte feigned shock. 'Oh, dear, was I supposed to do that? I've *tried* to block them from knowing about their competitors!' She giggled. 'Sadly, my efforts have been in vain. No, the competitors, real and fictitious, know of each other's ardent desire to obtain DP-47. The CIA made a most generous offer.'

'And if money was our only objective, we might consider them. As you know, there are other considerations. Tell me about the three final bidders.'

'North Korea's offer is the smallest, but they supplemented it with threats to destroy you—quite graphic—should you refuse their deal.'

'Heavy handed SOBs! So predictable. Will they budge on their offer?'

'I've bargained them up to a hundred million. The threats have increased proportionally.'

'Fools. I'm surprised China hasn't yanked their choke chain. I'd only accept their offer for the entertainment value. Who else?'

'The second one is fascinating. A spinoff group of disaffected terrorists from Al Qaeda. They call themselves'—Charlotte scanned the clutter of her desk—'I wrote it down.'

'Clearly memorable. What are they offering?'

'Ah, they say they'll top any other offer by fifty million.'

'We're up to one hundred fifty if we play them against the North Koreans.' Raynard smiled. 'But ...'

'I know it will come as a shock, but the Al Qaeda group doesn't have the money. Their offer is just bullshit and bravado. They can scrape up, maybe, fifty million. Maybe.'

'So far, the NoKos lead the bidding. Tell me you've saved the best for last.'

Charlotte smiled seductively. 'You know me so well. The Syrians. They haven't told me as much just yet, but they'll go to two hundred million.'

'The Syrians!' Raynard said, shocked. 'But surely they don't have that kind of money either. The entire country isn't worth two hundred million.'

'True. But they're *sooo* transparent. They're a front buyer for someone else.'

'Who?'

'The Russians.'

Raynard stiffened and swiveled Charlotte's chair so their eyes locked. 'Are you fucking serious?'

'Serious as a graveyard. I've tracked the Syrian's signal through a number of satellite bounces.'

'How many?'

'Pretty many, but not enough if their objective was to conceal the final destination. This is the big time. Moscow.'

Raynard spun around, arms outstretched. 'This is perfect!'

'I knew you'd be pleased.'

Raynard stabbed a finger at Charlotte. 'Tell them for two hundred, DP-47 is theirs!'

Charlotte stifled a phony yawn. 'I'm so ahead of you. They balked at one seventy-five, so I told them to stop wasting your time. We're now negotiating for two.'

Raynard grabbed her shoulders and kissed her deeply. 'There's my brilliant Charlotte!'

'They have conditions.'

'Naturally.'

'A final demonstration.'

'Acceptable, with *our* condition.'

'At the lab, of course. They're grumbling.' Charlotte held up her hand. 'In two days' time they'll agree.'

'The final act in our little drama.' Then Raynard's face clouded. 'No. One more to follow, and I should have said "tragedy."'

Charlotte reached up a hand and stroked Raynard's arm. 'You always knew how it had to end.'

Raynard glanced at her. 'It doesn't make it any easier. Finalize arrangements with the Russians—I mean the Syrians. I'll contact Carl.'

***

Two evenings later, a vicious blizzard filled the night with the howl of souls in torment, though the fire was warm and comforting. Raynard ruffled the fur around Cherokee's neck. 'Good night to be indoors, eh girl?'

A low rumble from Cherokee signaled agreement.

Charlotte pushed back from her desk and rolled her shoulders; a distinct crack was heard as she twisted her neck from side to side. She turned to Raynard with a smile. 'Six straight hours, but they finally caved. A sweet two hundred million. The funds will be transferred to an account prior to the demonstration at your lab, and we'll get verification through the bank. Access codes will be provided at the satisfactory conclusion of the demo. They leave with the product.'

'How much?'

'Twenty vials.'

'Hmm. They want to have enough to perform their own demonstration plus settle a few scores, I imagine, though the whole point of a weapon like this is intimidation. It's not meant to be used. I suppose they'll try to create more.'

'Certainly. Is something bothering you?'

Raynard smiled. 'Just details. We can control conditions at the lab, but let's be doubly on our guard in case the "Syrians" aren't being completely honest with us. They accepted a three-week delay before the demo?'

'Yes. They have some preparations to make.'

'You've done a magnificent job, Char.'

Charlotte smiled, then tilted her head to one side and gave a delicate sniff. 'I could use a shower.'

'Take a long, hot one while I prepare a feast. We'll celebrate.'

'I should help.'

'Nonsense. You've done your job for the day—for the year!'

Charlotte was nearly out of the room before Raynard asked, almost in passing, 'How soon before they try to kill me?'

Charlotte didn't seem at all surprised by the question. 'I've gotten a reasonable sense of these people during our negotiations. Once they have DP-47, that is, at the demonstration's conclusion, I believe they'll act.'

Raynard nodded. 'I have less than a month to live.'

***

The pristine coating of snow in London had already turned to grey slush, chased down the sewers by what was now a sleety rain.

'Jason, good to see you again,' Diana said, as he hung his dripping raincoat on a hook. 'Though you look like a drowned rat.'

'My looks match how I feel,' he said, with a crooked smile. 'Sometimes I think I'm getting too old for this shit.'

Diana kissed his cheek. 'Nonsense. You'll feel far better after a glass of scotch, neat. Come and sit. There's a nice fire going in the study.'

'I'd love to, but there's something I need to do first.'

'Ah. She returned the day before yesterday. Hasn't said two words since. You'll find her in the Triple S rooms, working.'

Stone raised an eyebrow. 'This late?'

'It's been her refuge, Jason. She barely leaves there to sleep. I'm afraid reality has hit her very hard. I know she'll be happy to see you.'

'Hmm. We'll see. Let me grab two of those whiskies and I'll find out.'

***

As predicted, light streamed from the open door of the Triple S offices, spilling into the shadowy hallway.

Stone entered quietly and walked past the conference table to a pair of glowing monitors. Yvette glanced up then turned back to her task, entering code into the predictive chaos model. Stone stood a few paces to the side, watching her fingers fly across the keyboard. When the algorithm was complete, she linked it and gave the command to run a series of baseline cases. Only then did she spin her chair around to face him.

'Sorry. Needed to finish that. These cases will run for at least twenty minutes.'

'Excellent,' Stone said, offering her a drink. 'Take a break.'

She hesitated a moment before accepting the glass and taking a sip. Her body gave an involuntary shiver. 'Bloody hell, I needed that!'

Stone flopped into a chair. 'Me too. Bad flights, bad traffic, and bad weather. Thank God for good whisky and good friends.'

Yvette took a deeper drink and closed her eyes. When she opened them, Stone saw the emptiness he'd seen in his own eyes many times over the years.

'I'm still a friend?' she asked. 'After everything?'

'A good friend. I have very few and I've learned to recognize them. You're one.'

'It was exactly as you predicted,' Yvette said. 'I was on fire with rage, eager to deal out justice. Eager to deal out death. It was ghastly, his ending. Exactly as I'd hoped it would be. A horrible, painful death by my hand. Then, just as it was nearing the end, it was as though my consciousness leapt out of my body and stood back watching this madwoman I'd become, committing this dreadful act. In that instant, I couldn't decide who I hated more, him or me.'

'I'm told good assassins don't feel that pain. I always have. I guess that means neither of us is a good assassin, but maybe it makes us something else.'

'What?'

He stood and smiled. 'Just people. Not all good, not all bad. People who still have a conscience.'

'Jason, I'm s-so s-sorry!'

Yvette flew from the chair and wrapped her arms around Stone's neck. 'So, so …' Sobbing choked off her words.

He could feel the heat of her tears down his cheek. She finally stepped away and was about to sit again, but Stone reached out and took her hand.

'It'll take time,' he said. 'Things will seem better, almost normal, and then a black demon will rear up and try to destroy you. Don't let it. You have friends who can help. In the end, even those ghosts will fade. Never gone, but manageable. Trust me.'

'I do,' she whispered.

Stone looked at their empty glasses. 'Guess I should have brought the bottle. What do you say we head back and join Diana in the study?'

'The simulation—'

'Will be there in the morning. And I'm going to need your help.'

'With what?'

'That'll wait till morning, too. C'mon. Let's not keep Diana waiting.'

***

The next morning, Arthur, man of many talents, prepared a celebratory breakfast to honor the return of the wayward sheep. It was the first time Yvette had eaten more than a muffin and coffee since she'd returned. And while Stone couldn't quite find the same enthusiasm for Spam, there were plenty of crispy bangers to go along with the eggs, toast, tomatoes, and orange juice.

Arthur, who was like an uncle to Yvette, joined Diana, Crandall, Yvette, and Stone. Luana had been called away on business, but sent her love to all and expressed her regrets at missing such a feast. Privately, she'd told Jason, 'I wish I was there, and not just for the breakfast, but I think your presence and the food is more what Yvette needs right now. You will keep an eye on her?'

'As always, whenever I have one to spare. I don't suppose you'd want to do some skiing in Breckenridge?'

'Absolutely. Are you available?'

'You called my bluff. But I will be, I hope, by spring.'

327

'I was bluffing too. Let's make it a date, though. Two weeks while there's still snow on the ground.'

The next half hour passed with no more dialogue than: 'More juice?' 'Pass the bangers please.' 'Yes, I'll take more coffee.' 'I couldn't squeeze in another slice of Spam ... well maybe a small one.'

When the plates were empty and the diners comfortably full, Yvette asked the question Stone had deflected the previous day.

'What is this mystery task you need help with, Jason?'

'Not much of a mystery, really, but it requires you to solve a mystery.'

'Intriguing,' Crandall said. 'Also confusing.'

Stone took a moment to collect his thoughts. 'Do you remember when we discussed the puzzle with the hole in the middle? At that time, there were a number of items—the rise to power of Carlos Velasquez and a break-in at the CDC among others—that seemed connected by this empty core.'

'There have been other significant events since then,' Crandall said.

'Yes. Like the transformation of the *Saint Martin* into the *Reina del Mar*. She had a short life after that when she became host to the second disease outbreak.'

'I remember the newspaper article you showed us the same day we discussed missing puzzle pieces,' Yvette said. 'The article relating the first outbreak in Guatemala.'

'At the time, it was the *only* outbreak,' Stone said. 'I know you updated the predictive chaos model to include the *Reina del Mar* and the third outbreak in Bangladesh. The first question is, are they all connected?'

'With high probability,' Crandall said.

'And the focal point?' Stone asked. 'The common factor to these events? Certainly not Carlos Velasquez.'

'No. Though Velasquez is one part of the puzzle. A well-known part.'

'No longer a player,' Stone said, with very little emphasis. 'Yet the puzzle is still incomplete. What's going on with this plague? What role does this Dr. Constantin Shukhov play?'

'He's legitimate,' Crandall said. 'A brilliant if eccentric doctor who left the CDC after some internal squabble. His companion—what was his name, Yvette?'

'Dr. Carl Heskin,' she said.

'Also a brilliant doctor, though less flamboyant than Shukhov,' Crandall said. 'He's still at the CDC, though no longer a rising star. Been shuffled off to the side, possibly because of some illness.'

'Where are you going with this, Jason?' Yvette asked.

'There's another player. Maybe the most important one. Powerful enough in his own right to defy the Viper. The name has come up. In fact, our crooked friends at the CIA and MI5 misidentified Heskin as our mystery man. If it weren't by sheer luck—Tyrone's friend Dr. Martha Zanders identifying Heskin's picture—we'd have assumed we finally had a picture of Jesse Raynard. We've tried to ID him before, with no success. So here's what I'm after, Yvette. Who completes the puzzle? And if it is Jesse Raynard, then who is he? How can someone who barely seems to exist be in control of everything that's happened? And why? My gut tells me someone is playing games with a deadly disease. Not a comforting thought. I need to have a long talk with Mr. Raynard, but to do that I need to know who he is and where to find him. That's the help I need.'

'Right,' Yvette said, rising briskly, 'I'll just get to it.'

Stone smiled. 'I was hoping you'd say that.'

***

Stone waited until 1:00 p.m., London time, before calling Chuck Johnson, who still answered the phone with a yawn. 'Thought you'd be up by now, Johnson.'

'Oh, I'm up, I'm just not awake. Still working on the second cup of coffee. What's up?'

Stone gave him a synopsis. When he finished, he heard the distinctive sound of Chuck running a hand over the thick stubble on his chin.

'You think this Jesse Raynard is the focal point with the *Reina del Mar*, the break-in at the CDC, even the outbreaks of this mysterious disease?' Chuck asked.

'That's my guess. Easiest way to confirm it is to question Raynard. Just two minor problems.'

'Yeah. Who is he and where is he? Trivial. And that bugs me more than anything.'

'What do you mean?'

'Think back to Smythe-Montgomery. He had his hands on action all over the globe, too, but the shadow he cast was bigger than a skyscraper's.'

'Interesting analogy, Chuck, but, if you'll pardon me, flawed.'

'Well, it is early in the morning. What's your beef with my analysis?'

'Smythe-Montgomery cast a huge shadow because he was huge. Everyone knew who he was and the press was all over him whenever he showed his nose. In our present case, we have the shadow, but no one is casting it. It's like there is no Jesse Raynard, just his shadow.'

Chuck chewed on this for a while before saying, 'I see your point. Could it be a group effort? A cadre of bad guys hiding behind the illusion of a single powerful person, this Raynard?'

'Maybe,' Stone said, 'though Yvette and Crandall believe it's one person. How often have you known a group of suspicious, egotistical criminals to operate efficiently together? Typically, rivalries devolve into violence till the strongest one takes control. Look at the Viper.'

'Point made. Can't say I believed the "board-of-directors" model either. But that just leaves us with the same mystery. Who is Jesse Raynard?'

'That's it. Well, I just wanted to keep you posted. Yvette's on the job. You can go finish your coffee and get a shave.'

'You sound like my loving spouse. Talk to you soon, Stone.'

***

It was nearly ten that same evening, and Stone was surprised to see light still streaming from the Triple S office as he made his way down the hallway. 'What are you still doing here?' Stone asked. 'We all missed you at dinner and here you are still cuddled up to a computer terminal.'

'Oh, nonsense, it can't be later than—' But as Yvette's eyes glanced at the clock, the word 'six' died on her lips. 'Bugger! Is that the time?'

'Sure is. Maybe it's time to wrap up.'

'There's something you need to see.'

'How 'bout in the morning? I was just going to take a walk to the end of Diana's driveway to clear the cobwebs, then call it a night.'

'Fine. But I'll burst if I don't tell you the gist of it. Mind if I join you on your walk?'

'Get yourself a jacket and I'll go raid the kitchen. I think there might be a Cornish pasty or two left over. You can eat while we walk and talk between bites. Deal?'

'Outstanding. Now you've mentioned food, I've grown peckish.'

330

***

Diana's family estate sat on over 100 acres of land. At one time, the long driveway from the road had been bordered by huge, majestic elm trees. The trees had been dead for years, victims of the Dutch elm disease that had wiped out the species in England in the '60s. Now they were grey skeletons that evoked memories of happier times. Richard Crandall had offered to pay for their removal and a planting of beech, oak, or linden, but Diana had politely declined.

Tonight, the air was damp and cold, promising frost by morning, but the old sentinels stood at their posts, as loyal to Diana as she was to them.

'My God, this is delicious,' Yvette exclaimed, biting into a pasty. Steam escaped the pastry pocket and curled away on the frigid night air. 'Thank you for heating them up, Jason. I didn't realize how hungry I was.'

They had just left the gravel circle near the front entrance, the fountain at its center quiet, the flower garden bare, turned earth. Yvette ate like a starving wolf, and the first pasty disappeared.

'Ah, better,' she said. 'I'll save the second one for the way back.'

'So, what did you discover about the enigmatic Mr. Raynard?'

'Very little about him personally. No birth records, so the name is obviously an alias.'

'Where did you search?'

'Here, the States, Australia ... I'm not done yet. And I should have said there are many records for Jesse Raynard, just none whose history suggests evil genius or megalomania. I suppose I'm jumping to conclusions that the name is false, but don't worry, I'll not give up till I'm positive.'

'If nothing pops up on the life and times of Jesse Raynard, then what?'

Yvette's demeanor changed in an instant, her words harsh, almost frightened, the playfulness in her eyes gone.

'I took a different tack later in the day. Started to focus on the plague ... I mean the disease outbreaks. It took a while. No doubt why I missed dinner.' She gave Stone a tepid smile. 'Got into some very dark places on the web. Don't worry,' she said, seeing the concern on his face, 'the Triple S servers are *well* protected. Richard and I made sure of that. Anyway, I followed several leads. Dead ends. The usual chatter from copycats, phonies. Then, at last, a solid track.'

'You make it sound like woodcraft, picking up the trail of a wild animal.'

'It's not so dissimilar, though without the cold, rain, and smelly droppings.'

Stone's laugh vanished as Yvette took his elbow. 'It's for sale,' she said.

He stopped dead. 'What's for sale?' he asked, though he already knew.

'The disease. The plague.'

'Who?' he asked, his voice gravelly.

'Jesse Raynard.'

'Good Lord.'

Stone was silent for so long that Yvette became nervous. 'Jason, what do we do?'

'Funny,' he said, a thin smile relieving the tension in his face, 'I was about to ask you that. I can be fairly effective if I have a target. I can even track one down, given time. This is different. If I knew who he was, where he was ... but that's old news. What can you do in Cyberville?'

'Cyberville! Never heard it put like that.' Yvette resumed walking and Stone fell in beside her. After another silent minute, she said, 'There are two options, not mutually exclusive. Being as there's only one of me, I'll recruit Richard.'

'What are the options?'

'The first is to try to hack in, disrupt communications, possibly disable their server. In the process of hacking in, it may—and I stress "may"—be possible to get a physical location.

'The second option is riskier. I pose as a buyer. Try to outbid the competition, whoever that may be.' She shrugged.

'You don't sound confident in either option.'

'I'm not. The second one in particular requires a complex backstory, complete with verifiable sources of cash.'

'Luana and I can help there, maybe. How much do you suppose a deadly plague would sell for?'

'I have no idea, but legitimate buyers would. And, Jason, I get the feeling we're coming late to the party. The seller, this Raynard, would let buyers compete. I may be able to see where the current bidding stands.'

'And the hacking option? I know for a fact you fucked up some NoKo servers with your super-trick anti-malware software.'

'This will be harder. The ransom to release my school computers was fifty thousand pounds. How does that stack up against the price of this disease, roughly?'

'A thousand times smaller, at least,' he said grimly.

'We can expect the protections to be proportionally more difficult.'

'Shit.'

'Richard loves a challenge,' Yvette mused. 'I'll tell him it's impossible. That'll put his hackles up. Then we'll see.'

Yvette spent three fourteen-hour days at the computer, often in the company of Richard Crandall. They'd been using a dark-web hacking algorithm developed by Pippa Browning ...

Chapter Nineteen

Hacking the Dark Web

Yvette spent three fourteen-hour days at the computer, often in the company of Richard Crandall. They'd been using a dark-web hacking algorithm developed by Pippa Browning, an IT expert who'd come up with the technique while hiking the Appalachian Trail, and they were making some progress. Stone had been in the office almost as much as Crandall and Yvette, but rarely spoke to them, not wanting to be a distraction. When they did acknowledge his presence, it was with no more than a nod and a grunt, their heads snapping back to the computer terminals.

Stone had rarely been more frustrated. He'd continued his own search for the identity of Jesse Raynard, calling in markers from all over the globe, searching data bases and birth records. Nothing but dead ends. In the small hours of the fourth morning, he'd finally thrown in the towel, exiting the Triple S office without acknowledging Yvette and Crandall, who hadn't even looked up as he stomped out.

Rather than go back to the more livable wing of Diana's estate, he instead turned off the hallway into the large dining hall that had once hosted a costume dinner. He found a nearly full bottle of single malt scotch on a wooden hutch, blew dust from a glass, and dimmed the lights. The inner courtyard was illuminated by a few colorful decorative lights, which caught the fall of snow outside.

For a long time, Stone just sat, sipping the whisky and watching the silent snow. At last, he let out something between a sigh and a groan and pulled out his phone.

'Hey, Stone,' Chuck Johnson said. 'What's up? Wait a minute. If it's eight o'clock in the evening here, it must be …'

'Really early in the morning here,' Stone said. 'Sorry to bug you, but I just needed to vent.'

'Are you drinking?'

'Naturally. Some of Lady Diana's best.'

'Rat bastard. Let me just grab a cigar and some cheap booze. I'll head outside.'

'Not snowing there, then?'

'A balmy sixty-two under a sky like polished crystal. Sorry, man.'

A minute later, Chuck continued. 'OK, cigar is lit, drink is at the ready. Let me guess what's bugging you. The infamous, invisible, nonexistent Jesse Raynard.'

'Good guess. Damn it, Chuck, I've been pulling out all the stops looking for this bastard, and can't come up with squat. Here's a guy who's knocked heads with Carlos the Viper and outlived him, developed a plague that can wipe out humanity, and is now negotiating to sell said plague to the highest bidder, and I can't even get a middle initial! I'm beginning to wonder if you're right, and he's nothing more than a figment. Just a name for some organization of equally invisible men.'

'And there's the problem. Organizations and their members are notoriously more difficult to hide than individuals. That thinking gets us nowhere.'

'Which is exactly where all my efforts to find Raynard have gotten me! Nowhere! It's maddening.'

'How about Yvette and Crandall? They having any more luck finding him through the dark web?'

'I'm gonna say no, since even if Yvette could refrain from yelling "Eureka!" in my face, Crandall couldn't. And every time I've seen him, it looks like he's bitten into a sour lemon. I'll have to talk to them tomorrow. I mean, later today. We may need to take another approach.'

'You've got one?'

'Not a good one. It's more like, wait for Raynard to make his next move; maybe get careless.'

'I suppose you still believe in the Tooth Fairy.'

Stone laughed. 'See,' he said, and Chuck could imagine Stone's twisted smile, 'I needed my good buddy to point out how screwed we all are. It takes a real load off.'

'Honestly, Stone, what else *can* we do?'

'That's it exactly. No point beating the same dead horse.'

'Look, why don't you talk to the local computer wizards. They may not have a name, address, and Social Security number for Raynard, but they may have something. Maybe something they don't even realize is useful.'

'Agreed.' Stone twisted in his chair and heard his back pop, a tiny jolt like electrical current stabbing down his leg. 'Ow! Sucks to get old.'

'You don't know the half of it, brudda. Call me soon, OK? With some good news.'

'I can promise you exactly half of that.'

***

Hot black coffee and Earl Grey tea, the drinks of choice for Stone and Yvette, who had crossed paths in Diana's kitchen.

'How long were you and Richard at it?' Stone asked, steam curling from his mug.

'What time is it now? Truth is, I don't know, though I remember a lovely sunrise. I took a walk down the drive before turning in. You?'

'Barely made it past three. But then, I'm older than you.'

'Hmph.' Yvette blew across her tea and took a cautious drink. 'Oh, praise the Lord.'

'I take it you weren't up till sunrise because things are going well.'

'No. For two days Richard and I played the role of buyer, trying to edge our way into the bidding, though we were late to that game. We thought we were making progress, but something must've spooked Raynard.' She took another drink of tea. 'I say "Raynard," though I have no idea who's providing the cyber services. Whoever it is, we were bested. Maybe it was our false link to the cash you and Luana offered as "collateral" for the purchase. It might have been a thousand things, though we were extraordinarily careful. Richard believes they simply didn't need or want another bidder because negotiations are complete.'

'That's bad.'

'Yes. It would indicate the sale will conclude soon, though ...'

'Though?'

'Well, assuming that all three previous outbreaks were designed to draw general attention of potential buyers, Richard believes no one would spend the kind of money it would take to win this bid without some final, private demonstration. I agree.'

'Interesting.'

'Since we've been ousted as a bidder, we turned our focus to hacking into Mr. Raynard's servers.'

'Any luck?'

'Need I remind you we were up all night?'

'So maybe a *little* luck?' Stone teased.

Yvette rubbed her eyes. 'Bollocks! They just won't focus. But actually, maybe, possibly a little luck.'

'What kind of luck?'

'A date, or rather several dates, that Richard and I believe represent possible purchase dates, still under negotiation. Also, mention of a lab as the location.'

'Where?' Stone said eagerly.

'Ah, I did say a *little* luck. Raynard's encryption is exceptional and he's more cautious than a fox crossing a field. We'll be back at it today. Perhaps by this time tomorrow we'll have something.'

'So, off you go! I'll bring tea and crumpets all day long.'

'I need Richard's help. In fact, I'm the helper in this. His algorithms are well beyond me. Before you say it,' Yvette said, holding up a hand, 'Richard has promised to skin me alive and burn my corpse if I wake him before noon. He, too, mentioned his advanced years.'

Stone laughed. 'Fine. But at 12:01 p.m. I'll haul him out of bed and sit him at the computer if he isn't already there.'

'And my tea has gone cold.'

'Allow me,' Stone said, tipping out the contents into the sink and refilling her cup. 'You should give Becky a call. I think she'd like to hear from you.'

Yvette raised a skeptical eyebrow.

'I talked to her a few days ago,' Stone said. 'She's at some conference in Paris. We buried the hatchet on how she played me like a fish, and I told her you were doing OK, reengaged in crucial world-saving shit.' He shrugged. 'She'd rather hear it from you.'

'I should have called long ago, but with work and the bloody time zones …' Yvette rubbed her eyes again before taking a sip of tea. 'If she's on the continent, I'll give her a call, though I'm sure she's too busy to talk.'

'She's at a conference. She'd take a robocall if it meant getting her out of some boring workshop.' He yawned. 'I'm on my way to the office to brew another pot of coffee and waste my time trying to discover the true identity of Jesse Raynard. Hah.'

'I'll be anticipating those crumpets, Mr. Stone.'

Stone's voice faded as he walked away, though Yvette thought she caught the words 'Hard work is its own reward.'

***

'Yvette, thank God you called,' Becky said. 'The speaker at my conference could bore a tree stump. How are you?'

The question was loaded with a depth of meaning from the simple 'How are you feeling *today*?' to the far more complex 'How are you dealing with Carlos Velasquez's death?'

'I'm well enough. Getting past the nightmares and the voices in my head calling me a murderer. Jason has welcomed me back into the fold and put me to work, side by side with Richard. The task is complex and difficult, which is exactly what I needed. Jason's so understanding of the stages I'm going through. I guess in his line of work, he's seen it all before. It gives me hope, though I still have some very black days. He told me you and he had … how did he put it? Buried the hatchet. I meant to look up the meaning, but it sounds like a good thing. A truce or a ceasefire at least.'

Becky laughed. 'More like the permanent end to our recent conflict. I was pleased he was willing to put it behind us. For what it's worth, his main concern was for our safety. He didn't give a rat's ass about that miserable excuse for a human, the Viper. "The world's a better place with that bastard gone." Not exactly his words, but close enough. Beyond that, he seemed stressed. No, that's not quite right. More like exhausted and discouraged, two words I never thought to associate with him.'

'Quite accurate, unfortunately.'

'I don't suppose you could spill the beans on what's made him that way?'

'Spilling beans? Oh, you mean fill you in. I probably shouldn't over the phone, especially if he hasn't.'

'Fair enough.' Becky hesitated. 'A little hint?'

339

Yvette laughed, which Becky noted as a good thing.

'It's complicated. You should come visit. I'm sure we could talk about it in person. You could help us tremendously if you know where to find the secretive Jesse Raynard.' Yvette's laughter died quickly, as there was no corresponding appreciation of her joke. 'Becky?'

'Did you say Jesse Raynard?'

Yvette tightened her grip on the phone. 'Yes, but I was only joking. We've been chasing his identity and his relationship to—other activities— since you first mentioned him. You don't mean to say you know where to find Jesse Raynard?'

'No, I don't.'

Yvette relaxed.

'But I know someone who might.'

Yvette's tension redoubled. 'Who?'

'The same person who first mentioned the name and helped me get the drone tech. Emma Lister.'

'I know she was Smythe-Montgomery's right-hand person. And now your business partner?'

'"Business partner" is a bit of a stretch. ARC does have some contracts from her. Avionics mods to commercial aircraft. A carryover from the Smythe-Montgomery days. She'd be the best business reason for a visit to London. I wonder if she'd agree to join us for dinner and meet a brilliant young scientist.'

'Who would that be?'

'You're kidding, right? I'm talking about you. No false pride, now. You are brilliant, you do fascinating work on predictive chaos modeling, and you're the sole heir to Lord Crandall.'

'She may have no great reason to love that name.'

'Bullshit. Smythe-Montgomery may have been good in the sack, but there are plenty of fish in the sea. She was glad to see the last of him.'

'Becky, you're an artist with words. I would love to meet Emma Lister, if she's willing.'

'Oh, crap, there's Gary, waving at me like a loon to come back to the meeting. I'll see what I can arrange and give you a call, OK?'

'Lovely. Enjoy your meeting.'

'That's just plain mean,' Becky said.

***

'What's put that Cheshire Cat grin on your face?' Crandall grumbled.

'I talked to Becky. She may be coming to London soon. Also, Jason promised me tea and crumpets.'

Crandall blew the steam off tea so black it looked like motor oil.

'Oh, really? Then what do you call this?'

Yvette stared at the box of biscuits.

'Hey,' Stone said, entering the kitchen at that moment. 'I see you found the crumpets. They look like cookies to me, but—'

'These are biscuits.'

'Biscuits? No way. I can tell a good buttermilk biscuit from a cookie.'

'The point is,' Crandall said, speaking slowly, 'they aren't crumpets.'

'Really? Shit. I've been looking for Arthur but couldn't find him. Took my best shot.'

'Your best shot?' Crandall said, exchanging a glance with Yvette. 'Your best shot is usually, umm, more effective.'

'You'd best ask Diana,' Yvette said, catching Crandall by the arm. 'We have work to do, don't we, Richard?'

'I could get the crumpets,' Crandall said.

'No, you could not. We have a polymorphic algorithm to crack. Off you go. Spit spot.'

'Bloody slave driver,' Crandall said, as he passed Stone. 'Fish and chips, Jason. A late lunch would set me up wonderfully.' His voice faded as Yvette hustled him away.

Stone eyed the cookie box. 'Not crumpets?' He grabbed one and took a bite. 'Well, their loss is my gain.'

***

Stone did manage the fish and chips, delivering them a half hour later. He received nothing but distracted grunts in thanks from Richard and Yvette, who sat hunched over keyboards, eyes locked on monitors.

I can take a hint as well as the next guy, Stone thought, leaving the two to their work. He glanced at his watch. According to Diana, Arthur should be here by now. She'd even mentioned he might be available to make fresh crumpets for afternoon tea.

Arthur was more than happy to oblige, though when he described a crumpet and how to make one, Stone had been unimpressed. 'I don't suppose you need my help?'

'No, thank you, Mr. Stone.'

'Excellent. I have a few things I need to do this afternoon.'

'I'll deliver them to the offices at the appropriate time, with your compliments.'

'Thanks.'

***

Arthur arrived at 4:00 to find Richard and Yvette pushed back from their chairs, taking a break. A tray with a handful of cold chips and fragments of fish indicated that, at some point, the two had eaten.

'Arthur, are those fresh crumpets and a pot of tea?' Crandall asked. 'Heaven!'

'Mr. Stone said he'd committed to providing them, as the two of you were dedicated to solving a difficult problem.'

'His word is good,' Yvette said, with a smile, 'though I'm glad he didn't try to make these himself. Join us, Arthur, and we'll tell you all about it.'

'Am I allowed to know?'

'What!' Crandall exclaimed. 'Good Lord, man, I'd trust you with my life.'

'He just needs to brag a little,' Yvette said, reaching for a crumpet.

'It was Yvette's idea, actually,' Crandall said, wiping crumbs from his mouth some ten minutes later. 'We weren't able to hack directly into Raynard's servers. They are quite well protected. However, with the bidding concluded, there has been nearly constant communication between the buyer and the seller.'

'Brilliant,' Arthur said, smiling at Yvette. 'You broke into the buyer's network.'

'Yes. It wasn't easy, but after a few hours of adapting algorithms, we managed it.'

'The trick, as I understand it,' Arthur said thoughtfully, 'is to get into a system and not be detected.'

'That's it exactly,' Crandall said. 'If the hack is discovered, your adversary can change encryption, satellite relays, or servers, and we're back to square one.'

'Worse yet, they could pass bogus information and send us off on a goose chase,' Yvette said.

'They haven't done that, have they?' Arthur asked.

'Unlikely,' Crandall said.

'They're very good at this,' Yvette warned.

Crandall placed his hands on his lower back and groaned as he stretched. 'As I'm painfully aware, Yvette.'

'Have you gotten the information you hoped for?' Arthur said.

'Not yet. A rather heated argument over the time and location for a final demonstration has set things back. We'll continue to monitor the negotiations.'

'Just so you know, Richard,' Yvette said, 'I'll be joining Becky Amhurst for dinner tomorrow.'

'Lovely. Where?'

'I never heard of it. What was the name? Ah, Paris Twilight.'

Arthur started, and Crandall stared at Yvette, his expression a mixture of surprise and envy. 'Paris Twilight! Top floor of what's now known as the Mountbatten Building, formerly the London offices of Smythe-Montgomery.'

'Oh. I suppose that makes sense. We're meeting Emma Lister.'

Crandall gave a nervous cough. 'Are you OK with this, Yvette?'

'I am. After all, she isn't Smythe-Montgomery and she's doing legitimate business with Becky's company.'

'Well, I, umm,' Crandall began lamely. 'I'm sure you'll enjoy yourself.'

'Thank you. I'm sure I will.' Yvette decided to keep the true purpose of this dinner a secret. Tomorrow night would be soon enough to dazzle him with the identity of the inscrutable Jesse Raynard, should Emma Lister be able to provide the information.

The three were seated at a table near a solid wall of glass that offered a view of the Thames and the London Eye, the entire riverside twinkling with lights.

Chapter Twenty

Raynard Unmasked

Wear your fancy duds, 'cause this ain't no burger joint,' Becky had said. Yvette settled on a long silver dress and heels, which, on her slender frame, made her look much taller than she actually was. Before she left, Diana caught up with her.

'Here,' she said, putting a necklace around her and fastening it. 'It was my mother's. Not overly formal. Not stuffy. Just dignified.'

Yvette looked at the string of alternating diamonds and sapphires. 'It's gorgeous, Diana. Are you sure—'

'Off you go. Don't want to be late.'

Yvette hugged her, walking out the main entrance and looking from side to side.

'Oh,' Diana said, as Arthur rolled up, 'I canceled your cab. And before you say a word, Arthur insisted. Go, go.' She made a shooing motion with her hands.

Arthur dropped her off at ten till eight and she caught the elevator to the top floor. When she stepped out, more than a few heads turned, disconcerting her for a moment.

When did I become self-conscious? she thought. *They're just staring at the necklace.*

Truthfully, none of the men (young or old) who'd been staring had even noticed the necklace.

'Well, this is a life lesson for me,' Emma Lister said, coming up and extending her hand. 'Never be seen with a woman younger and more beautiful.'

Becky grinned. 'I learned that one long ago. Yvette Crandall, Emma Lister.'

'Pleased to meet you,' Lister said. A cloud passed over her face. 'Wait, is this …'

'The young lady I mentioned. Colin Fishburne's friend. And, as it turns out, the person responsible for eliminating his murderer.'

Emma Lister froze. 'Good Lord! Lovely and the heart of a lioness.' She tightened her grip. 'Genuinely honored to meet you.'

Yvette glanced nervously from one to the other before collecting herself. 'The pleasure and honor are mine.'

'There,' Becky said. 'Now we've gotten past the stiff, formal greetings. Let's take our seats and get a drink.'

The three were seated at a table near a solid wall of glass that offered a view of the Thames and the London Eye, the entire riverside twinkling with lights. As they ate, Yvette grew more and more comfortable conversing with Becky and Emma, who both avoided business discussions that would have excluded her. When the dinner plates were removed and desserts ordered, Lister leaned back and gave Becky a knowing look. 'Would I be indiscreet to ask why you were so eager to get together? I've thoroughly enjoyed meeting Yvette and I've been quite impressed by the predictive chaos model she's helped develop. It's almost magical, like predicting the future, and as a side note, I wonder how it might be applied in the aerospace industry. But I sense another question lurking.'

'I believe you may have one, as well,' Becky said, a puckish smile on her face.

'Again, at the risk of being indiscreet, I would love to know all you're willing to share about the happy demise of Carlos Velasquez. I did, after all, obtain that wonderful drone from Jesse Raynard.'

Yvette stiffened at the name.

'Then let's share,' Becky said calmly. 'What we'd like to know is, who is Jesse Raynard?'

'Ah! A delicate question with no easy answer. Jesse was responsible for the rise of Carlos from a mere lieutenant to cartel boss of Mexico and Central America. But Jesse was never interested in the cartels or their drugs.'

'What then?' Becky asked.

Lister continued as though she hadn't heard the question. 'Jesse Raynard's motives are a mystery. We met only once.' A faint glow lit

Emma Lister's smiling face. She gave Yvette an assessing look. 'I'm a fairly good judge of character, and I doubt you'll be shocked by a confession of a highly erotic nature.'

'It's unlikely,' Yvette said.

'I met with Raynard and her assistant, Charlotte, at a beach resort in Mexico. To discuss the removal of the Viper, of all things. After our business was complete … well, the day was sunny and warm and we let down our inhibitions and enjoyed each other's company. Several times.'

'Raynard is something of an accomplished lover?' Becky asked.

'Oh Lord, yes.'

'Details, please,' Becky said. Yvette nodded seriously.

'Well, first off, she's a magician. She showed me a card trick I'd never seen before.'

'Wait!' Yvette said. 'You said "her" and "she."'

'I did. A beautiful woman with a will of iron, and the imagination of … What is it?'

'A woman,' Yvette repeated. 'How big of fools have we all been?'

'Gargantuan,' Becky said, flagging down the waiter in a very undignified manner. 'Get a bottle of cognac and a pot of coffee over here and leave them or I'll have your balls. Now beat it!'

The waiter left, an affronted scowl on his face, wishing the Yanks could learn some manners.

When he returned, his scowl vanished, replaced by a look of shock as Becky tucked a hundred-pound note into his vest pocket. 'Apologies. It's girl talk,' she said with a smile. 'Three of us, three of those bills—that is, two more—if you see to it we get some privacy.'

'Yes, ma'am,' he said. 'I'll not return unless you raise your hand.'

'Good lad,' Becky said, as he scuttled off.

She rounded on Lister. 'First, tell us anything you can about *Ms.* Jesse Raynard, then about your day at the beach. And don't leave out any details.'

Lister gave a lighthearted laugh. 'The day at the beach I can recall in great detail, and it will be a pleasure to share.' She gave Becky a hungry look. 'It could be used as inspiration. We're all women of voting age.'

To Yvette's surprise, Becky returned her smile and nodded. 'Perhaps.'

'As to who Jesse Raynard is, I may disappoint you.'

'You haven't so far,' Yvette said. 'You've already told us more than we've been able to find in months.'

'Hmm. Yes,' she said, drawing the word out slowly. 'Well, I know Raynard was working with the Viper, the man you so efficiently eliminated. As I mentioned, it was she who helped him rise from a faceless lieutenant in the cartels to the boss for most of Mexico and Central America. No mean feat. Almost magical, you might say.'

'Why would she associate with such a moron? After all, she helped eliminate him.'

'You know the expression "dumb as a box of hammers"? Well, just because they're dumb, doesn't mean you never use one. He was a useful tool in Raynard's hands—until he wasn't. She's very pragmatic. By the time we spoke, her annoyance with his idiocy had eclipsed his usefulness. For me, that threshold had been crossed long before. Raynard and I became allies. You,' she said, tipping her glass in Becky's direction, 'were an ally for obvious reasons, your friends being the target of the Viper's brutality. And Yvette, though Becky hadn't named you at the time, had as much reason as anyone to want him dead.'

Yvette hung her head, her jaw clenched.

'I am truly sorry,' Lister said. She drew a deep breath. 'Pragmatic. That was my point. Jesse Raynard is almost as much of a mystery to me as she is to you. And, in a sense, she's used me—and you two—as much as she used Carlos. I wouldn't want to get on her bad side.'

'But what is she ultimately trying to accomplish?' Yvette was tempted to say more, to bring up the mysterious outbreaks of disease. She wisely resisted. Even Becky knew nothing of Raynard's connection with that.

'Ultimately?' Lister said. 'I haven't a clue. Oddly enough, I'm not sure she does either.'

'What do you mean?' Becky asked.

'Perhaps nothing at all. Just an impression that she's been striving for something for so long that the striving itself has become her motivation. She's been a disappointment to herself and others, I'm sure. Probably when she was young. Now she's trying to compensate, to impress someone who no longer cares. Or harder still, she's trying to impress herself.'

'I don't suppose she left a mailing address?'

Lister laughed. 'No.'

'Is there any more you can tell us?' Yvette asked.

'She was quite good at card tricks.'

Becky smirked.

'I say it in earnest. I've never been impressed by magicians, but she did things with her hands that were astonishing, and not just for sexual gratification. From what Charlotte said, card tricks are only a tiny part of her repertoire. You may learn more by pursuing that line of inquiry—but I wouldn't.'

'Why not?' Yvette asked.

'I said magician, and that was inaccurate. She's an illusionist. I would be skeptical of anything you discover about Jesse Raynard. And cautious. As Carlos found out, she's a formidable enemy.'

'But an excellent lover?' Becky asked.

'Let me describe our day at the beach. You be the judge.'

***

At the end of a long, detailed account, which embarrassed neither Becky nor Yvette, Lister leaned back and smiled. 'I can see you both appreciate the finer things in life. Consider an invitation made, should you ever desire a relaxing evening.'

'We'll consider it,' Becky said. 'Seriously.'

'Lovely. Now, I've talked until I'm hoarse. I would like to hear some details of Carlos's final minutes, if it wouldn't be too distressing.'

Becky glanced over at Yvette, who nodded. 'I think I'm ready to talk about it. Jason said it would help.'

Lister poured more cognac. 'I'm all ears.'

***

It was after midnight before Yvette returned to Diana's estate, stuffed full of escargot, crab cakes, éclair, and information. She changed quickly and hurried down the long hallway to the Triple S offices, unsurprised to see light spilling out from the open door.

As she entered, Stone looked up, stifled a yawn, and said, 'You've just missed Richard. He left in a pretty grumpy mood. How was your evening?'

'His loss,' she responded, ignoring Stone's question. 'What are you working on?'

'Oh,' Stone said, with a wry smile, 'just a Sudoku.'

'Funny.'

'I'm still trying to track down the elusive Mr. Jesse Raynard.'

'Ah,' Yvette said, unable to suppress a grin, 'illusive is quite apt.' The change of spelling (and meaning) she kept to herself. 'You can stop.'

'Stop? Stop what? Looking for Jesse Raynard?'

'No. You can stop looking for *Mr.* Jesse Raynard. Jesse Raynard is a woman.'

Stone's jaw hung open as he took a few rasping breaths. Then he said the first words that came to mind.

'Bloody fucking son of a bitch!'

'Is there any coffee about?' Yvette asked. 'Fresh coffee, that is. I couldn't deal with any more alcohol.'

'Just made a pot. I was planning on a long, unproductive night. You're serious?'

'Absolutely. Jesse Raynard is a woman. Our fundamental search criterion was faulty.'

'No shit! I take it this intel came from Emma Lister. Do you think the information is accurate?'

'Right down to the mole on Raynard's … never mind.'

Stone poured two coffees and flopped back into his chair. 'Start at the beginning. And go slow.'

***

When Yvette finished, Stone shook his head. 'It sure as hell explains why we never got anywhere. A woman. A woman who's an illusionist! That would have been about twelve billion down on my list of possibilities.'

'We can search properly now. I'd be surprised if we can't find out who she is.'

'Unfortunately, a lot of this burden, at least early on, falls on you. It means you'll have to spend less time hacking Raynard's servers, and I'm not sure that's a good strategy.'

'Richard can continue along those lines. He's better at it than I am.'

'Did I mention grumpy? Tired and grumpy?'

'Tell you what. Let me get a few hours' sleep. I'll tackle Jesse Raynard in the morning—later this morning. I'll be shocked if I can't give you considerable information before noon. Information you can follow up on with Randy and Chuck. After lunch, I'll see if I can help Mr. Grumpy.'

'Can't say no to that deal. And the dinner was good?'

'Outstanding,' Yvette said. An impish smile lit her face. 'Plus, Becky and I were invited to participate in a ménage à trois. Or was it four? Can't think of the French for "four."'

'Too much information. Talk to you later.'

'Goodnight, Jason.'

***

The next morning, Stone wandered into the Triple S offices, stifling a yawn. Yvette was already working at a terminal. 'Up early,' he commented.

She glanced at the time—6:15—and grunted a non-reply.

It took a minute for Stone to recognize that her wrinkled clothes were identical to what she'd been wearing the previous evening.

'Wait a minute,' he said. 'Don't tell me you've been at it all night?'

Yvette gave him a bleary-eyed smile. 'I did put my head down for a few minutes. Might have drooled on some papers. But before you tell me the obvious, let me explain. I started pulling strings and one thing led to another. I just couldn't stop. I've found not *one* but *four* Jesse Raynards.' She shrugged. 'Only one of them goes by the name Jesse Raynard.

'The first was a frustrated girl raised by parents who were apparently never satisfied or impressed by anything she did. That girl's name was Jessica Prairie Reynolds. A brilliant student whose academic accomplishments were greeted with yawns.'

'How the hell could you know that?'

'I found her high school records. She was valedictorian, and there's a copy of her graduation speech online. Here's a snippet.'

Yvette picked up a wrinkled paper and gave Stone a sheepish look. 'Told you. Drool. Anyway, Jessica Reynolds said, "As we finish this stage in our lives, we all, I'm sure, look forward to life's new challenges with the firm support and encouragement of our families. Mom, Dad, you can stop yawning. Why did I think being class valedictorian would impress you? Maybe I should have tried pulling a rabbit out of my hat."

'It goes back to being a serious speech after that, but she was savaged in the school newspaper the following year, mostly because the principal banned student speeches at graduation ceremonies in perpetuity because of her. Of course, she was gone and had moved on to other things.'

'Pulled a rabbit out of her hat. That's a laugh,' Stone said, pouring himself a cup of coffee.

'She wasn't joking, Jason. At least, the second Jesse Raynard wasn't. She lived in Las Vegas and took college classes under several names, but that's not relevant. At least, not yet.'

'Sorry, you're losing me,' he said.

'I apologize. No doubt I'm thick-witted this morning. I'd love another cup of coffee.'

He poured her one, then glanced at the discarded grounds and filters in the trash can. 'How much of this have you drunk?'

'Far too much. I'll switch to tea—herbal tea—later today. Promise. For now, let me continue.'

'Can't say I'm not dying to know. Give me the short version.'

'Right. As I said, she attended school in Las Vegas, but, and this is the important part, she took the stage name Illusion's Master and began performing.'

'Pulling rabbits out of her hat? No shit?'

'She may have started that way. She worked the strip as a street magician, adding illusions and improving her technique, until she was literally discovered by a rich casino owner, who hired her and gave her the resources to perform some spectacular illusions.'

'Wait a minute,' Stone said, his eyes narrowing. 'I vaguely remember the story of a Vegas magician who came out of nowhere and became a superstar—David Copperfield or Siegfried and Roy caliber—then just disappeared. Quit for no reason or had a falling out with the casino owner or something. Foul play was even suspected at one point. After all, you don't stiff that Vegas crowd. Was that her?'

'It was certainly Illusion's Master. Gone, as you said. Run away or murdered. The mystery was never resolved.'

'Till now?'

Yvette smiled and rubbed her eyes. 'What you must remember … what I should have told you at the start, was that I'm telling this story as though I'm certain of every detail. I'm not. But it's so tedious to qualify every statement with "it's possible," or "I believe," or "it might be." It could take weeks to confirm my guesses, and even then, the trail could grow cold. I've made assumptions and outright blind guesses, and here I am. I'll jam everything I know into the predictive chaos model as soon as my eyes focus again. For now, you're getting the benefit of my intuition, such as it is.'

'Worth a fortune, in my book. OK, I understand the tenuous nature of what you're telling me.' He grinned. 'Please continue.'

Yvette returned his smile. 'The third Jesse Raynard, who went only by the initials I. M., made a name for herself in Hollywood. A good name at first, as a special effects designer. Then bad. There was conflict with the studio over graphically realistic scenes of torture and murder. Tabloid articles mentioned "high-quality snuff films." A comment in a media chatroom said, with sarcasm as thick as tar, that her work "undoubtedly made her parents proud." One of the responses, a match in sarcasm, caught my eye.' Yvette shuffled through papers, then read, '"Apparently, you don't know my parents."'

'I know,' Yvette said, with a thin smile, 'it's a pretty flimsy connection.'

'I disagree,' Stone said. 'Both the "I. M." moniker—a carryover from Illusion's Master, I presume—and the continued rejection by her parents. Or a perceived rejection. It hardly matters which. In her mind, Jesse Raynard keeps trying to impress her parents and keeps failing. Is it really just internal feelings of inadequacy? Her actions are what matter.'

'Why, Jason, you're quite the psychologist!'

'A student of life. I've known more than my fair share of screwed-up people.'

'Well, I concur with your assessment. Jesse Raynard is trying to impress someone; to achieve some recognition that is always out of reach.'

'The torment of Tantalus,' Stone said.

'Exactly.'

Stone rubbed his chin thoughtfully. 'Let me guess, I. M. disappeared from the Hollywood scene about this time.'

'Yes. And the fourth Jesse Raynard was born.'

'The one who went by the name. A completely new and unique name. Must have made it hard to make the connection.'

'Frankly,' Yvette said, 'it's the thinnest connection of all. However, there was Charlotte.'

'Charlotte, Raynard's assistant? Charlotte from the orgy?'

Yvette smiled. 'Yes, I suppose that's accurate. In any case, there was a Charlotte Shorewood—probably a stage name—who acted in several of I. M.'s early horror films. From South Africa, I think. When I. M. left Hollywood, apparently so did Ms. Shorewood. It's hardly a conclusive link, but it is something.'

'More than something. I swear, Yvette, what you've discovered is amazing.'

'Thanks. The breakthrough was discovering Jesse Raynard's gender.'

'Talk about a bad assumption. *Mr.* Jesse Raynard. So, what can you tell me about this fourth Jesse Raynard?'

'Well, as I learned from Emma Lister, Jesse orchestrated Carlos Velasquez's rise to power. She was the true brains behind the brutal muscle. Emma wasn't certain of Jesse's ultimate goals, only that she used Carlos. As we already suspected, Jesse was the agent behind the transformation of the *Saint Martin* to the *Reina del Mar*, which became the plague ship. It's safe to say Jesse Raynard was running experiments with an incredibly dangerous disease.'

'Still trying to impress Mom and Dad?'

'Who knows?'

Stone grew thoughtful. 'Something still doesn't fit. How does someone, even a brilliant someone with illusionist skills, develop a new bug? That's beyond what most epidemiologists could do. You don't just get up one morning and say, "Hey, I think I'll cook up a deadly disease today."'

'Carl Heskin, the man MI5 and the CIA misidentified as Raynard, might have the skill. So might the Russian doctor, Constantin Shukhov. Both were well-connected at the CDC. But ...'

'But?'

'I don't yet have a connection between either of them and Jesse Raynard, much less evidence of a nefarious collaboration.'

'But there *is* a deadly disease up for sale. Let's go with the working assumption that Raynard found the scientific help she needed to create this disease. There's a trail of bodies that testifies to its effectiveness.'

'Yes,' Yvette replied, though Stone caught the tone of hesitation in her voice.

'You don't sound convinced.'

She yawned. 'Oh, don't mind me. It's nothing I can put my finger on. You're right. The concern now is to stop the sale of this disease.'

'And to do that, we need to find the location of the lab where the sale will occur. I have a few questions for Jesse Raynard. Yvette, you've done wonders. Remember that puzzle with the giant hole in the middle?'

She nodded.

'You've filled it in. If you have any energy left today, work with Richard. We know enough about the four Jesses. We'll work with that as a basis, fill in details later.'

'It's risky, Jason. You know the expression "If you assume—"'

'"You make an *ass* of *you* and *me*." Words to live by, but time is our enemy. They also say, you can't win in Vegas unless you place a bet.'

'Everything on red?'

Stone smiled. 'Sure.'

At that moment, Crandall entered the room, squint-eyed and frowsy. 'Barely slept a bloody wink. Eyes feel like piss holes in the snow.'

'Good morning to you too, Crandall,' Stone said.

'Whoever thought to combine those two words should be drawn and quartered ... then shot. Ah, coffee!' He headed for the pot.

'Really, Richard, how can you drink that vile brew?' Yvette asked. 'A civilized Englishman. I'd prefer a cup of tea. Herbal tea.'

Stone gave Yvette a knowing wink and left them to it.

***

When he checked back later that afternoon, Stone was greeted by a slightly less surly Crandall.

'Ah, Jason, your timing is quite good,' he said. 'Yvette, why don't you tell him.'

'We have it, Jason. A location for the final demonstration.'

'And a date?' he asked eagerly.

'Yes, in a way.' She saw his face fall and quickly added, 'Don't be concerned. It's a one-week interval. We should have guessed as much.'

'OK, I'm lost. Any more of that coffee available?'

'Only the dregs, I'm afraid,' Crandall answered.

'The dregs will do,' Stone said, filling his cup with what looked like dark brown soup, then shutting off the pot warmer. He took a deep drink. 'Now, please explain why we should have guessed.'

355

'Simple,' Yvette said. 'Raynard is demonstrating a disease. The buyers are supplying the victim, and it will take several days to see the results.'

'That's fucking gruesome,' Stone said. 'But logical. The buyers would want to monitor the course of the disease. Watch it in action. When does the show begin?'

'Ah, a bit of bad news. Tomorrow, I'm afraid,' Yvette replied.

Yvette was surprised at Stone's reaction, which was no reaction at all.

'The location is in the mountains along the southwest coast of Costa Rica,' she continued. 'The nearest town is Savegre.'

'Never heard of it.'

'Nor had the buyers. It's a long drive from San José on mountain roads. They weren't pleased.'

'No choice, I suppose,' Stone said.

'No. The lab is located in the mountains overlooking the ocean, fourteen miles from Savegre. The facilities there are, apparently, suitable for this demonstration *without* exposing the buyer and seller to the infection.'

'Also makes sense.'

'Will you be going, Jason?' Yvette asked. 'A chance to get your questions answered.'

Stone only smiled. A moment later, Crandall let out a mighty yawn. 'You're welcome, Jason. I'll leave you two to discuss details. If Arthur is still about the place, I'm for dinner. Does anyone fancy shepherd's pie?'

'I do,' Yvette replied.

'Me too,' Stone said. 'But I believe it takes a while to prepare. I'll just finish my discussion here and we'll be right along.'

'A glass of Cabernet sounds good to whet the appetite,' Crandall said. 'See you two at dinner.'

'Richard,' Stone called out, as Crandall reached the door of the Triple S offices.

Crandall turned back. 'Yes?'

'Thanks.'

Crandall smiled and walked out.

'Jason?' Yvette said, when they were alone.

'Yes?'

Yvette frowned and air huffed from her nose. 'You know very well. Will you be going? It's your chance to meet Raynard. Question her.'

'Maybe,' he said thoughtfully. 'I'm glad it's just the two of us talking about this.'

'What? Why?'

'Because I don't want anyone else to know what I have in mind. It may be stupid. It's certainly nothing more than a hunch.'

'What do you mean?'

'It just doesn't feel right. The mysterious Jesse Raynard giving a demonstration for ruthless buyers who've brought their own victim. Will they be drinking tea while the man—or woman—dies? Playing cards to pass the time? Taking in the sights?'

'I see what you mean. But, Jason, it's all we'd hoped for. A location. A time.'

'And Triple S will act. I think Randy's been sitting on his laurels for too long. We'll send him to surveil the sight. If he needs backup, I can be there in twenty-four hours. So can Chuck.'

'And you?'

'If you think you can keep awake for a while longer, I have an angle I'd like you to explore.'

'Angle?'

'A line of inquiry.'

'Of course. What is it?'

'It's "who" actually. Charlotte Shorewood. Assuming her connection with Raynard is real, see what you can find out about her.'

'Other than her sexual proclivities?' Yvette asked, with a smirk.

'Sadly, yes. Can you do that? Just between the two of us?'

'Certainly. And the shepherd's pie?'

'Yes to that also. Randy, however, may have to skip a meal to catch his flight to San José.'

*True, he did have the gadgets: high-power binoculars, parabolic mics,
and the laser device that translated window vibrations to sound.*

Chapter Twenty-One

Randy and Stone Ask Hard Questions

James Charles O'Neil was howling in the background as Gail walked Randy to the door. 'You will be more careful this time?' she said.

Randy hesitated. He thought he'd been careful on his last international assignment. That was right before he'd been arrested, thrown into a Mexican jail, and offered to the Viper as a source of information. Since the Viper's methods of extracting information were quite painful, he'd been delighted when the local sheriff had seen fit to release him and fake his death.

'Randy?'

Gail's voice interrupted his musing and he grinned. 'I promise to be extremely careful.' He kissed her. 'James must be hungry. I also promise to take care of meals and diapers for a solid week when I get back.'

'Now that's a lie,' she said, with a laugh. 'Go on, or you'll miss your plane.'

***

Randy had plenty of time on the tedious flights to Costa Rica to wonder how he could conduct surveillance while being extremely careful. True, he did have the gadgets: high-power binoculars, parabolic mics, and the laser device that translated window vibrations to sound. He also planned to tap landlines and listen in on cell calls, though he wasn't sure if a cell phone would work in the remote location of Raynard's lab.

'At least I know what I'm looking for now,' he muttered to himself, as he negotiated the narrow, twisting roads after leaving the San José airport. 'A woman! Talk about feeling stupid.'

His brief moment of embarrassment passed as he thought through the logistical issues he had to solve before he could even begin his task. The primary consideration was finding a sheltered location where he could set up camp; near enough to allow him to do his job and yet not so near that he might be spotted by Raynard's security sweeps. Stone had been insistent on that point.

'Don't underestimate Raynard. She'll be on guard and well protected. Her guests aren't exactly scrupulous or trusting either. You might want to set up two or even three sites that you can move between.'

'That's assuming I can find even one.'

'You will. We've studied the satellite photos and you know there are at least four good options.'

'Yeah, sorry. Just bitching. Speaking of bitching, how come you're not on this little Boy Scout outing?'

Stone sighed. Randy was nervous and was being petulant to cover his fear.

'I'm playing another hunch. I'll be there as soon as I can. Chuck is standing by if you need backup.'

'Guess I'm still the *junior* vice president of Triple S,' Randy said.

'For now. Look, you'll do fine. Just remember, don't underestimate Raynard and under no circumstances engage either Raynard's people or the Russians. If you're made, run and don't look back.'

'Understood.'

He *had* understood. Stone knew his way around covert ops. The question was, what would he, Randy O'Neil, find when he got there?

'Guess that's the point of going,' he grumbled.

***

Randy rejected the nearer surveillance sites, though they gave the best view of the lab. He'd soon be grateful for this decision.

The more distant sites were acceptable, one as a base, one as a backup. He was crouching in the one he'd chosen to be his primary site, a narrow ledge that barely held him and his equipment, when two vans came up the twisty dirt road leading to Raynard's lab. The buyers.

Randy counted six hard-looking men, two geeks (scientists or accountants), and the guest of honor, easily identified by the bag over his head and the rough way he was being handled. The hard men had professionally deployed, two staying with the geeks, two searching the buildings, and two performing a determined sweep near the lab that, to Randy's shock, included those nearer sites. Had they pushed much farther, Randy would have been discovered. But at the end of two hours of beating the bush in a steady rain, the two sweepers headed back to the compound. Randy had no doubt a two-man team would be out daily.

Throughout the process, Randy had seen only three men from the compound, one who seemed to be the leader, but no sign of Jesse Raynard. Was she staying out of sight? Randy was certain there were more of Raynard's people inside. The other surprise Randy had gotten during those first moments was the sight of the prisoner as his guards yanked the sack off his head. Yevgeny Turgenev! A long-time political nemesis of the current Russian leadership, he was rumored to have died (of natural causes!) in prison. Apparently, that death was only postponed.

Twenty-four hours later, Randy was as miserable as a man could be. The rain came and went, and when it was absent, swarms of insects seemed to blossom from the ground with the sole mission of tormenting him. He had bites and stings on every inch of exposed skin and was certain he'd inhaled several of the smaller bugs. Once he thought he saw a centipede the size of his lower arm, but he could have been mistaken. It might have been a snake.

He'd been gathering intel the entire time, mostly with his laser device, as only two of the visitor's guards were outside, pacing a large balcony overlooking the coast. From what he'd heard, Turgenev was in a glass-walled room within a sealed section of the compound—a hermetically isolated part of Raynard's lab. Television cameras and microphones brought the only access to the observers, who were more than willing to have at least two layers of protection between themselves and the final experiment. Earlier that morning, the disease had been introduced into Turgenev's cell. Now, the observers would sit back and wait. They'd been assured that symptoms would appear in forty-eight hours or less, with death occurring within the next twenty-four to forty-eight.

Randy wondered how he'd be spending his time waiting for a man to succumb to a horrible disease. He got his answer the next day, when the hellish rain stopped and a damp sun appeared. First the guards and the two scientists appeared out on the porch, then several of Raynard's people set up tables and brought out coffee and breakfast. The man Randy thought was the leader accompanied them, talking as the scientists set up laptops. Randy could see they were monitoring the prisoner nonstop, as multiple images were displayed of his enclosure.

For the first time, Randy was able to make use of his parabolic mic, though the range was almost at the mic's limit. What he heard—or thought he heard—made no sense at all. As they sat drinking coffee and nibbling croissants, they kept referring to the lead *man* from Raynard's compound as Raynard! He listened intently for long enough to convince himself that this person was passing himself off as Jesse Raynard, and the buyers were accepting it. Randy stared through his binoculars. The man in question looked sickly: thin, pale, dark bags around his eyes. But he seemed vaguely familiar. Where had Randy seen him?

Suddenly it clicked. The man in the photos who had been mistakenly identified as Raynard by the CIA and MI5 operatives. The two men who'd been questioned by Stone. They'd given Stone a photo. It had been pure luck that Chuck had shown it to his friend Tyrone. Constantin Pavlovich Shukhov had been on all the news stories involving the plague, and there was no mistaking him. But the other man, the one the dirty agents thought was Raynard, had been identified by Martha, Tyrone's friend, as another brilliant scientist working out of the CDC, though not nearly as flashy as Shukhov.

Carl Heskin.

What the hell is going on? Randy thought.

Randy puzzled throughout the rest of the day, confirming that Carl Heskin's guests definitely believed him to be Jesse Raynard. But why the charade?

He also confirmed that Yevgeny Turgenev was dying horribly in his sealed room. Raynard's guests seemed pleased, though they were badgering 'Raynard' for access. Randy had caught a bit of this conversation from the patio that evening.

'We have hazmat suits,' one of the Russians said, 'and are willing to take the risk. We wish to begin testing.'

Heskin had coughed violently, struggling to regain his breath. When he did, he answered firmly enough.

'That was not the bargain. You can see the progress of the disease from the video and audio feeds, as well as monitoring his vital statistics from the data streams. When he dies, his body is yours and you may perform whatever tests you wish—at your facilities. You may also conduct any other experiments on the pathogen, which you will also have … AFTER payment is received and verified. By my estimation, this should be within forty-eight hours.'

'But—'

Heskin held up a hand. 'This is not a negotiation.'

Randy caught random grumbling in Russian, catching a few words that were a commentary on Raynard's legitimacy of birth as well as his predilection for children and small animals. If Heskin understood, he showed no outward sign.

That evening, Randy returned to the Range Rover, his base of operations, several weary miles away across difficult terrain. When he arrived, he contacted Chuck Johnson.

'We're running out of time, Chuck. Raynard may not actually be here, but Turgenev is dying, and when he's gone, there's no way the Russkis will take "no" for an answer. They'll send the funds, take the disease and the body, and scoot.'

The scratching of Chuck's hand over his nascent beard indicated he was thinking. 'You know,' he said at last, 'maybe we've been double punked. What if Heskin *is* Raynard?'

'A double life? I suppose. But what about the intel from Emma Lister?'

'Lister could be lying or she could have been punked.'

'But the other stuff Yvette found?'

'Come on, brother, that stuff was held together with cobwebs.'

'Stronger than steel,' Randy muttered.

It started to rain again and Randy stifled a curse before saying, 'Do we give a shit? I mean, he could be she or she could be he. Point is, a famous Russian dissident is about to croak and a deadly disease is about to change hands.'

363

'You're right. I'm heading your way now. I wish like hell I could guarantee I'll be there in time. If not ...'

'I'll see if I can slow things down, boss.'

'Do NOT get yourself dead, Randy.'

'Not my plan.'

'What *is* your plan?'

'I've got about a four-hour trudge back to the lab. If I don't have one by then, well ...'

***

As it was, Randy spent the four hours and another day trying to concoct a plan. He'd slept fitfully, thinking about the poor man whose imminent death would throw events into motion; events that might result in a plague being released on the world.

Dawn was struggling vainly against thick clouds and overcast the next morning. Randy shifted uncomfortably. Everything was wet and heavy; a smothering blanket over the world. He sat up straight, his heart pounding, as shouted orders filtered up to his blind. He clumsily pulled out his binoculars and wiped the lenses. When he focused, he knew immediately that something had happened. A Russian stood on the patio, repeating his order and gesticulating. Randy scanned the surrounding hillsides and saw the men assigned to patrol the perimeter making their way back to the lab. Another Russian came out onto the patio and interrogated the shouter, then both hurried back into the building. Only one event could have triggered this disturbance.

Shit! Randy thought. *I guess I'll come up with that plan as I go.* He rose stiffly and started down the slope towards the lab.

***

At Raynard's compound, tense discussions were occurring.

'Turgenev is dead,' a Russian doctor said, pointing at the data trace.

A statement of the obvious, since the prisoner, disfigured with weeping sores and bloody eyes, ears, and mouth, lay collapsed within his cell.

'Yes,' Heskin said calmly.

'So now we go to collect the body, and you deliver the pathogen.'

Heskin coughed, bloody spittle staining his handkerchief. 'I am tired and, as you can see, unwell. You will transfer the funds first.' He held up a hand as the Russian was about to protest, then pulled a small device from his pocket. An electronic remote. 'I don't even need to push this button. I've activated the failsafe and the pathogen will be released in thirty seconds. Too short a time for you to escape. I will continue to enter the abort code until I am dead—with you not far behind—or until payment is transferred and verified, as we agreed. At that time, I'll enter the disable code and you may claim the body and the pathogen. Say any other word than "yes" and I'll kill us all now.'

His finger hovered over the button.

'Yes.'

***

Randy had reached the outer wall bordering the patio, now strangely quiet. He put a hand to his hip. His primary firearm, an H&K nine-millimeter (Stone's recommendation), felt solid and comfortable under his palm. He then checked his backup. Also a nine mil, tucked under his left arm. *So much better to use only one caliber of ammunition!* He smiled briefly, but the smile slid from his face like bacon from a skillet. Not enough firepower. It was too soon to hope Chuck would be here, and there was no way Randy could deal with six heavily armed Russian thugs. Stone, maybe, could do it, but Randy wasn't Jason Stone.

He looked back over his shoulder, more than half hoping to see the aggressive, competent stare of Jason Stone just yards away. A vain hope.

Just me this time. And what can I do? He smiled grimly. *Slow them down.*

He crept up to the wall, took a deep breath, and set a hand on the top, preparing to vault over.

***

As Heskin watched the Russians grudgingly begin the payment transfer, his thoughts drifted back to his first meeting with the enigmatic Jesse Raynard. A dive bar in Atlanta. Carl drunk, or nearly so, and destroyed by hopelessness. Raynard had offered hope, though not for Carl. He had already been beyond hope. But his family! As the years had passed, Carl Heskin had come to trust and respect Raynard, then admire her, and finally, to become her friend. The final payment was now due, and Carl had no regrets. This day had been bound to come. He'd anticipated meeting it with despair. But now? Joy? All men die. Only some could say they'd provided for their family as he had.

Carl had several drugs to control his pain. He took one now, along with another that would produce euphoria and clarity. He felt its effects almost immediately as he entered the abort code for the last time. His staff and their special guest had quietly departed to the boat dock twenty minutes earlier. He could hardly wait to see the look of surprise on the faces of the Russians. *Ah, if only Constantin were here.*

'I said, the transfer is complete,' a grating voice repeated loudly.

Carl tapped a few commands on his computer, verifying the transfer of funds.

'Oh, well done!' he cried, unable to control his manic behavior. He typed several more entries. 'The lock to the enclosure is now released.' He went to a panel in the wall and pressed his thumb to a sensor, which blinked twice. The panel slid open revealing a cryogenic containment vessel the size of a coffee thermos. He placed it into a padded metal case not much bigger than a lunchbox and handed it over. '"Now I am become Death, the destroyer of worlds,"' he muttered.

'What's that?'

'A quote. Oppenheimer's words not long after the detonation of the first atomic bomb.' Carl grimaced. 'Get your suits. I'll get mine and we'll examine the body together.'

With the Russian guards gathered around the computers and the doctors going off for their suits, Carl slipped from the room.

Death isn't so bad, he thought. *Death isn't the end.*

***

Yvette tracked down Charlotte Shorewood faster than Stone had imagined possible. And since she'd told him Charlotte owned a cabin in the New Mexico mountains, Stone had become convinced he would find Jessica / Illusion's Master / I. M. / Jesse Raynard there. Raynard certainly wasn't in Costa Rica, at least by Randy's last report, and Stone had questions only Jesse Raynard could answer, not least of which was why she would put a deadly disease in the hands of those who might be mad enough to use it.

And that lingering 'why' was driving Stone now. He'd been forced to confide in Yvette. She was too damned smart for her own good. Stone smiled. The quote had been applied to him by his frustrated mother on many occasions. It had taken some time to convince Yvette to let him pursue Raynard on his own. Both knew Raynard was brilliant and more than capable of killing. Yet Yvette's experience with the Viper had broadened her understanding. Their conversation had been brief.

'Why are you pursuing Jesse Raynard, Jason?' she'd asked.

'I could say revenge,' Stone answered, 'for the trail of bodies, not to mention the threat to the world.'

'I'd understand if it was personal, like my obsession with the Viper.'

'But it is personal. Everyone is in danger. Luana, Richard, Randy … you. People I care about. I need answers.'

'Yes, I suppose. I settled for one man's death. It hasn't brought me the peace I'd hoped for, but that's just as you predicted. Will killing Jesse Raynard bring you peace?'

The question stung because of the dagger-like truth it contained.

Stone rubbed his temples, taking a long time before he replied. 'Good question. One that's kept me up at night. Many nights. Whether or not I *try* to kill Raynard—and I don't underestimate her ability to kill me—will depend on the answers I get to some questions. Something's still not right. So, my hope is to get my answers first. At that point, if circumstances require it, we'll face off at twenty paces.'

'Jason!'

'You're right,' he said, with a twisted smile, 'Twenty is too close. Fifty. Hell, we might both live.'

Yvette had kissed his forehead, wished him well, and agreed not to tell anyone of his plans. She hid the research on Charlotte's cabin and went back to work on autoregressive search algorithms for the predictive chaos model.

Stone had taken a series of flights that brought him to Albuquerque. And now here he was, snow falling as though it would obscure a river of blood.

He approached the cabin cautiously, having circled it several times since dawn, gradually closing the radius of his search. Though he kept a sharp lookout, the snow covered any tracks of humans or animals. Rumors that Raynard kept a vicious wolf-hound for personal protection might be exaggerated, but there was no knowing for sure what tricks Raynard might spring on unwelcome visitors.

It was well past noon when Stone made a decision. He was here and no one else's life was at risk. He'd approach the cabin and knock on the door if he had to, but he wasn't going to leave without some answers. The possibility of not leaving at all had also occurred to him, but he'd come as prepared as possible. He had his favorite H&K .45 tucked under his jacket, plus a small Walther strapped to his ankle. A knife at his hip and two others hidden in his clothing made him feel as comfortable as he could under the circumstances.

He'd just entered a clearing facing the house—and house it was, as big as his own in Breckenridge—when a large gray animal came around from the other side. Too big to be a dog, this was clearly the rumored wolf-hound. It froze as it spotted Stone, and he caught a good look at the glacial blue of its eyes. A low rumble filled the air.

Stone crouched down till he was eye level with the animal, lowered his head, and extended one arm. The rumble grew spotty then stopped altogether. 'Come on,' Stone said softly, 'check me out. I mean you no harm. I'm here for information, not blood.'

A full minute passed, and then the animal moved forward slowly, with no sense of fear or urgency, until its nose was inches away from Stone. It began sniffing, moving all around him, while Stone kept as still as possible, muttering soothing words that had very little meaning. At last, seemingly satisfied, it trotted back towards the house.

When Stone raised his head, he saw the dog standing close to a tall, attractive woman bundled in a parka, boots, and jeans. Long, dark hair tumbled around her shoulders.

'I'm impressed,' she said. 'Cherokee usually doesn't take to strangers. Maybe she senses something in you. Integrity?' The woman shrugged. 'But I'm being rude. Please stand. You're safe as long as you don't try to kill me. You're not going to try to kill me, are you, Mr. Stone? I suspect that would leave both of us in a *grave* position.' She laughed softly at her joke.

'How do you know my name?'

'Oh, please, our respective comrades have been hacking each other's systems for weeks. You're Jason Stone, one of the founding members of Stone Security Services.'

'And you're Jesse Raynard.'

'It depends who you ask. I heard Jesse Raynard was in Costa Rica conducting a deal with Russians.'

'I heard that was Carl Heskin,' Stone said.

Hurt swept across Raynard's face. 'He's a dear friend, one of very few, who was treated badly by a bloated organization and a corrupt government. Death stalks him now.'

'Yet he's masquerading as you. Makes me wonder why.'

'May I ask why you are here? If it's for blood, we'd best do that outside. Poor Charlotte will never be able to get the place clean if we do this indoors.'

'As I told Cherokee'—her ears perked up at her name—'I'm not here for blood, just information. Depending on the information, our next meeting could be very different. But I'm also not here to threaten.'

'Please,' she said. 'Ask away.'

'Why? Why create the deadliest pathogen the world has ever seen? Worse than the bubonic plague. Worse than Ebola. Why create such a thing, then sell it to people ruthless enough to use it?'

***

Before Heskin had been gone for a minute, allegedly in search of his hazmat gear, the Russian leader's computer screen changed. The body of a dead man in his prison was replaced with the image of Yevgeny Turgenev, alive and well, standing by a boat at a small dock.

The Russians exchanged glances. 'What the hell is this?' the commander said.

'You men are fools!' Turgenev said. 'Did Raynard just quote Oppenheimer? Of course he did. Speak, I can hear you.'

'You are dead. The disease!'

'Do I look dead?' Turgenev mocked. 'No, comrade, it is you who are dead. Perhaps it is best you step into the chamber and breathe death. Worse awaits you if you return home without your prize. *Do svidaniya*!'

The Russian leader spun towards the hall where, a moment before, Raynard had been standing. Gone.

369

'Raynard!' he thundered. He sprinted down the hall, waving for his men to follow.

In the outer courtyard, the deep rumble of a motorcycle filled the air.

***

Chaos erupted inside the compound. Randy vaulted over the wall in time to see drifting tire smoke and hear the howl of a motorcycle driven to the redline echoing in the courtyard. The Russians ran towards two Mercedes vans parked in the looping driveway. They never looked back, but jumped into the vehicles, more tire smoke and engine roar as they sped off in pursuit of Raynard.

Heskin, Randy thought. *His name is Carl Heskin. But the Russkis don't know that. What in the hell is going on?*

He ran to the outer wall overlooking the ocean. Far down the rugged slope, a boat was tied up at a small dock. Randy couldn't make out faces from this distance, though he guessed the people were the rest of Raynard's staff. *Heskin, damn it! And he's trying to join them.*

Randy spun around and faced the house. It seemed larger and more sinister up close. *Breathe, dumbass*, he scolded himself. *What would Stone do?*

This last thought calmed him. His hand went to his hip and he smoothly drew the H&K. *OK. So far so good. Priority? Stop the geeks from taking the disease. Good, good. How many left inside?*

An excellent question.

Randy's mind replayed the mad scramble of men to the vans. He counted silently. *One, two, three, four, five. Five. That was it.*

'Three more inside,' he muttered. 'Two scientists, one professional killer. First job, kill the killer.'

He moved towards the French doors opening onto the patio and reached out a hand. He paused, and the pause saved his life.

In an explosion of violence, a man burst from inside. Two shots passed close enough to be felt as a tug on Randy's clothes.

Randy was suddenly filled with rage. Why were these assholes always trying to kill him? Him! With a wife and family. He slammed the door back into the face of his attacker, glass shattering, then dropped to a crouch and fired up. One shot to the groin.

Blood splattered and the man fell back with a shriek. Cold as a glacier, Randy put the sights of the gun just below the bridge of the man's nose and fired. The back of his head flew off in a ruddy spray. Stone had suggested hollow-point bullets.

The man had barely hit the floor when Randy was attacked by an apparition from a sci-fi movie. But a hazmat suit was a poor costume for fighting hand to hand, and the man had no gun. Nevertheless, he clubbed at Randy with a small metal case, hitting him just above one eyebrow. The skin broke and Randy was soon blinking blood from his left eye, blood that sheeted down his face and dripped from his chin.

Randy pursued the man. In his anger and with his eyesight compromised, he ran through a heavy doorway into a large room, in whose center stood a glass and steel box, completely black inside. Off balance and partially blinded, Randy fired two shots. One connected and the man spun, the case flying from his grasp into a steel wall, popping open, and spilling its contents.

An alarm began to sound, and red lights flashed ominously.

When Randy regained his bearings, he saw two men in hazmat suits, illuminated at intervals by the lurid, strobing light. The man he'd wounded was pointing at the twisted case and another cylindrical container, open on the ground. He was screaming. His focus changed and he was frantically motioning to some point beyond Randy. A loud hissing competed with the alarm.

Randy dragged a sleeve across his bloody face, cursing, but before he could raise his gun the men barreled into him, sending him to the floor. They shoved and elbowed each other, trying to escape the room. Both made it out a moment before the pneumatic door slammed shut and the hissing ceased. A cold, detached voice now replaced the alarm.

A BREACH HAS OCCURRED. AUTOMATIC CONTAINMENT PROTOCOLS IN PLACE. A BREACH HAS OCCURRED. ALL HERMETIC DOORS SEALED AND LOCKED. A BREACH HAS OCCURRED.

Randy glanced from the flashing lights to the open container not ten feet away. An icy spider crawled up his spine.

***

Before he'd had a chance to wipe the blood from his eyes, check his surroundings, or contemplate the hideous death that now awaited him, Randy heard shots being fired, as though from a great distance. Then someone was calling his name. Randy struggled to his feet, noticing as he did so that the first two shots fired at him in the courtyard had done more than tug at his shirt. From the shoulder down, his left arm and sleeve were soaked in blood. He moved the arm tentatively, and pain erupted. But his joints still worked and he still had strength in his clenched fist. No broken bones, apparently. *Still*, he thought, *I might just bleed to death before the disease gets me. Probably a better option.*

'Randy! Where the hell are you?' a voice bellowed from beyond the sealed door.

Randy realized he didn't have the strength to make his voice carry beyond his prison—his crypt? Looking around, he saw an intercom on the wall next to the door. He thumbed the button. 'Chuck, is that you?'

'Where are you?' The shouted response.

'Use the intercom. Next to the door,' Randy said.

A few heartbeats later, Chuck's voice filled the anteroom. 'Randy, you in there? I dropped two would-be spacemen out here. Looks like you hit one first plus took out another guy who's just a plain mess. Hang tight, I'll get you out.'

'No!' Randy screamed. 'Don't open the door! The disease has escaped. It's loose in here.' His voice faded to a whisper. 'With me.'

'I don't give a fuck! I'm getting you out.'

Randy heard scrabbling outside the door, then gunshots followed by 'Mother fuck!'

The intercom returned to life. 'This fuckin' door is steel. Almost shot myself with my own bullets. Listen, there's got to be some controls somewhere. I'll find them, get you out.'

'Settle down, Chuck. You can't do that and you know it. Now listen. There are five more goons chasing Raynard—or Heskin—down the road. I don't know why. But when they take care of that, they'll be back to get what they paid for. Even you aren't that good.'

'I got me some backup,' Chuck snarled. 'Marcus came along for the fun. He's doing a perimeter sweep. And then there's you, once I get this damned door open.'

'More than ever, you can't open that door,' Randy said. 'You'd kill your own son and your own stupid self. Take the time you have and prepare for some very capable opponents. I don't know if there is more of this shit lying around, but you can't let them take any material out of here. Including my sorry ass. C'mon, boss. You know what to do.'

There was a long silence. 'Fuck you for a smartass,' Chuck growled. 'Hold on. Marcus and I will handle the Russkis then bust you out.'

He pictured the road ahead. Another short straight, a hairpin right-hander, and then a few short swooping curves would take him to the dock.

Chapter Twenty-Two

A False Premise

S tone's question hung in the air. Why create a deadly disease and sell it to people ruthless enough to use it?

Despite the seriousness of the moment, Raynard smiled thinly.

'You proceed from a false premise, Mr. Stone. There is no such disease. You and the rest of the world, including the would-be buyers, have been duped.'

Stone was stunned. 'If you're telling the truth, then it would be the greatest illusion the world has ever seen.'

'The greatest illusion the world has ever seen! You flatter me, but I must admit that was my goal. It's always been my goal.' Raynard's eyes narrowed. She was no longer seeing the world around her, but the debris of her past. The attempts and the failures. She shook her head and smiled. 'There, you've distracted me. Since you're not here for blood, let's go inside. It's cold.'

***

Stone was feeling a sense of overwhelming confusion, seated in a comfortable leather chair, a cognac on a side table and a fire blazing behind a wide hearth. The woman (man!) whom he'd been chasing for months and who'd left a trail of disease and death was now showing him the hospitality of an old friend, come for a visit.

Seeing his discomfort, Raynard smiled. 'I wasn't lying. There is no disease and the world is safe.' She considered this and shook her head sadly. 'It's as safe as it was before my illusion. Ask your questions, Mr. Stone, but don't expect me to give away all my secrets. You know the old saw about magicians!'

'Assuming you're telling the truth, I still have about a thousand questions, but the first is, why did so many innocent people have to die?'

'Ah. That's an impressive first question. Not "Why did you create the illusion of a plague disease?" or "What were you trying to achieve?". Cherokee's assessment was correct. You're a man of integrity—and compassion.' She ran her fingers through Cherokee's coat, and the huge animal rumbled contentment. 'Are you a reader, Mr. Stone? Of the classics?'

Stone gave her a puzzled look.

'I promise to answer your question, and I ask you to trust me for a few minutes.'

He hesitated a moment longer, then shrugged. 'I've read some. Maybe even some of the books my poor high school teachers couldn't get me to open under threat of physical punishment. Fact is, I've grown into it.'

'Excellent. And has this reading, perhaps, included some of the Russian greats: Tolstoy, Dostoyevsky, Solzhenitsyn?'

'It has.'

'Are you familiar with the book *Dead Souls*?'

Stone was completely lost at this point, but in fact he did know the book. Another Russian tome that he and Luana had read together. It involved a Russian scammer who was buying up dead serfs as part of an insurance con.

'I've read it. Nikolai Gogol, right?'

'Yes. So here is the answer to your question. No innocent people died.'

'Wait—what? The people in the Guatemalan village, the bordellos in Bangladesh. The *Flying Dutchman*!' His voice had risen half an octave as he rattled off the list of places where Raynard's demonstrations had left a long list of casualties.

'What was my illusion, Mr. Stone?'

'It was the illusion that you'd created the worst plague the world has ever seen.'

'Then how did these people die, if the disease was an illusion?'

'Well, I mean, I had assumed you'd … You mean to tell me you never killed anyone?'

'I never said that. There is blood on my hands just as there is blood on yours.'

Raynard rose and added several logs to the fire, moving them with a poker until she was satisfied with their position. 'Dead souls,' she said, still facing the fire. 'An equally important part of my illusion was the supposed deaths of innocents to demonstrate the existence of the disease. People die all the time. The poor and desperate are sometimes willing to part with the deceased—for a fee.'

'Dead souls!'

'Yes. Acquiring the bodies is the easiest part. My financial resources were more than adequate. I'm ashamed to admit that some of that money came from my association with Carlos Velasquez. In that sense, I am guilty of much, though I did what I could to moderate his worst abuses.' She turned back to Stone. 'A tip, for instance, regarding the *Saint Martin*.'

'You were the source of that intel?' Stone was astonished.

'Yes, though I had assumed the CIA and not The Salvation Army would respond. I had no notion of you or Stone Security Services at the time.'

'I need a drink.'

Raynard topped up his cognac.

'I'm pleased you never discovered the second part of my illusion.'

'So, the bodies in the village, the bordello, and on the ship—'

'The ship was a different story. The bodies of the villagers and those in the bordello were the unfortunate departed, purchased by me at a reasonable price. Bribes, blackmail, etc. facilitated the cooperation of the living. It wasn't easy.'

'I'll bet.'

'Giving the illusion of the dead having succumbed to a disease was also difficult, but I had help. I'm no epidemiologist.'

'But Carl Heskin is.'

'I had three possible illusions to spring on an unsuspecting world. Finding Carl caused me to choose the plague illusion.'

'There are two others?' Stone asked.

'Not currently active, Mr. Stone.'

'Please, call me Jason.'

'Thank you. You can call me Jess, if you'd like.'

'Your given name?'

Raynard smiled. 'If you only knew.'

Stone considered this for a while. 'You mentioned the ship was different.'

'Yes. Carlos the Idiot forced me to use his loyal captain and first mate, I suppose to keep an eye on me.'

'Didn't work out too well for them.'

'No. They died at my hand, but I'm not sorry. Two murderers, rapists, and human traffickers. I'd say they deserved to die, but who am I to judge? They did die, and they served me as did my dead souls to bring about my illusion.'

'But what about—'

Raynard held up a hand. 'I know. A thousand questions. If you're sure you aren't going to kill me, why don't you help me prepare dinner? Will venison be all right? Cherokee brought in a deer yesterday.'

'Beats dealing with all the crowds at the grocery stores,' Stone said.

Raynard laughed. 'It does. While we work, I'll tell you about Carl Heskin and his family. You should know he volunteered to work with me, knowing that he would die as Jesse Raynard.'

'That's the story I'd most like to hear … Jess.'

***

While they prepared dinner, Jess explained how she'd first met Carl and described the agreement they'd reached.

'So, the money from the Russians is going to his family?' Stone asked.

'Some. I'll be keeping a considerable amount to fund my hobby.'

'Creating illusions?'

'Exactly.'

'What about the Russian scientist, Constantin Shukhov?'

'A late addition to our cast of characters. Ego as big as a planet. Despised the bureaucracy of the CDC. He was a volunteer, participating for the mere fun plus for the publicity he'd receive. Not the sort of man I'd trust unless his own best interests aligned with mine. They did, for a while.'

Stone checked the venison steaks, sizzling under the broiler. 'About done, I think.'

A chime sounded and Jess checked her computer, gave a satisfied grunt, then typed several commands before returning to the kitchen for the salads.

'Carl's family is now *more* than financially secure.'

'The payment came through?'

'Yes.'

'You don't seem as happy as I thought you'd be.'

'For his family, delighted. But I thought you understood. My friend Carl … well, the finale of my illusion requires a sacrifice, an innocent death. It's my greatest regret.'

***

Stone and Jess were placing salads, venison steaks, and baked potatoes on the table when another alarm sounded on her computer. More insistent. More serious.

'Trouble?' Stone asked.

'A breach at the lab. Not part of the plan. Give me a second.'

Stone stood behind Jess as she pulled up surveillance cameras. Bodies lay on the floor, two in hazmat suits, blood pooling beneath all three. Next to a heavy door, a black man stood, looking both angry and terrified.

'Chuck?' Stone murmured.

'Friend of yours?' Jess asked. 'I should have guessed. Actually, I did guess. Fortunately, there's been no major change in plans, or I would have received a message from Carl.'

'But what about the alarm?'

'Let me check.'

Jess pulled up the cameras in the anteroom, showing Randy, bloody but still alive, standing near the intercom on the other side of the sealed door.

Stone was horrified, but Jess smiled. 'Now we come to it, Jason. Do you believe me? Your friend is in no danger, I swear. I can tell him so and release the door lock, but will he believe me?'

'Can I talk to him?'

Jess rose and motioned for him to sit. 'Just unmute the microphone when you're ready.'

'Randy, can you hear me?'

Randy stiffened, then turned his head from side to side. 'Stone, is that you? Where the hell are you?'

'New Mexico, having dinner with a new acquaintance. Listen to me. You're not going to die. There is no disease. My friend Jess will open the door and you can—'

'No! Chuck is here. So is Marcus. You could kill them both!'

379

'Hello, Randy,' Jess said calmly. 'Jason is right. You're in no danger and neither are your friends.'

'But the container is open. The alarms went off!'

'A way to discourage intruders. Listen, the material in the vials is inert. However, since you believe you are infected ...' She leaned over Stone and typed a command. A distinct *clatch* was heard and the brief hiss of air. 'The inner door is now open. I suggest you examine the body within.'

'Randy, what the hell is going on?' Chuck yelled into the intercom. 'Was that Stone? And who's the woman?'

'Give me just a second, boss.'

Randy warily went to the door of the inner room, kicking it open with his foot. The lights came on and flooded the room with a harsh brilliance, showing a collapsed body on the floor. 'There's a dead man here,' he called out.

'No, there isn't. Have you got a knife?'

'Have I got a knife? Are you kidding?'

'Cut open his shirt. If that doesn't convince you, cut his body anywhere you'd like.' She gave Stone a twisted smile.

A few seconds later, Randy was standing, eyes round. 'It's fake! What the ever-loving-fuck is going on?'

'Calm down, Randy,' Stone said. 'The body is fake 'cause the disease is fake. The whole damn thing has been an illusion.'

'Oh, yeah? Then how come the Russkis are chasing Raynard ... damn it! I mean Carl Heskin.'

'The final part of my illusion,' Jess said. 'The death of Jesse Raynard.'

***

Carl Heskin estimated his pulse to be 160 beats per minute. Given the advanced state of his illness, this heart rate was unsustainable for more than ten minutes. It didn't matter. He'd be dead in five. As it was, with the pain-control drugs, amphetamines, and mild hallucinogens running through his veins, he hadn't felt this good in years.

'Just another part of Raynard's illusion,' he muttered. But the manic smile wouldn't leave his face.

He powered around a tight curve, a rooster tail of dirt and rocks flung up behind him.

Slow it down, he thought. They need to get closer.

He reluctantly backed off as he passed the turnoff for the main road back towards San José, but his mind was elsewhere. He was eighteen, an up-and-coming motorcycle racer, competing on dirt courses, flat tracks— anywhere he could ride. He'd been full of life and immortal! Risking life and limb, laughing at insane risks. Other more important things had eventually calmed the speed junkie inside him: his passion for medicine, his love for a woman. Seeing the sick and broken man Heskin had become, Raynard had been shocked when Carl described this early phase of his life. A daredevil and master of two-wheel racing. Those days were just memories.

Still, Carl thought, *I may have a few skills left.*

As he descended a short, steep slope, he caught a glimpse of the first van in his mirrors. Flashes and a rattle of automatic-weapon fire brought a smile to his face.

Dumb bastards have finally caught up.

He slowed even further through a few tight corners. This had to be believable.

He pictured the road ahead. Another short straight, a hairpin right-hander, and then a few short swooping curves would take him to the dock. But he wasn't heading for the dock. His finger delicately brushed a button on the handlebar.

He accelerated down the straight, spatters of dirt erupting up around him. Perfect. Now, he would fly.

He twisted the throttle wide open and closed his eyes. *Goodbye my loves.* He pushed the button.

An igniter in the nearly empty fuel tank flashed and the tank exploded as Carl flew across the small runoff area and sailed out over the cliff, a streaking ball of flame that arced downward and crashed into the rocks below.

The two vans slid to a stop, the Russian commander leaping out. He exchanged his submachine gun for binoculars and studied the wreckage below. The bike was still burning, as was the rider, both broken and twisted on weed-covered rocks. As the commander stared, a wave washed, hissing, over the wreckage.

Jesse Raynard was dead.

Out to sea, speeding away rapidly, was the boat carrying Raynard's people and the State's number one enemy, Yevgeny Turgenev. He was gone, already out of range.

The leader snapped a command, and the Russians piled back into their vehicles. There was only one way to save the mission and their lives, and that was to bring back the pathogen. He would be forgiven for the loss of Turgenev, but would be beyond salvation if their true prize slipped away.

The commander never suspected he was already as dead as Raynard.

***

Chuck and Marcus had enough time to bind Randy's arm and slap a bandage over his bleeding eyebrow before the Russians returned.

'Damn eyebrows are the worst,' Chuck had said. 'Bleed like a stuck pig.'

Randy never got to ask Chuck how he knew so much about eyebrow cuts or stuck pigs. Chuck hustled him outside and they crouched behind a stone half-wall bordering the driveway loop.

'Marcus is on the roof,' Chuck called. 'Don't be standing up and getting in his line of fire.'

Randy turned and saw Marcus's grin before he slipped behind a chimney.

The three didn't have long to wait.

Engine noise preceded the two vans, both skidding to a stop and the occupants piling out.

Chuck's plan was simple. 'Kill them all. Don't wait, don't hesitate. If one happens to live, we'll bring him home, but my give-a-shit meter is on zero.'

Marcus dropped the first man, the commander, with a rifle shot from the roof. Two others were down before they knew what was happening. The last two took cover behind the open doors of the vans and returned fire.

Randy took careful aim at one's exposed feet below the door and fired. With a shriek, the man toppled to the side. Chuck put two more rounds into him.

The last man decided to make a break for it, and had slid behind the wheel of one of the vans. A rifle crack, and he slumped over the wheel, blood spilling from a massive head wound.

***

An hour later, the buildings and vehicles were wrapped in flames.

Chuck had discussed options with Stone and Jess, and this had seemed like the best solution. The hour it had taken them was to secure photographic and physical evidence of 'the late' Jesse Raynard's illusion. Prosthetics, videos, materials, detailed plans. They had even grabbed the supposed pathogen.

'I think it's best if Marcus delivers the evidence to the Agency,' Stone had said. 'No reason to bring Triple S into this.'

'No tickertape parades for the heroes who saved the world?' Randy grumbled.

'We didn't save the world, Randy, remember?' Chuck said.

'Must be my head injury,' Randy said, fingering the bloody bandage above his eye.

'The illusion is complete,' Jess chimed in. 'Or nearly so. In any case, the truth, as you've said, Jason, must now be shared. Maybe with a few magician's secrets held back.'

'What do you mean, "nearly so"?' Chuck asked.

'Jason knows what I mean, don't you?'

'I think I can speak for all of us, plus one other back in London. Jesse Raynard is officially dead. The perpetrator of the greatest illusion ever performed died in the final act.'

Chuck and Randy grunted their agreement.

'Just don't create another illusion without telling us,' Randy muttered.

'An interesting request,' Jess said. 'I'll discuss it with Jason over a much-delayed dessert.'

'Gotta believe Martha and Tyrone will want to examine this,' Randy said, patting the thermos containing the 'pathogen.'

'They're welcome to it,' Chuck said. 'And the Agency will be glad to take credit for debunking the biggest hoax ever.'

'Not a hoax,' Randy said. 'An illusion.'

Chuck nodded. 'So, all we need to do is hoof it back to the Rover. Marcus and I can pack the goodies. You OK to walk, Randolph?'

'They shot me in the arm, boss, not the leg.'

'Then lead on.'

***

Clouds shrouded the night sky, a gentle rain falling, when the boat beached on the pebbly shore. Two men got out, followed by a third who'd insisted on being part of this recovery.

Though his body was broken and partially burned, there was no hiding the look of peace on Carl Heskin's face.

The two men stepped forward, but the third said, 'Please, let me help. He saved my life.'

The other two silently grabbed Heskin's legs, while Yevgeny Turgenev took his shoulders, gently cradling his head. 'Thank you,' Turgenev whispered.

***

'You good with all this, Marcus?' Chuck asked, as his son prepared to leave for the airport and a trip back to D.C.

'Yeah. Let me see. I was visiting my dad when he invited me to vacation with him in Central America, where his current employer, Stone Security Services—'

'Watch it, son. I'm a vice president.'

Marcus waved this off. 'Your current employer, Stone Security Services, asked you to look into rumors of a drug smuggling operation. We discover there was no drug smuggling at all, and the operation's supposed headquarters turns out to be the lab of the mad scientist who'd—ostensibly—developed the worst pathogen since bubonic plague. I helped out and was imposed upon to deliver the evidence.'

Chuck ran his hand over his chin, feeling the thick stubble. 'Sounds like pure bullshit to me.'

'Ding-ding-ding,' Marcus said, putting a finger to his nose. 'You've got it! Fortunately, my boss's boss said he'd swallow that crap to get hold of the evidence. Once he gets it, I am so fired.'

'And you're OK with that?' Chuck reiterated.

Marcus shrugged. 'Got any job openings?'

'Hell yes!' Chuck growled, crushing his son in a hug.

'Hey. I think you cracked a rib! Hell, the Russkis couldn't lay a glove on me. Gotta go now, Dad. Oh, I'm glad Tyrone and Martha got a chance to look at that fake bug.'

Chuck grinned. 'Yeah. Seven of eight samples were unbroken. But you give your boss's boss the broken glass from the eighth, too. Shit, it's harmless.'

'A miracle!' Marcus said, his grin matching his father's. He turned serious. 'Wish I'd gotten to see Stone. Where's he been?'

'The old SOB is being mysterious. Imagine that.'

'But he's OK?'

'Sent me a text to confirm he's fine. Just some final business to attend to. You'll see him soon enough, being as how he'll be your new boss.'

'Kind of like the sound of that,' Marcus said. He glanced at his watch. 'Shit! Gotta go.'

As Marcus drove off, Chuck yelled out, 'Don't get your dumb ass on TV!'

'I'm not a glory seeker like my dad!' Marcus yelled back.

*'A jazz band? You tempt me, Jason. Would it shock you to know I play a
pretty spirited jazz violin?'*

Chapter Twenty-Three

A Funeral and a Party

There are Civil War dead in this cemetery from both sides,' Jess said.
'It looks more like a forest than a cemetery,' Stone replied. 'It's beautiful.'

The cemetery occupied a few dozen acres in the rolling, pine-cluttered hills southeast of Atlanta. A lazy stream flowed between them, the evening sun glinting off the rippling water. A small church perched atop one of the hills, and its bell echoed through the trees.

'I have to go,' Jess said. 'Are you sure you won't join me?'

Stone smiled. 'God might blast the entire church to fragments if I went in. No. I'll wait for you here till it's over.'

'I see Carl's wife,' she said. 'I'll be back soon.'

Jess, formerly Jesse Raynard, walked towards the church to attend the funeral service of her good friend Carl Heskin, who'd died after a long struggle with a rare disease. True enough.

It was a small gathering. Only family and, to Jess's surprise, Constantin Shukhov. She turned back after a few steps. 'You're a good man, Jason. Carl was a good man. I wish ...' She continued on to the church.

Stone took a slow walk around the cemetery, reading the headstones. Some were crumbling and moss covered, but most were still readable. More than a few men had been buried here after the battle of Atlanta. The dates ranged from July 23, 1864, the day after the battle, to August 15. Clearly, some of the injured had lived for weeks before succumbing to their wounds. Pain and suffering, followed by death.

Stone noticed the members of the funeral party moving the casket towards the burial site. He watched from a distance, not feeling right about intruding. What seemed a short time later, Jess came to his side.

'Do they know?' Stone asked, gesturing towards Carl's wife and daughters.

'How he died or who I am? No. I'm just a friend of the family. The money is from a wealthy, anonymous friend of Carl's who admired his work and his integrity.'

'That last part is certainly true.'

'Walk with me, please, Jason.'

Jess and Stone walked in silence, circling the cemetery grounds until Jess finally said, 'It hurts more than I thought it would.'

'Losing a friend always does. And the feeling of success? Of amazing the world?'

'Less rapturous than I'd hoped for, unfortunately. Foolish to think that the hurt I'd felt as a child and young woman could be so easily erased.'

'I like your friend Charlotte,' Stone said, motioning back to where she was still in conversation with Mrs. Heskin. 'What will you do now?'

'Back to New Mexico, I suppose. You?'

'Back to Tucson for a while. My wife is arriving from—somewhere. She travels a lot. We'll visit with our friends from Triple S before heading back to London.'

'Friends? Not colleagues. Not employees. That says a lot about you, Jason.'

'They are friends, despite the fact I shot the fiancée of one of them.'

'You *what*?'

'Only a graze. Long story. Hey, why don't you and Charlotte visit? Logan Fletcher has a little jazz band and they're giving a performance.'

'A jazz band? You tempt me, Jason. Would it shock you to know I play a pretty spirited jazz violin?'

'It would take a lot more than that to shock me now that I know you. Think about it, OK?'

'I will.'

***

A day before the concert, Martha was having lunch with Tyrone, who'd insisted she come into town for the performance. The two were seated at the bar of a hole-in-the-wall barbecue joint and tavern that Tyrone swore had the best ribs on the planet.

'My God, Tyrone,' she declared, after her first bite, 'I've died and gone to heaven! The meat is falling off the bones. And the sauce! If I could make barbecue like this, I'd weigh four hundred pounds!'

'Not bad, eh? Some advantages to living in the sunny Southwest. Hey, is that your dear friend Constantin Shukhov on the tube? He pointed to the TV behind the bar. 'Hey, Bosco, turn up the sound for a sec, will you?'

Bosco, the owner, bartender, and occasional cook, obliged. 'Friend of yours?'

'More like a giant a-hole,' Martha muttered.

Shukhov, dressed in his usual tailored suit, was talking to reporters in the wake of the full exposure of the disease hoax.

'Of course, it was soon obvious to me that the disease was fake. My skill at medical diagnosis borders on prescience. Naturally, I would have reported it sooner if I'd not been held back by the timid, ignorant members of certain governments, who actually threatened my life.'

A question was shouted at him by an eager newsman.

'The evidence? Pffh. Most of the evidence leading to the exposure of this fakery, I must say with all humility, was provided to the authorities by me. But I want no credit. Jesse Raynard was an evil, psychotic man. I'm only too glad he's in his grave.'

Having fulfilled his final promise to Carl Heskin, Shukhov waved the reporters aside and moved off.

'So that blowhard Constantin lands on his feet again,' Martha grumbled.

'Oh, to hell with him. Eat your ribs. Bosco, another round!'

***

This was a private concert. That is, the band was set up in Logan's backyard, which was now crammed with friends, some from around the world. Yvette was talking quietly with Becky while each sipped a Cosmo.

Logan and Cathie had catered the entire event, complete with four chefs, frantically preparing food over large grills, plus a half-dozen servers and three bartenders stationed strategically around their yard.

Martha and Tyrone drank a dark, lusty Cab from Logan and Cathie's wine cellar and continued abusing Constantin Shukhov, though Tyrone had looked up long enough to grin in response to Logan's 'ten-minute warning' sign. His big fiddle was already set up in the patio area just outside the huge sliding glass walls, now thrown open. Logan's grand piano wasn't going to be moved anywhere, but this approach, with him in the interior of the house and the rest of the band outside, had been tested, and the acoustics worked. Frank Burdan was tuning his guitar and Garrett Kittle was warming up and adjusting his drums, but Tyrone was a semi-pro. He could stroll up late and still outshine the others. Hence the grin.

Diana and Richard had elected to stay in England, pleading old age and inertia. Logan suspected they were relieved to get a few weeks of peace and quiet. Gail and Randy tolerantly showed off James Charles O'Neil to a crowd of cooing visitors. Chuck and Joy mingled, though Chuck was edging towards a small table near the band. Tyrone's licks were something to enjoy up close.

Other friends and neighbors moved around, talking, drinking, and eating appetizers. The sun hung behind a bank of low clouds, lighting the mild spring evening with a brilliant orange-gold that defied description. Logan put his arm around Cathie and was about to say something when he noticed Jason Stone, standing off to the side and drinking Guinness from a bottle. Stone's expression was unfathomable. Sadness, loneliness, and excitement were all strangely displayed on the man whose last name could be said to describe his persona. Logan was about to say as much, when Stone came alive, as though someone had tossed a match onto a leaf pile. Logan followed his gaze. Luana had just arrived, dressed to the nines.

Stone hurried across the room, having conjured a drink for Luana seemingly from thin air. A long hug, and Stone walked her towards a table, talking with surprising animation. At one point, Luana stopped and stared into his eyes, an incredulous look on her face, before a quick nod from Stone restored their motion.

Cathie shook Logan's arm. 'I *said*, aren't you supposed to introduce the band, like'—she glanced at her watch—'well, now?'

'Huh? Sorry, darling. I was just watching Luana.'

'What! And you, a doddering old married man. Incidentally, she's married to a man who could snap you like a twig.'

'He'd have to use both hands, at least,' Logan said. 'Point is, Stone and Luana are both acting kind of odd.'

'They haven't seen each other in a while. Maybe the two of us should try that, if it generates the electricity I'm seeing between them.'

'Funny. OK, time for intros. Wish me luck.'

Cathie kissed his cheek. 'Knock 'em dead.'

Cathie headed towards Joy and Chuck's table, while Logan edged slowly towards the mic, like a man towards gallows. *Jeez, Fletcher, lighten up. It's only, what, sixty or so friends and neighbors come to hear some jazz.* He took a few deep breaths and was on the verge of clawing back his equanimity when a hand on his shoulder made him jump.

'Holy gods, Stone, don't do that!'

'I need to tell you something before you start.'

'Yeah, well, I was—'

'Just listen, would you?'

Logan listened, his mouth hanging open. He glanced towards Luana, who waved at him. She was clearly enjoying seeing Logan as shocked as she'd been.

'You're certain?' Logan asked.

'Confirmation on my phone. From the airport to here is what, forty minutes?'

'Yeah, give or take.'

'OK. Can you work it in?'

'Yeah. We'll do a short set, let folks get some food, then ...'

'Remember. Use the name I gave you.'

'Got it. No stress at all. Maybe you'd like to tickle the ivories?'

Stone slapped Logan's back. 'Not in my job description.'

***

Logan's smile had returned by the time he reached the microphone. He tapped at it and said the usual ice breaker, 'Is this thing on?' Obligatory chuckles. 'Hey, thanks for coming out this evening. Please feel free to refill drinks, get some of the awesome food, or talk among yourselves. Just keep half an ear open while the Fourth Harmonics lay down a little smooth jazz. Let me introduce the guys.'

Logan made brief introductions and then the band dove right into 'A Night in Tunisia.' As always, once Logan began playing, the mellow jazz scared off the remaining butterflies. The music flowed smoothly. 'A Night in Tunisia' transitioned seamlessly into 'These Foolish Things,' the music carrying the band like a boat on a stream. Before he knew it, they'd finished the first set. The guests cheered and applauded. Becky whistled shrilly.

Logan was just about to seek out a drink and a few ribs when he noticed a tall, dark-haired woman, carrying a violin case, talking to Stone and Luana. Stone glanced up and waved for Logan to join them.

'Um, hi,' Logan said.

The woman reached out a hand. 'Sorry to crash your party, but I did have a surrogate invitation from Mr. Stone. I'm Jessica Carl. Happy to meet you. Please call me Jess.'

Logan took her hand. 'Logan Fletcher. My wife is'—he scanned the patio—'around here somewhere. I'll introduce you later. And any friend of Jason's is a friend of mine.'

'So, it wasn't *your* wife he shot?'

Logan looked stunned, then burst into laughter. 'No,' he said, pointing, 'she's the one with the toddler. Her husband wanted to kill Jason for a long time, but he got over it. Since then, I reckon they owe each other their lives—a couple times over. But enough about our hobbies. I presume what you have in that case isn't an Uzi.'

'No. It's an Amati. Far too good for my skills, but I have hopes.'

'An Amati? No shit? Pardon my French. And you play jazz?'

It was Jess's turn to laugh. 'I might surprise you. Can I see your playlist?'

'Oh, hell yes. Tyrone is gonna blow a gasket.'

Jess scanned the songs. 'I'm good to go for these, but it looks like you need a vocalist or two.'

'We have a guest singer. Our friend Judy Lewis.'

'This one could be a duet,' Jess said, indicating 'Route 66.'

'True, but … Wait. You can sing too?' He glanced at Stone.

'She didn't mention it to me, but I've learned not to be surprised by anything Jess says.'

'Well, hell.' Logan blew out a long breath. 'Jess, let me introduce you to the guys, then rosin up your bow.'

***

The music flew by, dreamlike.

At the end of the set, applause rocked the Casa de Fletcher. Logan stood, as though recovering from a trance, and headed for the wine bar, where he found Chuck and Stone engaged in a serious conversation.

'I'm not sayin' she's hard on the eyes, but do you trust her?' Chuck asked.

'I do. It was all an illusion, Chuck. I've been able to trace some of the "dead" villagers and "dead" prostitutes, and you can bet your ass she knew I would. Trust but verify. She didn't kill anyone you or I wouldn't have dropped in the blink of an eye. Shit, you're here and so is Randy.'

'Randy is where?' he asked, as he approached. 'Randy is getting a drink.' He glanced from left to right, then grabbed a bottle of scotch. 'None of that fermented grape juice. I'm shocked that you'd drink it, boss … Chuck. Damn it! Am I ever going to get over you being my Agency boss, boss?'

'I hope not,' Chuck said, with a grin. 'Let's drink to that!'

As the three drank and talked, Logan noticed Jess in conversation with Judy. *Is she really going to do it?* he thought.

Before he was even aware, Logan was back at the piano, wondering how his fingers were managing on their own while his mind was focused on the playful back and forth between Judy's soprano and Jess's alto. A light, musical banter. Tyrone joined in at the end, ripping through the intervals between the vocals, his fingers a blur on the 'big fiddle.'

At the end, hushed silence. Then shrieks and hoots of delight. More applause. But Tyrone had already led the band into the next tune.

***

At the conclusion of the third set, Randy noticed Stone staring at the day's *Arizona Daily Star*, pulled from the kitchen counter. Randy nudged Chuck just as Stone sensed eyes on him. Stone motioned for the two to join him. When they arrived, he flipped through the paper to page twelve and pointed to a small article above the fold.

When Randy finished reading, he looked at Jason, a smile on his face; a smile that vanished when he saw the grim expressions on Stone and Chuck.

Just then, Jess strolled over. 'What's up, boys?'

'This is how Stone finds "the next big thing,"' Chuck said. 'Old school. A newspaper and his gut. It's part of how he found out about you.' He handed her the paper.

Jess read the article twice. 'Poor editing,' she commented. 'Superfluous "ly" adverb.' She wasn't smiling when she turned to Stone. 'So, this is the next big thing?'

He shrugged.

Jess's eyes shone. 'I think you're going to need my help.'